WAYFARER

WAYFARER

Book One of *The Shekinah Chronicles*

A Novel by

MATTHEW DICKENS

Cover design by Valor Comics, Mario Ruiz, ValorComics.com.
Illustrations by Felton H. Allen.

Take note that the name satan and related names are not capitalized. We choose not to acknowledge him, even to the point of violating grammatical rules.

Destiny Image. Fiction

An Imprint of
Destiny Image® Publishers, Inc.
P.O. Box 310
Shippensburg, PA 17257-0310

ISBN 0-7684-2234-5

For Worldwide Distribution
Printed in the U.S.A.

This book and all other Destiny Image, Revival Press, MercyPlace, Fresh Bread, Destiny Image Fiction, and Treasure House books are available at Christian bookstores and distributors worldwide.

1 2 3 4 5 6 7 8 9 10 / 09 08 07 06 05 04

For a U.S. bookstore nearest you, call
1-800-722-6774.

For more information on foreign distributors, call
717-532-3040.

Or reach us on the Internet:
www.destinyimage.com

Endorsement

It is my joy to commend the writings of Matthew Dickens to you. In particular, I want to say a positive word about his newest work, *Wayfarer*. Anyone who reads this Christian fiction will be challenged to more carefully consider the glory of God and the evil world of satan and the demonic that opposes His plan at every turn.

Matthew Dickens is a creative and gifted writer. His imagination, tempered by biblical truth, carries us into a spiritual dimension that challenges us to seriously consider the claims of Christ upon our lives. Matthew's writings are lively and engaging from beginning to end. No reader will be disappointed with what they find in these pages.

Dr. Daniel L. Akin
President, Southeastern Baptist Theological Seminary
Wake Forest, NC

Character Descriptions

Applicable Bible References:

Antichrist References: Genesis 3: vs. 15; Job 41; Psalm 10; Psalm 52: vs. 1-7; Psalm 55: vs. 11-14; Psalm 74: vs. 8-10; Psalm 140: vs. 1, 10, 11; Isaiah 10: vs. 5, 12; (Isaiah 14: vs. 1-11 and vs. 16-21: refer to the Antichrist.) Isaiah 16: vs. 4, 5; Isaiah 25: vs. 5; Isaiah 27: vs. 1; Isaiah 30: vs. 33; Jeremiah 4: vs. 7; Lamentations 4: vs. 11-12; Ezekiel 21: vs. 25-27; Ezekiel 28: vs. 1-8; Daniel 11: vs. 36; Amos 3: vs. 11; Micah 5: vs. 5-6; Nahum 1: vs. 11, 12, 15; Habakkuk 2: vs. 4-5; Zechariah 11: vs. 12-17; (Cross reference Zechariah 13: vs. 2 & Matthew 12: vs. 43-45:) John 17: vs. 12; Acts 1: vs. 25; II Thessalonians 2: vs. 3; Revelation 6: vs. 8; Revelation 9: vs. 11; Revelation 11: vs. 7; Revelation 14: vs. 18; Revelation 17: vs. 8; Revelation 19: vs. 20.

Nephilim References: (Giants of the Naphal; also known as the gegenes gibborim.) Genesis 6: vs. 1-4; Deuteronomy 3: vs. 1-11; I Samuel 17: vs. 1-51; I Chronicles 20: vs. 4-8; Jude: vs. 6-8.

Lycanthropy References: (Shapeshifting.) I Chronicles 11: vs. 22; Daniel 4: vs. 28-34; II Corinthians 11: vs. 14.

The Scroll of Names

The Trinity: The Father, Son and Holy Spirit, also known as Us; see Genesis 1: vs. 26.

The Father: The Ancient of Days, the Father of Lights, Abba, the Spirit of Adoption, Jehovah-Jireh, Lord, and I am who I am.

The Son: Jesus, Immanuel, the Word, the Good Shepherd, Goel, Melchizedek, the Son of God, the Ancient of Days, the Son of Man, the Lion of the Tribe of Judah, the Christos Champion, The Living One, King of Kings and Lord of Lords, The Coming One, and I am who I am.

The Holy Spirit: The Spirit of the Lord, the Spirit of Wisdom, the Spirit of Understanding, the Spirit of Counsel, the Spirit of Might, the Spirit of Knowledge and the Spirit of the fear of the Lord; see Isaiah 11: vs. 2.

Lucifer: The Anointed Cherub, a Zoon, or Ha-Seraph.

Michael: Archangel; the Great Prince who protects Israel.

The Assassin: A shadowy protector of Lucifer's Imperial Court.

Gabriel: A prince in the Order of the Watchers.

Scriptos: Keeper of the Shekinah Chronicles.

Magnus the Lehohn: The Shekinah Champion.

Iscarius Alchemy: The Son of Perdition.

Simon Menelaus: Master of the Harness Magi.

Sodom: A Shadow King in the Council of Thrones and Master of the Nekros Order.

Tsavo: A Nephilimite giant; the last progeny of the second preternatural race of supermen spawned by fallen angels after the Second Great Deluge.

Empires & Hierarchies

The Saints: The Elect Ecclesia who will rule the universe in three distinct groups as regents of the Christos King; the earthly Jewish Wife {gune} the heavenly Jewish Bride {bethulah} and the Church. The Church is also known as the mystical Body of Christ, of which Christ is the Head.

Archangel: Crown Prince over all the elect angels in service to the Kingdom of God.

Cherubim: The living creatures who direct worship in Heaven and guard God's throne, also known as Seraphim or Zoa. Zoon, Seraph and Cherub are their singular designations. Seraph is also interchangeable with the word serpent in certain passages of Holy Writ, meaning shining or burning one. Compare Genesis 3: vs. 14-15, Numbers 21: vs. 6-9 and Isaiah 6: vs. 1-7.

The Twenty-Four Elders: Angelic rulers serving in the Kingdom of God.

The Watchers: The seven angels, i.e. spirit beings or eyes, standing before the throne of God in the Revelation of Jesus Christ; see Daniel 4 and Zechariah chapters 1-4.

Book Masters: Angels who record all that transpires in the whole of creation.

Hosts: Warriors also known as angels or the sons of God. They serve as guardians of the heirs of salvation.

Council of Thrones: Ten Shadow Kings ruling over the Kingdom of Darkness. The word king here is interchangeable with prince. It comes from the Hebrew word sar, which means ruler; see Daniel 10: vs. 13-21.

Thrones: Angelic rulers of the global order.

Dominus: Dominium Gate Masters guarding the entrances of galaxies and dominion pathways.

Powers of the Air: Rebel angels residing in the aerial regions.

Demons: Wicked spirits seeking union with mortals; also known as the Shedhim and the Seirim. They are not to be confused with rebel angels.

The Locust Cherubim: Winged, supernatural creatures with armored bodies shaped like horses that have the faces of men and hair like women flowing from beneath golden crowns, with each having tails like a scorpion; their likenesses possibly being linked to the post Flood Teraphim of the Assyrians. They are currently imprisoned in the Bottomless Pit.

The Brimstone Cavalry: A two hundred million strong army of fallen angels arrayed with breastplates of fire, jacinth and brimstone, riding upon horses that have lion-like heads and serpent-headed tails.

The Euphrates Strongmen: Four rebel angels bound in the Euphrates River, each waiting for the hour, day, month and year when they will be released to lead the Brimstone Cavalry in destroying a third of mankind; see Revelation 9: vs. 13-15.

The Gegenes Kings: Rulers from the third wave of Nephilimite giants to come.

The Harness Magi: An ancient guild of warrior priests and assassins. They also serve as guardians of the Covenant Harness.

The Illuminati: An elite class of men who control the world's Central Banks, also known as the International Bankers or Rex Deus; a coven of sorcerers falsely claiming descent from the House of King David, with key bases of operation located in Rhodes, Malta, London, Jupiter Island, and New Haven, Connecticut.

The Masonic Order: A Luciferian cult of cabalistic mysticism controlled by the Illuminati.

The Vampire Demoniacs: Covens of demon-possessed men and women.

The Idumaean Council of Princes: The royal houses of Europe with bloodline links to the Herodian Dynasty and members of the Illuminati

Apostate Israel: Those of the Israelite nation who reject the Messiah.

The Great Tree: The cedar of world government embodied in the Assyrian and his elect kings.

Assyria: The restructured Levant Land Bridge, and one of the empires beneath the boughs of the Great Tree, with capitals in Babylon, Tyre and Pergamos.

The Omega Group: A multibillion dollar megacompany created by the Harness Magi that has its international headquarters in the Turkish city of Pergamos.

Alpha Corps: A covert army of Red Horse Units created by the Omega Group.

Shadow Corps Intelligence: An intel agency created by the Omega Group.

Wolf Pack: Twelve-man Special Op units assembled by the Omega Group; the tip of the spear.

Sentinel Corps: Security forces providing protection for the Omega Group's corporate offices and international projects.

Special Services: An elite communications and electronic countermeasures team created by the Omega Group.

NGOs: Non-governmental organizations allied to the Omega Group and the Illuminati.

Cosmic Empires

The Kingdom of God: The universal kingdom.

The Kingdom of Heaven: Also known as the Millennial Kingdom; a period of time when the Lord Jesus will unite with Israel and reign over the Earth for one thousand years. This is the subject of the Lord Jesus' marturia testimony in the four Gospels and the Revelation.

Heaven: The glorious land.

Outer Realm: The circular universe beyond Earth controlled mainly by Lucifer and his fallen hosts who make up the Kingdom of Darkness, with rebel strongholds set up on barren planets and asteroids throughout space to block the Parade Route of the prophesied Conqueror to come.

Earth: The jewel of contention in the circular universe.

New Jerusalem: A jeweled city of cubicle design reaching fourteen hundred miles high, long and wide, nestled within a hovering sphere of transparent gold with a circumference measuring over eight thousand miles; the future capital of the universe. Its current location is in an undisclosed region within Heaven until the day of its earthly inauguration after the millennial reign of the Lord Jesus and his final judgment on the wicked.

Empire Holdings

Abraham's Bosom: A place of rest located in the same region as Hades, but is separated from the torments section by a great gulf; see Luke 16 vs. 19-31.

Dragylon: The Imperial Fortress of the Archrebel, which has its docking port in the airspace over Pergamos.

Hades: Also known as Sheol or The Grave; a temporary prison of torments for the damned located in the bowels of the Earth, controlled by the Kingdom of God.

The Abyss: A place of confinement for demons and rebel angels that fall in battle; see Luke 8 vs. 26-33.

The Well of the Abyss: Also known as the Bottomless Pit; a place of confinement for the Unclean Spirit, the Locust Cherubim and the Brimstone Cavalry.

Hell: Also known as the Lake of Fire; the final destination of the damned judged on the day of the second resurrection at the Great White Throne Judgment.

Worlds

The Pre-Adamic World: The original Earth where Lucifer was the Anointed Cherub of the threefold district of God's first Edenic Empire, the districts being Eden, the Garden of God and the Holy Mountain, foreshadowing the Outer Court, the Holy Place and the Holy of Holies in the Jewish Tabernacle and the Temples of Solomon and Zerubbabel. Applicable references can be found in Genesis 1: vs. 1-2; Isaiah 14: vs. 12-15; Ezekiel 28: vs. 11-19. Genesis 1: vs. 2 reads in the Hebrew, *The Earth became waste and a ruin*, which was caused by Lucifer's rebellion as shown in the other passages.

The Adamic World: The refurbished Earth where Adam and Eve walked in the Garden of God until sin entered in and caused the Fall of Mankind.

The Antediluvian World: The Middle East region and adjacent Nephilimite territories in the Levant Land Bridge destroyed during the flood of the Second Great Deluge.

The Ancient World: Land regions of the post Flood era where the focus of history was primarily on Africa, the Middle East, and Asia Minor.

The Old World: The continent of Europe.

14

The New World: The continents of North, Central and South America.

The Armory

The Sword of the Lord: A seismic power of earthly and supernatural destruction.

Dragaduceus: The war-blade of the Dragon Lord.

The Covenant Harness: A covenant garment of global power.

The Oracle of the Dragon Lord: An ancient staff of cosmic power wielded by the Masters of the Harness Magi.

The Trumpet of the Lord: A theocratic trumpet of cosmic ascension and assembly wielded by Prince Gabriel from the Order of the Watchers.

Preternatural Weapons: All manner of weapons forged with natural and preternatural materials such as swords, sickles, shields, armor, trumpets, crossbows, stellar explosives, flying chariots and galactic siege machines.

Adamantine: A preternatural metal of varying colors with great density and flexibility; an alloy that also served as the mold for the earthly Damascus Steel.

Christaloy: An alloy of different colors that is harder than adamantine.

Powers of the Shekinah Champion

Applicable Biblical References:

Immortal lifespan: Genesis 3: vs. 22, Genesis 5: vs. 27.

Indestructible against mortal weapons: Isaiah 54: vs. 17.

Seeing the supernatural: Genesis 28: vs. 12; II Kings 6: vs. 16-17; Revelation: chapters 1-22.

Wrestling with the supernatural: Genesis 32: vs. 24-30.

Supernatural speed: I Kings 18: vs. 44-46; Psalm 18: vs. 33.

Supernatural hearing: I Thessalonians 4: vs. 15-18.

Seismic power harnessed in voice: Psalm 18: vs. 7, 8; Matthew 27: vs. 50-51; John 18: vs. 6.

Supernatural strength and cunning: Judges 14: vs. 5-6; Judges 15: vs. 14-16; Judges 16: vs. 28-30; I Chronicles 11: vs. 10-24.

The ability to fly: II Kings 2: vs. 11; Psalm 18: vs. 29; Acts 1: vs. 9-11; Acts 8: vs. 39.

The ability to use His powers at will: Revelation 11: vs. 6.

Wrath in the Church Age: Romans 13: vs. 4; I Thessalonians 4: vs. 6.

The Shekinah Legacy

Lucifer: The first created champion of the Shekinah Legacy who brought desolation and darkness to the universe when trying to obtain equality with God.

16

Moses: A son of the House of Levi; the first to inherit the restructured mantle of the Shekinah Legacy who led the nation of Israel from Assyro-Egyptian bondage.

Joshua: The son of Nun whose father was a prince in the House of Ephraim; a champion who led the Jewish invasion of the Promised Land.

Othniel: The son of Kenaz; a champion and Judge of Israel who brought peace to Israel for 40 years after defeating King Cushan-Rishathaim of Mesopotamia.

Ehud: The left-handed son of Gera the Benjamite; a champion who brought peace to Israel for 80 years after slaying Eglon the fat King of Moab and leading the destruction of 10,000 of Moab's stout men of valor.

Shamgar: The son of Anath; a champion who slew 600 men with an ox goad.

Barak: The son of Abinoam of Kedesh; a champion who, with the guidance of Deborah the Judge, led the nation of Israel in a great victory over Sisera of Harosheth Hagoyim and his lord King Jabin of Canaan that brought peace to the land for 40 years.

Gideon: The son of Joash the Abiezrite; a champion who led 300 men in a great victory against the Midianites and the Amalekites that brought peace to Israel for 40 years.

Tola: The son of Puah of Issachar; a champion who judged Israel for 23 years.

Jair: A son of Gilead who judged Israel for 22 years.

Jephthah: A son of Gilead who was born of a harlot; a champion who judged Israel for six years and wrought a great victory against the Ammonites and the rebels of the House of Ephraim.

Ibzan: A champion from Bethlehem who judged Israel for seven years.

Elon: A champion from Zebulun who judged Israel for 10 years.

Abdon: The son of Hillel the Pirathonite; a champion who judged Israel for eight years.

Samson: A Nazarite from the womb who was the son of Manoah the Danite; a champion who judged Israel for 20 years and began to deliver them with great victories against the Philistines.

Samuel: The son of Elkanah of the House of Ephraim; a champion of judgment and prophecy who helped establish the monarchy of Israel by anointing Saul and David as kings over Israel during his life on Earth.

King David: The son of Jesse of the House of Judah; a champion of the greatest renown who reigned over Israel for 40 years, a throne to be established forever.

The Davidic 37: Thirty-seven champions fiercely loyal to King David who wrought great victories during the king's reign; some having slain hundreds of men at once while fighting alone.

Magnus the Lehohn: A prince in the House of Sheshbazzar and a member of the Shekinah Legacy who would foreshadow the return of the Christos Champion.

"If a trumpet is blown in a city,
will not the people be afraid?
If there is calamity in a city,
will not the Lord have done it?"

Amos 3: vs. 6

Prologue

The mouth of hell was bright with moonlight, shining the way for a gilded transport making its way through the spirit-filled night along the eastern boundary road of the Hinnom Valley; an ancient hole in the ground of human torment just outside the gates of Jerusalem. The transport was pulled along the road at a generous speed by a team of Friesian horses, escorted on all sides by a *quingenary* unit of Roman Cavalry known as the *Ala Quingenaria*. Banners bearing the crest of the House of Octavius flew near each corner of the transport's rectangular roof, billowing softly in the night wind as they mixed with the rest of the ensign-crowned poles being carried by the *quingenary's* other standard bearers.

A woman and her young son sat inside the transport's purple-padded interior, partially illuminated by moonlight filtering through small openings in the heavy drapes framing the windows. The woman was beautiful with smooth, milky skin and long red hair braided with gold rings, which draped down through the hood of her blue, palla cloak layered in folds over her white stola. She sat silently reading a scroll sent to her in Rome by her husband before his assassination several months ago, an act which also took the life of her firstborn. He had implored her to bring their younger son to Jerusalem for the Passover Feast.

Her youngest sat beside her solemnly playing a Jewish kinnor; a ten-stringed, pentatonically-tuned instrument he strummed with plectrums made of smooth bone. He was dressed in a white mantle with rainbow colored strips of cloth sewn around the edges of its large sleeves, a coat of many colors his father had given to him a year ago. A necklace with a round emblem made of pure gold hung from his neck, the bronze lion engraved in its center representing the royal seal of the House of Sheshbazzar; a line of nobility descending from the House of David.

The dark-haired boy stopped playing suddenly as an unearthly chill sifted through the transport's purple curtains, bristling the hairs on the back of his neck with a familiar feeling of dread.

He stared blankly into the cold shadows on the left. Tears trickled slowly from his emerald eyes as he clutched the kinnor close to his chest like a shield. It was as if some hungry predator lurked unseen in the shadows of the transport's interior; a recurring fear that was always coldest in his bedchambers at night, stalking him with whispers of a sharpened hate.

His mother turned to him when she noticed his playing had stopped, surprised by the tears streaming down his face. She laid the scroll aside and cupped his face in both her hands, turning it toward her. "What's the matter, my precious?" she asked.

His eyes trembled slightly as he looked up into his mother's flawless face glowing in the moonlight. "Abba...I...I miss Abba and James," he said.

She wiped away the tears on her son's cheeks with loving strokes of her soft thumbs. "I miss them, too, my Lehohn."

The boy bowed his head with a sudden look of shame when his mother addressed him by the proud surname given to him at birth. "I'm sorry, mother," he said.

"For what, my child?"

"For crying."

She lifted his chin gently, smiling with a look of supreme adoration. "Tears are not shameful, my son," she told him, her eyes brightening with a tender passion. "You have your father's heart. He was a compassionate man. A prince in the Tribe of Judah. That, as well as his and your brother's faith in this Christos Champion they were always writing to us about, this is what made them such a threat to King Herod."

The boy's eyes hardened through his tears suddenly at the mention of Herod Antipas, remembering his grandfather's words to his mother and him about how the Idumean King had hired an assassin to murder his father and brother.

"I hope Herod lives a long life," he said sharply.

The woman looked at her son with surprise. "What prompts you to wish that wicked king such fortune, my son?"

"That I may avenge Abba and James with my own hands," he replied.

"Vengeance is never the way, my son," she warned. "Blood is easily spilled. But it is not easily forgotten when it is done for personal gain. Be careful in what manner you choose to expose its color to your eyes…. Remember, you are the rightful heir to the throne of Judah now. How you govern your actions in personal affairs will determine whether or not you will rule as a wise king one day."

The boy's eyes fell from his mother's face.

"Look at me, my son."

His movement was slow, tears streaming down his cheeks.

She cupped her hands around his face again, wiping away his tears in the same manner as before. "Your grandfather is a very powerful man in the Roman Senate," she reminded him. "He has told me more than once that Tiberius' days as emperor are numbered. He is also allied to the enemies of Antipas that roam the halls of power in Rome, especially Herod's nephew Agrippa. He will see to it justice is done once Tiberius is gone, and Antipas no longer has an ally on the throne. Meanwhile, you must focus on your future, which will begin in part with your *probatio* training that will teach you the ways of the Roman Army. You will become an artisan of war and politics to prepare you for a future throne of your own. But you must never forget who you are. That is why I have brought you to Jerusalem for your first Passover."

"I will be a good king, mother," he said eagerly. "I will."

She smiled, pulling him close to her chest to hug him tightly. "I know you will, my Lehohn," she said, kissing him softly on top of the head. "Just remember what your father always taught you, '*Out of the mouth of babes and nursing infants God has ordained strength….*' Strength that will silence the enemy and the avenger."

A towering figure with wide shoulders and dark, collar-length hair stood in the center of the transport's rectangular roof, his burnished face emanating a bronze glow. He was dressed in a robe of royal-blue flax that shimmered in the moonlight. A linked belt of golden eyes was fastened around his tapered waist, supporting a broadsword in a silver sheath the size of a weaver's beam. A white pouch was nestled next to the sword on his belt, containing dozens of stellar explosives in the shape of small silver balls. On the right side of his belt was an ivory inkhorn and a large square holster containing a crimson-colored book of historical accounts about heroes and monsters, each bound by an ancient legacy.

Spirals of silver light filtered from the sides of his bright eyes as he stared up at the heavens. The clatter of shifting suits of armor filled the night air from the dust forces of the *Ala Quingenaria* traveling along in their formations on all sides of him, oblivious to his presence on the roof of the transport.

He slipped his hand over the hilt of his sword while watching a vast stream of rebel angels pass by above him, their eyes burning with red and yellow fires. He remained invisible even to them due to a special angelic and cherubic diffraction veil he was cloaked in, which allowed him to move unseen for long periods of time throughout the hidden realm.

A chorus of piercing howls filled the night air as packs of wolves in the surrounding hills announced the invisible approach of the powers of darkness, alerting the transport's armor-clad guardians to a more diligent watch of the shadowy groves of trees on each side of the road. Many of the rebel hosts landed on the spire-bordered roof of Zerubbabel's refurbished Temple rising into the night sky like a gold and marble beacon. Others took up positions on the battlements of the eastern wall looming high above the valley road, crowding together on the parapets between the blazing watch fires that cast ghostly spirals of light on the slope below, each anticipating a devilish spectacle to come.

The wingless angel glanced at the roof beneath his boots. His commission to protect and monitor the young prince below was about to carry him into the heart of darkness once more as it had done so often in the past. But on this night, the angels of the

Archrebel would focus the brunt of their destructive ways on the Christos Champion who had turned Jerusalem upside down with his messianic proclamations of divinity and salvation.

"Warnings to you, Book Master," a cold voice echoed suddenly from behind. "As the heavens are high and the Abyss is deep, so you can be sure that I haven't forgotten about the young prince in your keep."

The angel snapped his head up in a look of surprise, abruptly turning to face a legendary assassin who was both feared and respected throughout the ranks of holy and rebellious angels alike. He was a mountain of carved muscle, hovering near the roof between two of the cavalry's pole standards rising up behind the rear corners of the transport, his towering form glistening with a black, marble-like sheen in the moonlight. Slanted eyes of white fire glowed in the shadow masking his face, framed with golden locks of translucent hair. Sharply-tipped wings of bronze-colored adamantine protruded from his back, curving around his expansive shoulders in a liquid motion. Frigid vapors rolled down the vertical spines bulging from the exterior and interior of his metallic wingspan, spiraling around silver icons similar to the last letter of the Greek alphabet that were engraved hundreds of times between the spines of each wing.

The angel took a step back on the roof, clutching the breast of his robe, wondering if the assassin could really see him as he stared at the shadow masking his face.

"Worry not about your cloak, scribe. It remains intact," said the assassin, a vampiric smile of diamond teeth flashing into view beneath his white eyes. "But you can be sure that I can sense your confused presence."

The assassin hovered forward a pace, his smile increasing to a jester's width, eyes riveted on the space between the two banners flying near the opposite corners of the transport's roof. "Dark deeds transpire tonight, do they not, scribe?"

The angel's only reply was to grip the hilt of his broadsword.

The assassin's long hair swished back and forth around the sides of his shadowed face while he spoke, eyes flashing brighter with each word. "The hour of our casting out has come. But it is only temporary. For I assure you of this, the Heir will not make it to the *xulon* tree," he vowed. "He will not be allowed to fulfill his mission. He will either die by stones, or the scourging of leather-wrapped bones. I will see to that myself. Just as I will see to it that the young prince in your charge below doesn't fulfill his preordained path."

The assassin hovered forward a few more feet, drawing closer to the spot where he sensed the angel. "There is only one true champion. He was the first. The Anointed Cherub. The young one you protect will become a son of my heritage. Then he will die like the others before him. This I prophesy to you. For the shadow of the Dragon Lord's mark is already upon him," he declared, pointing to a bronze, two-headed dragon posted on top of an insignia pole being carried by a *vexillarius* standard bearer.

"There is betrayal in the night's air, scribe. Can you feel it? Can you feel the approaching destruction that promises to have its way over the Shekinah Legacy?"

He glanced up at the sky, laughing softly as the rebel hosts continued to streak toward Jerusalem. "Yes," he said, lowering his gaze again. "Even now the Son of Perdition proceeds with the deed of all deeds. A deed that will bring him into a dark and secret place to prepare him for the *Covenant Harness*."

The assassin threw open his wings suddenly, reflecting the moonlight in a bronze flare while floating backwards from the roof of the transport. "Remember this, Book Master," he said sharply. "The allure of silver is always brightest when offered in the darkness of opportunity. Opportunity prophesied and undenied. Prophecy fulfilled, yet doomed by unconquerable scheme and pride."

His laughter echoed through the air as a torrent of shadows spiraled up around him from the bottom tips of his marked wings. He vanished on the spot when the dark shapes exploded outward with smoky flakes of frigid light.

The flakes faded in front of the angel, giving rise to a prophetic tone in his voice just as the wolves in the surrounding hills unleashed their dreaded wails through the night air. "It begins."

Book One

Origins I:
Legacy

A lone warrior stood on a crag of rock that jutted out from the slope of Mount Scopus; a northern extension of the Mount of Olives also known as Lookout Hill that rose above the ancient city of Jerusalem. He was a statue of silence as he lingered in front of a thin grove of trees, gazing by the light of the moon at the watch fires burning on the siege banks built up between the broken walls of Rome's most turbulent province below.

The warrior, known as Magnus the Lehohn, wore fame and fierceness like few before him. Respect and honor had pursued him like a suitor since his graduation from the *probatio* training camps of the legionnaires. He would become the strongest and most cunning Praefectus Equitum in the *Alae Milliariae*, Rome's elite cavalry unit. To the dismay of family and friends, though, he had turned down posts in the Imperial Service and a seat in the Senate offered to him on several occasions by the Emperor Vespasian himself for his years of decorated service to the empire. He had chosen to remain an officer in the *cohorts* until he could finish out his term of service. His desire was to terminate his association with the evil oaths and icons associated with the Roman Army once and for all. Too often had his faith in the risen Christ clashed with such ideologies like the Mithraism cult of the Persian sun god introduced to the empire by the eastern legions that had helped bring Vespasian to power.

Though in his 40's, Magnus looked and lived with the vigor of a hearty young man of 30. The younger men in his *cohort* units would never forget the day when they saw him chasing a band of zealots on his horse at full gallop. He had come upon their flank as he chased them into a ravine, stooping dangerously low from his horse to grab a young, well-built zealot in full armor by the ankle, snatching him straight up into the air as he righted himself in the saddle with ambidextrous ease. It was a feat only one other in their ranks was known to have matched. Such horsemanship was first developed during the summers of his youth that were spent on his grandfather's stud farm famously known throughout the empire for its highly valued breed of centinarius champions.

Magnus stood six feet tall, a height that had helped him advance through the ranks when he was younger. His collar-length hair was black and wavy, arms hard and well-defined, tanned to a deep color of bronze from many years spent in the sun. Their strength had been forged during his post *probatio* days in the portable, thatch-covered arenas of the *hippika gymnasia*, a sporting competition waged between Rome's elite officers. A sleeveless, leather tunic mounted with bronze scales adorned his torso, with a purple-hooded cloak spilling gracefully over the armor's bulging shoulders. An auxiliary belt with silver squares was strapped around his waist, supporting a cavalry spatha; a slashing blade with an ivory, finger-grooved hilt. A Thracian scabbard of pure gold, pierced and engraved with scenes from some of the more famous battles he had fought in, sealed the weapon from view. Leather straps were wrapped tightly around his calves, extending down to his spiked, ankle-high boots.

Tears glistened in Magnus' emerald eyes while staring at the besieged and starving city below. Hundreds of zealots were impaled on both sides of the torch-lined road leading to the northern gate. The city's outer and secondary walls had been breached after five months of pounding by Scorpion catapults and other siege machines. The formidable tenth legion held the territory at the eastern extension of the Mount of Olives. The strongest portions of the army, though, had been lined up seven legions deep in a fortified position in the Kidron Valley below before moving in through the breaches in the city walls, with three ranks of his own cavalry units pulling up the rear behind them. Reserve camps stationed at the foot of Mount Scopus had all but been emptied in the conquest of the Antonia Fortress; the most strategic stronghold of the Jews. But the final assault was still to come, an assault on the Temple itself. And sadly, his wife, along with many others, were, for all he knew, still trapped in their homes near the Temple Mount between the forces of the zealots and those of the advancing legions. All that he held dear in the world was literally crumbling before him under the iron heel of the Roman Empire. An empire he had served valiantly since his first day in the *probatio* training camps.

Magnus leaned his head against the lance in his right hand, praying that his wife, Rachel, was still alive somewhere. He hadn't seen her since Rome's war with Israel's zealots began four years ago. Many had been trapped in the city at the beginning of the siege which came while they were celebrating the Feast of the Passover. He had secretly sent a messenger to his wife before the siege began, giving him a wooden slat with a fragment from part of Luke's Gospel cryptically urging her to flee to the mountains without betraying the military stratagems of his superiors. But confirmation of her having received the message never came. Such uncertainty about her whereabouts made his prayers all the more desperate.

"I believe you made a request to see me."

Magnus whipped around in surprise. There on the rocky slope before him stood the second most powerful man in the Roman world. He was a handsome, well-built man, arrayed in a crimson cloak and a gold breastplate of muscular design. A parazonium sword was strapped around his waist, a dress weapon of Romano-Hellenic design used only by generals and governors. The light of the torch he was holding illuminated his rugged face and his short hair.

"General Titus," said Magnus, snapping his weapon back against his shoulder, lightly rapping the scales of his *lorica* armor with a fisted salute as he acknowledged the Imperial Son. "I didn't notice your approach from below."

Titus made his way through the grove of olive trees to where Magnus stood in a small clearing. "I came along the eastern slope after my inspection of the tenth legion," he said.

"I thank you for coming, general."

"Only you, Magnus the Lehohn, could even presume to summon the son of Vespasian," he remarked.

Magnus smiled slightly, glancing past the Imperial Son at the guard detail lingering a few yards up the slope, with an old man standing in front of them.

The old man walked down to Titus' side when Magnus focused on him, stepping into the light of the general's torch. He was of formidable stature and build for his age, dressed in the sacerdotal robes of the Jewish priesthood, a white beard and a shaggy mane of hair covering his face and head.

"I believe you know Josephus," Titus remarked, gesturing to the old man at his side.

"We have never met," Magnus replied. "But I have often heard the deeds of the warrior priest who chose surrender rather than slaughter."

Josephus nodded warily. "I never surrendered my heart," said the old man. "I surrendered to sense, and to the academia of preserving my people and their history."

The old priest smiled with admiration at the hardened warrior before him. "But I think our people would have probably fared better under your leadership, brave prince," he continued, revealing his knowledge of the warrior's lineage in the House of Sheshbazzar. "I have seen and heard the deeds of Magnus the Lehohn as well. Your fame and nobility are even greater than that of Julian of the tenth legion."

"Your words are kind, priest," he said. "But fame in war is not the subject I wish to discuss at this hour."

Magnus turned his attention to Titus with a look of urgency. "I was hoping to speak with you privately, general."

Titus waved to his Praetorian Guard stationed beyond the grove. "Escort the scribe back to the Antonia Fortress," he ordered. "I will follow later."

Josephus nodded at the general and started back up the slope. He stopped short, however, and turned back around towards Magnus. "I have one question for you, Magnus," he said. "Who gave you the surname Lehohn?"

"My father," he answered. "It means *lion* in Greek.... The symbol of my father's house."

"I know.... And it suits you well since your first name means *great*."

The old priest looked at the hardened warrior with a wild and ominous assurance in his eyes. "I once saw a vision in the heavens before this war started," he remarked. "It was a group of stars in the shape of a sword. I thought it to be a sign from God that a champion would arise and deliver the people of Israel. And now I know that I was partially right. For he has raised up a champion. Only he has not come to bring deliverance.... But judgment."

Josephus turned and started back up the slope in a slow stride. "I will not soon forget you, *Great Lion*," the old priest told him, glancing back over his shoulder as he stopped again. "And neither will the world. Your name will be immortal in the pages of history."

Magnus said nothing, giving only a respectful nod to the old priest before he turned away again and joined the Praetorian Guard beyond the grove.

The detail turned into a clatter of clanging armor as the priestly scribe joined their numbers again, marching back to their horses stationed several yards away on a higher ridge. The torch-line above their heads faded slowly from view as they mounted their steeds and rode away towards the main path down the mountain.

Titus took several more steps down the slope until he was only a couple of feet from Magnus, propping his hand on the pommel of his sword as he locked gazes with the warrior. "I can see the concern in your eyes, Magnus," he noted, the light of his torch illuminating both of their faces. "This campaign is a difficult one for you, is it not?"

"To be sure, general."

"I understand," he said. "However, you are the most highly decorated Praefecti in the Imperial Army.... Your father may have been a prince in the Tribe of Judah, but your mother was the daughter of a Roman Senator. Don't let the dynasty of a broken kingdom cloud your judgment. Its days of glory will never come again."

Magnus pulled a small leather pouch from his auxiliary belt. Several pieces of silver could be seen peeking through an opening at the top of the pouch. "I will always belong to the House of Sheshbazzar," he replied, looking back up at Titus. "But fear not, general. I am of Solomon's lineage, and merely a prince of the royal bloodline, as my father and brother before me. I have no claim to the throne because of the past sins of King Jehoiachin.... The last and greatest of all the kings of Israel came through David's other son, Nathan. He was a *Root* from a powerless and *dry ground* that had become the line of David. This was something my mother did not understand when she was grooming me for the throne of Israel. But I know my place now, and I hold no allegiance to the zealots who wish to control my homeland.... All wickedness in Jerusalem must be wiped away."

"And what, to you, is wicked in fair Jerusalem, Magnus?"

"The plague of apostasy, sire," he answered, clinching the pouch in his hand tighter. "I remember when my mother brought me back to Jerusalem as a boy at my father's request to experience my first Passover. And though it was against Jewish tradition to tabernacle among Gentiles during the celebration, my mother felt it would be safer to stay at the Atonia Fortress, due to the hostility shown to my father's house by King Herod. And it was there that I first saw the Son of the living God. The last and greatest King of Israel who came through Nathan's line."

"You mean the Carpenter from Nazareth?"

"Yes," he answered, turning sideways to gaze at the city below. "I watched from a secluded place in the Praetorium as he was interrogated by Pilate and scourged mercilessly under that cruel art of the *flagrum taxillatum*."

Magnus opened the pouch in his hand, letting the Imperial Son see one of the shekels inside that was engraved with the right profile of the curly-haired image of the Phoenician god Melkart on the shekel's obverse, with an eagle standing on the rudder of a ship inscribed on the reverse side. "These 30 shekels of Tyrian silver, is what the Sanhedrin paid to betray their own Messiah. My mother obtained them from a merchant who had sold his potter's field to the Sanhedrin for the same shekels forsaken by the Master's betrayer. She'd heard how the chief priests had refused to keep blood money. Considering my father and brother were followers of the Lord Jesus, she sought out the merchant who had sold his field and made him an offer for the shekels he couldn't refuse. She often used them during my childhood education as tutorial reminders of the price of cowardice and betrayal. They were lessons meant to prepare me for the dangers of leadership."

Magnus paused, remembering every detail of the day his Savior died for him. "With my mother's approval and the commission of a small detachment of the *Ala Quingenaria*," he continued, "we followed Jesus from the Gabbatha Pavement after he was sentenced to death. The mob celebrating his death sentence followed as well. Never before had I seen such hatred and cruelty from the kinsmen of a condemned man. The spirit of *Death* was everywhere, rolling with a crushing pitch that was barely kept at bay by the soldiers assigned to the execution detail. But the Lord remained utterly determined during his march to Golgotha. I have seen much in my warlike days, but I have never seen anyone suffer like he did, and then die with such heroism and power. The whole Earth shook at his passing."

"But it didn't end there," he added. "I didn't see it with my own eyes, but I know he rose from the dead, just as the Apostle Paul told me years ago. For the Spirit of the Lord bears witness with mine that he is seated in glory. He will return to this world at the appointed time to fulfill his Word, and to bring forth the righteousness of his rule."

"I have heard the story of this…new god," Titus spat out. "His followers have spread this doctrine to the four corners of the Roman world. But my father is the ruler of all men, as it was prophesied when he received divine visions in the Temple of Serapis. It would not bode well for the rest of your military career to forget that, especially considering Rome's distaste for this new Jewish religion."

"This is not a religion, sire," Magnus replied. "He is *The Way*. He is God incarnate. He forgave me of all my sins…. It is through Him that I have eternal life."

"As you say," he replied with a wave of his hand. "Just remember where your loyalties are rooted."

"I will, general." Magnus turned around fully towards the city. "As I said before, I have no allegiance to the apostasy of Israel. And I hold no loyalties toward the zealots and their guild of Sicarii assassins who are trying to revive the glory of the past," he assured him. "I only wish that my wife, and others who have no part in this conflict, be spared from death."

Titus stepped to Magnus' side, resting his hand on the warrior's shoulder. "I have done all I could to preserve the lives of the innocent already," he answered, his face hard and remorseless in the light of his torch. "These zealots have been deceptively barbaric from the start, though. They do not abide by the rules of war. And because of it, I have been forced to treat them in the same manner. But I will do what I can to make sure nothing foul befalls your precious Rachel. If she is still alive as you hope."

Magnus looked into Titus' stern face, a small gleam of hope in his emerald eyes. He wasn't sure if he could trust the general to take such measures in the heat of war. And though Titus was greatly loved and respected by his men, he still remembered how brutally the general had treated his own soldiers whenever they were put to flight by the zealots during a battle.

Magnus held the general's quiet stare while he pondered those realities. He also knew of Titus' rumored dislike for having to tolerate a half-Jew in the hierarchy of his army's command structure. The rumor had spread throughout the Imperial Army shortly after the beginning of the siege. But the general vigorously denied the rumor when approached about it. Instead, Titus lauded him with praise and assurance that he held the same respect for him as the rest of the empire did.

In the end, however, it didn't really matter what Titus thought of him. He was a freed man in the risen Christ. Because of this, he was compelled to do what was right, even in war. By that compulsion, he himself would protect as many of the innocent as possible.

"General," said a voice from behind.

Magnus and Titus turned at the sound of a gruff voice coming from the upper side of the grove. The silhouette of a towering figure captured their gazes as it emerged into the light of Titus' torch. He stood two feet taller than Magnus, chest wide and heaving, arms long and sinewy, his streamlined jaw covered by a thin black beard. His dark olive, skin glistened with a watery sheen. A long mane of braided black hair dangled to his waist. His silver breastplate was ancient Egyptian, with gold eagle wings crossing at the center. A white schenti skirt with sheer-like pleats was fitted around his waist, splitting up the middle to reveal a blue tunic of the same material. A curved shotel sword hung from his jewel-studded belt.

Magnus stood amazed at the warrior's unusual size. Never before had he seen the likes of such a man as they locked gazes.

"You must not travel alone in these parts, general," the giant urged, his voice deep and soulless.

Magnus stepped forward, placing the pouch back in his belt, gripping his lance with both hands to confront the stranger. "Who is this...man, general?!" he asked, stepping in front of Titus like a shield.

The warrior folded his thick arms across his armor, giving Magnus an utterly fearless smile that revealed unusually sharp incisors among his white teeth.

Titus stepped around Magnus, pressing on his arms to lower his weapon as he passed. "Relax, Magnus," he said. "This splendid beast of destruction is my newest recruit. One of my couriers managed to lure him away from his mercenary alliance with the Scythian Nomads. And as one of few exceptions to certain ethnos requirements, he's now part of a secret *cohort* I'm developing within the Praetorian Guard."

Magnus held his lance to the side, studying the titan before him. His stature wasn't the only unnatural trait about him. His eyes were hidden in small shadows, defying the light of the general's torch illuminating the rest of his face. His whole appearance reminded Magnus about the tales of the evil *gibborim*.

Titus stepped up beside the warrior, slapping the dark bicep on his right arm with his introduction. "Magnus, I want you to meet the most relentless and fearless warrior I have ever come across, present company excluded, of course," he smiled. "He is the terror known only as Tsavo. I first heard about him when I was in Alexandria several years ago."

Magnus stood quietly unimpressed, his suspicion building as a veil of silence fell over the small clearing where they stood.

Titus moved back down between the two warriors locked in a dead stare with one another. "Wait for me outside the grove, Tsavo," he ordered. "I'll join you in a moment."

Tsavo did not move. There was only the appearance of a fierce scowl on his bullish face to show he was unwilling to yield position.

"I said leave us, Tsavo!" Titus repeated, his tone rising with authority, eyes dancing royally in the light of his torch.

The giant took in a breath through his large nostrils, releasing it in a slow and indignant manner, lightly rapping the breast of his armor with a fisted salute before walking back to the other side of the grove.

Titus turned to Magnus again. "There is no need to feel threatened by Tsavo's presence, Magnus."

"I am not threatened in the least, sire."

"Then what is it, other than Tsavo's sudden appearance, that unnerves you?"

Magnus glanced at the large figure lingering in the shadows on the other side of the grove. "There's something about him that I don't trust, general…. Something unnatural."

Titus looked back at the giant. "He is a rare feast for the eyes, isn't he? There are wild legends about him that abound throughout Egypt. It's even been said that he's over three thousand years old, and that he is one of the Titans spawned from seed of the gods that hover in the heavens around us."

Magnus squinted at the large silhouette in the distance while listening to Titus' tale.

"Such stories seem to carry a weight of possibility when you first behold him, don't they?" The general noted, glancing back at Magnus with a sardonic grin.

Magnus didn't notice the general's smug demeanor because of his intense focus that was still trained sharply on the giant's darkened silhouette.

Titus stepped in front of him, demanding the warrior's attention with the flames of his torch. "Give no more thought to Tsavo this night, Magnus," he ordered. "I need you at your best tomorrow when you lead your *cohort* units in support of the first wave against the zealot defenses at the Temple. Crush all who resist you. But do not take the Temple. That is mine to conquer. At this point I don't want it damaged. I feel a certain inclination to preserve it as a trophy to the glory of my father's reign."

Magnus' gaze fell toward the ground when he suddenly remembered the significance of what day and month it was. Regardless of Titus' desire to capture the House of the Lord intact, he knew the oracles of the Prophet Daniel and the Gospel of Luke concerning the destruction of Zerubbabel's refurbished Temple were on the verge of coming true. Numerically true. For this very night was the eve before the centuries-old anniversary of Nebuchadnezzar's destruction of the first Temple.

"Do you have a problem with your orders?" Titus asked, snapping Magnus from his haunted stare.

Magnus shook his head. "No, general."

"Good."

Magnus' expression became heavier with concern the more he thought about the destruction to come. "I will hold you to your word, general," he replied.

"My word?"

"Concerning my wife," he reminded him.

"Yes, of course," he said. "As I told you, I will do what I can."

Magnus nodded his thanks, still unsure what measure of cooperation his request would truly receive tomorrow in the heat of battle.

"There will be a brief conclave with Tiberius and the other commanders of the army in the morning before the assault on the

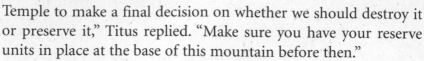

Temple to make a final decision on whether we should destroy it or preserve it," Titus replied. "Make sure you have your reserve units in place at the base of this mountain before then."

"I will, general."

With that, Titus started to leave, only to stop and face him again with a final word. "You're my best officer, Magnus…. I'm counting on you to remember your place in the scheme of things tomorrow. I will not fail in this siege of Jerusalem as Cestius Gallus failed in his."

Magnus rapped the breast of his armor with a fisted salute as the Imperial Son turned and hiked back up the slope, Tsavo taking to his side the moment the general exited the grove.

Magnus looked back at Jerusalem again after the general and his strange escort rode away. He sighed in a tired breath, bowing his head against his lance.

Magnus stood on the flat ledge of rock for another hour, lost in the memories of his past while gazing back and forth across the expanse of the city in the vicinity of the Temple area, hoping for some sort of signal from his beloved to tell him that she was still alive. But the distance was just too far for him to bring the house he had inherited from his father into focus.

Distracted, Magnus didn't notice the change in the night's atmosphere. The moon had grown brighter somehow, the sky ripening to a purple hue, teeming with stars shining like stones in a rippling brook.

Magnus began to notice the changes taking place all around him. He was surprised by a shaft of light descending from the sky in front of him, landing on the rocky slope several feet away, concentrating on one spot as it expanded like a circular curtain.

He took a step back on the flat ledge, raising his lance as the heavenly vision swirled majestically before him. The shaft of light rolled for several seconds before dissolving, revealing an enormous figure of a man clothed in a luminous robe of sky-blue flax. Heavy armaments could be seen outlined beneath the stranger's ethereal garment.

Magnus lowered his lance slowly, the Lord's Spirit softening his defenses. The stranger was taller than the giant he had encountered earlier even though he was standing on the slope beneath his ledge of rock.

"Who are you?" Magnus asked respectfully, trying to see the stranger's face cloaked beneath the robe's large hood.

The stranger walked up to Magnus, looming higher than the warrior without actually standing on the overhanging rock. "You're not frightened by my appearance?" Asked the stranger, his voice like an echo from a deep well.

Magnus was visibly stunned by the stranger's words when he spoke in a tongue never uttered for his hearing before. But somehow he understood. The texture of the language was similar to a form of ancient Hebrew he was taught as a child.

The stranger could see the confusion on Magnus' face. "I speak in the language first spoken by Adam," he said. "You understand it because I speak to what is buried within you."

Magnus' confusion melted into awe. He was beginning to understand a measure of what was happening, hoping this stranger before him had come with the answer to his prayers.

"Are you not yet frightened by my appearance and strange words?" he asked.

Magnus thought for a second before answering. "I should be," he answered. "I should be on my face as a dead man…. But I am not."

"And why is that?"

Magnus answered more boldly as the Holy Spirit who lived within him hardened his Adamic frame with the proper strength and response. "I have seen God in the flesh. And I fear neither man nor angel. I fear only him. I bow…only to him."

"And that is why I have been sent to you, brave one," he said.

The stranger lifted his hands that looked like bronze-colored glass, each as large as Magnus' head. He gripped the sides of his luminous hood, pulling it back slowly to reveal a burnished, man-shaped face chiseled to a stony countenance, accented by disheveled locks of black hair that emanated with a rainbow-colored aura for a few seconds before fading. Solid-blue corneas burned brightly in his eye sockets, shimmering with golden irises and diamond pupils. "I am Michael, a servant of the Lord Jesus, the risen Christ," he told him.

"Michael?" said Magnus, the name ringing with great power and familiarness. "You…are the great prince the Prophet Daniel wrote about…. God's Archangel."

"Yes. And I have come to you with an urgent commission from the Most High."

Magnus drove his lance into a cleft in the rock beside his foot. "The campaign…. That's why you're here, isn't it?"

Michael nodded. "This night I must once again stand aside as outside forces in the terrestrial realm seek to destroy the Children of Abraham. The hopes of the zealots for self-rule and the establishment of a new dynasty will be crushed. But Israel's seed will not be obliterated. It will flourish in other nations as it has in the past."

"I have no wish to be part of this campaign," Magnus replied. "But I have no love for the zealots or their political regime. What happens to them now matters little to me. I only wish for the safety of the innocent. That is what weighs heavily upon me. War shows little mercy to those caught in the middle."

"You have seen much during your life here on Earth. And you speak from a heart as large with compassion as it is with valor and loyalty. You have been endowed with a passion which cannot be bound by the words or deeds of other men. That is the reason why I have come to you. It is time for you to inherit the Legacy ordained for you from on high."

"I don't understand," Magnus said. "I thought you were here to answer my prayer for the safety of those who have nothing to do with the zealot's revolt."

"I have always protected those who belong to the Most High," said Michael. "But that is not why I have revealed myself to you this night. I am here to coronate you with the holiest of mantles. It was first held by the Anointed Cherub. But it was forsaken when he sought equality with the Lord Most High. His pride and jealousy lured him into a delusional darkness forever. And because of it, he and all those who followed him in his rebellion will one day be confined to the depths of Hell forever."

Michael paused for a moment, lifting his eyes to the stars. "But our Lord, in his divine wisdom, would not let that mantle be destroyed with the evil one's rebellion," he continued, looking back down at the warrior. "He would shape and hammer the mantle into something new, passing it to the hands of noble men at the appointed time. Moses was the first to inherit it; Joshua would be his heir. It was later passed to the judges of Israel such as Shamgar, Samson and Samuel. King David and his 37 men of valor were next in line."

Magnus stepped back a pace, somewhat daunted by any comparison of himself to Israel's most revered patriarchs. "These are great men whom you speak of. But what do they have to do with me?"

Michael drew a step closer to the flat rock where Magnus stood. "They were each special champions with different powers and mission objectives," he answered. "And you have been chosen to continue the Legacy. To be...the next Shekinah Champion."

43

"Shekinah Champion?"

"Yes," Michael nodded. "A champion of light.... A role you were marked for before you were even born. It was the same with the others."

"I don't understand. The Christos One was the ultimate champion. What need is there for another?"

"You speak with truth and loyalty from the depths of your heart, Magnus. And that is why the Lord delights in passing this holy mantle to you." Michael took another step closer. "He desires to see your faith flourish throughout the ages. And to watch as you discover your destiny as a living foreshadow of the wrath to come."

"Wrath?"

"Yes," Michael replied. "You will be a living foreshadow of divine judgments to return in full after the Ascension of the Church."

"What about my wife?"

Michael placed his hand on Magnus' shoulder. "Remember our Lord, and hold not to the things of your present life that will become the former."

Magnus bowed his head. The vision of his wife sung to the heart of his youth, whispering the sweet memory of when they first met in Jerusalem's marketplace. But the cries of the Carpenter nailed to the *xulon* tree for his sins quickly overpowered the image, wrapping around his thoughts with the suffocating pitch of his sacrifice. Its embrace was a piercing reminder, resonating in his spirit with Blood-soaked thunder as it cut through the flesh of his own desires. He knew he could deny his Lord nothing.

"What does the Lord require of me?" he asked as he lifted his head slowly.

"Rest easy, Magnus. Your precious Rachel, like the rest of your family, belongs to the Lord. He will always take care of her."

Magnus stared at him. He knew his words were true. But his assurances of her ultimate safety did not vanquish his desire to do what he could to protect her himself.

Michael took a step back and held out his glassy hands, palms facing up. A bronze bowl appeared between his hands in a flash of spiraling flames. "Take this," he said. "It is Shekinah Wine. A vintage of stored up wrath. It will sustain you for as long as you walk the road of the *Wayfarer Call*."

"How long will that be?"

"It is not for you to know the times and seasons, Magnus."

"But…."

"Take it," he urged. "It is your destiny. It is what you were born for."

Magnus took the bronze bowl with both hands, pressing his fingers to some of the fiery-blue symbols of ancient Hebrew etched around the bowl's lip. He rolled the bowl between his fingers, stirring the dark-blue liquid sparkling inside it. The sense of honor and duty instilled since childhood called out to him from his rugged reflection in the wine.

He closed his eyes and inhaled the sweet aroma of the sparkling wine, pressing his lower lip against one of the sets of flaming symbols near the bowl's rim representing the gematria of

999. The liquid rushed over his tongue with a taste as rapturous as the fruit, exploding with a powerful jolt of electricity while making its way down his throat in one long gulp, coursing throughout his entire body in a matter of seconds. The bowl disappeared in a flash of spiraling flames as the sudden jolt of added power brought him to his knees in a clap of thunder. The wine's Edenic enzymes surged throughout his body, their chemical reactions instantly enlarging his lung capacity and blood flow, fortifying his immune system with a stalwart shield against human disease.

Magnus rocked backwards where he had fallen, arms outstretched, mouth gaping slightly at the sight of the moon and stars growing brighter with each passing second. The mountain's olive trees loomed over him, sentry-like. Another fiery sensation electrified his skeleton while he peered at the strange anomalies around him, his back arcing in a sharp snap from the shock of his flesh and bones hardening to a preternatural density. Thousands of pin needles of light danced across the surfaces of his emerald eyes simultaneously, pulsing up and down. The heavens burned with fire as the needles of light parted at the center of each eye, dissolving away as the Holy Spirit who lived within him allowed the Shekinah Subconsciousness of his mind to roll back the veil to the spirit world like a scroll.

Michael placed his right foot on the ledge of rock and leaned into the champion's line of sight, resting his hand in the center of his *lorica* armor.

Magnus could see countless winged beings stretched out against the field of stars behind Michael's head, with horseless, fiery-wheeled chariots and siege ships of the strangest design streaking by beneath them while they made a slow descent from the sky.

"Rise, Magnus."

The champion focused on the Archangel's ethereal eyes at the sound of his deep voice, his mind teeming with increased brain activity.

Michael offered a hand to help him to his feet.

Another small clap of thunder rolled through the air as Magnus slapped the Archangel's forearm with a hearty embrace of his

45

hand, feeling as though he could catapult himself over the city below from the immense power flowing through him.

Magnus released the Archangel's forearm, taking a step back, staring at his right hand with a look of awe, feeling the added power from on high flowing through his veins like a fiery flood. The aches and pains of his impressive mortal frame acquired from a life of endless training and military campaigns were gone. To be 25 again would not compare by any measure to the sensation of the wine that now consumed him.

He looked up at Michael. "This is incredible," he remarked with a shrug of his shoulders. "I can hardly feel the weight of my armaments.... I feel almost naked."

"The power of the Shekinah Wine has bonded with your blood," Michael replied. "Your human limitations in this realm are almost nonexistent now. And the fighting skills you mastered in your *probatio* training and the *hippika gymnasia* have been amplified a thousand times over."

Magnus thought about the ramifications of inheriting such strength and skill. "This cannot be good," he said, holding both hands in front of him. "This is too much. This kind of power could make a man feel like...a god."

Michael placed his foot back on the lower slope again. "But you are not a god," he noted. "You have simply received a greater portion of power from above just as Elisha did when he inherited Elijah's mantle. Your fear of the one true God, and the fact that the Holy Spirit dwells within you, will help keep you in line with your calling like Moses and the others before you. Always remember the source of the power given to you when you're tempted to believe more of yourself than you should."

"I will."

Magnus moved to get a better look at the new picture of Jerusalem burning brightly behind the Archangel. "I can see you're not alone," he said, pointing at the wingless angels hovering above the city in fiery ranks.

"No, I'm not," he answered, turning toward the city.

Magnus peered up at the darker angels with the glowing eyes and the strange siege ships spread across the upper atmosphere of the surrounding mountains. "Then they belong to the evil one."

"Yes."

"They're as fierce-looking as I've always imagined them to be…. Every bit the monsters haunting the shadows of my childhood."

Michael turned back around with a nod of his head. "Your knowledge of the Scriptures serves you well. And that knowledge, with the Holy Spirit's guidance, will enhance greatly as you continue to study the Word. You will…."

A sudden chorus of crickets distracted Magnus from the Archangel's instruction, echoing loudly in his ears from the grove of trees behind him. "My ears…. The sounds of the night are like thunder," he marveled.

"It's one of the many changes your body has undergone," he explained. "Your skin and the density of your bones have already hardened to a preternatural state. And your eyes will forever glow like coals of emerald fire in the shadows. It's an effect similar to the Shekinah Glory that shone on Moses' face when it wasn't veiled. But the powers you have yet to discover will be the most extraordinary effects of the wine you will experience."

"Such as?"

"With a simple thought, you can soar through the air with angelic speed," he started. "Your strength is as great as 20 of my best warriors, if not more. And the only things that can draw your blood are weapons and flames of preternatural design. But rest assured, no mortal weapon in this age, or the ages to come, can harm you. The hottest of mortal flames and the coldest of environments cannot touch your life, either. But you can still feel their bite to a tolerable amount. Your clothing will have a measure of protection from impacts and forces of speed applied to them by the Shekinah Wine that feeds the energy stored up in the ionic bonds of sodium in your skin."

Michael paused for a moment, conveying a sense of caution with his piercing stare into Magnus' bright eyes. "And be sure to guard the level of your voice," he warned. "For it is now the *Sword*

47

of the Lord. At its top pitch, you can cause an earth-shattering shockwave that will devastate everything before you for as far as the scope of your eyes can behold, including the rebel hosts of the evil one. Its power is harnessed and unleashed according to the content of your targeting thoughts. So beware."

Magnus touched his lips lightly with his fingers at such a warning. "I will be careful," he said softly.

"In time, you will learn to master the range of these powers. For they are powers that do have limits as the Holy Spirit will teach you."

Magnus nodded, desiring to explore his powers. "I want to fly!" he exclaimed, looking down with wonder to see his spiked boots beginning to lift off the rock before even voicing his desire.

He rose slowly, floating breathlessly above Michael's head with outstretched arms. He ascended faster with a thought, the wind rushing against his dark head, his purple-hooded cloak flapping wildly behind him. He spun around in a corkscrew motion, the mountainside twisting below as he rose above the tops of the trees. He stopped in mid-twirl above one of the trees bordering the grove, the top branch brushing against the spiked soles of his cavalry boots.

The bones of his body felt bloated with air while hovering in place, smiling like a child. He peered out across the landscape, noting the hosts in the distance positioned rank and file above Jerusalem, oblivious to any care he had for the moment.

The pull of Michael's voice snapped him from his sudden rapture. "Come down, Magnus," he called.

Magnus twirled around and projected himself backward, arms and cloak shooting over his head as he dropped like a stone. Flying had become second nature to him in a matter of seconds, controlling his descent with subconscious ease.

At the last moment before impact, Magnus slowed the rate of his fall, floating down gently on the ledge in front of Michael. "I love this feeling! It's majestic."

"It does have a limitation, though," said the Archangel. "You cannot ascend past breathing level. Though you could hold your breath for an inordinate amount of time, the lack of air in the upper atmosphere would eventually render you unconscious."

"What are my other limits?"

Michael rolled his wide shoulders. "You must remember that you have been gifted with a tremendous power, to see and hear the activities in the realm of the spirit. You can touch this realm and bring judgment where the Holy Spirit leads. But it can touch you as well," he pointed. "Which will be to your advantage at times."

"It will?"

"Yes," he said. "Physical matter can affect angels when we're engaged in combat. Even though the atomic sparks of life that make up the structural substance of our spiritual bodies are filled with a great deal of empty space that can be manipulated, it is sometimes difficult for us to pass through solid objects once our minds are locked in a heated battle. That will be a great equalizer for you since you are unable to move through solid objects at any time in your present state."

"Why is that not one of my powers?"

"Because you haven't been glorified yet," he answered. "Your body has great power and is impervious to the weapons of man, but it is not the same as the Shekinah Body that our Lord had at his resurrection. You will inherit that glorified state when the *Trumpet of the Lord* heralds the Ascension of the Church."

Michael drew closer to Magnus. "The evil one and his forces will oppose you with great prejudice," he continued. "They're powerful. And they're not to be underestimated. They have created a vast empire in the first and second heavens known as the Outer Realm, as well as the *cosmos* systems of human government that dominate this planet. It is a dominion allotted a time of sufferance until their cup of wickedness is full. And because of it, you will always be behind enemy lines. Never let the illusions of physical might blind you to that."

Magnus nodded silently, listening to every word carefully as if he were a teenager again in the *probatio* training camps being taught his first lesson in the art of war.

49

"You must take guard against the mercenary *gibborim* of the evil one," Michael further warned, "especially the one called Tsavo. He's a shapeshifter…. The last of the original giants from the second wave of Nephilimite Conquerors spawned by rebel angels after the age of the Antediluvian World. And though he is a champion of the fallen ones, his sole desire is to wear the *Covenant Harness*; a beastly headdress with a mantle of flexible armor that was shaped by the hands of the evil one himself after the decline of Nimrod's empire. It is promised to the one known as the Great Tree who will rule over the kingdoms of the *latter days.*"

Michael took note of the enemy ranks still making their slow descent from the heights of the upper atmosphere. "This armor was placed in the care of an *ashshaph* from the Order of Tammuz in the land of Shinar," he went on, looking back down at Magnus. "The sorcerer was charged with protecting the *Covenant Harness* from pretenders to the throne. To help with this task, he formed a secret brotherhood of *chakhamim* warriors known as the Harness Magi to help protect the mantle throughout the centuries from mercenaries like Tsavo. But the giant's knowledge of the covenant mantle has made him desperate to prove he alone is worthy to rule over the kingdoms of men. His taste for blood and power is insatiable. So beware."

Magnus nodded, giving place in his mind to the vision of the bull-like warrior. "By what means can he be destroyed?"

"Though ancient power flows through him, he is not indestructible," he answered. "You can destroy him by way of drowning or the taking of his head as David did with Goliath."

Magnus thought for a moment, imagining what it would be like to go hand-to-hand with the giant as David had done with the mighty Goliath.

Michael drew even closer, his face and eyes burning with purity. "At the appointed time, you must seek out the iron sarcophagus of King Og of Bashan. The Holy Spirit will lead you. In it, you will find a weapon of adamantine lore. It was a blade once held by Goliath, to be used against the Israelites. But it was captured by David when he defeated the giant in the Valley of

Elah, only to be secretly placed back in Og's tomb after the Shepherd King's death. Use only the knowledge of its riddle in the shaping of your own weapons of war. But remember this.... Blood-stained spikes are the keys to unlocking the greatest power you have."

Michael placed his large hands on the warrior's shoulders. "Use all your powers to defend those who are weak," he urged. "Go where the Spirit of the Lord leads you. Preach the Gospel and administer judgment where God demands it. But be careful about revealing your powers to others. Misdirection will help keep the enemy at bay. And a degree of anonymity will be health to your bones."

Magnus nodded silently.

"A final word of warning to you, champion. No matter what you see in the light of the day to come, do not interfere with the campaign against the zealots.... The Temple will be destroyed, and many will be scattered."

Michael noticed the champion's eyes trembling with a lover's fear. "Hear me, Magnus," he said. "The horrors of this world and the effects of the *Wayfarer Call* will tempt the emotions of your Adamic nature like never before.'...."

Michael stepped back from the champion with that warning, reaching behind his neck with both hands to pull the hood of his luminous robe back over his head. "But fear not, you beloved son of *The Way*. 'The Lord is with you always, even unto the end of the age.'"

Magnus stood silent, watching the Archangel turn and retreat along the mountain's rocky slope. "Michael, wait. What about my wife? What will become of Rachel?"

Before Magnus could move, Michael was consumed in a fiery blaze, shooting into the sky like a blue comet. The Archangel cut a bright path through the heavens, disappearing through the ranks of rebel hosts descending from above in a rumbling flash of light.

Magnus searched the units of horseless chariots and siege ships speeding back and forth in the upper atmosphere, bringing the images of the rebels closer with a simple, concentrated

51

thought. The faces of the rebels were of differing shapes, but similar to the veneers of men. Their eyes were completely black except for their irises that were shaped like five-pointed stars, each rotating counterclockwise in the center of their orbs, glowing like red and yellow suns.

Lightning flashes from drawn swords and exposed fangs suddenly filled the spectrum of his magnified vision.

Magnus struggled to find any trace of Michael in the descending ranks of evil, clenching his fists in frustration.

"Michael," he called out again, careful to control the power of his voice. "Come back!"

Magnus shot up into the air suddenly, the wind rushing hard against his bronze face. The sight of the descending ranks mattered nothing to him at the moment, Mount Scopus quickly becoming a distant speck beneath him. Michael's earlier warnings about flying too high went unheeded. His breaths quickly became strained when he neared the strange chariots of the descending horde, eyes draining of their moisture as a spell of dizziness started to set in, lungs constricting.

"Michael," he called, his voice muffled by the thin veil of oxygen. He could see nothing but the fiery wheels of the chariots and the countless eyes of glowing menace that consumed the positions of the stars. The frigid winds of the rebels showered him from above in a stinging mist, bringing him to a stifled hover.

Magnus turned as the chariots sped by him in lightning intervals, rotating wildly, the frigid vapors from above becoming thicker, mixing with his exhausted breaths. Chaos filled his mind. Never had he seen such evil wonders before. Horseless chariots and siege ships blew by on each side of him like infernal cavalry, the howls of rebel angels thundering with blasphemy and contempt in his ears.

His head slumped forward as the thundering chaos and the frigid mist from above caused him to black out, severing the power holding him in the air. He fell backward between the speeding chariots, arms and legs flailing about while he plummeted toward the ground, the wind swishing and slicing around him in furious wails.

Mount Scopus thundered softly as Magnus crashed to the spot where the Archangel had been standing only moments ago, sending clouds of dirt and jagged debris flying high into the air as his hardened frame created a deep crater on impact. The large slab of rock where he had been standing earlier broke off from the mountainside and shifted down the slope from the force of his crash, with several trees from the surrounding grove following. The large slab slid over the mouth of the crater, sealing Magnus in the Earth.

Beams of sunlight peaked through the cracks around the oblong-shaped slab of rock covering the crater's mouth. Magnus shifted his head when he felt the warmth of the sun prick his fingertips that rested near the upper edges of the crater's interior. A burning aroma seeped in with the small beams of sunlight as well, swirling around his nose with the dust he stirred by the slow movements of his arms.

Magnus started to shift the rest of his body beneath the slab, his senses awakening to the burning smell seeping into his shallow tomb. He lifted his hand flat against the belly of the slab, sliding the ton-heavy rock to the right with an unconscious ease, the full force of the sun hitting him in the face. His bright eyes quickly resumed their normal color in the daylight.

He could tell it was well past the fifth hour of the day from the sun's descent towards the west. A single name gripped his thoughts suddenly as a hot wind swept across the mountainside where he lay, slicing over his exposed face in a smoky stench.

"Rachel," he muttered, her name quivering off his lips as the scent of smoldering flesh filled the air.

Magnus sat up quickly. His eyes fell on a merciless display of impaled bodies that had doubled in number on each side of the city's northern road. Flames and blustering clouds of smoky ruin soiled the sky above the walled province beyond the groves of torture. The Scorpion catapults once used to launch showers of iron-tipped darts were abandoned in front of the siege banks. Black plumes of smoke circled the towers of the Antonia Fortress as

Zerubbabel's refurbished Temple burned uncontrollably, the fire having spread throughout its intersecting structures and the columned pavilion of the Royal Stoa on the southern wall of the Temple Mount.

Magnus sprang to the rim of the crater with a quick push of his hands, ripping his ragged cloak from around his neck as he landed on the slope. "Rachel!"

He vaulted forward with another quick leap, cutting a high arc through the air before landing back down on the mountain-side again, his mind taking quick action to control the adrenaline mixing with the heavenly wine coursing through his veins. He drew his spatha blade in his dash down the steep slope, swinging it like it was a natural extension of his hand while leaping over craggy outcroppings with the ease of a deer. The landscape around him blurred in his race through the groves of tree stumps where mighty palm, olive, and myrtle trees had once populated the lower sides of Mount Scopus.

A trail of dust followed as he crossed the Kidron Valley at the foot of Lookout Hill in a matter of seconds.

Magnus' speed slowed to a normal pace almost immediately when he reached the northern road where the first zealots were impaled, the wall of dust behind him subsiding.

The rawest stench of death and bile-layered decay descended on him in a heavy cloud at his entry into the pathway of dead and dying zealots. Roman soldiers standing at the bases of the wooden pales recognized Rome's most decorated Praefecti walking into their grove of torments, talking in hushed voices with one another while he passed in front of them.

Magnus stopped in the middle of the pathway, staring up to his right at a haggard, torn face of a young zealot hanging in the familiar pose of impalement, wrists spiked through on the sides of his rood just above his head, feet doubled over and fastened in similar fashion. Needles of light pulsed across the champion's eyes suddenly as his mind subconsciously tore back the veil of the spirit world. A hulking apparition appeared on top of the pale above the zealot's head in the form of watery flames rolling out-ward like a scroll, the split fire vanishing in small plumes of light as the formidable shape of a rebel angel became more defined. Black eyes of rotating fire stared back at him from the top of the rood, their glow shining through tresses of long hair framing the sides of the rebel's predatory face. An infernal crossbow hung from the right side of the armored apron fastened around his waist, with a sickle sword hanging on the left. A round black shield was attached to his left arm, with gold, antiquarian markings of angelic origin inscribed on its rolled-out center to signify his membership in the Nekros Order; an elite group of rebel hosts specializing in the art of search and destroy.

The rebel flashed his sharp, iron-like teeth at the champion with a sneer of laughter, the bottom tips of his wings billowing with motion on each side of the zealot's head hanging beneath his perch, looking as though they weren't natural appendages, but rather illusions of assumption.

A cold chill swept over Magnus' body as thousands of similarly-armed rebels materialized on each side of the road, perched in identical crouching positions above the heads of the impaled zealots, their strange wings billowing outward from the tops of the pales like black banners.

He watched as more fallen angels burned into view. The fiery chariots and the siege ships from last night filled the sky in rings of spaced-out regiments, stretching like a hovering net across the airspace of the entire city. There was no sign of Michael or his warriors anywhere as pillars of black smoke continued to climb high above the city walls. The sounds of war and human agony spreading over the groves of the executed in thick clouds of ruin, eclipsing the sun in smoky intervals. He felt utterly alone, stranded at the mouth of a hell on Earth. Michael's words that he would always be behind enemy lines echoed through his feverish mind as sporadic flakes of human ash and city debris began to rain down on him.

Magnus was unable to mourn the city of his Jewish heritage. His thoughts were fixed on his wife, and the promise Titus had made to him. But his failure to show up and lead his men in the final assault on the zealots would have consequences. His fear was not for himself, however. He had been called to a higher purpose;

no man could strike a death blow against him now. Few had come close to doing so even before his induction into the Shekinah Legacy last night. But that was not true for the ones he loved.

He quickly started forward, splintering the ivory hilt of his spatha sword with an increased grip, beads of cold sweat rolling down his face. His eyes searched left and right, keeping watch for the slightest movement from the rebel angels or the soldiers on either side of the road.

The champion walked for what seemed like hours, listening to the hushed voices of the soldiers ringing clear in his powerful ears through all the weakened moans of the impaled.

The pitch of the war reached its peak for Magnus as he rounded a bend in the road, walking into the shadow of a ten-foot rood planted in front of the northern gateway's blackened arch. The sword fell from his hands, tears flooding his eyes at the sight of his wife hanging in a broken pose above him, smoke and flames ascending behind her on the other side of the blackened gateway. Rachel's arms were stretched above her head and nailed to the sides of the pale. Her black hair masked the sides of her head which dangled toward a familiar sword lodged deep in her chest. The blood ran thick along the blade and ornate hilt of Titus' parazonium blade, soaking her fringed dress as it dripped heavily over her knees.

The rebels perched on top of the other pales roared like ravenous wolves when Magnus fell against the rood's knotted trunk.

He dug his fingers into the dead tree beneath his wife's feet, the tears blurring his vision as he splintered and cracked the knotted wood with his hands, snapping the trunk's base in half while the demons roared triumphantly behind him. He caught the transplanted tree in its teeter to the left, gently wrapping his left arm around Rachel's body while laying the broken trunk on the ground. He pulled the spikes from her wrists carefully, casting them aside. He then removed the blade from her chest in the same manner and flung it behind him.

Magnus knelt beside her body, pulling her to his chest, stroking the hair away from her face that was matted with blood and dirt, the glory of her raven-like mane tarnished forever. The moment he had feared most and prayed vehemently against since the beginning of the siege had come true. Brutally true.

He could only stare at her broken body in disbelief. Even in his worst nightmares, he never imagined she would suffer such a death. She was the flesh now stripped from his bones; one of the tenderest blooms of life and human love he would ever know.

"Avenge her, young one," a cold voice said from above. "Avenge her with all the power at your disposal."

Magnus looked up through his tears, feeling the blackest depths of despair creep over his soul. A golden-haired rebel with metallic, crimson-colored wings encrusted with carved feathers, jeweled eyes, and silver symbols stood before him. His golden eyes were those of a dragon, with black, six-pointed stars rotating counter clockwise in the fang-like irises of crimson fire burning in the center of each eye.

"Avenge her," the rebel repeated, his frigid voice echoing in the champion's mind rather than his ears. "Claim your legal rights of vengeance, young champion.... Claim them!"

The moment was quicker than the eye as the mysterious rebel vanished in a hot wind of dust and smoke-layered shadow, his unspoken invitations swirling around him in fading whispers and vapors of stringed music.

Magnus stood to his feet without a word, his mind overwhelmed with confusion and despair. The howls of the rebels subsided into sharp snickers as he turned around from the blackened gateway and started to walk away, his wife cradled in his arms, tears rolling down his face.

The taunts of the rood-perched rebels and the murmurings of the Roman soldiers standing below them faded to mere echoes as Magnus walked along the road. His tears fell onto Rachel's face, mingling with the flakes of ash raining down on them.

A small contingent of the rebels exploded off some of the pales on the left side of the road when a scarlet-colored power from the Council of Thrones hierarchy swept down from the sky, following the champion from a distance.

Magnus fell to his knees at the foot of Mount Scopus, defeated, kneeling beside a shallow grave dug with his own hands. He was holding Rachel in his arms, stroking her raven-colored hair. She was a pale reflection of her former beauty, her brown skin sullied and tortured at the hands of men he thought he could trust; the words of Vespasian's son ringing with a hollow resonance in his mind.

His emerald eyes clouded as he thought of the impoverished life she had lived before they met. She had been abandoned as a child, forced to survive among beggars and lepers scrounging for food left over in the fields of wheat merchants. She was nearly half his age when they first met in Jerusalem's marketplace. But the attraction was instant. Her beauty had caused great commotion in the marketplace that day as her guardian, an unscrupulous merchant, put her on the auction block. He remembered the fierce bidding, the highest offers coming from the caravan of an Ethiopian prince. But he quickly trumped the prince's offer, doubling the bid to the crowd's great astonishment. The merchant refused to believe that Magnus, a Roman officer, was able to pay such a price. But when he revealed the seal of his mother's house, the deal was quickly closed. Rachel responded with tears and surprise, not knowing what to expect from a master who would pay so much for one with as seemingly little value as she. Her biggest surprise came later when she was set free. In addition, he had given her double the fortune paid for her, making sure she would be taken care of for the rest of her life. They wed a year later, two years before the beginning of the Jewish War.

Magnus pulled her to his chest. He closed his eyes and kissed her blood-dried lips tenderly, the sweetness of their fruit having faded. "Holy Father," he whispered against her mouth, "please bring her back to me.... Please, Father, restore her.... Please, Father!"

Silence was the only reply from Heaven.

The champion leaned forward and placed her body in the grave. He then looked upward with pleading eyes, placing his hands on the wound in her chest as if to allow the immense power already flowing through him to be God's instrument to raise her. Tragically, such powers of resurrection and healing, like those given to the Apostles for the testimony of authenticity, would not be found amongst the arsenal at his disposal.

Magnus sobbed softly at the continued silence from above, his bloodied hands trembling against her chest as he waited for the miracle he knew deep within him would not come.

Time seemed to stand still until he reluctantly pulled back his hands. At that moment a shadow fell over his face from the bowing of his head, the tears drying against his face in the heat of a building rage. His own heart thundered in his ears with thoughts of tearing Titus limb from limb, a power that did reside within him.

"Yessss," a voice hissed from behind. "Destroy him, champion."

Magnus opened his eyes with a bright and hateful glare, slowly rising to his feet. His demeanor hardened when he turned and came face to face with a towering angel. The scarlet-colored rebel was a mountain of sleek muscle that shimmered like Morganite stone, his deceptive wings rustling through the air behind him, the tips of his oil-dark hair looped with golden rings. The black eyes of his humanoid face blazed with star-shaped irises of yellow fire rotating in counterclockwise patterns, fangs emerging in a jester's smile. A scale-armored apron with a sickle sword on one side and a preternatural crossbow on the other was fastened around his waist beneath a muscled breastplate of black adamantine, with a miniature, jewel-marked shield of gold nestled between the breastplate's pectorals; its markings signifying his authority over the Nekros Order.

"Leave me, spirit," Magnus growled, his fiery eyes piercing the other warriors hovering in the air behind the lead rebel in a submissive silence.

"A Shekinah Champion for only one day, and already you speak with season."

"Leave me!" he repeated.

"Very well. I will leave you to your anger." The rebel leaned close to Magnus' face, his black eyes flush with the heat of rotating stars. "Do your worst, champion. Do your worst."

59

The rebel drew back in a windswept fluster of wings, rising backward into the air amongst the Nekros warriors with howls of spiteful laughter. The motley crew streaked across the sky in a wide arc, descending toward the chaos still bubbling at the heart of the ancient city.

A cloud of dust rose from the road of the impaled zealots beneath the band of retreating rebels, marking the approach of a small unit of horsemen.

Magnus focused on the cloud with a vengeful scowl, clenching his fists, hardening his stance in front of his wife's grave, her blood dripping through his tightened fingers, echoing in his ears with each splatter on the ground.

The cloud of dust faded as 16 of his own men from the horse-archer *cohorts* thundered to a halt some 20 feet away. Armed with javelins, they moved to surround him.

Magnus' eyes settled on the one who led them, watching as Titus himself positioned his familiar mount in the middle of the unit's circling formation, barring Magnus' path. But he had no intention of running from this confrontation.

Titus dismounted and strode toward Magnus with a certain swagger, casting a military issue writing slat made of wood and a set of iron shackles at his feet.

Magnus looked down at the shackles first before glancing over at the familiar, veneer-thin slat of folded wood. A stylus-tooled depiction of his father's royal seal was positioned beneath the knot of the cord tied around the slat, with a half broken clay replica of the seal's lion's head lumped on top of it.

"One of my spies intercepted the secret message you sent to your wife prior to the siege," Titus revealed. "And as you know, I am quite fluent in both Greek and Aramaic. I had hoped to orchestrate your downfall in front of my other officers once the city fell. But it seems your cowardly absence has given me the opportunity to destroy you in front of those who truly adored you: your very own men."

Magnus lifted his head with a smoldering stare. "You murdered…my wife," he said lowly, gritting his teeth.

"Yes…. Yes, I did," he replied with relish. "She's been in my custody all along. But it wasn't until today that I was able to hear her scream for mercy."

Magnus held his ground, the inner rage building to a fever pitch.

Titus drew dangerously close to the champion, squinting with disdain. "I always suspected that your loyalties were divided when I found out you had been allowed to keep from taking the mark of the empire. You're as much a barbarian as those zealots who foolishly set those fires in the inner court of the Temple. And I have tolerated your presence in my army because of my father's friendship with the House of Octavius. But no more. I have found the nail to pin your hide to the wall," he sneered, poking his finger against the chest of Magnus' scale armor. "All I needed was patience, and to watch for treason. Your days of usurping the son of Vespasian are finished!"

Titus swung his left hand to the side, striking Magnus on the jaw with a quick backfist to humiliate him even more with a show of his own strength. The champion's head didn't move, though, as the general grunted in a painful grimace from the hearty blow. It was like striking the side of a marble pillar.

Magnus grabbed Titus' offending hand, his movement too fast for the general to see. He crushed it with a simple squeeze, filling the air with the sound of cracking bones.

Titus fell to his knees, screaming in torment.

The archers took aim at their former commander without hesitation, hurling their javelins with great speed and strength, striking Magnus in the arms and back in perfect unison. Each javelin buckled into splinters against the champion's hardened frame, their impacts merely chipping off some of the scales of his armor as the broken weapons bounced off of him.

The archers gazed at one another in disbelief.

Magnus continued to squeeze while Titus writhed in pain at his feet, his wife's blood running through his fingers down along the general's arm. "The murderer of my earthly father and brother found mercy in Caligula's exile of him years ago. But you

61

will find no such quarter with me," he said with finality. "To torments I send you!"

Magnus drew back his other hand that was tightly drawn into an unforgiving fist.

A force of immense strength caught Magnus' arm before he could deliver the blow to the general's head. "No!" commanded a voice from behind.

Magnus glared over his left shoulder to see Michael holding his wrist, still clothed in the luminous robe from the night before. "You said she would be taken care of, Michael!" he cried, pulling the Archangel forward a step with his attempt to jerk his arm free.

Michael increased his grip, looking almost surprised by the raw power flowing through the arm of the new champion. "No, Magnus!" he repeated. "His life is not yours to take! Vengeance belongs to the Lord!"

Magnus glared down at Titus, refusing to relinquish his hold on him. He looked around at the paralyzed archers on their mounts, confusedly watching the strange scene, glancing back and forth at one another as they each wondered who would dare to make the first move to help their general. They were all more than accustomed to Rome's frequent changes of power in the last few years, and it was always important to make sure you were standing on the right side when the smoke cleared.

"Let go of him, Magnus!" Michael repeated.

Magnus looked back at the Archangel just at the moment the voice of the Holy Spirit whispered to his heart. "*Obey*," said the Lord.

The urging of the Holy Spirit spoke of Rachel's home with the Father above as well, reminding him, too, of how his Savior suffered at the hands of unjust men without striking back with the fullness of divine power.

He let go of Titus' hand, tossing the Imperial Son backward in the process.

Michael released his hold on Magnus and vanished once more.

Titus crawled to his right, pulling himself up by the ankle of one of the archers, tucking his broken hand beneath his arm. "Bind him!" he panted, falling against the horse's side.

The archer steadied his horse as Titus fell against him, looking to his comrades for help. None of the other archers seemed willing, each reining their steeds backward several paces.

Magnus felt the cold sting of his loss making one last stab at his broken heart, faint tears hardening in his emerald eyes with his gaze heavenward, the rage of it all exploding through his quivering mouth. "FATHER!!!!" he shouted, Michael's warning's from the previous night getting lost in the cloud of his emotions as the *Sword of the Lord* was unleashed.

The ground around Magnus' feet collapsed into a five-foot crater 40 feet in circumference as the shout exploded from his mouth in a seismic wave, rippling like a watery, funnel-shaped explosion. The wave widened when Magnus lowered his head in the motion of the collapsing ground, just missing Titus and the others as the shockwave gathered a rolling wall of sand and other debris in its earth-shattering course.

The rebel angels that were still perched on top of the roods in the distance vaulted into flight as the roaring wave raced toward them, its power cutting the groves of impaled zealots in half, tossing debris in every direction. The wave suddenly shifted upward before striking what was left of the battered city, pulled to a new course by the unseen Will of Heaven which caused the hovering chariots and siege ships to break from their formations. It rushed through the air above the smoking remains of the city, catching some of the rebel hosts by surprise while they sped back and forth across the rooftops in their evil pursuits. Black explosions pulsed throughout the wave as its razor-sharp pressure tore rebel angels in half, their remains falling into a swirling portal to the Abyss that opened in the ground in the center of the city below.

The wave eventually melted away into the horizon.

The air at the foot of Mount Scopus was calm. Magnus was still on his feet in the center of the crater. Titus and his men lay scattered all around him, their frightened horses stirring together in a small herd off to the left.

Titus managed to pull himself to the top of the crater, standing, gazing incredulously at the splintered pales scattered across the landscape in the distance, the bodies of the zealots jumbled together in mounds of flesh and wood.

Titus steadied himself the best he could, tucking his injured hand beneath his other arm as he turned back briskly. "On your feet!" he shouted to his men who lay dazed and sprawled out in the crater. "Show your allegiance to the masters of Rome, and bind this traitor!"

Magnus was horrified at what he saw above the rim of the crater, ignoring the general's orders to have him bound. He touched his lips with trembling fingers where miniature, raised symbols in Hebrew burned with an ember's glow to spell out the gematria phrase, *My Wrath*, before eventually sinking into his flesh again. He could only imagine the full destruction that could have been wrought had the Lord not obviously intervened.

He turned around with a sudden thought, finding his wife's grave completely submerged beneath the crater's wall of sand and dirt.

The words of the Lord came to him again. "*Obey and submit, my son.*"

Magnus swayed at the words while staring at the spot where he had dug his wife's grave, dropping to the sand on his knees at the divine command.

The archers slowly stood to their feet as Titus continued to rant above them.

"He doesn't breathe fire!" Titus shouted. "You've seen sand storms and earthquakes rise up suddenly before!"

The archers glanced at one another, unsure of what to believe.

"I said bind him!" Titus repeated.

One of the archers grabbed the shackles that were partially covered with sand and dirt at the center of the crater behind

Magnus. The other men each drew a second javelin from their side hanging quivers, shoring up their lingering superstitions with a well-trained posture to shock the champion with impalement should he resist. The archer with the iron bands placed them around the wrists of his former Praefecti nervously, trying not to look him in the eye in the process. He then pulled him to his feet with an easy jerk, turning him around to bind his ankles with the other set of shackles that were connected to the wrist bands by a hanging chain.

Titus walked back down into the crater and stood in front of the bound champion, smiling victoriously while endeavoring to hide the pain in his hand. "I may have not been able to capture the Jewish Temple intact as a trophy for my father, but you can be sure of this one promise that I make to you now, brave prince," he sneered, mocking him with Josephus' words from the previous night. "Your slow destruction will be my prize as your name is blotted out of every book and pillar that recorded your fame. Others will be honored for your noble deeds. History will never know you even existed."

Titus drew closer to his bowed head, reaching out toward him with a renewed boldness as he snatched the pouch of silver from Magnus' belt. "This is all that you have left in this world," he said maliciously. "Tutorial reminders of the lesson you didn't learn about the price of cowardice and betrayal. You can ponder their weight as you spend the rest of your life in chains…. Exiled on the Isle of Patmos."

⊷•••☒○☒•••⊷

Magnus lay sprawled on his back in a deep sleep on a wooden bench in the belly of a Roman slave galley, stripped of his armor and rank. His face and chest were covered in sweat, arms and legs hanging down toward the hull floor, bound by chains that could have been crushed into powder at any time he so desired. A lantern swung back and forth above him, its motion flowing with the galley as it rolled on the sea in a fierce storm, stirring the damp, nauseating cloud of decay permeating the holding quarters from all the bodies of the other slaves that lay dead and dying in the shadows around him. The stench of death, rather than the chains binding him, had kept him flat on his back, sitting heavily on his chest like an abysmal reminder of the blood and carnage of the past few days that had changed his life forever.

Memories and chains were all that remained now. Power from on high to exact complete vengeance rested within him. But it had been surrendered to men of low estate. Men of evil design whose form and skill had touched the shores of his life once again, exacting an even greater price than the one he had paid as a boy born to a royal house with Herodian adversaries.

A scene of strange images emerged in his mind while he slept. He could see himself standing on a moonlit crest of a rocky hill overlooking a beach of burnt clay being assaulted by heavy surf. Blood and water dripped from the tips of his hair, pelting his sleeveless, thigh-length armor of large, signet-like seals of gold rolled up on the sides like lumps of pressed clay, inscribed with bronze symbols of Hebrew in their flat centers beneath the lumped borders of each thickly-hammered seal. The armor was fastened together by a seam of crown-engraved buckles of refined silver arranged single file down the middle of the flexible garment rather than the side like the *lorica squamata* armament he was accustomed to wearing. A helmet partially made of bronze was tucked under his left arm, with emblems and a ceremonial face mask cast in a heavenly color of gold. A slightly curved, single-edged blade was strapped around his waist. To crown it all was a leather, crimson-colored cloak with golden emblems that was draped over his shoulders, its liquid hem swirling around the lion claws looped around the tops of his boots.

Magnus grasped three Blood-stained spikes between the fingers of his right fist, watching the stony ground in front of him yawn with a thunderous cracking noise. The granite opened in a counterclockwise motion as if the rocks were turning to liquid. A blast of black smoke bellowed from the pit which hardened to a six-foot diameter. A large paw rose up over the jagged rim of the opening, followed by another one as they each clamped down on the stony sides of the pit explosively. An enormous, black griffin with red wings emerged slowly through the pit's swirling thicket of smoke, hunching its muscular shoulders forward in a crouching position, its golden eyes shining with the shape and power of a dragon. An iron chain hung around its neck that had a diverse display of beastly body parts dangling from the chain's thick links. The winged lion growled at the champion with an old hatred as familiar shekels of silver dripped from its fanged jaws, splattering in the blood that was bubbling up from beneath the rocks where the beast was crouched.

Magnus showed no fear of the beast as another entity ascended through the smoke of the pit. The spirit of a beautiful woman decked in precious jewels and seductive garments of purple floated up behind the growling beast. She held a wicker ephah in her hands, and had a dragon-twined cross branded on her forehead with the words *Mother of Harlots* written in Akkadian above it. The word *harlot* was also inscribed on the lead covering that sealed the basket she was holding. But the inscription was written in Hebrew instead of Akkadian, crowning the other engraving in the center of the lead cover that depicted two, stork-winged goddesses carrying an ephah like the spirit woman before him.

His gaze traveled down the slope of the hill where he was standing as the images before him faded into ashy currents of wind, drawn to the waves crashing violently on the beach of burnt clay below. The great sea exploded in front of him as a black and red dragon with two heads ascended through the surface in a funnel of water, its crimson-colored wings arcing high above each head, shimmering with ancient symbols, jewels, and eagle-style feathers that were carved like worked metal between the vertical spines of each wing.

The dragon was perched on a Babylonian cross of translucent gold that rose slowly above the surface of the crashing waves, flexing its sinewy limbs in a hateful stare, flames billowing in clouds through the sides of each fanged jowl as golden blood dripped from three slash wounds on both heads. At the same time, the dragon's rising seemed to cause the moon in the sky of his dreamworld to move to the right of the hill, revealing the image of a nighttime sun hidden behind it.

Magnus rocked back and forth on the wooden bench slowly as the dragon hovered before him in his mind, seeing his image on the mountainous hill reflected in the translucent surface of the cross. The flames of the dragon's dual jaws spiraled down around the cross, taunting him with the promise of a funeral pyre.

"What do you see, Magnus?" a voice whispered suddenly from the shadows.

Magnus didn't respond, unaware of a pair of silver eyes emerging from the shadows of the corner at the foot of his bench. Burnished hands slid into view from the shadows a second later, clinging to each wall of the corner just beneath the ceiling. The hem of a royal-blue robe fluttered through the air from the corner as the galley rocked back and forth on the sea, the stranger's glassy face appeared briefly in the strobes of light while the lantern swung from side to side, illuminating the intersecting walls he clung to like a spider, his thick shoulders and chest protruding forward.

"What do you see, Magnus?" the stranger probed encouragingly, his cosmic voice booming softly at the core of the champion's sleep-submerged consciousness.

Magnus heard the distant voice this time. "I see a beast and a harlot…. And a beast with two heads," he said groggily.

"And what does it all mean?" the stranger asked, his eyes flashing with silver bursts of fire as his voice continued to fill the inner hull with ghostly echoes.

"I…. I don't know," he answered.

"That which you see is not a new revelation," the stranger answered. "It is a riddle of images drawn from your knowledge of the Scriptures. Number their strength against you…. A beast, a harlot and a dragon. They shall be the triangle that tasks you in both form and legend."

Solitary tears trickled from the corners of the champion's eyes as the images in his mind started to spiral together with those of his shattered life. "I…. I don't understand."

"You will," the stranger replied, kindly. "…In time you will understand it all."

The stranger's silver eyes melted back into the shadows of the corner, his glassy hands sliding along the hull's wooden beams as he slowly disappeared. "I am Scriptos," he echoed softly, "a servant of the Lord Jesus, the risen Christ…. And I will write your story."

He was pursued on high to
suffer much for his Courage.
To inherit a Mantle prepared
for him before the foundations
of the world were laid.

The Legacy of his course has
aged well against the Wayfarer
Call, but the darkness of the
Dragon Lord grows. The wars
weigh heavy upon him.

The Shekinah Chronicles
Book Master entry: Lisbon, 1755 A.D.

Book Two

Origins II:
Resurrection

Ceaseless waves splashed against the time-worn shore of Magnus' mind, thundering with memory that froze his thoughts in the past for a moment. The jagged bluffs and smooth, gray slopes of the Isle of Patmos, a small island formed by a volcanic eruption in the Aegean Sea, rose into view in his mind while he sat silently on a flat rock in a moonlit grove of cedars. The small isle had been his home for a hundred years after his initial banishment to its shores.

Magnus sank into the memory of his last day on the small island. Rome still ruled the world at the time. But Titus and Vespasian had long since died. Emperors had come and gone, but he had survived them all without aging a single day in appearance or strength.

He saw himself that last day standing on the island's ash-covered beach at sunset, the volcanic cliffs and hills looming behind as he faced the sea, the tide slapping gently against the legs of his deer skin pants, the salty breeze blowing through his collar-length hair and the thick beard covering the lower half of his sleek face. He was twirling a wooden staff in front of him that was hollowed out at each end, with several holes carved into the exterior of the staff's two ends. Ballots of air whistled through the holes in the staff as he spun it back and forth in front of him, whipping it around his back in circles while passing it from hand to hand with a virtuosos grace, filling the salty air with a sharp melody.

Magnus stopped when a flash of light and wind swept across his face. He crouched defensively with his staff, snapping his head to the right. An enormous figure of a man stood on the beach only a few feet away, appearing out of thin air, clothed in a luminous robe of sky-blue flax that had the outline of heavy armaments beneath it.

"Keep those senses sharp, you beloved son of *The Way*," the hooded figure replied, his voice echoing softly with a familiar dialect. "Your greatest threat will always come when you least expect it."

Magnus nodded his head while maintaining his defensive stance.

"I am Gabriel, a servant of the Lord Jesus, the risen Christ," the tall visitor said, pulling back the hood of his robe to reveal a burnished face framed by disheveled locks of platinum hair, eyes bright with colors of blue, white, and gold.

Magnus lowered his staff, driving it into the sand beside him, the Holy Spirit assuring him the angelic visitor was telling the truth.

"The time has come for you to leave this place," Gabriel told him.

The angel reached inside his robe and pulled out a copper scroll and an old soft leather case with the mark of a *flagrum taxillatum* whip master branded on its flap. "Take this scroll," he urged, offering the rolled copper first.

Magnus reached out and took the scroll from the angel's hand. "What is it?" he asked, taking note of the Hebrew symbols hammered into the rolled copper.

"It is a map to the riches that were buried with King David beneath Jerusalem," said Gabriel. "You will need it to replace the wealth of your mother's house that was stolen from you. There is a special vest of armor and a helmet hidden among the treasures as well. Be sure to take them with you...for they are the symbols of your authority."

Magnus shook his head, remembering the legends he'd been told as a child about the secret treasure Solomon had supposedly buried with his father King David. "I am not worthy of such riches," he replied.

"You are a prince in the House of Sheshbazzar, Magnus. They are yours by right of inheritance. But take only what you need. A mere portion of such treasure will make you the wealthiest man on the face of this Earth.... For you shall be a nomadic king of great travels to foreshadow the wrath to be poured out at the return of the King of Kings."

Magnus fell silent, glancing out at the ocean as its tide sliced softly around his feet. He could only imagine what waited for him beyond the horizon.

Gabriel offered the leather case next. "And take this," he told him. "But do not open it until you are instructed to do so. Keep it somewhere safe until the appointed time."

Magnus took the case by its strap and held it in front of him. "Dare I ask what this is?"

"You will know at the appointed time."

Magnus didn't argue. He simply nodded his head and secured it across his chest by the strap it dangled from.

"After you have secured the treasure of your inheritance," Gabriel continued, "seek out the tomb and the iron sarcophagus of King Og of Bashan. You will need the mystery of the ancient sword in Og's tomb to help you shape your own offensive weapons of war as Michael instructed. But make sure you are not followed to the tomb. This particular sword must not fall into the wrong hands after you reseal it in the sarcophagus."

"Why?" he asked.

"You will know the reason why once you have held it in your own hands."

With that said, Gabriel pulled the hood of his robe back over his head and began to walk away. "Farewell, you beloved son of *The Way*," he said, his voice echoing across the beach. " 'The Lord is with you always, even unto the end of the age.' "

"Wait," Magnus pleaded, reaching out for the angel just as he had done with Michael so long ago, countless questions still plaguing him about the life set before him.

Gabriel shot into the air in a bright streak of light before even one of those remaining questions could be posed, arcing across the twilight sky above.

—•—••——◼◻◼——••—•—

The sounds of the night echoed softly in Magnus' hearing, slowly drawing him from the ancient memories of his last day on the Isle of Patmos.

He stirred sluggishly, massaging his eyes as the image of the angel faded from his mind. The rock where he was sitting was positioned on the ridge of a small wooded hill in southern Lebanon overlooking an enormous crater in the center of a grove of trees below. His hair was short and slickly parted to the side, eyes bright with a millennial glow. He wore a full-length frock coat of brown velvet, accented by a dark blue sweater and jeans to help ward off the cold air that swept down from the fossil-lined mountains of limestone looming all around him in the distance. Tall cedars with thick, sweeping branches towered over both sides of him like the mythic spires of a Gothic castle, their dark green tops brushing against the night's twinkling canvas. The moon was unusually bright, casting sporadic shafts of lunar light down throughout the rolling grove of cedars below.

The grove was one of the last of Lebanon's famous conifers, located near the small valley town of Bshirre. A larger remnant of these once proud giants had survived millenniums of war, plunder and exporting, only to be almost totally annihilated while being used as fuel for the Beirut-Damascus Railway from 1914 to 1919.

Magnus leaned forward stoically, focusing on the center of the crater's stony floor where one of the shafts of moonlight fell. It looked as though it had been filled by hand with a dark patch of soil that didn't match the dirt of the cedar-lined ridges around the top of the crater. But the most curious element of the different-colored soil was the enormous six-pointed star of Rosicrucian symbolism constructed from smaller five-pointed stars symmetrically drawn in the center of it, surrounded by a wreath-like depiction of 13 Babylonian eagles clutching olive branches and arrows of belomancy in their talons. The five-pointed stars making up the larger star were blazing sbas of demonic power he knew well, the origins of their first recorded appearances in the Ancient World tracing back to the pyramids of Egypt and the Dog Star of Anubis, with links to the star of Remphan mentioned in the Book of Acts. It was also an image visible on the flags and currencies of the world's most powerful nations.

Even stranger was the phrase *Akeldama* written in front of all six points of the main star, an Aramaic passage from the Scriptures meaning place or farm of blood. He knew the phrase as well as he knew the origins of the star. What he didn't know was that the dark-colored soil had been taken from the real *Farm of Blood* located outside the ancient walls of Jerusalem, a plot of land purchased by Judas with money stolen from the Apostolic treasury. This was the very same place where Judas would eventually hang himself, yet differing in location from the potter's field purchased by the Sanhedrin with the 30 pieces of silver forsaken by the Lord's chosen betrayer.

Magnus scanned the shadows of the tree-lined border on the opposite side of the crater. There was no movement in the towering crop of trees. He imagined this would change as the evening progressed, having been drawn there from Iraq by the Holy Spirit.

Like the Massorah Magna in the margins of Holy Writ, Magnus had seen much from the peripheral corners of history's last two millenniums. But bearing witness to the conflict that was clearing the way for Babylon's resurrection was something he'd been anticipating for centuries. Napoleon had schemed to resurrect her, but was denied, as were others. It was a dream of all secret societies linked together by the evil legacy of that land. But it wasn't until now, with the direction of the Harness Magi's front company the Omega Group and the bank-rich families and fraternities of the Illuminati and their Masonic Order, that such dreams were finally being realized.

With the exception of others connected to his world of uncommon existence, Magnus had seen and learned more than anyone could dream possible. Time and again he worked behind the scenes, exacting judgment, empowering the weak against cruel men with global ambitions.

But at times an old loneliness would set in, prompting the desire to know the loving touch of his wife again. Such longings for companionship were only made worse when a brother or sister in Christ passed on to glory, leaving him behind to continue his sojourn through the world. The pressures of the *Wayfarer Call* and the potency of his Adamic nature were by far the most difficult of his wars. But the double-edged sword that had become his life often sang with a bittersweet promise of release, especially when it openly clashed with the razor-sharp edges of mankind's wickedness.

Such were the wars he greeted with both dread and welcome.

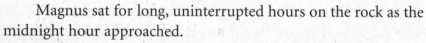

Magnus sat for long, uninterrupted hours on the rock as the midnight hour approached.

He glanced up through the treetops of the cedars surrounding his elevated perch as a frigid wind swept across his stony face. A distant beacon of multicolored light caught his attention as it fell slowly from the stars in the Outer Realm. It appeared to be a meteorite at first, but the anomaly grew brighter as it fell. He lost sight of it behind the mountains before he could magnify it with his preternatural vision.

He figured it to be a host of some kind. The heavens over the Middle East had been filled with a greater intensity of angelic activity ever since the beginning of the war to raise Babylon from the ashes, especially when the Imperial Fortress of the enemy arrived over the city of Al-Hilla.

He leaned forward, training his gaze on the trees opposite the crater, hoping to discover the reason he had been led to this dark hole in the world.

He soon did.

"Careful, Magnus," a voice echoed softly from behind. "The darkness can master you with too much study…. Especially on this Christmas Eve night."

Magnus sat up slowly at the sound of the frigid voice, eyes darting back and forth. He didn't turn as a pair of white, slanted eyes appeared behind him in the shadows, followed by the bronze silhouette of sharply-tipped wings. The assassin's burning eyes hovered about 10 feet high in the air, his wingspan filling the space between two trees behind the rock, covering his mountainous shoulders like a rippling suit of liquid armor.

He kept his gaze straight ahead, confused by the fact his sensitive hearing and acutely tuned perception of the angelic realm had failed in warning him of the rebel's approach. But the overwhelming veil of dread filling the atmosphere around him clearly told him what sort of host he was dealing with.

Magnus didn't move, ready to defend himself in the blink of an eye as he decided to question the rebel to gauge any other hidden strengths he possessed. "How is it that you know my name, fallen one?" he asked, glancing back out of the corner of his left eye.

A fanged smile appeared in the shadow beneath the flesh-peeling heat of the assassin's white eyes. "It's my business to know," he answered.

"Really? You must be Old Scratch himself, then?"

A muffled chuckle shrouded Magnus from behind, the assassin's eyes pulsing malevolently. "No…. But you can think of me as the *Devil's Fiddler*, if you like."

Magnus gave little heed to the assassin's boastful comment, keeping his mind trained as sharply as possible on the position of the entity's voice. "Let me warn you, rebel. I have little patience for games tonight."

The assassin hissed with a soft laughter. "Such arrogance…. I like that in a man."

Magnus swivelled sideways, catching a glimpse of the sharp edges of the assassin's metallic wingspan outlined by a shaft of moonlight. "Your blood-soaked plunder of this world will not last forever. Judgment is promised. And it will be a swift and unforgiving hand that deals it."

The assassin smiled widely again when he saw something approaching the crater's opposite ridge. "Promises are meant to be broken," he said, pointing, revealing a thick arm that glistened like black marble in the moonlight. "Behold those who would welcome the Dragon Lord's age of uncontested rule...."

Magnus was slow to turn, keeping his mind tuned to the assassin's position. His eyes fell on the crater once more. An unusually tall and brutish man dressed in a black overcoat and suit walked to the crater's edge, stopping in a shaft of moonlight that fell between two trees along its rounded border. He wore a small skull and crossbones pin on the left lapel of his coat. His hair was short and black, fashionably slicked to the side, his face dark and olive-colored. The portals of his eye sockets appeared empty beneath the depth of shadows veiling them.

Magnus immediately recognized the giant. He hadn't crossed paths with the Nephilimite known as Tsavo since the night of his coronation. But he had encountered many of the vampire demoniacs and secret societies allied to Tsavo since then, with one of the more notable of such skirmishes taking place on the outskirts of London during the Great Plague of the 17th century as he sought to recapture a dark and ancient sword from his past.

A downward rush of wind fell suddenly through the surrounding trees as another power entered the wooded arena.

A scarlet, black-winged prince fell to the center of the crater from the night's brightly lit canopy, his taloned feet stirring up a clap of thunder with his touchdown next to the six-pointed star. The rebel was arrayed in a jeweled, black-muscled cuirass, flashes of yellow fire rotating in the center of each shadowy eye, fangs glowing in the shafts of moonlight blanketing the spot where he stood. He relaxed his wings, turning his back to Magnus' lofty perch on the tree-lined hill to face the giant standing above him on the crater's opposite ridge, motioning him forward.

Magnus watched intently as Tsavo leaped to the stony floor of the crater, landing on the other side of the star across from the familiar rebel. The Nephilimite stood eye level with Sodom, saluting him with a quick bow of his dark head. No words were exchanged as they both stepped back from the star several paces. Their attention was drawn toward the star at their feet, as if waiting for something to happen.

Magnus didn't move, trying to keep his focus on the rebel still lingering behind him.

The assassin moved closer to the shaft of light where he had unveiled his arm, allowing his towering form to become more defined. "Behold, champion," he said, holding out his large left hand to reveal the ashes of an ancient corpse. "Behold…the rise of Perdition's Son."

Magnus stiffened from a wind stirred up around him, spoken into existence by the rebel's voice. The wind scattered the pile of ashes in the assassin's hand, gathering them together in a cluster of shadows that swept toward the center of the crater. Tsavo and Sodom stepped back from the star again as the wind encompassed them, the shadows swirling in and around them, howling fiercely as they pierced the shafts of moonlight, mixing with the eagle and star-shaped symbols of the darkly-colored soil at the center of the crater floor.

The ash and dirt-filled shadows circled the crater's center as a flash of divine lightning struck the middle of the crater like an atomic key. The ground opened with a thunderous cracking from the force of the strike that continued down through the Earth, creating a fissure that stretched deep beneath the floor of the Mediterranean Sea miles away. The rim of the hole turned counterclockwise as the fissure formed beneath it, its stones churning like water.

Black smoke bellowed from the hole as the sides of the newly formed pit quickly hardened to a six-foot diameter, releasing a funnel of wind that rocked the tops of the surrounding trees, rippling the night's starry stream with a fervent heat.

Tsavo and Sodom stood their ground outside the host of shadows circling the opening in the crater floor, listening to Teraphimic wails exploding from the mouth of the pit like the roar of a thousand cannons.

The opaque arm of a human spirit emerged slowly through the smoke, beckoned from a place of wandering imprisonment in the *well* of the Abyss, fingers wide and probing as they clamped down on the stony sides of the pit. Another arm followed, its hand gripping the stones in like manner, with the head and shoulders of the *nephesh*-crowned spirit emerging next.

The pit closed in a clockwise motion behind the man-shaped spirit after he climbed free, severing the smoke and tormented winds of his prison.

Sodom and the giant stared at the resurrected spirit wailing at their feet.

Above the crater, Magnus stood, horrified. "It can't be," he whispered.

The assassin laughed. "But it is," he assured him. "Behold… '*The Beast that was, and is not, and yet is!*'"

The assassin's words echoed down the slope with his quote from the Book of the Revelation, stirring the circling ashes around the spirit as he rolled over on his back in the center of the crater, mummifying him in the orbiting vapors of new life. The ashes from the ancient corpse and the dirt from the *Farm of Blood* began forming a skeleton over the spirit's shady form, knitting the joints together like simple building blocks, rib cage snapping together in a flash of light. A new brain covered the spirit's opaque mind, its rippled substance literally drawn into existence by one of the smoky fingers of the orbiting ash. A smooth skull appeared afterwards, formed in the same manner. Cerebral tendrils extended from beneath the skull, attaching to the spinal cord as the rest of the needed organs and blood vessels emerged from the molecules of the ancient corpse's ashy remains, giving rise to muscles and other tissue that bloated and stretched in and around the skeleton, completing its intricate network. Eyes swelled into view beneath closed lids while the exterior flesh of the spirit's new body was being created, followed by long tresses of black hair mixed with translucent highlights of gold that sprouted from his scalp. The ashy vapors swirled around his face, leaving behind a smooth layer of flawless bronze skin as the dirt and ash-filled shadows dissolved at the bottom of his feet.

The resurrected man lay motionless in the center of the crater as the howling winds died away, entombed in his new flesh, awaiting the final fusion between body, soul, and spirit.

Sodom stepped forward, reaching to the belt of his armored apron and pulling out a golden drinking horn of metaphysical design. It was an ornate cup shaped like a winged lion, with the rear half of its body extending up through its wings in the shape of a gilded horn with a wide mouth and diabolical markings of archaic skill.

Sodom knelt beside the head of the resurrected man, pulling back the lid of the drinking horn with his sharp fingers as he lowered it toward the open mouth of the body's flawless face that was identical to one he had worshiped for ages. "Receive all that the great Seraph offers, Lord Judas… *'For out of the serpent's root shall come forth a cockatrice, and his fruit shall be a fiery flying serpent,'* " he said, quoting a passage from the Book of Isaiah.

The liquid was a black, blood-like crude alchemized from the jeweled substance of the Dragon Lord's own body. It rushed down Judas' throat like a pathogenic flame, filling his new organs and blood vessels with its thunderous charge, hardening his entire body inside and out to a preternatural state, merging his soul-crowned spirit with the carbon-based brain of his new body in a completing jolt of power.

Sodom stood after pouring the last of the blood into Judas' mouth, securing the drinking horn on his belt again.

Stars filled the spectrum of Judas' blue eyes as his eyelids flew open suddenly, mouth gaping open even further with the first rush of air into his ageless lungs. The memories of his last night on Earth flooded his newly formed brain. His breaths became shorter and faster at the passing image of a familiar Carpenter who stood bound in the Garden of Gethsemane. The memory of a crooked tree quickly followed. A thick, twisting rope was clenched in the left hand of his former body as he saw himself standing beneath the tree. The image of the Tyrian shekels paid to him by the Sanhedrin had been his last thoughts in the land of the living, their silver luster shattered by a quick snap of twine. The memory of the sudden snap caused him to scream when a blistering abode darkened the vision in his mind.

His screams stopped abruptly as the vision of darkness in his mind quickly gave way to his earthly surroundings, his thoughts drawn to the cool breeze brushing over his sleek-muscled frame, arousing his senses with prickly prods of new life. The reality of his long-desired freedom was almost unbelievable at first, after wandering through the dry places of torment in the well of the Abyss for the last two millenniums.

He lifted his hands to his face as the sweet sensation of freedom swept over him, the dust-size particles of his old body falling from his fingers, dissolving with a familiar scent of judgment that had cankered his spirit for centuries, hardening him to the core with a purpose as dark as the prison that had held him for so long. This was a purpose he could never have understood before his fall. But Jesus had known. He had even declared it boldly before all the Apostles. The memory of that day had tortured him with the same viciousness as the darkened flames of the Abyss. But his memories of the Old Testament Scriptures spoke to him in his torment like never before when he was alive, revealing to him a future time when he would be allowed a season of opportunity to challenge God for control of the universe and its focus of worship. It was an opportunity he had anticipated with great scheme.

Judas pulled his knees toward him, rising from the center of the crater slowly without using his hands or bending at the waist, quickened by the immense power of the Dragon Lord's blood flowing through his darkened mind. He stood six feet tall, the tresses of his ethereal hair twisting slightly in a gust of wind.

Pin needles of light exploded across his blue eyes the moment he sensed Sodom's presence. The armored rebel stood before him in all his dark glory, his false wings swaying in the soft currents of the night air.

Judas strutted toward the rebel angel, raising his arms as if to embrace him. He looked up into Sodom's black eyes, gazing at the mirror-like irises of yellow fire reflecting his new veneer, the dual images contorting like the flickers of a candle light. "A god and not a man," he said, focusing on the rebel's face with a vain smile, his voice devoid of accent as it echoed softly in a rapid-fire succession of every language spoken among humans, angels and the Cherubim. "I was speaking of myself, of course."

Sodom bowed. "Of course," he agreed. "Such godhood warrants my devotion to you, Lord Judas…. That is why we have been sent to you. To prepare you for your anointed place as the Great Tree who will rule over the nations."

Judas looked at the giant standing silently to his right, receiving a reluctant nod from him. He could sense the giant's immediate jealousy of him, and he liked it. The mere size and regal bearing of the giant, coupled with the Dragon Lord's supernatural knowledge of Tsavo flowing through him, told him that he was one of the old ones; a Nephilimite like the conquerors of renown from the Antediluvian World. With obvious jealousies and added knowledge aside, such a lineage alone made the giant one to be watched carefully.

"The master has also sent you a gift," said Sodom, turning to the trees behind him.

Judas and Tsavo both faced the border of trees as Sodom gave a guttural command to the shadow-filled spaces between the cedars above the crater's rim. A man dressed in a silver robe with a large hood stepped through the tall cedars, followed by twelve demon possessed men arrayed in hooded, black capes draped over panoply mixtures of Assyrian, Babylonian and Persian body armor.

Tsavo growled softly when the leader of the small band of men appeared, glancing back at Sodom suspiciously.

The man in the silver robe walked down into the crater, carrying a large, ancient chest in front of him. The others behind him followed his lead to the crater floor.

The leader stopped when he reached the bottom of the slope, waiting for his men to march ahead and form their lines of tribute. The men turned and faced one another in two lines, making a quick draw of their sickle swords before dropping to one knee in a unified clatter of armor, extending their shimmering blades across the crater's floor.

The leader made his way slowly through the aisle, keeping his eyes on the curved lid of the chest he was carrying. The chest was crafted from lacquered acacia wood and fitted with ornamental emblems and hinges of pure gold. No key hole was visible on the front of the lid, but rather a large thick seal of silver. A carving of a lion's head protruded from the seal, its fanged mouth open as if to strike, eyes large and hollow.

The leader stopped at the end of the aisle, dropping to one knee with the others, placing the chest on the crater floor. He glanced at the rebel angel towering to his right, seeing the same terrible appearance he had observed many times before during the dark rituals of his secret order, designed to prepare him for this very moment. The men behind him were each Adeptus Exemptus magicians versed in a perversely titled system of *magick* known as the Enochian Key; a subordinate sorcery of invocations giving them the power to steel themselves when looking upon rebel masters. It was a power acquired through intense training that included memorizing the Satanic Grimoires; ancient books of sorcery like the infamous Necronomicon.

"Bestow the gift," Sodom ordered.

The leader pulled back his hood, revealing a mark on the back of his right hand. The mark was shaped like a black griffin cresting over the top of a golden cross, constricted by a black and red dragon with two heads. The leader's silver hair and tanned face had the appearance of a countenance halted at middle-age, preserved in that state by an ancient power flowing from a staff known as the *Oracle of the Dragon Lord* strapped across his back in a long quiver.

Judas recognized him from images in the Dragon Lord's blood flowing through his brain.

The leader focused on the chest in front of him. He reached into his robe and pulled out a small pouch made of leather, fishing out two large diamonds from inside, inserting them into the hollow eyes of the lion's head emblem protruding from the chest's silver seal. Small flashes of light pulsated through the diamonds when he inserted them into the eye sockets, with air spewing from beneath the seal's thick border.

Tsavo watched with an almost salivating interest while the chest was being opened.

The leader pushed the rounded lid back slowly, reaching inside with both hands. He stood up, pulling a blackened lion-skin garment from the chest, tailored by Satan himself from a rare breed of lion descending from the Genesis lineage of its species that had been spared destruction in the Second Great Deluge.

The *Covenant Harness* hung like a cloak in the leader's hands as he made sure not to touch the black, scale-like lining of the skin's interior. It was designed in six, wing-like segments, with silver-tipped bear claws looped to the tapered hem of the front and back wings. Red, eagle-style feathers were sewn to each segment of the harness by vertical threads of adamantine, with nine types of eye-shaped jewels embedded like scales throughout the feathered segments in a vast display of wealth. Silver crescent moons arced over each jewel to complete its armored look. Dual leopard heads were fastened to both of the garment's shoulders, with their lower jaws having been removed in the design process. Each beast once weighed two hundred pounds more than their modern day descendants now ranging from the plains of the Serengeti to the rim of Mount Kilimanjaro's Kibo Crater.

A blackened cowl constructed from the head of the lion skin harness itself hung forward from the back segments of the garment, its lower mouth having been removed like the garment's beastly shoulder crowns, with its original eyes replaced with the golden orbs of a dragon. The cowl's upper mouth dangled from an iron chain with a Quicksilver enamel, connecting the space between the garment's front segments, anchored to sun-shaped emblems of embossed gold depicting black and red dragons intertwined in poses of broken infinity. Gold engraving plates were molded in the centers of the chain's thick links, displaying bronze-colored titles of authority such as *The Assyria*n, *Prince of Tyre*, *King of Babylon* and *The Son of Perdition*; each written with a stylus-tooled precision in various Semitic languages. Another emblem of gold depicting a black and red shepherd wrapped in the mantle skins of a wolf hung down from the chain's central link, with a long, silver-coated spike that was squared in its design hooked to the bottom. The words, *The Nail,* were carved in a single column of black Hebrew letters on the front of the spike; the same one once used to hold the third and final disputed epitaph

89

above the head of the Lord Jesus, which read, *This is the King of the Jews.*

The symbols of the harness had been added to the original garment over time, with each holding great significance. The garment's beastly shoulder crowns represented the great Leopard Kingdom of the future, and not that of Alexander the Great's empire that was divided up after his death between his four generals Ptolemy, Cassander, Lysimachus and Seleucus. The bear claws dangling from the split hems of the front and back wings were also future in their symbolism. The feathers of the harness represented the eagle standard once used by the Serpent Tribe of Dan; a segment of people who disappeared from the nation of Israel as a formative group thousands of years ago when Tiglath Pileser III of Assyria invaded the land and took a great number of Danites into captivity. The lion's-head cowl was a symbol of a future power as well. But the garment as a whole was meant to represent the entire global kingdom to be embodied in the person of the Great Tree. This messiah would reign over the world through ten kings from joint commands in Babylon, Tyre and Pergamos, all overseen by the fatherly eyes of the dragon.

Tsavo stepped to the side of Judas several paces to get a better look at the garment. Though he had never seen it before, he knew he was looking upon the garment of his ancient lust for the first time.

Judas' blue eyes danced with delight as he, too, recognized the garment. Its legend in the Ancient World had no equal. Its wearer would inherit the covenant power of the Archrebel himself, a covenant revealed to him during his torturous wandering throughout the Abyss.

The leader showed no concern for the giant's sudden edginess upon laying his hardened eyes on the ancient treasure for the first time. Though Tsavo was a formidable force to be reckoned with, he had been easily denied from obtaining the harness for millenniums by each of the Magi Masters. Tonight would be no different.

The leader formally offered the armor of promise to the future king. "To you, Lord Judas, I present the *Covenant Harness.*"

Tsavo growled with a low, guttural hate at the leader's words. His desire for the *Covenant Harness* was insatiable. He'd always known it would be unveiled one day. But he had expected its appearance to come just prior to Judas' ascension to a global throne. Not now. Not at a moment when he was unprepared to take action.

Sodom gave Tsavo a fiery stare, flashing his large, wickedly-sharp fangs in silent laughter. He turned fully toward the giant, resting his black-nailed hand on the hilt of his blade in a threatening gesture.

Tsavo's fists clenched at his sides as the leader passed in front of him. He glanced at Sodom in his threatening pose, quickly peering back at the garment so very near to him, his heart thundering with primordial instinct.

Scores of Sodom's best warriors began to surround the crater's ridges, their red and yellow eyes appearing in the shadows like scattering embers.

The giant took his eyes off the garment, growling under his breath at the sudden arrival of the Nekros Order. There would be no escape should he act to seize the harness now. He could only stand by and watch while it was presented to Judas, his strength having been contained by superior numbers.

Judas tilted his head back as the leader lifted the garment's chain above him. He spread his arms outward to let the vestment's black-scaled lining slide down over his arms and back, gasping with a sudden delight when the fabled harness came to a rest on his shoulders with a velveteen weight, its pendant and spike sliding down to the center of his chest, the garment's tapered hems with the dangling bear claws swishing down around his knees.

The leader walked in front of Judas, waiting silently.

Judas looked ahead regally as he reached behind to pull the sides of the beastly cowl forward. The two ivory fangs of the cowl's upper mouth sank down on each side of his eyes as the crown came to a rest on his head, revealing the word *Alchemy* inscribed in golden letters on the forehead of the lion just beneath its arcing mane of black hair; written in several Semitic languages.

In similar manner, the phrase, *The Lie*, was carved in red on each fang of the cowl.

The sides of the lion's hollowed-out neck surrounded his throat the moment he lowered his hands, the harness' crown amplifying the power within him in a sudden jolt of energy. The whole garment gave him the appearance of a fierce cherub.

The leader motioned to his men behind him to stand up as Judas relished the crown's amplifying power. "I, Simon Menelaus, Master of the Harness Magi and keeper of the *Oracle of the Dragon Lord*, bid you welcome, Lord Judas," he replied. "And we bring you tidings of Babylon's rise…. All phases of Operation Assyria and Project Palladium are proceeding according to the master's plan."

"I know," said Judas. "And I am well pleased."

"We of the Magi, as our deceased brethren of the Cainites of long ago, have clung to the prophecy of the ascended masters that you would rise again one day. We believed you would stand up against the Lion of the Tribe of Judah himself as in the past. For that, we are your servants. And we have come to worship you."

Simon bowed his head and knee with a worshipful decree. "O king, live forever."

The other Magi behind Simon prostrated themselves in the same manner, raising their swords as they repeated the sorcerer's words. "O king, live forever!!"

Sodom bowed and repeated the chorus of praise himself. "O king, live forever!"

"Yes!" Judas replied rapturously. "Honor me!"

Sodom lifted his head from where he knelt, peering over at the giant who refused to relinquish his proud stance.

Judas turned toward the giant at the same time, hardening his pose against the defiant Nephilimite as he spoke to him for the first time. "I am your king now, Tsavo," he commanded. "I must increase. But you must decrease…. Honor me."

Tsavo glared down at the Beast with a restrained hate. His movement was slow in the bowing of his knee and head. "Hail to you, Lord Judas," he said lowly, fists clenched tightly by his sides, black blood seeping through his fingers from the bite of his razor-sharp fingernails.

Judas laughed with delight, turning toward the others kneeling before him. "I accept your honor," he replied, glancing at the fiery eyes that lingered in the shadows around the moonlit crater. "But hear me. Though the gravity of the Abyss still chains me from ascending higher, I am no longer the man the world briefly knew. No longer the zealot in a drama that branded me a traitor. No! Judas is dead. I am the new shepherd. The world will yield to the crook of my staff. They will follow me, Iscarius Alchemy.... And they shall worship me as their god!"

The rebel angels in the surrounding trees erupted in a unified roar of praise. "HAIL THE ALCHEMY KING!!! HAIL THE ALCHEMY KING!!!"

◆━◦━ ━◻◦◻━ ━◦━◆

Magnus stood galvanized by the unholy nativity unfolding in the crater below. "The Unclean Spirit," he said in a haunted voice, recalling passages from the books of Zechariah and Matthew. "The Antichrist."

"Yesss," the assassin hissed behind him. "The Fisher King has come. The Phoenix of Phoenicia. The Superman of the Serpent Tribe of Dan.... The Cockatrice of the Chaldeans."

Magnus spun around to face the rebel behind him for the first time.

The assassin pulled his wings back into the shadows, allowing only his white eyes and diamond fangs to be visible.

"Who are you?" Magnus demanded, squinting to try and penetrate the darkened veil covering the rebel's face.

Laughter echoed throughout the forest as the assassin sank even farther into the shadows.

Magnus stood paralyzed by an old boyhood fear as a familiar and frigid gust of wind swept across his confused face, watching the mysterious entity melt completely into the shadows as if he were one with them.

Magnus whipped back around, unsure of what to do.

Alchemy turned toward him suddenly, sensing his presence for the first time above the cheers of the rebel angels. The Master's betrayer locked gazes with him the moment he spied his tree-covered position on the slope high above the crater.

The image of the Beast enlarged when Magnus focused his stare, zooming in on his flawless face beneath the lion's-head cowl. He looked puzzled as the Beast smiled at him, choosing not to alert those worshiping him at the center of the crater. It was clear from his devilish smile that Judas somehow recognized him from the dark power flowing through his mind.

Magnus remembered the dream he'd had of the Beast while imprisoned in the belly of that Roman slave galley.

He turned his back to the Beast, searching the darkness again for a glimpse of the mysterious rebel, wondering who he really was.

Magnus was slow to face the crater again. The Beast just smiled at him as silently as before, still choosing not to alert his presence to Sodom and the others. The whole scene was even stranger than the ancient dream given to him in the bowels of that Roman slave galley. It was a nightmare beyond all his expectations.

The words of the Holy Spirit came softly and unexpectedly as Magnus stared at Judas. " '*Behold the Assyrian was a cedar in Lebanon with fair branches, and with a shadowing shroud, and of an high stature; and his top was among the thick boughs. The waters made him great, the deep set him up on high with her rivers running round about his plants, and sent out her little rivers unto all the trees of the field, and his boughs were multiplied, and his branches became long because of the multitude of waters, when he shot forth. All the fowls of heaven made their nests in his boughs, and under his branches did all the beasts of the field bring forth their young, and under his shadow dwelt all great nations.*' "

Magnus almost swayed while the Spirit-breathed words of the Prophet Ezekiel echoed in his mind, intoxicating him with a divine confirmation that what he was witnessing was not a dream.

Judas nodded at Magnus as if to tip his crown, whispering the full translation of the champion's name and surname in the same soft manner as the Lord's voice that had just spoken to him.

Magnus stiffened in his posture at the Beast's apparent mimicry of the Lord's voice. He snapped the lapels of his coat together angrily, leaping into the air with a quick thought to distance himself from the flesh-born nightmare. The forest canopy was beneath his boots in a matter of seconds. He held his head low while gripping the lapels of his coat, the wind rolling along the contours of his face.

He knew no matter how far he flew he could not escape the reality of what he'd just witnessed. The Beast was alive. Many pretenders to the ultimate throne of evil had preceded him throughout the centuries. But things were eternally different now. Judas had returned as the Scriptures foretold he would. The rebel fowls of the air had been setting things in motion for centuries, waiting for the day when God would allow *The Lie* to rise from the *well* of the Abyss. A day that had finally come.

Magnus closed his eyes. The factions of peace and horror were already at war within him.

"*The end is not yet, my son. 'And now you know what is restraining, that he may be revealed in his own time. For the Mystery of Iniquity is already at work; only He who now restrains will do so until He is taken out of the way,'*" the Lord whispered through the wind, reminding him of who was in control. "*'And then the Wicked One will be revealed, whom the Lord will consume with the breath of His mouth and destroy with the brightness of His coming.'*"

Magnus sank into the starry sky with a slumbering flight, the Spirit of the Lord guiding him across the horizon like countless times in the past. The dream of ascending from the dark road he had traveled for so long was nearer than ever before.

"Woe to the worthless shepherd,
Who leaves the flock!
A sword shall be against his arm
And against his right eye;
His arm shall completely wither,
And his right eye shall be
totally Blinded."

Zechariah 11:17

Book Three

Origins III:
Ichabod

Tower Valley, a small, prosperous town of twenty-two thousand located north of San Francisco near the Oregon border, was sprawled out on a slightly rolling plain drenched in spring sunlight. The town was surrounded by thick forests and a range of mountains shaped like a natural coliseum, the slopes and cliffs of the granite peaks covered with towering pines stretching down around the foothills all the way to Pacific Coast Highway 101.

Once known long ago as Tsidkenu Valley, the town had since become a picture of progressing economic achievement since its expansion from the original site on the eastern mountain range; a settlement founded in 1860 by Jewish Christians. The town was a small metropolis with the grandeur of the old and the new intertwined in its structures. The streets were paved with fresh asphalt. Traffic was moderate as the town's citizens roamed back and forth between the different shops along Main Street. South of the business district were rows of brilliantly carved balustrades, towering pillars, second floor porticos, shingled cupolas, daunting arches, emerald green lawns, and black, wrought-iron fences. These were the crown jewels of the posh Victorian homes dominating that section of town. Most of the older structures were nestled in the heart of the town's executive community known as Imperial Lane, each differing with a signature roofline.

The local courthouse stood at the northern core of the town. It was an imposing sight, modeled after the likeness of London's Westminster Abbey, with gothic spires towering into the sky on each of the rectangular structure's four corners. Hundreds of stone arches covered the frontal facade, enclosing portals of reflective glass. An enormous clock tower made of smooth, gray stone, with an obelisk-crowned roof and a horizontally ribbed exterior, reached hundreds of feet into the skyline from the middle of an open courtyard in the center of the square-shaped courthouse. Men on steel scaffolds surrounded the lower half of the tower, slowly making their way upward while overlapping the stone exterior with strips of pure ivory carved with intricately detailed images of winged, Virgoan goddesses riding upon Taurus bulls.

Four identical glass buildings surrounded the courthouse, the clock tower rising high above their flat roofs. L-shaped tunnels of plexiglass extended from the sides of the buildings, connecting each of the new structures that were surrounded by more men on steel scaffolds completing the final stages of a year-long construction plan. Like the monuments of Egypt and Washington D.C., the four glass buildings, as ordered by the Omega Group, had been aligned according to ancient astrological blueprints of the Zodiac. Even the streets intersecting with the courthouse square, designed by the town's first Masonic insurgents over a hundred years ago, mirrored the cosmic causeways of Rome and Babylon in their north-south trajectories. The transpatial archeometry of the buildings and the streets intersecting with the courthouse were designed to mark the town as a stronghold for demons and rebel angels; an esoteric *magick* found in varying forms in government buildings and churches across the globe, perpetuating the motto of the ancients: *As above, so below.*

A steady stream of armored SUVs with tinted windows roamed back and forth throughout the town, taking care of business for the Omega Group; an international conglomerate secretly established by the Harness Magi on December 24, 1913 with the billions of dollars in gold and other natural resources horded over the centuries by the predecessors of their mystic order. Crews from the Omega Group's Special Services Corps, an elite communications team responsible for installation of electronic countermeasures, were busy installing fiber optic EMP charges beneath the roads throughout the town and surrounding valley. The charges would be capable of instantly crippling vehicles of any size with an electromagnetic pulse.

Black Hawk helicopters flew back and forth from a small air base built just outside of town at the foot of the valley's northern mountain range, with a set of railroad tracks located nearby that had been limited to supply traffic only. The base was fenced off with the tightest of security, complete with barracks large enough to house a small team of elite soldiers recruited by the Omega Group. A heavily protected gatehouse was built next to the fenced off facility, guarding entry to a road leading up to a wide plain in the foothills of the northern mount where a 17th century-style French chateau could be partially seen looming above the air base, its shingled roofs cresting just above the treetops on the mountain's lower slope.

—··— ▤○▤ —··—

Rebel angels hovered unseen high above the bustling town, formed in a ring consisting of 24 elite warriors from the Nekros Order. They rotated slowly around the clock tower's black-numbered face that was enclosed in a leafy trim on all four sides, counseling with one another telepathically in great anticipation of the arrival of their Shadow King from the port city of San Francisco.

The rebels had infiltrated the town during its expansion of the original settlement, paving the way for one of the temples of the Masonic Order that put its roots down in the valley at the turn of the century. The Masonic newcomers to the town turned out to be not only allies and relatives of California's Railroad Barons and Silver Kings, but also wolves from an ancient order of cabalism that had veiled themselves in the folds of the Church and various charities since the days of the Apostles. The Gold Rush of 1849 first brought them to the state, increasing their wealth, and allowing them to gobble up territory for their own personal use and development. Their land grabs would eventually bring them to the valley. And with the lure of their formidable resources, they would gain influence with some of the children of the original settlers holding prominent positions in the town's government. Their lust for control spoiled 40 years of peace by pushing those from power who were spiritually aware of their Luciferian doctrines cleverly masked in charity and religion. Most of those who resisted them in one form or another were murdered. These dark deeds were conveniently covered up by the town's new, Masonically-contracted police and judiciary branches of service brought in from San Francisco in the year 1900. The majority of the town, however, would conform to the Pergamos and Laodicean spirituality that had crept in amongst them with the purpose and drive of progress at any cost; a compromise foreshadowing the corrupting spirits that would assault the seven future Jewish assemblies of Asia Minor the Apostle John had written to in the Revelation of Jesus Christ.

As a result of such apostasy, the town was later marked for total darkness by an epitaph that had mysteriously appeared above the archway of the town's house of worship. It manifested sometime between Halloween and the morning eve of the Babylonian holiday All Saints Day, exactly six months and *thirteen* days after the great earthquake that struck San Francisco in 1906. The word *Ichabod* had literally been cut into the sanctuary's granite stonework; an Old Testament curse which meant the glory of God had departed. And it had. For there had not been a trace of true Faith in the town for over a hundred years.

Gabriel, one of the seven princes from the Order of the Watchers, stood unseen in the belfry of the town's clock tower, awash in a mix of shadows and rays of sunlight pouring through the belfry's stone arches. Crisscrossing beams of wood filled the belfry's vaulted ceiling above him, with long-stemmed pistons and steel spindles hanging down between them, supporting three large brass bells hovering above a square opening in the wooden floor beneath them.

Heavy armaments were outlined beneath the luminous robe of sky-blue flax he was wearing, his platinum hair accentuating the glow of his burnished, man-shaped face. Swirls of light emanated from his gold pupils and white irises, pulsing back and forth across the surfaces of his solid-blue corneas, filtering outward from the sides of his eyes in vaporous streams while he watched the rebel angels circle the tower. His presence in the bell tower went undetected by the rebels thanks to an angelic and cherubic diffraction veil the Order of the Watchers and the Book Masters of Heaven were gifted with. But it was only a temporary veil.

Gabriel turned his head to the right suddenly as he sensed a familiar presence. His peripheral vision allowed him to see a dark-haired figure of a man sifting through the belfry's middle bell in fiery ripples, the train of his long, royal-blue coat of modern design swirling down around his legs in the draft of his sudden appearance.

"Did you get the deed?" Gabriel asked.

The angel bowed his head. "It is done, my prince," he said. "The old sanctuary on the valley's eastern mountain range has been secured for the champion. All records of its existence have been destroyed as you ordered."

"Were you detected?"

"No, my prince."

"Well done, Scriptos.... Well done."

Scriptos stepped to Gabriel's side in front of the open arch where the Nekros warriors could be seen circling the tower, the menace of their red and yellow eyes rolling in through the belfry like the embers of a suffocating furnace.

"This town's curse is a heavy one," Scriptos commented, silver light streaming from the sides of his eyes as he watched the rebels circle the tower.

"Yes," Gabriel agreed. "The task will be grim, especially with the imminent arrival of Sodom the Sullier."

"I understand there is activity in the Outer Realm because of the activity here?"

Gabriel nodded. "The evil one's Dominium Gate Masters are fortifying their positions. But that's not unusual at this late hour. They've been fortifying their blockades since the allies of Apostate Israel started clearing the way for the kingdoms of the Great Tree."

105

Gabriel gave the angel a stare of warning. "But the evil one and his Alchemy King are not satisfied with their advances," he added, slowly turning his attention back to the rotating ring of rebels. "That's why they've invested so heavily in this valley project."

Scriptos turned to the arch again. "I dare say the champion will feel the full force of the evil one's triangle here."

"To be sure. For this town's cup of wickedness is almost full."

Both focused silently on the *Ichabod* epitaph cut into the stonework of the town's sanctuary that was being torn down a few blocks away from their position. They had both witnessed the consequences of such wickedness many times throughout history. And the result was always the same. Wrath and judgment.

"Such a curse is not so easily removed," Scriptos remarked, watching a large crane and wrecking ball go to work on the sanctuary's small bell tower.

"No…. It never is."

Gabriel lifted his line of sight again. The Nekros warriors were starting to rap violently on their shields with their sickle swords, howling with goblin shrills in celebration of the collapse of the sanctuary's frontal facade where the *Ichabod* epitaph had been carved.

Gabriel turned away from the arch and started toward the bells. "Come," he said. "Our season in this hell is finished for now."

They strode across the belfry floor with ghostly steps, rippling through the middle brass bell like pools of fiery water, dropping down through the square opening in the floor beneath the bells, disappearing into the darkness of the tower's four-hundred-foot well.

"Depart from Me, you cursed,
into the everlasting fire prepared
for the Devil and his angels."

Matthew 25:41

Book Four

Chapter One

A cheviot-red Aston Martin DB7 screamed around the winding curves in the forests of Tower Valley's southern foothills, its halogen headlights slicing sharply through the night. The milky-skinned driver glanced into the rear view mirror, her hazel eyes squinting from the glare of the pursuing headlights reflected in the glass. The perfect features of her face were tense and desperate as she brushed away the auburn locks from her face, tossing them over the shoulder of her blue Chanel suit. She scanned the road ahead, jamming on the clutch, shifting through the gears frantically. A surge of adrenaline pumped through her toned legs while working the pedals repeatedly, the steering wheel trembling softly in her hand with each stomp on the gas.

April Wedding, a gifted scientist and mother of a six-year-old daughter, was running from a future threatening to steal all traces of her identity, and ultimately damn her soul.

"Hang on, baby," April replied, glancing at her daughter buckled in the passenger seat beside her, bracing her hand against the child's chest as she whipped the Aston Martin around another sharp curve, tires squealing as the tachometer reached 90 mph.

"Stop, momma! Please!" the child begged, crushing a fluffy toy lamb against the breast of her denim overalls.

"Everything's gonna be okay, Megan," she said, glancing back at the relentless headlights in the rear view mirror. "We just have to get away from here as quickly as we can."

The black Suburban behind her rocked back and forth, struggling to keep pace through the tight curves in the road, headlights fixed on high beam to blind her.

The chase continued for several minutes through the treacherous turns until a long stretch of road with steep banks on each side opened up before the speeding vehicles. The Suburban was able to close some of the distance between it and the Aston Martin, narrowing the margin to about five car lengths.

April reached up and slapped the rear view mirror downward in a fit of rage, severing the blinding lights it reflected. She pressed her petite-heeled foot on the gas even harder, the car's speed dangerously passing 100 mph.

Megan looked at her mother with frightful tears. "Momma, stop! We're going too fast!"

April dared not take her eyes off the road at such speeds to attempt to console her daughter, painfully ignoring her pleas to slow down.

"Momma, please!"

April stared straight ahead into the darkness. "Megan, momma needs you to be quiet right now," she said desperately.

"No! I'm scared."

"Megan, please!"

Something in the distance caught April's attention while she argued with her daughter. Another set of headlights exploded into view a quarter of a mile away from a second SUV. It slid sideways to block the road, causing her to let up on the gas instantly to slow the speeding car.

April started to panic as she was suddenly faced with the prospect of being captured. She tried to muddle through her jumbled thoughts of what to do. With a steep drop off into the wooded meadows on each side of the road, there was no way she would be able to swerve around the vehicle ahead.

The more she searched for a route of escape the slower her speed became. The Suburban behind her closed its distance even more until it was nearly on top of the rear bumper, its lights splashing the car's windshield with a mind-numbing glare.

"What's happening, momma?" Megan cried, wiping away at the tears in her eyes.

April didn't answer. Tears just rolled down her face. She had no choice but to slow the car's speed below 40 mph, the vehicle ahead getting closer by the second.

She palmed her eyes to dry the tears, only to have more follow when the car was brought to a stop about 20 feet away from the blocking vehicle. The other Suburban veered to the right behind her, backing up and parking sideways like its twin to block the road from behind.

Four men in dark gray suits got out of the Suburban blocking the car from the front. Each wore sunglasses equipped with Starlite night vision lenses, allowing them to easily penetrate the darkness. Their angular faces were ghostly as they stood side by side in the bright glow of the car's headlights. Each was armed with a Heckler & Koch .9 millimeter SMG, a potent and easily-used weapon with a curved clip and a ball-like handle fixed on the end of the short barrel, complimented by a pistol grip that allowed its handler to spray a target with a full range of mobility.

April could feel the rhythm of her heart in her ears as the gun-wielding men stood before her. She turned to see four more men emerging from the other Suburban.

"Momma, who are those men?" Megan asked.

April looked at her daughter in the glow of the dashboard lights, placing her smooth hands around Megan's face. "Baby, momma's gonna get us out of this… I promise."

April looked up to face the obstacle in front of her, noting the idling purr of the car's supercharged engine, her mind pondering the unthinkable, envisioning the bodies of the four men before her flying over the hood of the car while plowing through the vehicle ahead.

A sudden rap on the passenger side window startled April and her daughter before she could enact her desperate plan. Megan screamed out for her mother, drawing away from the leathery face with deeply set lines hovering at the window.

April looked to her right in terror to see a familiar man pointing the barrel of a gun at her daughter. The nameless man that had stalked every corner of the town with his security agents on a daily

113

basis, sliced across his neck with a single finger while pointing the weapon, gesturing for her to cut the engine immediately.

She closed her eyes, the tears coming faster than before as her head fell in a defeated stupor. She had wasted too much time thinking when she should have been acting. The engine died suddenly as she turned off the ignition, severing her hopes of escaping the nightmare she had been living in for almost two and a half years since the Omega Group's takeover of Tower Valley.

April hesitated to hit the unlock button, Megan's fearful cries reminding her of the alternate and most desperate part of her planned escape.

Another rap at her daughter's window shocked April's amber-colored eyes open again. She looked over at the window slowly, her frightened stare meeting with the man's dark and merciless eyes again.

"Get out of the car, Dr. Wedding," the man demanded, his voice ringing with an accent from Europe's eastern block.

April held her finger on the door's unlock button lightly, hesitating to relinquish what little power she still had to protect her daughter.

"Now, Dr. Wedding!" he said, pulling back the round action bolt on the side of his HK to load the clip's first full metal jacket into the firing chamber.

April took a deep breath, wiping away the tears with her other hand. She thought her heart would burst through her chest as she hit the button, popping the locks that echoed like gun shots in her ears.

The man walked around the front of the car and stopped beside the door on the driver's side.

"Momma, don't go," Megan pleaded, tugging at her arm.

"It's okay, baby," she said, wiping at the tears on her daughter's face. "Momma's just gonna talk to these men for a few minutes and then we'll be on our way."

"No!" Megan cried. "Don't leave me."

The driver side door opened suddenly from the outside.

April didn't turn to look, taking her daughter's head and kissing it on top, pressing her close to her chest. "I love you, sweetheart," she whispered. "I love you."

Before April could finish comforting her daughter, the lead agent ducked into the car and unfastened her seat belt, grabbing her by the arm and snatching her from behind the wheel, the wails of her daughter trailing behind her.

April struggled to keep her balance while being dragged around in front of the car's headlights where four other security agents formed a semicircle around them. They looked like clones in their identical suits. Black omega symbols from the Greek alphabet were sewn on the left breast of their coats, arcing over another insignia threaded in a silver, serpentine design. Both were icons she had come to loath over the last few years.

The lead agent loomed over April, wrenching her left arm to pull her closer. "Where is it, doctor!" he demanded.

April grimaced with pain, but remained silent.

The lead agent looked at one of the four men closest to him, giving him a quick nod. The other agent stepped forward at the silent request, pulling out a black device similar to hand held metal detectors used in airports, complete with a digital meter and tiny sensor lights.

This was the moment April had feared, trembling as the agent waved the beeping bioscanner in front of her from head to toe, a device she had developed.

"The prototype isn't on her, sir," he said, unable to find the magnetic signal he was looking for.

The lead agent grabbed April by the arm and jerked her forward again. "Where is it, Dr. Wedding?"

She remained silent as the tears streamed down her face, fear paralyzing her ability to speak. Months of planning their escape had been lost in her hesitation to plow through the roadblock earlier. Courage had been sharper in the preparations to flee. But such armor had been stripped away the moment she unlocked the car. The instinct to protect her daughter from being injured in a crash had crippled her choices in the heat of the moment. A moment when her daughter's very life mattered the most.

"Where is it?!" he shouted.

He jerked April backwards by the arm, slapping her down on the road's narrow shoulder of grass. She braced herself with the palms of her hands as she fell to the grass in a weakened stupor, blood trickling from the corner of her mouth.

The lead agent turned to his men still positioned behind the Aston Martin. "Search the car!"

They moved without hesitation at the order.

"No, wait!" the leader said suddenly, looking through the glare of the car's headlights to focus on the shadowed outline of the crying child still buckled in the passenger's seat. "A Lilliputian engineer wouldn't conceal such a priceless commodity by ordinary means."

He turned to one of the darkly dressed agents to his left. "Bring the girl to me!"

The agent obeyed instantly, walking to the passenger side door and jerking it open. He unfastened Megan from the seat and snatched her from the car by her arm, ignoring her terrified screams.

April was hypnotized in a moment of dizzying pain, head teetering backwards onto the road's grass bank, her auburn locks spilling down the slope. She instinctively lifted a hand to the side of her face that was red from the blow as she lay sprawled on the bank, the stars slowly coming into view above the treetops through her clearing vision. Seconds seemed like hours.

A single gun shot exploded through the night air suddenly. Another sound followed, its pitch like that of something metal striking the road's surface.

April struggled to sit up on the grass bank as the marauding sounds echoed in her ears. The glare from all the vehicles' headlights stunned her for a moment.

April crawled forward a bit, only to stop in a look of unbelievable horror once her eyes adjusted to the car's headlights.

"N…. NOOO!" she screamed, looking at her daughter lying motionless in the middle of the road, blood bubbling up over the chest of her denim overalls. "Megan!! Megan!!!"

The lead agent stood over the child while holding a machete in his hand, HK strapped over his shoulder. He bent down and picked up the little girl's right hand he had severed with the shiny blade, tossing it into a small plastic bag. "You should have never hidden the prototype there, doctor," he said, casting a cold look towards the child's horrified mother.

April cried as if panting for air.

"Remember," he said. "You created this calamity."

April choked on the unthinkable, face pale and death-like. The shock of the moment hit her in a wave of unpardonable guilt, eyes wide and tear-filled as she reached out towards her slain child, face puffing from all the tears.

The lead agent glanced to his left and motioned with his hand. "Load up," he said, handing the blade and the small plastic bag to one of his men.

He walked over to where April was sprawled sideways on the grass on the verge of collapse while the other agents were loading up, squatting in front of her.

She bowed her head in heaving sobs, feeling nauseated by the closeness of the man's remorseless face.

"You will be allotted a time of mourning," he told her in a matter of fact way. "However, your presence is still required in the lab Monday morning."

He paused, grabbing her by the hair, jerking her head back to make sure she was listening. "And a word of warning…. Try to run again and you will join your daughter."

He released her head with a downward push and stood to his feet. He then straightened his coat before reaching into the left breast pocket for a small business card that he tossed to the ground in front of her. "Mr. Scythe is the best mortician in town," he said, his face stone-like and serious. "I highly recommend him."

April cried uncontrollably as the man walked away and got into the Suburban that was blocking the Aston Martin from

behind. The other vehicle passed by on the left side of the road to follow it back to town, leaving her alone with her daughter's body still highlighted in the glow of the headlights from her own car.

Chapter Two

Magnus walked down the long stretch of valley road at a solid pace, tugging at the lion's head cuff links fastened to the French cuffs of his white shirt. Locks of his hair caressed the sides of his bright eyes as a passing breeze bloated the split train of his navy blue coat that circled around the tops of his knees. The soles of his laced boots clicked and crackled against the asphalt that was covered in pine needles. The smallest of noises from his wardrobe were amplified in his ears, the cotton of his shirt sliding against his hardened skin, the fabric of his jeans shucking with the motion of his legs, coat slicing through the night air ushering around him in swirling breaths of distraction.

He scanned the stars while he walked, questioning in his mind why he had been led to this relatively unknown valley in Northern California. He hadn't been near this part of the state since the San Francisco earthquake of 1906; a time of judgment when the palaces of thievery and dens of whoredom of the Barbary Coast gangsters were swallowed up in the devastation. It didn't just touch one class of the city's population. Thieves, bankers, merchants, whores, commoners and the religious had found themselves all lumped together in the same fiery pit of chaos. It was a story often repeated throughout the centuries, usually involving the same cast of characters, but with little lasting effect or reflection from the surviving afflicted. Cities of commerce and residence could be rebuilt to their original splendor or even greater with hard work. But such was not the case when dealing with the depravity of humankind's Adamic nature.

A sudden rush of wind pressed against the champion while he thought about the past, gripping him with an icy embrace that stopped him dead in his tracks in the center of the road. He lowered his chin into the wind, immediately sensing an old and familiar presence. The stench of *Death* was scented with innocence as he lowered his gaze and focused on the road ahead of him, concentrating on dual sources of light over a quarter of a mile away. He stood like a statue staring into the night, his pupils moving with the motion of camera lenses, enlarging the appearance of a vehicle and the lone silhouette of a woman bending over something in the middle of the road.

His reason for being called to the valley at this point of the journey was at least clear, he thought. Offer hope to the stranger in the distance.

Magnus clenched his jaw and burst forward into a blinding run, literally disappearing from view.

Magnus materialized like a ghost several feet from the crying woman, staring down at her in complete silence after having covered over a quarter of a mile of asphalt in a matter of seconds.

After all the senseless suffering and persecution he'd seen visited on the weak throughout the last two millenniums, it was still almost like seeing it for the first time when he saw closeup what the woman lamented over. The body of a little girl was sprawled out in a pool of blood in the middle of the road, her right hand strangely missing.

He said a silent prayer for the grieving woman, noting the grim irony of a toy lamb clutched in the child's left arm, its curly coat soaked with innocent blood.

April cried uncontrollably, head hung in despair, the locks of her auburn hair brushing over the breast of the child's blood-splattered overalls. For the moment, she could not feel the pain of the rugged asphalt burrowing into her knees. The only thing she could feel was the stab of guilt. She had done this. She had caused this calamity just as the lead agent had told her.

His words rang cruelly through her very soul, shaking her physically. She rocked backwards on her knees, crying with desperate, inhaling breaths that struggled to pass through the swollen canals of her nose.

April glimpsed a pair of boots through the haze of tears. She fell back in a panicking fit, retreating into the glow of the headlights, rubbing her eyes profusely to see the man standing before her more clearly. His shadowy head lingered just above the line of the headlights, allowing only his tall, sleek-muscled frame to be outlined by the car's halogen beams, eyes glowing with emerald pyres.

She crawled backward until her back hit the car's front bumper, holding her bloody hands up to protect herself from expected blows. "LEAVE US ALONE!!" she screamed. "Just…just leave us alone."

Magnus said nothing. He knew words at that moment would not be convincing. Action would be the only breakthrough method. He slipped off his long coat slowly, bending over the child's body and covering her petite frame with the large garment. He then walked respectfully around the body, stopping several feet from April's position against the car's bumper.

He squatted in front of her, allowing his bronze face to be illuminated in the headlights, eyes softening in their bright glow. "I will not deliver more harm to you," he said softly. "I am a friend…. Permit me so to prove it."

There was a calm honesty resonating in the man's voice that allowed April to drop her blood-covered hands. Her voice trembled when she spoke. "Don't…don't hurt me," she said weakly.

"Who did this to you?" he asked.

The question barely registered in April's jumbled thoughts. She looked away, wiping her face again. The magnitude of what she was involved in could hardly be explained in a fluster of tear-choked words. "It doesn't matter," she replied, a sense of finality teeming in her strained voice. "Nothing matters any more…Meg…Megan is gone. I broke my promise…I couldn't save her."

121

Magnus glanced back at the covered child, pausing for a moment of silence at the mention of her name. A coldness welled up deep from within, visiting him with a familiar sorrow.

He looked back at April, quickly wishing away the image of his murdered wife before it clouded his thoughts. He cocked his head to the right a bit, training his augmented hearing on dual sounds in the distance. The low hum of two powerful V-8 engines whispered in his ears like a passing wind.

With a gentle and hasty movement, Magnus grabbed the grieving woman by her shoulders. "I won't hurt you," he reassured her, looking into her wide eyes as she gasped with an expression of shock from the sudden gesture, appearing as though she had just noticed him. "I'm going to put you into the car until I get back."

"Who are you?"

"The cavalry."

"There's nothing you can do," she replied, her head falling to the side again. "The Omega Group is too powerful…."

Magnus' expression hardened even more with her words. "The Omega Group? What are they doing here?" he asked in surprise.

She did not answer.

Magnus lifted her off the road with a look of urgency, experiencing no resistance as he carried her to the passenger side door of the car. He opened it and placed her in the seat where her daughter had been sitting earlier, reaching across her to flip off the headlight switch to snuff out the sight of the child's body still lying in the road.

Magnus grabbed the keys from the ignition and knelt beside her. "Stay in the car and keep the doors locked," he said, pushing the universal lock button in a hurried breath. "I'll be right back."

April said nothing. She simply looked out the driver's side window, defeated.

Magnus closed the door and put the keys in his pocket.

He walked to the rear of the car and eyed the long road before him with a hardened stare, fixing his hearing on the sounds of the retreating vehicles again. His body stretched forward in a hazy blur as he broke into another lightning run, disappearing from sight.

* ··· ⚊◯⚊ ··· *

The yellow lines on the long stretch of road blurred together in one wide bar beneath Magnus' hypersonic feet. His arms and legs were distorted and wavy in his race across the asphalt, the wind shear rolling over his bronze face, hair whipped straight back. The trees on each side of the road merged into 70 foot tall picket fences in the wake of his speed, the stars above him running together in streaks like wet paint on the night's dark canvas.

Several miles ahead of him, traveling single file at steady rates of 60 and 70 mph, were two Suburbans, their red tail lights glowing like afterburners.

Magnus honed his focus on the rear vehicle and closed the distance easily, cutting his velocity in half to keep from overshooting the target.

The tinted windows on the vehicle's rear double doors shattered as Magnus plowed into the right side tail light with his left shoulder, shearing away the quarter panel like wrapping paper. The Suburban swerved to the left on impact, tires squealing as it flipped over into a violent roll down the road's left side bank, headlights twirling in every direction. The SUV crashed upside down into a cluster of pines, killing all four men inside instantly.

Magnus didn't watch the Suburban crash behind him, moving quickly to overtake the other vehicle ahead before the occupants inside had a chance to respond to their comrades sudden demise. He leaped forward in an arc over the Suburban's rear doors, tucking his knees into his chest while sailing over the long roof in cannonball fashion. He kicked his legs straight down once he cleared the windshield, the oval toes of his boots piercing the vehicle's hood like a pool of black water, sheet metal rippling all around him as he hammered through the engine, ripping gashes in his boots and the sides of his jeans as he pushed the V-8 block halfway through the pavement.

123

The vehicle jolted to a deafening stop, as if slamming into a brick wall, its rear end flying up off the ground. The lead agent burst through the windshield head first from the passenger's side, flying by Magnus in a shower of glass, hitting the asphalt face first in a 50 foot slide. The other agents were killed instantly as their heads slammed against the roof of the bouncing vehicle.

A hushed silence of death shrouded the valley road around Magnus as he stood unmoved at the center of the hood's crater, boots resting on top of the V-8 engine that was driven into the pavement, legs wet with antifreeze and transmission fluid. He was gazing into the open portal where the windshield used to be, its crumpled edges surrounded by a border of jagged, glass teeth. The twisted and bloodied bodies of the other three men were sprawled across the tops of the seats.

Magnus turned toward the road where the lead agent lay groaning with muffled, dying breaths. He punched through the rippled sheet metal in front of his waist with his fingers, gripping the hood from underneath, tearing it down the middle in a single shear that echoed throughout the surrounding forest. He took a step forward and kicked through what was left of the radiator, booting the entire front end, bumper and all, several hundred feet down the road.

Magnus walked slowly over to where the man lay dying, his boots grinding glass and other small debris into the road's surface with his forceful steps.

He stood over the man briefly, his emerald eyes bright and merciless, fists clenched at his sides.

Magnus tucked his left boot under the man's right arm and flipped him over, barely recognizing the leathery face that was ground to a bloody pulp. "Phinehas Kaiser," he said in a low voice.

Kaiser, a ruthless wetwork operative and lead agent of the Omega Group's Sentinel Corps, lay helpless at Magnus' feet, spinal cord severed, right eye torn from its socket. His left eye was half-closed, the scope of his vision blurred and dense, confusion overwhelming him as fiery tentacles pulled at the very essence of his hardened spirit.

Magnus bent to one knee, drawing close to Kaiser. He grabbed him by his blood-covered throat.

Kaiser choked on his own blood as the mysterious enemy lifted his head and shoulders off the pavement. The vision in his remaining eye cleared enough for him to see Magnus' bronze face. He didn't recognize him. But he did recognize an otherworldly mystique in the stranger's phantom eyes only a select few of his superiors in the group had displayed in the many dark rituals he had participated in during his employment.

"That's right," said Magnus. "You don't know me. But I know you, Phinehas Kaiser. I have watched your kind from behind the scenes for nearly two thousand years. Brazen and merciless puppet masters of nations. Cowards who manipulate the weak while dancing on strings of your own, controlled by powers more wicked than yourselves."

Magnus grabbed Kaiser's chin with his other hand while holding his shoulders off the pavement. "Why did you kill that woman's daughter?"

Kaiser kept a disciplined silence with what little strength he had.

"Why is the Omega Group here in this valley?" he pressed.

Kaiser tried to force a refusing smile between the stone-like fingers that gripped the sides of his chin, clinging to his silence as if to insure his place in the next world.

Magnus would not push the issue any farther. "Keep your allegiance to your dark masters, then," the champion replied. "But know this, Kaiser. I am of the Ancient World…. I share in a legacy that was once a plague upon the mighty Philistines. A legacy that sheds the blood of evil men both great and small…. Men who have no reward in eternity."

Magnus spun Kaiser's head around with a quick twist of his hand just as a look of terror welled up in the agent's remaining eye, the bones in his neck snapping loudly as his face was turned toward his back.

The champion stood up and let Kaiser's turned face crash squarely into the asphalt.

He lingered in the middle of the road as blood dripped from his fingers, watching a small portion of the road beneath Kaiser's head liquify, turning counterclockwise. A plume of black smoke billowed from the opening as the sides of the small hole hardened for a moment, the smell of brimstone filling the air. The back of Kaiser's head collapsed slightly with a quick suction emanating from the gateway, pulling his soul-crowned spirit down toward Hades.

Magnus turned and started back down the road while the portal closed behind him in the same liquid motion as it had opened. He could hear the distant cries of Kaiser's spirit descending into torment, mixing with the echoes of blood dripping from his fingers that splattered against the lid of the agent's asphalt casket.

Chapter Three

Tsavo stood before the glass wall in the board room of Seraphim Enterprises' newest corporate office, a major holding company for the Omega Group. The board room was located in the executive wing on the top floor of the Omega Group's glass structure facing the southern facade of Tower Valley's elaborate courthouse.

The room's decor was lavishly masculine, complete with a floor of gray marble having a circular map of the world painted in multiple colors at its center. The sapphire-laden words, *As above, so below*, were written in Akkadian and several other ancient languages beneath the map's Zodiac border of gold. Red velvet drapes were pulled back into the shadowy corners of the glass wall. The other three walls were made of dark-paneled oak polished to a glossy sheen. The ceiling was vaulted and coffered in a honeycomb design, with halogen lights positioned in every other dark and lifeless comb. Granite statues of famous warriors stood like sentries in front of every other panel on the right and left side walls. Alexander, Attila and Hannibal were among the most notable. But the muscled sculpture of Goliath in his Aegean armor and those of King Og and the Sons of Anak rose above the others, prominently positioned at the center of the right-side wall.

An enormous, trapezoid-shaped table of redwood was anchored on top of the map in the center of the floor, with wing-back chairs of dark leather tucked neatly around its longest sides. A 36-inch computer projection screen was embedded in the center of the shiny table, facing the ceiling. A throne-like chair of smooth granite occupied the space at the head of the table near the glass wall. Rubies and onyx stones were configured in wrathful phrases of ancient Nephilimite languages on the throne's rolling arms, its symbol structure resembling angelic cuneiform. Carved in the chair's stone backrest was the picture of a large sword with a dragon-marked hilt that had its blade driven through a fiercely sculpted lion's head. The sword's tip pierced the forehead and right eye of a man's face partially hidden behind the beast's fangs.

Tsavo remained still and silent before the glass wall, staring at the clock tower rising from the open pavilion at the center of the courthouse. His olive-skinned reflection stared back at him, his short hair slicked back, eyes dark and probing. He was clothed in a gray suit custom-designed to fit his mountainous frame, with a hooded robe of black silk with gold embroidery hanging open over his double-breasted coat. The robe symbolized his most exalted position as the town's only Ipsissimus Master of its Masonic Temple. With such an exalted place in the Satanic Brotherhood, the administration of the temple and its order was left to the town's mayor, who himself was a Druid high priest. The mayor was also a descendant of one of the aristocratic families of the Railroad Barons who fought the valley's original settlers for control of the town's future at the beginning of the 20th century.

Tsavo stared into the midnight sky stretched out over the town's clock tower, gazing into another world that lay hidden from the eyes of mortals. The multi-winged forms of 24 rebel angels burned into view across the backdrop of a large autumn moon teetering just above the peak of the clock tower's *asherah* obelisk; a rallying point of phallic symbolism in the Masonic mysteries.

The rebels orbited the clock tower slowly, engaging in some sort of urgent telepathic conference with Sodom the Sullier who stood on top of the tower's obelisk, wings arced high above his head while basking in the glow of the moon. The tower's stone exterior, at Sodom's order, had been completely refurbished with an ivory finish of Virgoan goddesses and Taurus bulls that gleamed brightly against the moon. The new clock face displayed blue and gold images from the Zodiac orbiting inside the circle of numbers, with the depiction of a moon moving mechanically on the outside of each number. The moon followed an arcane orbit that always positioned it above the 12 and the golden sun fixed in the middle of the clock at special tolls of the hour. This was done to symbolize the path of the invisible dragon the Earth's moon was thought by early astrologists to orbit upon. The clock's orrery was powered by an underground water source similar to the Tower of Winds of ancient Athens and the astrological clocks of the cathedrals built during the Renaissance.

The moonlight reflecting off the clock tower bathed the middle of the board room in a wide shaft, falling on most of the statues lining the walls. Tsavo glanced down at a vellum scroll sitting on top of a Sumerian prism dating back to the year 2000 B.C. that was placed against the center of the glass wall, its chipped and cracked sides giving a detailed history of 10 kings who ruled during the age of the Antediluvian World.

Tsavo snatched the scroll off the prism, rolling it out in his hands with a desire to relive the pleasure he had experienced only moments ago when it was first delivered to him. The scroll was a message sent to him through a secured courier from a prototype agent of the Omega Group's Project Nietzsche program. The giant had personally dispatched the agent to Egypt months ago, responding to an important tip he'd received from one of his powerful allies in the country. The message read: *The pride of Og has been recovered. Proceeding to the rendevous point in Venice to meet with our ally from the Carpathian Mountains.* The giant gave a low growl of laughter at the text coded in the language of his Nephilimite nativity; a text only he and the esoteric mystics of the Ancient World could possibly decipher.

Tsavo crumpled the scroll with his hand, making a tight fist around it, boiling the Nephilimite blood beneath the thick skin of his palm with a commanding thought, expelling small plumes of fire between his fingers to incinerate the evidence of his secret maneuvers for obtaining the ultimate power.

The oak doors on the farthest end of the room suddenly opened. A thin, red-haired man entered the room cautiously, the doors hissing like an airtight hatch being depressurized. He had the look of an accountant with his wire rim glasses and the pushed up sleeves of his white shirt.

Tsavo didn't turn from his position in front of the glass wall, letting the ash of the scroll scatter from his hand while glancing at the man's reflection in the glass. "Report, Mr. Specter."

Specter, Deputy Director of Valley Operations, stepped forward hesitantly. He pulled out several satellite surveillance photos from the brief he was holding, his voice cracking in his reply. "Uh...Mr. Chairman, I just received the latest update from Shadow Corps Intelligence."

"Has the prototype been retrieved?"

Specter shook his head. "That's why I brought these surveillance photos, sir," he answered, laying his brief on the table and spreading out the pictures. "Something went wrong."

Tsavo turned his head so that part of his stone face could be seen in the reflection of the wall's glass. "What?" he asked calmly.

Specter hesitated, scratching nervously at a serpentine symbol recently tattooed on the back of his right hand. He'd always been intimidated by the giant, long suspecting him to be a product of some sort of supersoldier program, possibly serving as a precursor to the Omega Group's current biogenetic experiment known as Project Nietzsche. He was also a high-ranking practitioner of the illumined rites known by only a select few of the group's top brass.

"What went wrong, Mr. Specter?"

"Well, sir," he said nervously, "from the looks of the space-based infrared photos we just obtained, it would appear as though Kaiser and his team were completely annihilated."

Tsavo turned full tilt toward the man, eyes set with shadows, his face an expressionless picture of the unforgiven. "Elaborate, Mr. Specter," he ordered.

Specter's gaze fell toward the table under the giant's terrible scowl, hands trembling slightly while sifting through the photos. "Sir, it would appear these shots the town's satellite took a few minutes ago show....well...."

"They show what?"

"They show two Suburbans on the valley's southern road. Both have been completely destroyed.... The engine for the lead vehicle was actually driven straight through the road's surface somehow by the looks of some of the magnified shots."

Tsavo was silent for a moment, staring coldly. He clasped his large hands behind his back, pulling the mid-section of his loose robe back around his waist, his wide shoulders and chest stretching the fabric of his suit. "Where is Dr. Wedding?" he asked, showing no concern for Kaiser and his team.

Specter stuffed the photos back into the leather brief. "The last report that Shadow Corps Intelligence received from Kaiser and his team before the initiation of radio silence was that they were chasing her towards Pacific Coast Highway 101."

"What about the tracking lock on her implant?"

"That's the problem, sir."

"Problem?"

"Yes, sir," Specter answered nervously. "It seems Dr. Wedding removed her and her daughter's manufactured chips and injected them into a couple of the lab's test specimens to keep us from tracking their special magnetic signatures. As you know, the prototype that she stole doesn't have the same magnetic signature as the manufactured chips programmed into the company satellite."

"Why would she make such a bold move?" the giant snarled. "She would have needed help from someone with resources and links to our intelligence network."

The giant took a step forward, a low growl gurgling under his breath. "There's been a breakdown in our security structure somewhere, Mr. Specter."

Specter swallowed hard. "We're working on it, Mr. Chairman," he said. "The only time she left the town was when she was authorized to go to Silicon Valley for research materials for the second prototype.... Kaiser was supposed to let her go after he retrieved the chip to see if she would lead us to the individual helping her. I told him to make sure he gave her plenty of reason to keep running."

Tsavo's glare changed to a look of surprise. "Who authorized you to defy the security protocols of Project Palladium with this

131

ridiculous plan? Dr. Wedding and her daughter were to be killed immediately once they were detained!"

"I understand, sir," he answered respectfully. "But last minute orders came down from the brass at Shadow Corps that preempted our usual protocol for this project. Everything was hectic when she suddenly decided to make a run for it. However, the plan was to capture her and her contact at the same time, and inject them with the alpha serum to find out just how far the breach of security extended. We were going to eliminate them after we had the information we needed."

"Whoever is helping Dr. Wedding doesn't seem to be abiding by Shadow Corps' planned containment, Mr. Specter."

"Sir, it's quite possible that Kaiser and his team did retrieve the prototype before they were killed," Specter offered. "The satellite images do indicate that they were headed back to town. It could have been destroyed in the wreckage."

"I don't need possibilities, Mr. Specter," the giant growled softly.

"I understand, Mr. Chairman," he said. "Shadow Corps Intelligence is in the process of realigning the satellite to try and track Dr. Wedding visually if she's still on the move. Our radar station at the base reports no breach of airspace to indicate she was airlifted out of the valley. All EMP charges beneath the valley's southern road that were installed by Special Services have been activated. But I'm afraid we may have received our intel too late for those countermeasures to be effective at this point since the EMP charges do not extend throughout the entire the road. I have alerted our agents outside the valley of the situation. And I have the Wolf Pack and a team of Black Hawk helicopters prepped on the tarmac. They're ready to pursue at your command."

"No," Tsavo said calmly.

"Sir?"

"I will see to the recovery of both Dr. Wedding and the chip myself."

Specter gave a quick bow of his head, knowing not to question Tsavo's reserve. "I understand, Mr. Chairman," he replied, tucking the brief back under his arm. "I assume you'll be using one of the Black Hawks, then?"

"No, I won't."

"Sir?"

"Did you not hear me, Mr. Specter?"

Specter nodded slowly. "Is there anything else I can do?"

"Have the final arrangements for the conference been prepared?"

Specter was dazed for a moment at Tsavo's question, fumbling over his words, trying to keep pace with the conversation as it switched suddenly from the matter of the security breach. "Ah…yes…. Yes, sir," he stammered, pushing his glasses up further on his nose. "Lodging at the chateau on the northern mount has been prepared for the dignitaries' arrival day after tomorrow."

"Good."

Specter breathed a little easier knowing that the intimidating figure before him found reason to be pleased in spite of his intelligence report.

Tsavo narrowed his glare on Specter. "And what of Mr. Alchemy's itinerary?" he inquired.

"It remains the same, Mr. Chairman," he told him. "He's due to leave the Omega Group's headquarters in Turkey the same day the dignitaries will arrive. His private plane will land in San Francisco after midnight. From there he will be driven to the valley so the FAA won't have a record of his flight pattern to our location."

"Good," said the giant. "You can leave."

Specter left the room quickly, gently closing the heavy doors behind him.

Tsavo turned and faced the glass wall again, staring out at the dark summit still taking place at the clock tower. His shadowed stare grew even colder when he focused it solely on Sodom, growling with a low, guttural hate as the fallen angel stood tall on the crest of his ivory throne, embraced by his elite-numbered force.

"Secure your hatred, old friend, lest your enemies hear its silent thunder," a cosmic voice warned.

Tsavo turned his head to the right to see rotating irises of red fire sift through the wooden panel near the corner of the statue-lined wall. Black, flame-ribbed wings followed, invading the moonlight.

Tsavo watched as Bastion, Dominium Gate Master of Dragylon, emerged fully before him. "Anger is what fuels my passion, ancient one," he said proudly.

Bastion was an impressive sight in the moonlight, looking as though he were a fluid statue of granite, his holographic wings licking at the ceiling. A muscled cuirass of pearl was fastened to his stone-colored chest, with a small black shield fixed in the center of the armor displaying gold markings to signify his authority. Similar markings were detailed on the scale-covered strips of black linen that formed an armored apron around his waist, its belt supporting a shotel sword of gold adamantine and pouches of stellar explosives. Long black hair framed the sides of his gargoyle face, looped with golden rings at the end of their curled tips.

"Your passion will only bring you peril, Tsavo," the rebel cautioned, the red irises of his stone face rotating with star-shaped flashes of light with each word.

"I have had to bide my time for far too long," he sneered. "I have played the master's game while others who were never my equal were brought to power over me…. The *Covenant Harness* should be mine by virtue of my sufferance and my service. With it, I could change the very core of the prophecies that are set against us!"

"Simon and the Harness Magi will always oppose your desires for the crown as they have done in the past," said the rebel. "As will the master."

Tsavo growled under his breath at the rebel's reply, turning back to the wall while trying to shield his thoughts from Bastion's powerful mind. He could envision the Lake of Fire awaiting them all if the prophecy of God's Word wasn't changed. But that goal seemed closer to being achieved now because of the cryptic message sent to him from his man in Egypt.

Bastion looked at the scheming giant with a sharp grin, sensing his efforts to shield his thoughts. "Ambition, as long as it is in submission to the master's designs, is a virtue we have always nourished, Tsavo," he continued. "The fact that you haven't acted fully on your ambitions is the only reason the master hasn't already dispatched you to torments.... A truth you should ponder before acting foolishly."

Tsavo was unmoved in his resolve. "When Alexander the Great lay on his deathbed in Babylon he was asked to whom he would bequeath his empire.... 'To the strongest,' was his reply."

The giant looked at the rebel with unflinching arrogance. "I am the strongest," he boasted.

"Time will tell, Tsavo...time will surely tell."

Bastion whipped his wings of black fire in front of him as he levitated backward, melting through the wall slowly, his black and red eyes still visible while uttering a final word of warning. "I suggest you make haste, old friend," he said. "A new power has come to Tower Valley, a power that threatens all our plans. And from what I have heard, he is no ordinary host...if he is even a host at all!"

Tsavo appeared puzzled by the rebel's parting comment, glancing back at the urgent conference still taking place at the clock tower.

Bastion's words echoed in the giant's millennial subconsciousness, unearthing the memory of an adversary believed by many to have died long ago. He walked to the paneled wall lined with the life-size statues, standing in front of a six-foot skeleton lacquered in a golden solution for preservation. He had come across it in the ruins of an underground Templar stronghold in England in 1755 while searching for a sword even older than the *Covenant Harness*. A helmet of great antiquity crowned the skeleton's skull. It had been perfectly preserved in the ruins of the stronghold where he had found the skeleton, and needed no solution to keep it from deterioration.

135

The detail of the helmet alluded to the identity of a nomadic king greatly feared among the powers of darkness. It was round and crafted of the greatest metallurgical skill. It was made of Christaloy bronze, a preternatural substance of varying ores known to be harder than adamantine, and found only on the Mount of the Congregation in Heaven. A slightly raised spine arced over its crown, inscribed with jeweled symbols of a Hebrew signature. Other raised emblems were etched on both sides of the helmet, each special fitting having been shaped with Christaloy gold. Narrow side flanges of this same gold framed the sides of a gilded mask hanging down in front of the helmet. Small, warlike zoons were engraved in bronze on the flanges and the man-shaped mask, one pictured on each flange and one beneath both eyes of the helmet's sculpted veil. A miniature sword of bronze sporting a micro-intricate hilt of white Christaloy was carved vertically over the center of its closed mouth.

Tsavo glanced at the golden image of a palm tree etched on the right side of the bronzed helmet, its victory palms sparkling with 12 priestly jewels shaped like fruit. The giant slowly turned his attention to the image of a lion's head etched in gold on the left side of the helmet. A ring of silver fire was clenched in its diamond jaws that had two jail-style keys, each basaltic in color, hanging from the bottom of the ring. The key on the left had the word Death written in deep, red grooves on its long stem, while the other one was inscribed with the Hebraic inscription Sheol.

Tsavo leaned toward the helmet's golden face mask. "No," he said. "The worms have long since eaten your flesh.... Haven't they?"

The giant whirled around in a sudden fluster, his black robe whipping out behind him while racing for the tall doors at the other end of the room. A rush of wind exploded against the glass wall in the wake of his speed, rustling the heavy drapes as he vanished from the room in a blur.

A pair of slanted eyes of white fire appeared in the glass wall's left corner as the drapes settled, flashing with disapproval. The sharp edges of a metallic wingspan stretched forward from the shadows, curving around the sides of a cloaked entity.

The eyes hovered in the corner, watching the room's heavy doors close with hisses of air.

A slow, haunting wail filled the room as the assassin sank back into the corner again, frigid vapors rolling off his retracting wings, falling to the floor like sizzling pellets of sleet as he disappeared into the shadows once more.

137

Chapter Four

April awoke to the smell of burning kerosene, struggling to sit up in what appeared to be a sleeping bag wrapped snugly around her. She fumbled for the bag's zipper, ripping its cord slowly with her hand. She rubbed her eyes as she pulled her feet out from under the flannel lining, sitting up slowly. Twisting around, she noticed she was sitting in the middle of an old abandoned church building. Kerosene lamps were positioned in groups of three across the floor's dusty planks, with a large space heater sitting several feet away.

April rose, still feeling a bit dazed, wondering if she was dreaming. She studied the 30 by 60 structure, heels grinding with an echo from her slow pivot, eyes adjusting to the light. The interior's dingy, gray walls were cracked and peeling. Eight-foot-tall windows, each boarded up from the outside, spanned the left and right side walls of the small sanctuary. A 30 foot vaulted ceiling with exposed, crisscrossing beams loomed above her, giving the cramped auditorium a sense of space. Several web-covered pews were scattered about the sanctuary, each on the verge of falling apart. Beyond the pews was a small pulpit chamber sunken into the back wall, its entrance crowned by a pointed arch.

April pivoted around toward the entrance of the sanctuary, turning her back to the pulpit. Before her, about 15 feet away, were a pair of rotting doors. In front of the doors were four slender posts that supported a lofty balcony spanning across the building.

She tilted her head back to study the balcony, staring briefly at the fence-like rail stretching across the front of the balcony.

On the rear wall of the balcony, barely in sight above the railing, was a wide, half-arched window missing some panes of glass. Several shafts of moonlight pierced the aged glass, cutting a path through the center of the sanctuary's vaulted ceiling, playing havoc with the infestation of shadows in the ceiling's crisscrossing beams.

April lowered her gaze, allowing it to wander to the right of the doorway. As she stared into the shadow cast by the balcony's overhang, she noticed an enclosed staircase, minus its door, spiraling upward.

She stood there staring, rubbing her arms with her hands, feeling the warmth of the space heater pressing against her back. Her head dipped slowly, eyes catching a glimpse of blood smeared on her white blouse. Slow, heaving breaths began to build within her, the dried blood of her murdered daughter stinging her awake from the dream state she thought herself to be in.

April released her arms, hands trembling as she started to remember the horror that had become her life. She closed her eyes to fight the tears, clamping both hands over her mouth to keep from screaming aloud.

"What can I do to ease your pain?" a gentle voice asked from behind.

April whipped around at the sound of the voice, nearly falling backward from the sudden turn, the boards from the old plank floor creaking with a ghostly echo as the heels of her shoes ground against the aged wood. In front of her, standing beneath the arch of the pulpit chamber, was the dark-haired stranger who had come to her aid on the valley road. He stood beside the pulpit's lectern, emerald eyes glowing brightly in the shadows of the sunken arch. The coat he'd used to cover her daughter's body was held to the side, wet with blood.

April stared at him silently, noting the blood on his white shirt as she backed away several steps, glancing at the rips in the sides of his jeans reaching from the knees all the way down to the cuffs. He appeared even stranger than before behind the dim glow of the kerosene lamps.

She couldn't remember much of what had happened. Images of the moment her daughter was killed flashed across her mind, followed by glimpses of the man before her helping her into the car.

"Who are you?" she asked.

"A messenger," Magnus answered, stepping down from the chamber's raised platform.

"A messenger?"

"Yes," he replied patiently, placing the blood-soaked coat on a pew out of sight while walking over to the space heater. "A messenger of the Living God."

Magnus took the cap off a thermos he held in his hand as the young woman stared at him with surprise, watching him pour a steaming liquid into the thermos' blue cup. "Would you care for some soup?"

April shook her head, eyes still wide. "No," she said softly.

"It will warm you."

"No," she insisted, the tone of her voice rising with frustration.

"You have no reason to fear me."

141

"What have you done with my daughter's body?!" she demanded.

Magnus lowered the cup, placing both it and the thermos on top of the space heater to keep their contents warm. He was silent for several seconds before answering. "I felt obligated to give her a proper burial," he replied. "I gave her body rest in the graveyard out back. And my Father, who is in Heaven, has given her spirit sanctuary within his house."

April stared blankly, face ruddy from the smeared makeup. Her head dipped as she thought of her daughter's last terrifying moments on Earth. "Why are you doing this?" she asked, looking back up. "And why are you trying to console me with a cheap eulogy?" Her voice rose in anger and confusion. "Who are you?!"

"I am a messenger of the Living God."

Flustered, April turned to the left and right. "Stop it!" she replied, backing away several steps. "Save that junk for someone fool enough to believe it, and just tell me where my car is."

Magnus held up his hands. "Please…. I only want to help."

"Where's my car?!!" she screamed, eyes wide.

"It's parked out front," Magnus answered patiently.

April spun around and fled for the rotting doors beneath the balcony's overhanging floor, darting between the two central beams supporting it.

"*Go,*" the Lord whispered to the champion.

Magnus burst forward in a blur at the command, like a wind rushing by her.

April screamed suddenly, stopping short as the stranger appeared in front of the double doorway before she could reach it, arms folded across his chest, the night's lunar rays outlining his form as they crept through the spaces between the sanctuary's sagging doors. Her mouth dropped a little, looked back over her shoulder at the space heater to see that he had indeed beaten her to the entrance. The rhythm of her heart was frantic when she looked back at the doorway, face chilled by another sudden wind whisking by to the right of her, eyes widening when she saw that the stranger had disappeared again.

April stared at the rotting doorway for a moment. Slowly, she turned back toward the heater, shocked to find the ghostly stranger standing there in the same manner as before.

April walked out of the shadow of the balcony, her anger giving way to an unbelieving expression. "Who...who are you?" she asked, mouth trembling. "Wha...what are you?"

"As I said before, I am a messenger of the Living God."

"God?" She paused, squinting with a bewildered stare at the stranger who didn't seem to have a trace of any kind any kind of an accent. "Are you trying to tell me that you're an angel?"

"Not in the sense you suggest," he refuted quickly. "I'm something else."

April glanced back at the doorway. "How did you do that?" she asked, looking back at the stranger while pointing behind her.

"With a power beyond the scope of mortal comprehension," he answered.

"Obviously," April remarked softly, the wonder of what she had just witnessed eclipsing her pain for the moment.

Magnus stepped toward her, extending his hands in a friendly gesture. "It would be easier trying to explain this if I knew your name."

April stared at him quietly for a moment. He was definitely not the contact she was supposed to meet outside the valley, she thought. His display of some of the same superhuman skills that Seraphim Enterprises' R&D department was rumored to have developed in its Project Nietzsche program was unnerving at best. But he didn't seem heartless like the other agents working for the Omega Group. The tone of his voice and his actions appeared sincere.

She brushed her hair to the sides of her face, wiping at the smeared eyeliner on her face with her hands. "My name is April," she said with a sniffle, clutching her arms.

"Thank you. My name is Magnus." The champion stepped to the left of the space heater, gesturing with his hand. "Are sure you wouldn't like to warm yourself with some soup? There's plenty for the both of us."

"No…I'm not hungry."

Magnus nodded, smiling politely at her defensiveness. "I understand," he said. "Is there anything I can do for you?"

April looked around at the sanctuary's shadowy interior, rubbing her arms with her hands. "No one can help me," she said, still unsure of the situation.

"I would like to try."

April took a cautious step forward, focusing on Magnus' bronze face, imprisoned for a moment by the magnetism of his emerald eyes. "Who are you?" she asked again.

Magnus clasped his hands behind his back. "That…is a story of wondrous complexities." He stepped toward April. "I think it would be more prudent for your sake, though, if you answer some questions of mine first…like why you are on the hit list of the Omega Group?"

"You know of the Omega Group?"

Magnus nodded. "I have tracked the comings and goings of the Omega Group and its shadow masters for quite some time,"

143

he replied. "Which is why I am rather curious as to the group's purpose for being here in this valley?"

April looked away, still holding herself with her arms. "That, too, is a story of wondrous complexities," she answered, glancing around at the church. "Where are we, anyway?"

"We're in the house of worship that was built by the valley's first settlers in 1860," he said, stepping to the side to survey the decaying surroundings as April did. "To put it geographically, we're on a plateau located about halfway up the western face of the valley's eastern mountain range. And from what I know, this is the only remaining structure of the original settlement before it expanded to the valley floor in the year 1900."

April peered over at the sleeping bag on the floor. "I don't remember the drive here," she said, looking back at Magnus with a hint of suspicion.

Magnus could feel the leeriness in her voice even before he turned to face her. "You passed out on the way here," he told her, eyes piercingly honest. "It was no doubt induced by the shock of what you have been through tonight."

"How long have I been unconscious?"

"Just over four hours. It's about midnight now."

April lifted her hands to her face, rubbing her forehead with the tips of her fingers, gently bringing them down over her eyes to massage them. "They will come for me," she mumbled, fighting back the urge to cry some more.

Silently, Magnus closed the space between April and himself, his movement faster than the sound of the boards that creaked in the light aftershock of his footsteps. He placed his strong hands on her petite shoulders, startling her with his gentle touch. She gasped as Magnus embraced her with his hands, eyes wide. "Relax," he said. "I only want to help."

"Then let go of me," she insisted, pulling back with her shoulders.

Magnus complied immediately, holding his hands back in a nonthreatening manner.

April was surprised he let go.

Magnus placed his hands behind his back again to allay any fears she had of being touched again without permission. "You must be in a lot of trouble if the Omega Group's Sentinel Corps is after you?"

April prodded the inside corners of her eyes with her fingers as if to pinch away the sudden pain in her head. "It's all an experiment," she sighed. "The entire population of the valley is involved."

Magnus folded his arms across his wide chest. "What exactly do you mean by an experiment?"

April hesitated to say any more, unsure if she could trust him with what she knew.

"I only want to help, April," he said, seeing the fear in her. "If I was with the group, we wouldn't be here discussing these things in such a manner, now would we?"

"But who sent you?"

"I have told you who sent me," he reminded her. "And that's the truth."

April sighed.

"I know you're hurting, April. And I really want to help you. But you've got to tell me what's going on."

She looked up at him once more, faint tears of desperation clinging to the bottom of her eyes. "The town itself is a testing ground," she told him.

"Testing ground?"

"Yes," she answered.

"What sort of testing ground?"

"The group," she started, voice cracking a bit, "has made the town of Tower Valley, the place I was running from, a so-called perfect society. The group's top brass officially refer to it as Project Palladium. It's supposed to serve as a model for the nations of the world."

Magnus squinted suspiciously. "What does this 'experiment' include?"

April's head lowered in shame when she thought of her part in the madness that had engulfed her life. "For the past two years and five months every facet of life in Tower Valley has

145

been dramatically transformed, supposedly for the best." She lifted her head. "But it's more like the controlled atmosphere of a laboratory."

Magnus' mind was racing, hanging on every word the beautiful young woman was speaking, somewhat leery of where she was headed with her story.

"I personally don't know much about this organization, but I assume, since you say you know a lot about the Omega Group, that you're familiar with the Masonic Order?"

"Yes," Magnus nodded. "I have followed their activities for quite some time as well. Their mystic teachings are grounded in second and third century Gnosticism, Manichaeism and the teachings of the Cainites who composed the Gospel of Judas. Their structural roots originated with the Knights Hospitallers and Templars of the First Crusade; the *Rex Deus* priesthood who, according to the botanical reliefs carved into the stones of Rosslyn Chapel in Scotland, explored the Americas before Columbus did. The Masonic Order masks themselves in charity, good works and the promotion of brotherhood. In actuality, they're an ancient Luciferian cult. They're linked to the Druid *oak men* of old. Their reach of control extends to the highest levels of the G8 nations and most of the world's other governments, including the Oblonica secret society of Masonic assassins and thieves known as the *Mazzini autorizza furti incendi avvelenamenti*; a splinter group most people refer to as the Mafia. This cabal was assembled in the 19th century by Giuseppi Mazzini, author of the Palladium Rites. They're somewhat similar to the Sicarii assassins of ancient Israel. The highest level of the Masonic Order, however, is famously referred to as the Illuminati; international financiers who control the world's Central Banks. Along with their serfs in Europe's Idumean houses of royalty, they hold great sway over the world's other numerous secret societies. But it is the Harness Magi and their masters among the rebel angels who rest near the peak of this elaborate trapezoid of power. The *nugae* messages and secret symbols of Rosicrucian power that identify these different groups are embedded in the walls of cathedrals and government monuments across the globe to mark their territories.

Flags bearing the five and six-pointed stars are the most visible of these archaic symbols. And though some of the more recognizable of these groups are often seen at odds with one another in public, I can assure you that they are all bound together beneath the surface in a universal Satanic Brotherhood, which has one of its most influential power bases right here in the state of California."

April looked at him dazedly, amazed at his ability to rifle off such an intricate web of conspiracy without a shadow of doubt in his eyes. "I…. I don't believe in any of that stuff," she replied. "Not to that degree anyway. But I have seen some very weird things since I moved to the town. And I do know that a local chapter of Masons loyal to the Omega Group easily swayed the town's religious and financial institutions into committing to the experiment. In other words, the group literally bought the entire valley from the Masons who already seemed to control everything, threatening to foreclose on the mortgages of the few who had thought to resist the less than subtle takeover of the valley. All resistance evaporated when the group revealed the astronomical prices they would pay each citizen for their homes and businesses…."

"Money that would go right back into the local banks controlled by the International Bankers," he remarked.

"Yeah, exactly," she said, brightening. "And all they had to do to collect was agree to a contractual participation in Project Palladium, which meant giving up all control of family, money, health, government and religion to the group for the duration of the experiment that was specified in their contracts."

"A synarchy…."

"A what?"

"Synarchy," he repeated. "It means to be ruled over by shadow masters of the state."

Magnus thought for a moment, his countenance turning grim as the Scriptures swirled in his mind at such implications. "Tell me…by what means is this control manifested?" he asked, his voice heavy with dread.

That question brought forth the deepest regret in April's expression. "As you can tell by my signing bonus parked outside, I was hired at a hefty price by the director of the Omega Group's nanotechnology and biometric programs to develop the means for controlling the population of the town." Soft tears streamed down her face in what seemed to be an endless night of emotional release as she explained her role in everything happening in the valley. "With what seemed like a limitless amount of funding, I led a team of Lilliputian engineers, along with the group's own MEMS and STM technicians, in the creation of the A-6 Mark…."

April's words struck a chord deep within the champion. His stare was attentive, teeming with horror and excitement.

"The A-6 Mark," she continued, "is a Quantum nanochip the size of an uncooked grain of rice that can be injected into the body. In more complicated terms, it's a miniature tube of chloroform fluid that contains molecules of carbon and hydrogen atoms. The tube itself is a nanotech nuclear magnetic resonance machine. Its magnetic coil spins the atoms of the fluid, allowing it to do calculations trillions of times faster than the newest Pentium chips."

"Where are the chips … inserted?" he asked hesitantly.

"They're either injected into the forehead or the palm of the right hand," she answered. "Those were the only two choices that the group would give the townspeople. I have no idea why they were so insistent on those particular places for the implants."

"I do," he said softly.

"How?" she asked.

"That's not important right now," he said, shaking his head solemnly.

He paused, listening to a soft wind moan against the old walls of the sanctuary, its rotting timbers wailing with soulful creaks while he brooded over what had been revealed to him.

Magnus walked back to the space heater, turning sideways, the lamps on the floor casting a dim shade of yellow light over him. "What exactly were you being chased for?"

"I stole one of two prototypes for the A-6 Mark," she answered bluntly.

Magnus turned his head sharply, surprised by such a daring act. "What prompted you to take such a risk?"

"I was tired of the control."

"Control?"

"Yes," she said. "Everyone in the valley was required to receive an implant," she revealed. "But I was able to remove the implants my daughter and I were injected with before making a run for it. And I did it just in time. The group had started giving permanent marks on the skin to coincide with the placement of the chips, forcing the few remaining women of the town who weren't already members to join the Order of the Eastern Star, with their children being forced into groups called the Order of De Molay and Job's Daughters. I knew there would be little hope in trying to flee if I was made to take the visual mark and join that organization. The group increased the Masonic leadership's power of influence over individual citizens by introducing them to a new course in mass hypnosis known as Alpha Rhythms Meditation. Like the truth serum sodium Pentothal, this mass hypnosis technique alters the alpha brain waves between eight and 13 vibrations during visualization rituals, prepping the mind for binding hallucinations and commands controlled by the voice of an outside handler."

"I am familiar with this course in mass hypnosis. There are many ecumenical and evangelical organizations throughout the world that have covertly introduced their members to these practices. But tell me more about these permanent marks. What do they look like?" he asked with a raised eyebrow.

"They're two inches long and an inch wide," she answered. "The ink dye they use can never be removed. Not even by surgery. And to add to that, someone's name, along with a secret three digit nanite numerical code, referred to as *gematria* consonants from an ancient form of Hebrew, is encoded into the main structure of the mark so they can't be reproduced outside of the valley's labs. The code can only be read by a special black light developed by one of my teams."

"Does that mean what I think it does?"

149

April nodded. "Yes. Someone's blood was mixed with the dye. I was told it was part of a fail-safe identification process in case the CNO systems linking the nanochips suffer an electromagnetic or cyber attack. The visual mark itself is shaped like the number 8 in mixed colors of black and red, with its top curve broken in the middle. Two dragon heads with separate sets of wings extend from the broken ends, suspended in an attempt to reconnect the symbol, it seems. My team developed a device that would administer the visual mark at the same time the nanochip is implanted for future projects. But I haven't the faintest idea why they chose such a strange image to coincide with the placement of the implants."

Magnus bowed his head with a deep sigh. "I know why."

"Explain it to me then. And don't tell me it's not important right now."

He crossed his arms as he looked back at April. "What you're describing has little to do with *gematria*. It's a system of enumeration rather than computation. The symbol is a Stigma. It's a deified icon of the Egyptian and Assyrian empires, along with a host of other lesser civilizations that passed across history's stage. It's linked to the *SSS* mark of the ancient mysteries. It gave rise to other serpentine images like the hollow dragon heads of the Sarmatian *draconarius* standard bearers of the 2nd, 3rd and 4th century armies of Rome.... Such likenesses have struck fear and respect across the world since the fall of mankind."

April bowed her head with a look of disbelief.

Magnus took a step toward her. "I need to know more," he prodded.

"Why?" she asked.

"I need to know everything that's going on if I am to help you."

April clutched the sides of her head with her fingers as she walked over and sat down on one of the old pews beside the space heater, her head still aching from the chaos of everything that had happened. She rested her elbows on her knees, burying her face in her hands, still unsure if she could trust her feelings about the stranger.

Magnus walked over and squatted in front of her. "Let me help you, April," he implored.

She looked at him with the greatest fatigue. "All right," she said softly. "All right."

April took a slow breath as she submitted herself again to his desire to know more. "After removing the manufactured chips from my daughter and myself," she continued, "I injected them into a couple of the lab's rat specimens to throw them off our trail. No one can come and go without being tracked by the group's company satellite."

"Then what made you think you could escape with the prototype?"

"Because the prototype doesn't have the same magnetic signature as the manufactured chips. It was never meant to be programmed into the company's satellite."

"I see…. You must have had a source you were going to reveal all this too, then? Someone you thought you could trust?"

"Ye…yes," she stuttered, somewhat stunned by his deduction. "I was allowed to leave the town five months ago on a research trip to Silicon Valley. Under supervision, of course. But I managed to make contact with someone very powerful on the outside, someone I knew who was rumored to be investigating the group's private projects. With his help, I was able to delay my return to the town for a few days, citing various technical reasons my guardians couldn't quite grasp at the time."

"A lie?"

"Yes," she said. "And it worked. We were able to determine the best opportunity to escape with one of the prototypes. We decided it should be this particular week."

"Why this week?"

"I knew if the group could ever be distracted long enough for me to make a run for it, it would be this week while they were preparing for a secret conference being held here in a couple of days."

"What sort of conference?"

"It's a meeting of political heavyweights who are interested in the project."

The champion nodded with understanding, allowing another breath of silence to fall between them before prodding any further.

"Where is the prototype now?" he asked.

April could hardly bring herself to answer, holding her mouth as she closed her eyes. "It's back in the hands of the group. After I removed my daughter's manufactured chip, I hid the prototype in its place." She stopped for a second to choke back the pain. "I knew they would search me for its magnetic signature if they caught us, but I figured if they couldn't find it, I could use the promise of its return to bargain for our freedom. I never dreamed they would suspect that I would use my own daughter to smuggle it. They knew how much I loved her. I was counting on that…but I was a fool."

Magnus was respectful in his tone as he spoke of her daughter, knowing that her backup plan to use the chip as bargaining power was nothing more than desperation in a hopeless scenario. "So that's why they killed Megan and took her hand?"

"Yes," she said in a near whisper. "I could have removed the prototype back at the lab, but they killed her just to prove how much in control they really are. I was even told to be back at work by Monday morn…." April stopped cold in the middle of her account, eyes widening with suspicion suddenly as she looked at Magnus. "Wait…."

"What is it?"

She stood up slowly, moving to the side of him, walking backward toward the church's sagging doors.

Magnus stood also, wondering what he had said to scare her. "What's the matter?"

She studied the blood on Magnus' clothes for a moment, eyes darting back and forth. "How did you know my daughter's name?" she asked, a sudden convulsion of fear and conspiracy gripping her heart with an icy clench.

"I heard you mention it when we were on the road."

"No," she said, unable to remember having mentioned her name before. "You are one of them. That's why you're helping me…you're trying to gain my trust!"

Magnus was taken aback by the sudden twist in the conversation, holding up his hands as he retrieved his last step. "What reason would I have for doing that?"

April was frantic. "You want to know my source too! That's why they didn't take me back to town themselves!"

"Listen to me, April," he begged. "Your contact is probably already dead."

"No," she said, shaking her head in disbelief.

Magnus lowered his hands slowly. "You're in a state of hysteria right now, April. And considering the circumstances, it's quite understandable. But I assure you, I only want to help."

"No…. Stay away from me!" she screamed.

April twirled around and raced for the doorway, barely remembering through her muddled thoughts the displays of speed Magnus had exhibited moments ago. This time he didn't bar her path, and allowed her to burst through the sanctuary's rotting doors with the force of her outstretched hands. She was engulfed in an explosion of moonlight, refusing to look back.

153

Chapter Five

Tsavo squatted next to Kaiser's broken body, clutching the back of his head, twisting his face back around in front of his torso. He studied Kaiser's shredded face, pondering the fierceness of the act it had taken to kill him. A host of Heaven could have done this, he thought. But it was unlikely.

The giant flicked Kaiser's head to the side, grabbing the lapels of the dead agent's splattered coat before standing back up. He lifted Kaiser in the air like a piece of cardboard, tossing him into the woods to his left.

Tsavo turned and walked toward the wrecked Suburban sitting in the middle of the road, eyes dark and calculating, his black robe swirling in circles behind him as a strong wind swept down through the trees. He walked up to what was left of the vehicle's front end, carefully examining the jagged crater in the center of the crushed hood and the large engine driven halfway through the asphalt below it.

He surveyed the twisted scene on the other side of the shattered windshield. The broken bodies of his men lay sprawled over the seats, the smell of blood and progressing rigor mortis saturating his heightened sense of smell.

With a squint and a growl, Tsavo walked around to the second passenger door on the left side of the Suburban, fists clenched. His dark eyes were set with determination as he tore the door from its hinges, flinging it behind him with child-like ease.

He reached inside the vehicle, stretching his thick arm across the dead body closest to him. His eyes saw inside the dark interior with a piercing clarity, easily spotting the small plastic bag sitting on the floor behind the driver's seat. He grabbed the bag and pulled it into the open.

Tsavo moved back half a step to inspect the bag's contents by the light of the moon. He opened the bag's seal, pulling out a child's severed hand and holding it in front of him between his fingers. The giant plunged one of his fingernails into the tender flesh, twisting it back and forth in a probing manner before pulling out the small, rice-shaped nanochip hidden beneath the layers of the skin.

Tsavo held up the chip in front of him, blood streaming down over his merciless fingers. With a snap, he crushed the chip between his thumb and index finger, rubbing it into dust with his otherworldly strength. He tossed the hand aside, flinging it deep into the woods.

In anger, he turned and reached down beneath the Suburban, grabbing the vehicle's foot bar where the door had been torn away. The giant roared as he stood upright again, lifting the Suburban like a toy, flipping it over the embankment on the other side of the road with a toss of his hand. The thunder of the rolling vehicle echoed throughout the night as it crashed into the trees at the bottom of the steep bank.

Tsavo stood there staring at the moonlit pavement stretching before him. He lifted his right hand with the child's blood on it, sniffing his fingers as he stared at the road ahead. A low, guttural growl escaped his hardened mouth when his nose caught the scent of the mother in the texture of the child's blood. The giant lowered his hand and stretched his arms behind him, letting his black robe slide off his shoulders. He stripped himself of his tailored clothing and shoes.

Tsavo stood silent for a moment, the scent of the child's mother pulsating vibrantly in his senses. He was a marvel of exposed muscle from head to toe, chest cut with an indestructible width, arms and legs long and thick. The giant began to chant in the language of his father's angelic tongue, commanding the power within him to beckon a beastly shape with which to hunt his prey.

His body began to contort in the middle of his chanting, facial bones cracking with realignment. His sharp fingernails increased in length as bristles of black wolf's hair shot through the pores of his skin like darts. His flesh was quickly covered by the prickly strands of hair, muscles bulging through the new covering, the irises of his eyes morphing into yellow pools of light. He howled with laughter as he thought about the hunt, lifting his gaze to the moon above as sharp fangs emerged in his frothing mouth, his face still contorting with transformation.

April stumbled through the waist-high grass in front of the old sanctuary, trying to make her way to her car parked on the dirt road about 10 yards away from the sanctuary's entrance. Her shoe heels broke in half the second she made it to the road, slowing her down instantly.

April grabbed for her left shoe, hopping on her right foot as she pulled it off. She kicked off the other one as well, running full speed for the car, collapsing to her knees beside the driver's door. She reached up for the door handle, but it was locked.

April started to search the pockets of her suit coat until she remembered the stranger had driven her. He no doubt had the keys. A saving thought managed to pierce her confusion. She had a spare key in a magnetic box hidden on the car's frame beneath the driver's door.

April reached under the door frame to search for the miniature box, her breaths rapid with exhaustion. The box was nowhere to be found. It had obviously been dislodged in the chase.

"No!" she cried, beating on the door with her fist.

"I believe these are yours," a voice said from behind.

April turned and jumped to her feet. The mysterious stranger she knew only as Magnus was standing beside the car's rear bumper, holding her keys out toward her.

Magnus took a step forward. "I won't hold you against your will, April. They will catch you, though. You know that. And they will not spare you for their use this time, especially when they find out what I did to Kaiser and his Sentinels," he warned.

April looked at him confused, breathing rapidly.

"They're dead, April," he said, noting her look. "The enemy will be looking for the both of us soon enough."

April shook her head in disbelief, lunging forward suddenly to snatch the keys from Magnus' open hand. She paused in place after drawing back with the keys, surprised by the fact she wasn't met with a last minute act of resistance.

Choosing not to ponder the weight of his warning, or the sincerity of all he had done, April turned and jammed the key into the lock, flinging the door open. She flung herself into the driver's seat, reaching back with her left hand to grab for the door's handle. She glanced back at Magnus while starting the car.

"Stay," Magnus replied. "I can protect you. Just as God obviously protected you when you contacted your source. How else do you think you were able to make contact with the outside world unless he had blinded them to what you were doing? You should know better than anyone that the group was surely monitoring every move you made when you were in Silicon Valley."

"If your God was so helpful why didn't he blind them to my escape as well?"

"I can't tell you why your escape has turned out the way it has, but I know from experience God is using it to help you. So don't put yourself in even more danger by trying to run before you see the whole picture."

April ignored his plea by slamming the door shut. She turned around in the seat and jerked the car into gear, flipping her lights on at the last minute just before stomping on the accelerator. The car spun off with a supercharged roar, swerving back and forth on the dirt road that snaked down the mountain, leaving in its wake a cloud of dust and airborne rock.

Magnus watched the car's brake lights disappear around a bend of pines.

He frowned at his decision to let her leave. Though he had only known her for a brief time, he could relate to her pain. The searing loss was always the same, burning a hole of fear and separation deep within the spirit of the living. There would be no peace in his heart tonight, especially not after learning what was transpiring in the town below.

Magnus looked heavenward. "What purpose brings me to this dark place, Lord?"

159

Chapter Six

April gripped the wheel of the car with both hands, trying to control the vehicle as it swerved back and forth. The headlights flashed across the trees on each side of the road, scarcely lighting the way in time as the road's curves raced toward the car out of the darkness.

She could tell she was nearing the bottom of the mountain by the rapidly declining landscape all around her. She stepped on the accelerator even harder, taking the time to wipe the strands of hair from her eyes, ripping through the gears at a maddened pace. Her only hope to see to it her daughter didn't die in vain was to make it to the contact she hoped was still waiting for her outside the valley.

April screamed suddenly, slamming on the brakes as something large and animal-like dashed across the road in front of her.

She sat dazed for a moment from the sudden stop, wondering if she had hit something.

Dust from the road curled around the car's halogen beams as she peered out the windshield, searching for signs of a carcass.

Nothing there, she thought.

April reached down to shift the car back into first. Just as the car started to roll forward, a force from above came crashing down through the hood, bouncing the automobile's rear end off the ground.

April was thrown against the ceiling before she knew what happened, the impact nearly knocking her unconscious.

April sat up slowly from where she lay slumped across the passenger seat, nursing a knot on top of her head. She peered over the steering wheel with a look of disbelief at the smoking crevice that was once her hood, the mangled engine beneath it sizzling with the sound of draining fluids. The headlights were out. There was only light of the moon to see by now.

April's heart sank at the sound of a low, bubbling growl coming from the other side of her door. She slowly turned to her left, only to see a pair of yellow eyes and an elongated jaw of sharp teeth rising into view. The moment was one of shock and stark terror as soundless tears rolled down her cheeks.

The jaws of razor sharp teeth snapped at her suddenly with a terrible growl.

April screamed, turning to crawl to the passenger seat. Before she could reach the door, the roof of the car started to collapse in a sudden crash, the vehicle's windows exploding outward in showers of glass. She cried hysterically, clawing her way to the jagged opening in the passenger-side window, the car bouncing up and down as the beast pounded from above, pressing the roof down with relentless blows.

April threw her arms over the window frame and pulled herself up through the opening, falling forward to the dirt road as the window's frame collapsed behind her, her shoeless feet barely clearing the roof's final collapse. She rolled over and crawled backward on her hands, pushing gravel with her feet until her back hit against the trunk of a large pine.

April's breaths came frantically as she looked up at the beast standing in the moonlight on top of the car's flattened roof. The creature was enormous, almost mythical in size, covered in black, prickly fur. Its head was that of a wolf, with the shapely chest, arms and legs of a man. Its hands were nothing more than long, razor-sharp nails meant for tearing.

Tsavo's yellow eyes blazed wildly at her, the moon hovering like a crown above his pointed ears, fangs dripping with saliva. He bent forward on the roof on all fours, extending his long neck over the crushed edge.

"Leave me alone!" she screamed.

Tsavo exploded with a salivating growl, jaws widening, a soulless hate swelling in his luminous glare.

April scrambled to her feet, screaming for help as she darted into the woods.

Magnus jerked his head up from his silent prayer, fixing his gaze on the mountain's wooded path before him. He had been motionless for about 20 minutes until the faint cries of trouble registered in his powerful ears.

Without thought, Magnus burst forward in a lightning-fast run, quickly disappearing down the road around the same bend of trees April's car had vanished behind earlier, leaving a quiet wake that gently swayed the tips of the tall grass in front of the old sanctuary.

April ran with all her might, stumbling over tree roots, struggling to keep her balance, rocks digging into her feet while dodging back and forth between the pines. The mountain's rough terrain was visible before her from all the lunar shafts penetrating the forest.

She could see a flat rock in the distance that seemed to connect with a wide clearing. Beyond the clearing, through another smaller section of pines, she could see the main road.

April swung her arms frantically, running full tilt, glancing back at the sound of the branches snapping behind her. The beast was in a pursuit, slowly closing in on her, seemingly enjoying the chase.

She turned her head just before reaching the large rock. To her surprise, the rock was not connected to the clearing. It was a bluff overlooking a meadow of wheat-style grass some 20 feet below.

April fell forward over the edge before she could stop herself, tumbling head over heels, seeing a sudden rush of jumbled images. She landed sideways on her left arm, screaming as it broke on impact.

Magnus stood in thin spirals of smoke that rose up from the front end of the Aston Martin, bending over what was left of its hood while running his hand along the large crevice in its center. It looked as though it had been caused by a double-armed blow.

He took a mental note of the damage, comparing it to the carnage he'd unleashed on Kaiser and his Sentinels. Someone had left him a message, he thought. Someone with nerve enough to taunt him.

A fierce howl suddenly electrified the mountain air.

Magnus snapped his attention in the direction of the howl, spotting a path of broken limbs through the mountainside's thick foliage of pines, wildly forged by a terrible strength.

The dimensional makeup of his face stretched like a bronze beam of light as he disappeared through the jagged pathway in a desperate race to offer April one last chance of hope.

April lay motionless in the meadow's darnel grass, the night's gentle winds swaying the tips of the grass in circular motions. She moaned from the stabbing pains of her broken arm and the shortness of breath from having the wind knocked out of her.

She tried to sit up, only to fall on her back.

Another fierce howl ripped through the air high above her, giving her strength enough to look up and see that monstrous black shape crouching on the flat bluff above the meadow, its yellow eyes shining with omens of primordial wrath. The moon seemed to follow the beast, still hovering in a stationary orbit above its head.

April managed to turn herself over on her stomach with all the strength she could muster from her right arm, trying to ignore the pain of her broken limb while crawling for the road, clawing frantically at the tall blades of grass for leverage.

She dug her nails through grass and dirt, heaving with panicked breaths as she caught a glimpse of the road that was visible through the trees in front of her.

A clawed hand latched onto her right leg suddenly, lifting the right side of her body off the ground. She struggled to scream for help while being dragged backward to the center of the meadow.

Tsavo flipped April over by her leg.

Her chest heaved up and down with terrified gasps for air as the beast crouched over her. Its eyes glowed like embers, fangs emerging in a web of saliva.

There was nothing before her but the blackness of impending death. This was all her life had come to. She thought to call out to the very God she didn't believe in. Her mouth could only quiver with a muted plea for mercy, though, before fainting at the sight of the hellish teeth poised to tear the life from her.

Tsavo opened his jaws wider when April fainted, breaking the web of saliva in a quick lunge to consume her flesh.

He stopped short of sinking his teeth into April's throat, snapping his head toward the cliff where the flat rock was, listening to the rumble of a snapping thunder coming down the mountain toward him.

165

Chapter Seven

Magnus could see a clearing in front of him as he darted between the trees. He increased his speed, the appearance of his face a blur in the shafts of moonlight, his bright eyes remaining solid, fixed firmly on its target.

He was almost clear of the pines when he vaulted forward, decreasing his speed in midflight, smashing through trees in his path, snapping one of the pines in half with a fist as the image of his body resumed its original shape.

The sound of crashing timbers filled the foothills as Magnus sprang clear of the wooded slope, arms winging outward, the ripped sides of his jeans bloating with plumes of air in his downward glide. He spotted April lying deathly still in the middle of the tall grass below as he passed over a smooth ledge of rock.

Magnus landed in the tall grass beside April's motionless body, kneeling over her with frantic hope, turning her face so he could see it fully. He could hear her heart still beating with life while he inspected her cuts and bruises, taking note of her left arm that looked considerably disjointed.

He closed his eyes with a prayerful word that her injuries didn't seem to be life threatening. "Thank you, Father," he whispered. "Thank you...."

Magnus was suddenly aware of something moving behind him while he huddled over April. Conflict had been expected.

"Welcome back from the dead, great king," a voice cried from the darkness.

He opened his eyes in a heated glow, lifting his head slowly as the hellish voice shattered his moment of thankfulness. Hearing that particularly thick, soulless voice behind him was unexpected.

Magnus stood and faced the trees in the distance just as a giant figure of a man stepped from the shadows of the meadow's surrounding pines. "Tsavo…you bloodthirsty maggot."

Thickly-cut muscles rippled from shoulders to calves as the giant walked forward into the open. "It's been a long time, champion," he said. "I never really believed you were still alive, especially when I found those bones and that helmet of yours in the ruins of the old Templar stronghold in England in 1755. I remember how the bells of London rang out as the ground trembled beneath my feet the very moment I picked up that helmet. It was as if the powers of Heaven had been offended by my disturbance of your resting place."

Magnus said nothing. He knew the real reason why those bells rang so long ago.

"The rumors of your parabolic existence continued to persist, though, despite finding your helmet," the giant continued. "But I foolishly dismissed those contrived tales as the fearful fantasies of weak-bodied men glimpsing the wrath of one of Heaven's avenging angels. Had I known you were the new Shekinah Champion, I would have forsaken my command over the Praetorian Guard and accompanied Titus when he confronted you…. Had I only known, you would have surely died that day."

"Well, here's your chance," Magnus challenged. "But know this: I am not an avenging angel. I am a living foreshadow of the Lion who destroys abominations such as you. Millenniums may pass, but God doesn't forget. The gavel of his judgment is always swift to fall when you least expect it."

"Judgment? I am judgment!" he roared.

The giant crouched forward, chanting for his lupine shape to return, growling, face contorting, bones popping with realignment.

Magnus reached to his left instinctively for his weapon, only to remember his ancient sword was tucked away in his war-cabinet back at the old sanctuary. Ironically, after all the time that had passed since his first encounter with Tsavo, he would now find out what it was like to go hand to hand with the giant.

He started to leap forward to meet Tsavo head on, but stopped cold before his feet could leave the ground, catching a glimpse of something out of the corner of his left eye. A shadowy blur with a bronze gleam streaked into view, cutting a path across the backdrop of the meadow's border of trees.

The giant lunged forward in the middle of his transformation, unaware of the anomaly racing toward him. The shadow's metallic trim whistled like a buzz saw as it passed behind the leaping giant, slicing through his thick neck with the accuracy of a laser beam. The apparition disappeared in a flash of light as it exited through Tsavo's neck.

Tsavo fell forward in the tall grass on his knees, head rolling from his shoulders on impact, his enormous torso crashing to the ground with a loud thud.

Magnus stood still, waiting, gazing back and forth at the trees with a puzzled squint, posture remaining rigid and battle ready.

There was nothing to be discovered, though, only the silent whispers of the night wind.

With a notable caution, the champion moved forward quickly, knees plowing through the darnel grass in a parting frenzy. He stopped and stood over the giant's naked body, watching the lupine hair retract back through the pores of his thick skin, the smell of brimstone filtering through his nose as a portal to the Earth's penal core was closing in a liquid fashion.

He looked back up at the border of trees, searching for signs of an angelic presence. There was still none to be found.

Magnus studied the giant's large head that was soaking in the black crude at his feet. After millenniums of evil schemes, the giant's demonic spirit had finally inherited the torments of the Abyss. It was a fall, though long in the waiting, that had come by the strangest of means.

" 'A presence, dark, invades the fair…. Giving horses ample scare….' "

Magnus' heart froze in a surprised breath as another frigid and familiar voice ripped through the silence of the killing field. He lifted his head toward the trees again, the scope of his vision settling on two large pines 15 yards away at the border of the meadow. An ominous figure with a metallic wingspan stood between the twin trees, nearly filling the expanse with his black, marble-like shoulders. He towered to 10 feet or more, his slanted eyes burning like white fire through the shadow masking his face, shining as brightly as his crown of golden hair blazing with a translucent luster.

Magnus was taken aback by the assassin's sudden appearance, remembering quite vividly how he had only experienced such stealth once before on the night of Judas' resurrection from the *well* of the Abyss.

The assassin's poetry replayed in Magnus' mind with a haunting echo, allowing him to pick up on the middle portion of the verse. " '*Chaos reigns,*' " he said slowly, " '*and panic numbs….*' "

" '*When something wicked this way comes,*' " the assassin finished, smiling with a vampiric gleam through the shadow covering his face.

Magnus gestured at Tsavo's decapitated body. "Why?" he asked.

"You know why, young one," the assassin replied. "He was a pawn who thought himself a king worthy of the *Covenant Harness*; a caged wolf who sought to dominate his handlers with submissive subterfuge."

Magnus concentrated his powerful vision on the mysterious rebel, trying to penetrate the shadow covering his face. "I know you," he said. "Lebanon…. That Christmas Eve night of the unholy nativity…. You were there."

The assassin laughed with a bubbled hiss. "Yesss," he answered. "There…here…everywhere."

"You're not omnipotent," Magnus replied. "You may have caught me off guard, but you're not the Almighty!"

The assassin grinned in a beastly manner. "I am more like him than you could ever imagine, brave champion."

An unnatural wind swirled around Magnus as the assassin assaulted him with his vanity, penetrating the flesh of his mind with his sleekly-cool voice, plaguing his soul with the echoing hints of a perfection long since lost.

Magnus' head bowed dizzyingly. He couldn't understand why he was feeling a sudden sense of sympathy for the rebel. His thoughts were crushed between the fingers of some sort of telekinetic grip it seemed, his reasoning teetering toward a maddened appeal as the enemy's eternal plight for justification reached out to him.

He lifted his head, only to be stunned by another undetected move by the assassin, causing him to falter backward a bit in his stance.

Before he could recover from one trance, Magnus found himself drawn into another. He stood in awe of the assassin towering over him a few feet away. He eclipsed the scenery behind him, his bronze-colored wings curving around the shoulders of his black-muscled physique, reflecting halos of moonlight as frigid vapors rolled along their liquid spines. His face remained veiled in an impenetrable shadow, hair billowing with a golden glory as smoky tentacles of light trailed from the corners of his bright eyes

Magnus found it difficult to think again, feeling that same shadowy fear of the unknown which had haunted his boyhood for a season after his father's murder. But he was able to notice symbols resembling the last letter of the Greek alphabet etched in silver on both sides of the assassin's bronze-colored wingspan, looking strangely similar to the marks of another cloaked rebel he hadn't seen since Jerusalem fell to Titus.

The assassin laughed with the coldness of space while the champion stood hypnotized before him. He started to float backward toward the meadow's border of trees, his laughter trailing behind.

The spell over Magnus broke when the assassin melted through the shafts of moonlight, sinking into the shadows on the other side of the trees. He started to pursue, only to stop short of leaping through the air when he spotted a set of headlights through the trees coming down the road. He glanced back at April as she lay unconscious behind him, quickly snapping his head back toward the trees where the mysterious power could no longer be seen.

He looked at the road again. The headlights were coming closer. He had only seconds to make a decision. Get April to safety first, or pursue the mysterious rebel?

Magnus turned without another thought, running back and scooping April up in his arms, taking several quick steps through the tall grass before leaping high into the air.

━·━ ☰◇☰ ·━━

Magnus floated to a limb near the top of a tall pine beside the flat bluff overlooking the meadow. He skulked behind several large branches to hide himself from a low hovering UH-60M Black Hawk helicopter shining a spotlight on the area below. April was safe now back at the old sanctuary. But he had lost his chance to pursue the mysterious rebel.

He watched another group of Sentinel agents walk down the slope from the valley's southern road where two SUVs were parked, joining the four already standing around Tsavo's decapitated body. A tall brutish man with a crewcut and a communications ear and mouth piece walked in front of the second group of agents, carrying a large body bag under his arm.

Magnus listened through the turbines of the chopper hovering in front of him to the muffled tones of disbelief coming from the first group of agents congregating around the giant's body. They had discovered the kill zone while patrolling ahead to provide security for the clean and clear crews sent out to collect Kaiser and his team, calling for backup to help contain the area until they could extract the body.

The brutish-looking man leading the other group started barking orders to the agents standing around the body, unfolding the large bag under his arm, throwing it out on the ground beside the decapitated giant. The agents from the first group shouldered their HKs as they were ordered to secure the corpse and its severed head. They struggled to put the giant inside the bag, barely raising him above the tips of the tall grass blowing back and forth in the wind of the chopper's rotors.

Magnus picked up on a radio transmission coming through the chopper's com-link as he watched the agents. They and the ground units were being ordered back to town by someone in charge on the other end. The pilot acknowledged the order and radioed to the lead agent below, informing him to evacuate as soon as possible.

The Lord spoke to Magnus suddenly while he was listening to the transmissions, urging him to take immediate action to protect his stronghold from being discovered.

The car, he remembered. April's car was still on the mountain road. Even though the road had fairly good tree cover from above, there was still a chance the car could be discovered if the chopper decided to do a sweep of the area, which would lead them right to the old sanctuary.

Magnus turned and vanished from the treetop, racing back up the mountain to retrieve the wreckage.

173

Chapter Eight

Sodom the Sullier stood alone in one of the middle arches of the clock tower's belfry, removed from his pinnacle above, his 24 warriors posted in groups of six on the four glass buildings built in a square around the courthouse and its tower. The bottom tips of his false wings billowed in and out of the archway in a silken motion, fangs locked in a savoring smile as the moon filled much of the belfry with its waning beams of light.

He feasted on the street lights below with a supremic glare. Even with the majestic mountains and thickly forested landscapes surrounding the town, it would never have the total night time grandeur of his Bay City province of San Francisco. But it would do for now.

No, he thought. It would more than do. For he had built this town into a monument of his own design just as he had rebuilt the halls of corruption along the Barbary Coast destroyed with the rest of San Francisco so long ago, a loss he would never forget. The sudden assault upon his most prized province had swept down from the north out of the seclusion of the state's sparsely settled region of redwoods, its true origin having been divinely masked along the San Andreas Fault Line.

A frigid voice surprised Sodom from behind, blistering his winged back with its coldness. "A Shadow King and his *rural seat of various view*.... Tis a sight for the lips of blind Milton to dictate."

Sodom fell to one knee in the middle of the arch, his bright eyes descending toward the tower's ivory exterior in a reverent bow of his head. He had come to know that cosmic voice well since taking over the reign of Tower Valley.

White eyes of slanted fire appeared in a veil of darkness behind the rebel king, preceding a pair of metallic wings splitting into neighboring shafts of moonlight, frigid vapors rolling off the long spines of each wing from the intercontinental forces of speed applied to them.

Sodom spoke slowly. "I received word, my lord, that the matter of Tsavo has finally been resolved."

"Of that you can be sure," the assassin replied. "Cardinal Menelaus will be assuming his role for the first day of the conference."

Sodom lifted his head. "We will be ready for his arrival, my lord."

A sinister smile sliced the darkness beneath the assassin's white eyes. "Really?"

"I am aware of the matter that has prompted question in your voice, my lord. My warriors have informed me of the arrival of a new enemy. It seems Kaiser and his team were destroyed in a most violent and personal fashion. Such carnage makes one wonder if we're not dealing with something other than one of Michael's warriors."

The assassin stepped closer to Sodom. "You can be certain we are not dealing with a mere angel from Heaven."

Sodom looked back to his right with a suspicious squint. "Could it be the champion, my lord?"

"Without question," he answered coldly.

"But I thought he died a long time ago?"

"I have destroyed him many times in the pages of fiction. But in life? Not yet."

Sodom glared threateningly across the landscape of his precious town. "I will have Tribune Massakur and my other warriors hunt him down and destroy him before the sun rises!"

"No!" the assassin snapped. "You will do nothing. He is mine to deal with."

Sodom quickly nodded his head in a submissive bow. "And the scientist?"

"She will be easily dispatched when I'm done with the champion."

Sodom offered no debate. "As you wish, my lord."

The assassin shuffled his metallic wings. "See to it that the Lamb's seven eyes do not penetrate the town's borders during the conference."

"There are no spies within the town limits, my lord," he said, his voice sharp and reassuring.

"Do not forget the curse that was placed upon this town, Sodom," he warned. "The Watchers and the Book Masters are always near to monitor such things whether you see them or not. You would do well to remember that."

The warning scolded him. But it gave him pause to consider the possibility. He peered down at the spot several blocks away where the town's sanctuary of worship had once stood, the place where the curse had been inscribed. An elaborate brick structure with white pillars stood in its place, serving as the town's central bank.

"What else do you require of me, my lord?" Sodom asked.

There was no answer from behind.

"My lord?"

Sodom stood up slowly when no reply was given. He was hesitant to turn in the direction of the belfry's interior, wings bloating backward through the arch in a receding wind. He searched the spacious loft, but there was no trace of the assassin.

Sodom turned back around in the arch, reining in his wings, eyeing the soft glare of streetlights below. "You were foolish to come here, champion. Foolish."

⸻ ◈ ⸻

While Sodom surveyed his town, a tall figure of a man was stooped over inside the belfry's middle bell, clinging quietly to its long-stemmed chime, his boots resting lightly on the percussive ball.

With the aid of his angelic and cherubic diffraction veil, Scriptos had managed to penetrate Sodom's valley defenses unseen. It was a limited cloak, however. The energy of his elect purity would eventually flow outward after lingering in one concentrated position for too long, alerting his presence to other

cosmic minds in the area. But exposure was no longer a risk. He had heard all that needed to be recorded.

Scriptos peered down at the open shaft below, following the chime's thick chain that descended into the tower's four hundred foot well of darkness. He quietly wrapped his long, royal blue coat around his legs and sword, careful not to disturb the bell as he dropped through the opening and disappeared.

Chapter Nine

Magnus sat against the gray, plaster-peeling back wall of the sanctuary's pewless balcony. The first rays of the morning light were billowing through the panes of glass in the wall's arched window just above his head. He held his right leg back with his arm, knee tucked into the chest of his blood-stained shirt, head hung low. An antique trunk with polished brass fasteners was sitting open to his left. In the corner beyond that, near the top of the balcony's stairwell, was a portable closet made of clear plastic shaped like a rectangular box with white canvas sides. Dark frock coats, along with several suits and other changes of clothing, filled the bulging closet.

To the right of the portable closet was his wardrobe-style war cabinet, hand carved from polished acacia wood. It was six feet tall, with small wheels protruding from the clawed pads of its four legs shaped like those of a lion. A round emblem of pure gold sealed its rectangular doors, with a lion's head protruding slightly from its center. Inside the cabinet was an array of priceless, ancient armaments, including one of two violins made specially for him by Antonius Stradivarius in the year 1713.

Magnus was deep in meditative thought as he replayed the course of events from the previous night in his mind. He watched the dust particles floating in the shaft of sunlight coming through the window overhead, admiring their flight as they were raptured from the bondage of the balcony's dark floor with the slightest shuffle of his feet, swirling, rising into the warm glow like freed souls drawn to Heaven. The simplicity of the dust's freedom to rise from a place of decay was the flight he longed for.

He looked to the right with a sigh. April lay unconscious in a sleeping bag beside him. He had done his best to set her left arm, broken in her fall from the ridge, putting it in a sling formed from one of the shirts in his portable closet. Bandages taken from his supply crates downstairs were applied to the minor cuts on her feet, with black tube socks pulled over top of them to keep her warm.

Magnus reached over and stroked her forehead gently with the back of his hand, pulling it back with another sigh. He thought about his wife and the scores of people he wasn't able to save in the past. Though he possessed great power and wealth, he was still bound by the reality of his Adamic heritage. He lived in a world of fallen souls that couldn't be saved by might, but by Blood.

Magnus turned his head and picked up a SATCOM phone sitting on the dusty floor to his left. He dialed a San Francisco number, offering a quick prayer that his call would be shielded from intercepts while he waited for the connection.

180

———◆—■◦■—◆———

An early morning phone call woke the owner of a Victorian townhouse in San Francisco's posh Pacific Heights. A short, heavy set man with thinning, gray hair rolled over onto his side in the four poster bed where he had been sleeping. He flipped back the 30 years still nuzzled up to the brow in covers, sleeping peacefully through the ringing that shattered the quiet of their pearl-colored bedroom.

Louis Barrows, a lawyer once part of a prominent investment management firm, reached for his robe as his feet hit the bedroom's lightly warmed hardwood floor. The bulldog wrinkles of his face sagged wearily as he stood up slowly, sliding his hairy arms into the sleeves of a blue robe.

The digital ringing emanating from his office alerted him more keenly to the difference in the rings compared to his regular phones. He knew there was only one person who would be using that particular phone system in his office. He shuffled to the foot of the large bed hurriedly, stepping down several stairs into a small, cupola-shaped nook adjacent to the bedroom soaked with the fresh rays of the morning.

He sat down in a leather chair behind a well-ordered desk. A large bay window sporting a view of the Golden Gate Bridge circled around behind him, its tall panes of glass reaching all the way up to the bedroom's vaulted ceiling. His own gruff reflection stared back at him in the computer screen on his desk as he picked up a special iridium phone. "Mr. Lehohn?" he mumbled, rubbing the sleep from his eyes.

"We must be brief, old friend," Magnus replied from the other end, "lest we find ourselves at the mercy of prying ears."

Louis straightened in his chair at Magnus' urgent tone. "Is something wrong, sir?"

"It's nothing I can discuss right now," he answered.

Louis leaned forward onto the desk, looking as though he had been in that position for hours worrying about some crucial brief of business. "Have your trunk and your other supplies arrived yet?" he asked.

"Yes…I'm settled in for the moment."

"Good. Another one of your mysterious friends appeared in my office and offered to make the delivery as usual."

"I wouldn't have it any other way."

Louis turned in his chair toward the bay window, cupping his hand around the mouthpiece of the phone to keep his voice from carrying through the acoustics of his sunken office. "If I may ask, sir," he inquired, squinting with concern, "why have you decided to stay there in that old sanctuary? From the pictures I saw of it given to me by one of your associates, it looked like it should be condemned."

"Let's just say it's safer than staying in town."

"That's what concerns me," he replied. "Something doesn't feel right about that place. I had this Tower Valley checked out. But I could scarcely find out anything about it. It doesn't even appear on the state maps."

"It's probably best that you don't probe any further," Magnus suggested. "Things could get out of hand before my business here is finished. And I don't want any of my transactions traced back to you or your family."

Louis hesitated a moment before agreeing to his suggestion. "Very well, sir," he said. "I know that you keep me in the dark about most of your dealings for my own safety. And I know you to be an honest and caring man; one who has blessed me with great fortune. However, could one person still have so many enemies as you seem to have after all these years?"

There was a brief silence from the other end. "Unfortunately, old friend, my enemies seem to increase as time goes by."

Louis shook his head as he stared out at the San Francisco Bay. "Your life continues to be one of great mystery to me. Maybe one day you will give me a little deeper glimpse into it."

"You will know everything about me when the time is right. But for now, I have my own mystery to unravel. And while I'm doing that, I need you to prepare for a guest. She'll need all the necessary arrangements."

"Yes, sir."

"I will call you back in a few days with more details."

"I'll be ready."

"Good," Magnus replied. "Stay sharp, and take care of yourself."

"You too, sir…I'm here if you need me."

Magnus leaned his head back against the rear wall of the balcony as he placed the phone on the floor beside him with a sigh. He stared up into the shaft of light above him again. To tell his friend the truth about his ancient legacy was something he longed for. But he was forbidden by the Holy Spirit from doing so. He had revealed himself fully to others in the past. But for the majority of those he'd met and befriended in his sojourn across history's landscape, Magnus had been forbidden by the Holy Spirit from telling them of his powerful legacy. God, as was the case most of the time during the Church Age, would use the normal pathos of life to bring the elect to faith in his Son, with glimpses of the supernatural to help open the hearing of a few in crucial moments of decision. But the age of patience and petition was seemingly coming to a close. Soon the King would return for his children, leaving the rest of the world to suffer a time of wrath and judgment while the *marturia* testimony of Jesus Christ was proclaimed by the Jewish Elect.

Magnus glanced at April with those thoughts of impending judgment, only to be reminded of the mysterious rebel who seemed to be taunting him with a battle yet to come.

Chapter Ten

A Black Hawk helicopter roared past the courthouse's clock tower, its tail kicking sideways as it passed around the clock's northern face. The chopper quickly realigned for a descent, dropping through a torrent of updrafts as it made its way towards the Omega Group's glass building on the south side of the clock tower.

Specter stood on the roof waiting for the chopper to land, the wind of the churning blades pressing down on him as it came to a rest on a helipad a hundred feet away from where he was standing. He turned away while the Black Hawk powered down, its dying winds whipping his dark-colored tie against his face.

The slick's main door slid back as the rotors ebbed to a slow whirl. Bishop Kane, a brawny, bull-faced man dressed in black fatigues and wearing a Marine-style cover, stepped down from the slick and walked over to Specter.

Bishop grabbed Specter by the shoulder and spun him around, his face almost plunging forward into the chest of Kane's ammo vest. "What's the word, Mr. Specter?" he demanded, his voice loud and commanding.

Specter bounced back a step from the merc, pushing his glasses back up on the bridge of his nose. "The clean and clear crews have taken care of Kaiser and his men," he answered. "But we have another problem, sir."

"What problem?"

Specter was visibly shaken as he looked up into the cold stare of the Omega Group's Director of Covert Operations. "Mr. Tsavo...is dead, sir."

"What?!"

"Yes, sir," he answered.

"Who was responsible?!"

"We don't know, sir," he replied. "The clean and clear crews found his body several miles away from the first kill zone on a forward sweep of the valley's southern road. He was decapitated, sir."

Bishop's face was frozen in a scowl, eyes darting back and forth with disbelief. Never had he come across a man, or a group of men for that matter, that could have possibly posed a threat to the giant.

"I received word from one of Mr. Alchemy's regents in Rome," Specter continued, "and they believe these killings are the work of only one operative, sir."

"Impossible!"

"That was my first reaction as well, sir," he replied. "But we do have something else to go on, though. Shadow Corps Intelligence picked up on an outgoing call from a SATCOM phone earlier this morning...."

"And?"

"For some reason they couldn't get a fix on it when they first picked it up. Only a few words were discernable during the transmission. But with a little more legwork, and data that is forthcoming from our intelligence linkup with the NSA and the ECHELON listening post in England, we should be able to at least track down its point of origin."

"This isn't a game, Mr. Specter!" Bishop roared, bending his head forward to poke his large nose in the slender man's face. "You don't have time for a little more legwork. The security of Tower Valley has been compromised."

"We're working on it, sir," he assured him. "We've already doubled the town's security for the duration of the forthcoming conference. And we have ID checkpoints set up on every road outside the valley by agents posing as state police. But we're lacking the extra manpower needed to search the vast terrain of the valley and its mountains."

Bishop took a step back from Specter. "What's the word from the brass?"

"Cardinal Menelaus is already enroute from Rome to take over the conference's first day of proceedings. Masonic agents from the group's P2 agency in Italy will be accompanying him to provide security for the dignitaries until Mr. Alchemy arrives."

"What about the mission in Lebanon?"

"The next phase of Operation Assyria is still a go as scheduled," he answered. "The Red Horse Units of the Omega Group's Alpha Corps Army are waiting for you on a small fleet of TSVs in the Med. Electromagnetic resistant Comanches and Apache Longbows will provide close-range air support, with a small mechanized unit of Panzer and Stryker vehicles providing ground ordnance. F-117 Nighthawks will soften your targets before the main strike."

"And the blackout?"

"Taken care of, sir," he answered. "Our lead agents in the brass at CENTCOM will see to it that the Common Operating Displays at Joint Command and all AOR stations are inoperative at the appointed time. They, along with our operatives at the CIA and those in command at the other ISR forward bases located along the *Arc of Instability*, have guaranteed us a 48-hour intelligence blackout of all Middle East surveillance, including suspension of all coalition forces patrolling the border between Syria and Lebanon. Shadow Corps Intelligence has also acquired the transponder encryption codes of the remaining elements of the Syrian Air Force that fled to Lebanon when the coalition forces took control of Syria. The codes will help delay any response they posture once your aerial units cross the border."

"And what of our special equipment?"

"We have Arabian and Quarter horses stationed on the northern border of Israel for our mounted divisions that will lead the southern front, with Friesian mounts to be used in the mountains of Lebanon. Our RHU legionnaires have been equipped with their gladius and spatha blades, with crossbows issued as secondary ordnance. Our R&D metallurgy techs were able to fashion the blades from CT-20 armor piercing metal as ordered. They also developed shields for the cavalry units that are resistant to puncture from the standard NATO rounds to the 20mm, dual warhead jackets some of your own forces will be using in their OIC smart guns."

"And the evac?"

"Chinook helicopters will meet your forces at the designated LZs. You will be extracted and dispersed throughout the forward base systems in Macedonia and Vicenza, Italy that NATO command turned over to the European Military Union. Shadow Corps Intelligence will cover your tracks in the guise of a training mission."

Bishop smirked with approval. "Good. But you still have a mole to burn, Mr. Specter," he replied, resting his hand on top of the .40 caliber Glock 27 strapped to his right side. "And I suggest you do everything the brass tells you to do in finding Dr. Wedding and this operative who has penetrated the valley. Is that clear?"

Specter nodded silently.

Bishop started for the chopper, stopping just short of its open bay, turning back for a parting word. "Have you ever met Iscarius Alchemy, Mr. Specter?"

Specter shook his head. "Not personally, sir," he answered. "His scheduled arrival for the conference will be my first opportunity."

"Do you remember what Mr. Tsavo was like?"

Specter nodded warily, the color draining from his face a bit.

Bishop grinned at Specter's sudden paleness. He turned back around without saying another word and hopped back into the chopper, leaving Specter to ponder Alchemy's shadowy myth that haunted the corridors of power within the Omega Group with an even more pervasive darkness than Tsavo's had.

Chapter Eleven

A motorcade of black Suburbans, six in number, made their way into the town limits of Tower Valley. A gray Rolls Royce limousine traveled at the center of their single file formation as the motorcade rolled through the southern entrance of the town, turning right on Imperial Lane. The Omega Group's glass buildings quickly rose into view above the shingled cupolas and sloping roofs of Tower Valley's executive district. The courthouse's clock tower loomed behind the buildings, rising into the afternoon sky above the walls of glass like a mythic citadel, its ivory-ribbed exterior reflecting the sun's light with a blinding gleam.

A strong autumn wind swept through the tall oaks hemmed in behind the cobblestone sidewalks on each side of the street, showering the motorcade with a storm of red and gold leaves as it rolled slowly through the picturesque neighborhood. The residents of Imperial Lane wandering about in their yards gave little notice to the fanfare wheeling down their street. Parades of luxury had become common in their town.

The motorcade circled the glass buildings and headed north outside the town limits, traveling for about 20 minutes before turning off onto a heavily-guarded road that ran alongside the Omega Group's air base. Each side of the road was covered with thickets of pines. It quickly became an incline leading up to a flat plateau in the foothills of the northern mountain range's southern slope.

As the lead Suburban crested the top of the road and leveled out onto the plateau, a French-style chateau made of limestone came into view against the backdrop of the rising mountain range. It sat in the center of the plateau's six hundred open acres. Its A-shaped roofs and domed turrets were covered with dark shingles hand crafted from aged wood, their covering reaches spreading wide over the chateau's open-armed embrace of the plateau's core. A fifteen-foot-high wall made of solid limestone surrounded the chateau's perimeter, including a vine-yard behind the house covering over a hundred and twenty of the six hundred acres.

The motorcade rolled up to the chateau's limestone archway, the lead vehicle stopping short of the entrance. A black iron fence with tall spirals filled the mouth of the arch, barring the motor-cade's approach.

On the other side of the spirit realm's light-bending veil, stood Bastion, Dominium Gate Master of Dragylon. He was poised behind a stone statue of a fierce griffin posted on top of the archway.

Bastion fixed his fiery gaze on the VIP behind the tinted win-dows of the limo, the wrought-iron gate in the arch below open-ing with a heavy clatter the moment he spread his arms in a welcoming gesture.

The motorcade rolled slowly through the gate into the chateau's square courtyard of light-colored brick. The extended halls of the mansion's frontal facade were like arms on the sides of the courtyard, hugging the spacious opening. At the center of the square was a section of plush grass, with three shittim trees aligned in a triangular pattern at its epicenter. An infinity-shaped bench of stone was positioned at the center of the trees' formation like an altar.

The motorcade circled around the courtyard, stopping in front of the chateau's imposing entrance. Twisting strands of ivy covered much of the chateau's frontal facade, wrapping around the house's tall portals of segmented glass. The strands reached as high as the towering, A-shaped roof that curved outward on both ends above the main entrance's limestone arch.

The driver of the Rolls Royce, a large Italian dressed in a black Armani suit, stepped from the car, shielding his eyes with a pair of sunglasses while walking to the limo's rear passenger door.

He pressed down on the limo's silver, S-style handle, stepping back as the suicide door swung open.

The French doors of the chateau's main entrance opened at the same time the driver was opening the limo's passenger door. Specter stepped out onto the entrance's stone patio, looking less wrinkled than normal as he made sure his tie was straight.

The limo driver stood at attention behind the open door, bowing his head as Cardinal Simon Menelaus stepped from the car.

The sorcerer was dressed in a black cassock and high-heeled shoes with golden buckles, making him appear taller than he actually was. A purple cape was draped over his sleek shoulders, with a pectoral cross designed from the mystic Tau of Tammuz hanging around his neck, matching the color of the golden biretta pinned to the top of his head.

He carried a six-foot staff in his right hand known as the *Oracle of the Dragon Lord*. It was made of ancient wood shaped from one of the support beams found in the ruins of the Tower of Babel. It had been crafted by the hands of the first Master of the Harness Magi, lacquered over with a black liquid alchemized from the Dragon Lord's own preternatural flesh, which gave the staff a colossal weight no mere mortal hand could wield. A Babylonian cross of pure gold crowned the top of the staff, with a black griffin cresting over the cross' petibula bar, its jaws frozen in an open snarl between the winged heads of a black and red dragon wrapped around the cross in a pose of broken infinity.

The staff was an instrument of great power passed to each Master of the Harness Magi throughout the millenniums, kept in reserve for the last master of their ancient order who had yet to *come up out of the Earth* to claim what was his just as the *Covenant Harness* had been kept for the Son of Perdition. Those within the Magi knew nothing of Simon's original date of birth, only that the *Oracle* he'd inherited always gave those who wielded it a mystical longevity of extended life.

The original Master of the Harness Magi had been there at the beginning to help lay the foundations for the first Babylonian Empire. Each master after him had successfully resurrected the mystic traditions of the Babylonian Order whenever a new

191

empire arose, spanning from the orient to the undiscovered tribes of the Americas. The Kingdom of Israel would be their central target in the Ancient World, though, as they polluted the holy people with astromancy and false prophets such as the priests of Jezebel. One of their greatest achievements would come at the hands of the Roman Emperor Constantine, founder of the pagan Church of Rome. They would guide the Masonic Crusades and the Catholic Inquisitions, persecuting the true Saints such as was done against the Christians in the Valley of Rora in the 17th century; a people remnant in size who stood valiantly against the professional armies of the Papacy under the fearless and unparalleled leadership and biblical stratagems of the great Joshua Gianavel.

With the history and success of each Magi Master resting firmly upon him, Simon was the living embodiment of all the false prophets of the past. But another greater than he, the last of the Magi's masterial line, would rise in his place one day, using the full weight of their evil legacy to lead the people of the world into worshiping Judas as God in the flesh. Those who refused would suffer unto death, with the brunt of the Dragon Lord's wrath being poured out on the seven future Jewish Assemblies of Asia Minor and the remnant in Jerusalem.

Simon stepped to the edge of the limo's open door. "Thank you, Mr. Buragatti," he said in a deep voice, speaking in such perfect English that it masked any trace of nationality. "Take the convoy and return to San Francisco. The dignitaries will be arriving soon."

"Yes, your eminence," Buragatti nodded.

The driver quietly shut the door and walked back around to the driver's side of the limo, turning up the left lapel of his suit coat to speak into a miniature communication piece pinned to it. "See is secure," he said, speaking cryptically of the cardinal's secret mastery of the Vatican. "Move out."

Simon focused on Specter as the small caravan began to pull away behind him. He smiled from ear to ear in his trek up the steps in front of him, the golden sphere on the bottom of his staff clicking regally on the stones of every other step. He held out his right hand to Specter when he reached the top, letting the sapphire ring on his third finger catch a glint of sunlight.

Specter took the cardinal's hand, bowing his head submissively to kiss the ring on his finger.

"I understand Project Palladium has been experiencing some complications of late, Mr. Specter?"

"Minor complications, your eminence," he answered, lifting his head.

"Isn't it true that one of the prototypes for the A-6 Mark was stolen by its creator?"

"Yes, your eminence. But we programmed the company satellite with the magnetic signature of the other prototype a few hours ago. Tracking indicates the signature signal for the one that was stolen was terminated late last night. It seems that Mr. Tsavo was successful in destroying the chip before…."

Simon looked at Specter with a raised brow. "Before his body was found headless?" he said with another smile, finishing Specter's statement for him.

"Yes, your eminence."

"And what have you done with Tsavo's body?"

"We have it on ice in the old stone bunker beneath the town's courthouse," he answered. "It was suggested by our R&D department that we preserve it for research to be used in the Nietzsche program created by Mr. Tsavo."

"No," the sorcerer replied. "There will be no research performed on Mr. Tsavo's body."

"What shall I do with it, then?"

"Keep it where it is until Mr. Alchemy arrives," he ordered. "He will instruct you on what to do with it."

"Yes, your eminence."

"Good. Now what about our other problem? I understand that Dr. Wedding made contact with a very important media personality on the outside before she fled."

"Group agents following all our known enemies in the media discovered late this morning it was Nicholas Forrestal himself, after Commander Kane left for the Mediterranean."

"Yes," he replied. "Our most staunch adversary of the printed page."

"Shadow Corps Intelligence found out that he had chartered a seaplane to land near the salmon fishing port of Shelter Cove outside the valley along the Pacific Coast Highway."

"And was he dealt with properly?"

Specter drew closer to the cardinal, his voice almost a whisper, as if he feared for his own life for what he was about to say. "Mr. Forrestal's personal security team helped him slip by our agents before he could be eliminated. But I received another secured communique from one of Mr. Alchemy's regents in Rome just before you arrived," he said, his mind alive with dark accounts of mysterious assassins from an ancient order that were known to work for the group from time to time. "A unit of the Harness Magi has been sent in to take care of him once and for all."

Simon was completely stone-faced as he played along with Specter, knowing that it was he who had sent each message. "What about Dr. Wedding and this mysterious agent who has penetrated the valley?"

"That's the strange part about the communique," he said. "The regent ordered me to sit tight, and that the hunting down of Dr. Wedding and the operative helping her would be handled by other means."

"Then carry on as you have been instructed, Mr. Specter," Simon told him, his brown eyes flashing with silver flecks of fire as he gazed back at the familiar rebel standing on top of the chateau's gateway. "I'm sure the problem...is well in hand."

Chapter Twelve

Magnus lingered in the glow of the moonlight pouring through the balcony's arched window. He was dressed in a long coat of Moroccan leather and a snug, dark blue sweater and jeans. He was perched on top of one of the post supports of the balcony's old railing, playing a custom designed violin crafted for him by Antonius Stradivarius himself.

He watched April as she slowly woke from her unconscious by the pull of the music. She hissed painfully, moaning when she tried to lift her left arm from beneath the folds of the sleeping bag covering her.

"Careful," he said tenderly, lowering his violin "Your arm has been set."

His words were distant echoes in April's mind as she sat up in the sleeping bag with a sudden jolt, the nightmare of her fight to escape the raging beast crashing back down on her with instinctual timing, her mind blurred by the terrible images of the monster hovering over her with its gaping jaws. The pain in her arm increased with her sudden movement, sending her reeling against the balcony's rear wall.

"It's okay!" Magnus told her. "You're safe."

April looked up to see Magnus squatting on top of the balcony's railing, her head and arm pounding with a steadying nag of sharp pains. "What happened?" she mumbled, glancing at her left arm, held snugly in a makeshift sling.

"Tsavo nearly killed you. But you need not fear him anymore. He's dead."

"Wha...what are you talking about?" she asked, situating her arm gently in her lap as she pulled her knees towards her beneath the sleeping bag. "What does the Chairman of Seraphim Enterprises have to do with that thing that attacked me?"

"He was the thing that attacked you, April."

"What?"

"Tsavo was the last of the Nephilimites born after the fall of the Antediluvian World. His *gegenes* predecessors were a race of superhuman giants spawned by fallen angels who ruled that age...an Atlantean age mixed with both achievement and fornication."

"Please...don't start this again," she said, bowing her head in frustration.

"You wanted to know what happened, April. So, I'm going to tell you everything."

"Tell me everything about what?"

"About the world you're living in, and the part you're playing in the cosmic drama surrounding it."

Magnus paused for a moment, standing to his feet on top of the railing's post support. He moved forward slowly, floating down to the balcony's plank floor.

He walked over to where she was sitting against the balcony's back wall, setting the violin down on the floor beside him as he squatted in front of her. "We live in a world inhabited by spirit forces of both good and evil," he continued, his emerald eyes brightening even more in the shadow of the wall beneath the window. "They're all around us. God is real, April, and so is Heaven. But Hell is equally as real, as is the Devil. And he has used you to help create a mold for bringing about a visible mark of allegiance he will force upon the world in the future."

April stared at him with a terrified expression. "Who are you?"

"As I told you before, my name is Magnus...Magnus the Lehohn. I was born a prince in the House of Sheshbazzar in 24 A.D., and have walked the Earth from that time forth. I am not Longinus or the Wandering Jew. They are myths. I am something else. One who was chosen by God to be a living foreshadow of the wrath to come at the end of the Church Age. But most of all, I am a disciple of the risen Christ."

April shook her head. "I don't believe it...I won't believe you. You're insane."

"Am I?"

April stared into his bright eyes, unable to escape the fire of truth glowing hotly in them. "Why is this happening to me?" she sobbed.

"God is reaching out to you, April."

She held her head in a weary and silent stupor.

"April," he said, reaching out toward her, lifting her chin gently with his hand, "I'm telling you the truth."

"Truth? I'll tell you the truth," she said. "Megan was all I had in this world. And that's the only truth I really care about right now."

"You have no other family?"

"No," she told him, her countenance growing even more sorrowful. "My mother was not married when she gave birth to me. She died soon after I was born due to complications. I ended up in an orphanage where I spent the first eighteen years of my life. I was told that my mother didn't have any known relatives at the time of her death. And I never had the opportunity to find out what happened to my father. But I refused to let myself be a victim. I excelled above all my peers in school, which earned me a full scholarship to Stanford. The only thing I kept from that miserable childhood of mine was my name. I have always found it interesting that my mother chose to name me April before she died...April Wedding."

"Names are very important," he remarked. "When chosen with love and care they speak of something great that has been prepared for its bearer before they're even born. And your name tells me that your mother loved you very much."

April said nothing as his words brought only a small measure of solace.

"What about Megan's father?" he asked.

April wiped at the tears on her face. "We never married. And I never kept in touch. He was a mistake I made when I was doing

197

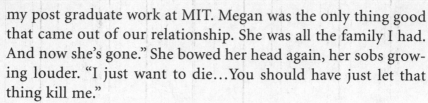

my post graduate work at MIT. Megan was the only thing good that came out of our relationship. She was all the family I had. And now she's gone." She bowed her head again, her sobs growing louder. "I just want to die…You should have just let that thing kill me."

"April, if you wanted to die you would not have run."

"Please, just leave me alone."

Magnus breathed a long and patient breath, listening to the voice of the Holy Spirit prompting him from within. "Listen to me, April," he said.

She lifted her head slowly, unable to keep from being drawn into the rapture of his bright gaze when he leaned closer.

"Do you believe what you have seen and experienced?"

"I don't know. I've seen so much that I can't explain. I just don't know if I'm willing to believe you're really two thousand years old, and that all of this has something to do with God and the Devil. I'm a scientist…at least I was. And I believe in what I can prove."

"I see. Then answer me this: Is the sky blue?"

"What?"

"You're a scientist, aren't you? You believe in the power of knowledge, right?"

"Yes."

"Then tell me: Is the sky blue?"

April stared at him for a moment before answering. "No," she said.

"I don't believe you."

"But it isn't."

"Prove it."

"What?"

"Prove it," he repeated. "Tell me why the sky isn't blue."

April huffed with a look of frustration. "The sky is actually black," she started. "White light from the sun penetrates the Earth's atmosphere about eighteen miles above the planet's surface. The light is composed of all the colors of the rainbow. When it connects with the air molecules in the atmosphere it scatters blue and violet light wavelengths. The other colors pass on to the surface unaltered. This phenomenon spreads from molecule to molecule. The perception of our eyes is determined by these combined wavelengths because we're sensitive to the blue light. That's why the sky appears blue."

"I am almost two thousand years old, April, and I think I know more than you," he chided. "And I don't believe a word you're saying."

"It doesn't matter if you believe me or not!" she replied. "It's the tru…."

April stopped cold in the middle of her defense of the truth, staring at the champion who held his ground with a silent strength.

"You see," he said softly. "You know the sky isn't really blue. And I'm also sure during the course of your elite education you have discovered, as your peers before you, that evolution isn't true either, a doctrine that defies the physical laws of entropy itself. A doctrine which also demands that you cling to the ridiculous theory of uniformity in the fossil record you no doubt know to be false due to all the evidence of a universal flood. A flood which upset the fossil record with all its hydrostatic windstorms, volcanoes, cross currents, whirlpools and other hydraulic hemorrhages unleashed on this planet when the fountains of the deep were opened. And shall I comment on the cell structure of the human body as well, or the half-life of palonium halos in granite which also disprove Mr. Darwin? And lest I be remiss, shall I touch upon the Fibonacci phenomena in botany, music and art? Perhaps, since you are a quantum physicist, we should discuss just how much of our universe is constructed from *dark matter*? Or shall we talk about the introns and epigenetic marks of DNA? Or better yet, should we discuss the physics of the *Roche Limit* for the Earth's moon, and the retrograde motion of the planets? But even those providential laws, as concise as they are in light of the entropyric effects ordained to be inflicted upon them with the fall of mankind, cannot be compared to the Lord's supernatural superiority over his creations."

April said nothing, eyes downcast. His remarkable insight into the truth about the origins of the universe was humbling.

She knew the scientific community's denial of the truth was meant to protect their flow of grant money. They couldn't risk losing the funds which helped prop up their research and their prominent pulpits from which to shape public opinion. But what she didn't know yet was that such public hypnosis was secretly beginning to be reshaped with a new strategy by the source managers of the scientific community's cash flow. A strategy which would acknowledge a different and more inclusive power cleverly masked as the creator of the universe, thus preparing the masses for the full resurgence of *magick* and the age of dark miracles where the world would openly worship the Dragon Lord as they had done in days of old.

"My little experiment wasn't meant to be vindictive, April," he told her. "But you know what I've said is true. Your mentors defied the very laws of the science they claimed to have practiced. But it's not enough to just know the truth. What matters is whether or not you believe on the God of truth as Savior."

"Like you?"

"Yes…like me."

"You're supposed to be two thousand years old, right?"

"Almost," he smiled.

"Okay, then…. Did you see Jesus rise from the dead?"

"No," he said. "But I did see him on the fourteenth of Nisan, the day he died. A day when darkness covered the whole Earth. I remember how he hung on that gnarled tree for six hours in the middle of four other condemned men, unflinching in the strength of his love. Even the soldiers who had nailed him to that rood were amazed at his prowess, and how he died at his own time of choosing. But it would be years later before I was led to faith in the risen Christ during an encounter with the Apostle Paul when I was a young cavalry officer in the Roman Army."

"How do I know you're telling me the truth about any of this?"

He paused for a second, answering her question by posing another one to her. "Have you not seen what I can do?" he asked in a baiting manner. "Where would I get such power if everything that I've told you weren't true?"

"Science is capable of many things today. Russia and the U.S. Military Industrial Complex have been experimenting with supersoldier programs for years. And the Omega Group has been the funding muscle behind most of it. They're even rumored to be responsible for all the so-called alien abductions for the last fifty-some years."

Magnus leaned closer, eyes burning brightly in the shadows, knowing that the truth of everything she said was far beyond anything she could possibly realize. "You did well with your reply. Signs and wonders are quite deceiving in this current dispensation. But answer me this," he challenged.

April's heart skipped a beat as his ghostly eyes bore down on her.

"Can you think of any other man or so-called god whose recorded words and deeds literally changed the entire course of history as Jesus' life, death and resurrection did? Or perhaps you believe the Apostles simply made everything up? A lie that would be the most elaborate hoax of all time. But suppose they did make up a lie of such magnitude. This would still leave us with one question. Why would the Apostles make up a lie, and then suffer and die for it themselves for some future earthly fame and fortune they couldn't even enjoy?"

"What about all those religious nuts in the Middle East who blow themselves up for their beliefs?" she asked.

"There have been many religious leaders throughout the centuries who have brainwashed their followers into dying for the glory of their false doctrines," he answered. "But how many of those same religious leaders in the Middle East today blow themselves up for what they believe like they teach their followers to do? Would you die for something you knew wasn't true? Or would you prefer to continue making a profit off the deaths of others like Mohammed and the leaders of his religion have done since that wicked man's murderous regime of slavery and war first plagued the Middle East? Men who conspire behind the scenes with their sworn enemies."

"What about the many empires that have conquered other nations throughout history for personal gain while flying the

Christian banner?" she asked pointedly. "Empires as cruel as any other radical nation or group of people claiming they're on a divine mission from God."

Magnus was patient with his reply. "First of all, the Church does not have a banner or a flag that is ordained from on high. That was added by the Roman Emperor Constantine, which gave birth to the so-called Christian flag we know today. And secondly, have you ever *actually* read anything Jesus said?"

April started to answer, but fell short, appearing to be caught off guard by his sudden inquiry into her personal reading habits.

"Jesus said there would be many who would come in his name," he continued. "But he also said they would be wolves clothed as sheep. This is something you have seen firsthand with the Masonic Order of this town, is it not?"

April stared at him. The glow of his eyes was ghostly, but warm, reaching out to her with a passion fueled deep from within. She had seen too much to discount everything he was saying. But she could still not bring herself to believe the totality of it all even though she had tried to call out to God for help when she thought she was going to die in the jaws of that beast.

Magnus could see her lingering doubt. "Hear me, April," he pressed. "It is not my custom to weigh in on someone with such a parlay of apologetics. But I have seen the vanity of man's wisdom broken with the passing of Da Vinci, Voltaire and Twain, men who thrived on the Hermetic heresies of the Renaissance. And too long have I had to weather the irreverent deification of such fools. Fools who knew nothing of the boundless enormity of the objective truth of God's Word."

April looked down at her arm in the sling. "I'm just not ready to believe."

Magnus reached out and touched the left side of her face. "I understand. But know this," he said, lifting her face gently. "Jesus gave his life to save those who were given to him before the world even began. I don't know what your future is, April, but I have done what is commanded of me. I have presented you with the truth of the Gospel. And regardless of the outcome from what I have shared with you, I will do what I can to protect you."

April touched his hand pressed against her cheek. "Thank you…and thank you for what you did for Megan, too."

"I assure you of this, April. Your daughter, along with my parents and my wife, are at peace with my heavenly Father."

"You were married?"

"Yes," he said softly. "But that's a long story for another time. Think about everything I have told you while I'm gone."

"Where are you going?" she asked, clasping his hand tighter against her face.

"I have to find out why I'm here before the enemy finds out where we are."

"And how are you going to do that?"

"I'll know more once I see the town for myself."

"No! You can't. They'll kill you on the spot."

Magnus smiled. "I will die only when the Father wills it," he told her. "And I doubt it will be tonight."

"Who is this Father you keep talking about?"

"God is one in three persons," he answered. "You have God the Father who is distinct, yet the same as God the Son. God the Holy Spirit is to be thought of the same way. But the revelation deepens with the incarnation of Jesus as God's only *begotten* Son, which means he shares the same substance of being as God the Father and God the Holy Spirit."

Magnus pulled away from her hand slowly and stood up in the moonlight, leaving her somewhat confused with his complicated explanation. "You should be safe here while I'm gone. The sanctuary has perfect tree cover from above. And I'm sure this old house of worship has been long since forgotten for the time being."

"How do you know?"

"Some associates of mine who secured this place for me are always careful to cover their tracks. One of those associates will watch over you until I get back. You won't be able to see him, but I assure you he's here."

April glanced around the balcony with a puzzled look.

"There are crates of food and water downstairs when you get hungry," he told her. "I also have some other supplies that may help ease the pain in your arm. Just help yourself to anything here. Oh, and I hope you don't mind the black tube socks. They don't exactly match that Chanel suit of yours, but they'll keep you warm. They'll keep the bandages snug against those cuts on the bottom of your feet as well."

"Thank you," she said, looking down at the socks she hadn't noticed before.

April spotted something square and compact sitting in the corner to her right. It was red and made of metal, with what appeared to be car tires and star-shaped wheels smoothly embedded in its sides.

"Is that my car?" she asked in a surprised tone, recognizing the winged emblems of her Aston Martin in the center of one of the embedded wheels.

"I had no choice. I didn't want to leave it on the mountain's road to be discovered. I'll see to it that it's replaced when my mission here is done."

"But how did you do that?"

"With my hands," he said simply.

April stared at what used to be her car. "Your hands?"

Magnus squatted in front of her again. "Remember," he told her. "Think about all you've seen and heard. Ask yourself why you've been allowed to witness such events."

She looked at him in utter amazement, nodding with a hint of hesitation.

With that concession, Magnus jolted up, whirling around in a quick manner. He ran toward the rail and vaulted over it, pulling his knees toward his chest, the train of his coat flying above his head as he fell into the darkness below.

April sat against the wall in total awe, waiting for the sound of his boots to come crashing down on the floor below. But the only sound she heard was that of the sanctuary's sagging doors creaking shut.

She pulled the sleeping bag up around her legs as chill bumps coursed over her skin, staring into the abyss of shadows in the rafters of the sanctuary's vaulted ceiling, searching for Magnus' mysterious associate he said would be watching over her, wondering if all he had told her was real. "God? The Devil? All this can't be true. It just can't be," she whispered.

A cold draft of air swept through the sanctuary while she stared at the rafters, shadows stirring all around her, the wind whistling softly through some of the holes in the balcony's peeling walls. She pulled the sleeping bag up around her snugly. The atmosphere of the old meeting hall was growing cold and darker in Magnus' absence. He was the only remaining light of hope in her life, she thought, looking back over at the squarely-compacted car sitting in the corner. A strange and inexplicable light, but light, nonetheless.

She curled down inside the sleeping bag as the wind continued to whistle in low shrieks throughout the sanctuary. "Why is this happening?" she whispered aloud, covering her head to weep again for all she had lost. "Why is this happening to me?"

A pair of silver eyes burned into view in the rafters above the balcony's rail as April covered herself, recording every word and movement. Always recording.

Magnus hovered high above the valley's southern road, perched on the branch of a tall pine, arms wrapped around his bent knees. Two other pines were snuggled next to his perch, shielding him from view with their branches which crossed in front of him. His dark clothes helped him to blend with the nighttime landscape. The moon and stars were bright above him, forming a jeweled dome over the surrounding mountains.

The town was a mere half-mile away from his position. The vaulted rooftops and shingled cupolas of Imperial Lane were the first objects to fall into the scope of his magnified focus. He quickly scanned across the tops of the town's bright lampposts, training his bright eyes on the four glass buildings hedged in around the courthouse and its clock tower, shimmering with an ivory glow from the strategically-placed spotlights. Red approach lights flashed on the corners of each of the glass buildings, serving as beacons for group helicopters.

Magnus shook his head. With the Omega Group's help, the town had become a nation unto itself, complete with its own military to protect it from outsiders.

Magnus tilted his head, picking up on muffled sounds from above. He looked up to see the running lights of two Black Hawk helicopters passing overhead, both operating on some sort of hybrid stealth mode while patrolling the valley's airspace.

He turned his attention to the courthouse's ivory tower as the choppers passed by. The starry backdrop around the clock tower burned like a fiery scroll before him as the Holy Spirit allowed him to roll back the veil to the spirit world with a commanding thought. A ring of 24 rebels came into view, circling the tower's obelisk where another rebel was perched on top. He recognized some of the shield-bearing warriors circling the tower when he magnified his vision, but none more than the rebel prince standing above them. But Sodom and his elite-numbered force, although formidable from what he knew of them from the past, seemed arrogant at best considering what April had told him was happening in the town.

It looked too easy, especially considering the group's mortal defenses which would be child's play for him. But there was still that mysterious rebel from last night who wasn't numbered among Sodom and his elite warriors, which gave him reason to pause and wonder whether or not he was being lured into a trap since they hadn't come looking for him by now. He would definitely be the wild card to watch for.

Magnus thought about the dream he'd had while imprisoned in the belly of that Roman slave galley, remembering the triangle that would task him in both form and legend. A beast, a harlot and a dragon.

Those words and visions had followed him across time as that triangle of evil did indeed task him in form and legend, serving as archetypes of greater things to come. And the town before him seemed to be an archetype greater in form than any he had seen in the past. It was, from what April had told him, exactly what the world was to become in the future.

Magnus closed his eyes. "Father," he prayed softly, "I have been a wayfarer on the roads of time for almost two millennia, and I have seen many foreshadowings. Now I see the model for what the world is to become. And so I ask, Father, what duty is left for me in this wicked world, especially here in this town? The enemy doesn't even seem concerned by my presence yet. And now that mysterious rebel who was in Lebanon for Judas' nativity has reappeared."

He stopped to listen for a moment. But there was no answer from above, only the sounds of the autumn wind whistling around him in soft currents.

"What more do you require of me, Lord?"

The night air continued to swirl around him as the Spirit of the Lord spoke to his heart. " *'A good understanding have all they that do his commandments,'* " the Holy Spirit told him, reminding him of God's Word which had been faithful to lead him into righteousness when vexed with enigma or selfishness during missions of the past.

Magnus looked at the town again, sensing in the words of Holy Writ a certain design meant to prepare him for the fires of trial. "Lead me, Father," he whispered through the breeze. "In Christ Jesus' name, lead me…. Amen."

Magnus stood up on the limb slowly, coattails flapping in the breeze. He jumped forward suddenly, rustling the branches of the surrounding treetops with his quick burst of speed, vanishing toward the town.

⊷·⊷≡○≡⊷·⊷

The assassin was poised on a flat bluff near the top of the valley's northern mountain range, standing guard over the sleeping town like a watchful reaper. The locks of his golden hair swayed gently across the shadow over his face, swishing back and forth in front of his white eyes. His adamantine wings were relaxed at the sides of his titanic arms, their sharp tips rising above his head in a slight arc. The moon was at its crest above him, its light falling on his sharp wingspan through the mountain's foliage. Tall pines towered all around his small lookout, concealing most of his perch,

providing him a vantage point which enabled him to see the inner workings of the central valley floor.

He peered past Sodom and his ring of warriors, focusing on the town below them. The corner lights on the Omega Group's glass buildings blinked as a consistent beacon for the Black Hawk helicopters patrolling the valley from above.

Streams of white light were squeezed from the corners of his eyes with his concentration on the rooftops south of the court-house's ivory tower. His marble-like chest expanded to a greater width, inhaling something familiar entering the town with great speed and stealth. The presence of purity and power from on high had slipped through the Omega Group's preliminary boundaries, even passing beneath the senses of the rebel angels protecting the town from a closer vantage point than his. But the intruder had not slipped past him.

A fanged smile of diamond light flashed across the assassin's masked face. "Let the games...begin."

Chapter Thirteen

Magnus squatted on the rail of a fire escape bolted to the side of a two-story clothing store. He hovered over an alleyway leading out to a section of the town's main strip of road. To his left was another brick building of equal height to the one where he was posted. In front of him, above the rooftops of the darkened storefronts across the street, he could see the upper halves of the four glass buildings surrounding the courthouse and its clock tower.

The sound of an approaching vehicle suddenly snapped Magnus' focus to the street. The lights of a black Suburban crept around the left corner of the alleyway, slowing to a stop on the street adjacent to the alley's entrance.

He lowered his arms from around his knees as the vehicle stopped beside the alleyway entrance, balancing himself on the rail with his boots. A spotlight mounted on the lower window frame of the vehicle's passenger door rotated slowly toward the alleyway, flooding the bottom level with a rush of intense light. The spotlight's wide beam searched the alley, all the way back to the bricked-up dead end. The beam retracted slowly, sweeping up along the alley wall to his left, probing the brick all the way up to its roof.

Magnus remained perfectly still as the beam swept back down the wall of the building beside him, gliding across the alley's pavement towards his position. He was still motionless as the beam began to climb the wall toward his perch on the fire escape.

He waited until the last moment, just as the beam touched the fire escape's grate floor behind him. He swiftly turned and leaped toward the other building across the alley, the train of his coat just missing the shaft of light as it swept up across the fire escape's railing.

Magnus landed on top of a cement arch protruding over a window in the neighboring wall, balancing himself flat against the building to keep from having to hover out in the open.

The spotlight finally clicked off when its illuminated reach found nothing out of the ordinary.

Once the patrol was gone, Magnus was able to squat down on top of the arch in a more comfortable position. The town had been easy to penetrate so far. But he knew he wasn't near the heart of power yet. And the enemy was more than just aware of his presence in the valley. Sodom and his warriors no doubt knew who he was by now.

The white eyes of that black rebel from last night stared at him in his mind when he considered Sodom's knowledge of his presence in the valley. Until last night, he hadn't even seen the mysterious entity since Judas rose from the *well* of the Abyss.

Magnus shook his head to clear his mind of the rebel's image, but only partially. Not knowing what shadowed corner those white eyes would be coming from would be something to keep him on edge.

He teetered forward a bit, turning to the left to look at the clock tower where Sodom and the other rebels were posted. Never was a target larger than the one before him, he thought. But what to hit that target with was still unclear.

Magnus leaned back against the brick wall. "Guide me, Father," he prayed. "Show me what you desire of me."

"*Follow Me,*" the Spirit of the Lord instructed.

The champion's eyes flew open in a fiery determination as Heaven spoke. There was no great detail in the answer. But it was an answer, nonetheless.

He pushed out into the open in a flurry of speed, letting the Holy Spirit lead him from within, descending low toward another system of alleyways across the street. He was in the open for less than a second before disappearing in a stretched blur.

Chapter Fourteen

Magnus lingered in a narrow alleyway in the shadow of a small pharmacy. He stood behind a tall utility pole with his back pressed against the right side wall of the building. Across the town's main strip of road leading to the courthouse square, he could see a two-story brownstone structure lit up in the glow of antique lampposts positioned along the sidewalk in front of the building. A trapezoid of steps led up to a small grove of Roman-style columns that bordered the portico of the structure's entrance. The compass, square and capital "G" icon of the Masonic Order was carved in colors of blue and gold in the center of a vaulted gable shadowing the portico from the tops of the columns. Beneath the gable, standing on each side of the temple's black, oaken doors, were two brazen pillars. The pillar on the left side was crowned with a carving of the globe and all its continents and islands. The one on the right was crowned with a globe of five-pointed stars; both being identical in design to the stone pillars positioned in front of the entrance of the Masonic Memorial Temple on San Francisco's historic Nob Hill. Above the doorway was a carving of a winged-sun disk and the Assyrian god Asshur, with the phrase, *The Dead Shall Be Raised*, written beneath it.

The roof of the temple was on an even grander scale. It had the spire bordered architecture of Solomon's temple, forming a hedge around four huge redwood trees stationed at each of the roof's four corners. They sprouted straight up through the building itself via the atrium-style holes at each corner which had form-fitting glass melded into each of the tree's vertical segments of thickly rolled bark. The four redwoods were once part of a small private park located in front of the town's first temple built on a smaller scale in the year 1900.

In the center of the roof, from what he could see at street level, stood a dragon-marked altar of stone 21 feet square and seven feet tall, accessed by a set of six steps ascending eastward. Each corner of the altar was flanked by a fierce cherub, the tips of their wings coming together to form a single horn on all four corners. Most of the stone edifice appeared to have been blackened by intense flames that no doubt rose up from a pit he couldn't see in the center of the square-shaped altar, completing the temple's grim panoply of Hebrew and pagan imagery which gave more than an evil whisper of the so-called mysteries practiced by the elite of their secret order.

Magnus took notice, too, that the elaborate temple was on the east side of the town in strict accordance to the esoteric practices of transpatial archeometry. The members would enter and worship in their dark chambers toward the rising sun of the east, with the west and south holding minor importance in their ceremonies; a practice, along with Easter sunrise services, that had been condemned by the town's original settlers. But it was the north, the scriptural location of the Mountain of God and his throne as recorded by the Prophet Isaiah, that was considered the place of darkness by Masons. Regardless of the symbolic disdain for the north in the order's rituals, it was that very place the evil one himself, the true master of the Masonic Order, had longed to have as his own since he first schemed to rebel.

Magnus watched several men move from the shadows of the alleyway to the right of the building, each dressed in Druidic robes rather than the usual Masonic garb. He enhanced his vision, focusing on the leader of the small band, zooming in on the man's robust, white-bearded face through the folds of his hood, glimpsing the visual mark for the nanochip April had described to him last night branded squarely in the center of his forehead. He could detect the spirits of demons hidden within the leader and the others with him, their eyes bearing the scars of wrecked houses.

The group of men quickly turned the corner and entered the temple through the front entrance.

The temple, from what April told him, had become the new center of worship in the town, helping the Omega Group wield an iron fist over the Blue Lodge members that no doubt made up the majority of the adult male populace, with the women and children being subject to the order's Eastern Star affiliate and its junior auxiliaries.

Magnus sighed from his place of hiding as the doors close behind the small band of Druids, sensing a familiar dread in his spirit. Samhain, the Druidic holiday known as Halloween, was only two days away. The leader of the small band of men was no doubt preparing their sanctuary for the ceremonies and the human sacrifice to be offered to the evil one and the rest of the powers of darkness on Halloween. Such ceremonies were some of the wickedest he had ever come upon in his millennial travels. The Druids were well-known for their savagery. Even the Roman Empire was fearful of them when its armies came face-to-face with their vicious bands of tattooed warriors known as the Picts; Celtic barbarians from Northern Scotland who waged some of the fiercest battles the Romans had ever experienced in their long history of domination.

Magnus reluctantly turned his attention away from the temple, hoping the Lord would allow him the chance to prevent their diabolical plans as he had been called on to do several times in the past at other sites dedicated to human sacrifices such as Stonehenge.

He looked to the main road leading to the courthouse square that was several blocks away. The road ran through a lighted tunnel built into the central base of the glass building facing south. Above the tunnel, on the building's top floor, was a crop of lights illuminating some of the large panes of tinted glass. Magnus stared at the dimly lit panes, figuring it to be the operations center for the town's security.

It would take excellent timing and perfect cover to make it inside the courthouse square, he thought, giving Sodom and his warriors a quick look as they held their positions at the clock tower.

Magnus stood in the shadow of the building between the wall and the utility pole for several minutes just staring, planning his method of entry. As he studied the glass building an idea dawned on him. His bright eyes fell down to the road in front of him, focusing on a manhole cover in the middle of the street. The sewer system would probably be the best and only way to get any closer without being detected. That is, of course, if the Omega Group didn't have the sewer tapered off with a laser sensitive security system, he thought, peering up at the sky as a pair of Black Hawks passed overhead. But that seemed unlikely since the town's mortal defenses appeared to be concentrated from ground level up.

Magnus concentrated on the manhole cover, devising his method of movement into the open without being seen.

With a calculated aim, he released his targeting thoughts through a muffled whistle of force. His targeted breath penetrated the finger holes on top of the steel cover, lifting it up on its rounded edges with its power, spinning it on the opposite side of the hole's rim like a coin on a table.

He quickly vaulted from his place of hiding, not even taking time to glance at the clock tower where Sodom and his warriors were gathered. He glided low over the street like a wind-swept shadow, pulling his legs together at the last second, coattails flapping above him as he dropped down into the hole past the spinning manhole cover. He caught the top handle of the ladder fixed to the round wall beneath the manhole's rim, lifting himself back up in time to catch the falling cover, quietly lowering it back into place.

———— ❈❖❈ ————

Magnus dropped through the vertical access tunnel, splashing down in knee deep water. His eyes quickly adapted to the thicker shadows, illuminating the path before him. He found himself standing in a long tunnel of aged cobblestones that arced over his head for as far as he could see. Spiral shafts of moonlight fell through the finger hole slots of the manhole covers spaced out through the tunnel's ceiling in front of him. The water he stood in ran for miles in front of him through a maze of wide trenches.

Magnus lifted his arms beside him, palms facing the arced ceiling. With a simple thought, he rose to the water's surface, the train of his leather coat dripping heavily. He started forward, the pressure from the soles of his boots rippling the surface of the water in the force of his slap-gentle stride.

He made his way slowly through the tunnel, taking time to plan his entry into the glass building that had shown signs of activity. His eyes were intense, darting back and forth, probing for the enemy in every nook and cranny in the sewer's stones. He noticed something familiar in the stones as he walked. Countless lines traced the walls and curved ceiling of the sewer system, streaking up and down in wavy patterns. But they had not made by the hands of men. They were stress fractures obviously caused by some seismic event in the past. One such event sprung to mind with first-hand intimacy. The great San Francisco earthquake of 1906; a cataclysm which ruptured three hundred miles of the San Andreas Fault Line. The town, though it was hundreds of miles north of San Francisco, had no doubt absorbed some of the after-shocks of the quake, fracturing its subterranean foundations not easily seen by the casual eye.

Magnus crossed an intersection of tunnels as he followed the lines, his boots slapping the water in soft echoes as he approached the ribbed arch in front of him.

A pair of white, fiery eyes appeared suddenly in the pools of Magnus' footsteps just as he was starting to pass beneath the arch, a diamond smile stretching beneath them, both fading quickly as the ripples flattened.

Magnus stopped abruptly on the other side of the arch when a cool breeze suddenly swept through the tunnel before him, shifting his coat and hair in its twisting current. The water beneath his soles sloshed forward in waves from the force of his sudden stop. Spirals of moonlight fell all around him from the finger hole slots of a manhole cover directly above him, closing around him like a lunar prison while he scanned the tunnel in front of him for trouble.

A dark and stealthy shape started to ascend from the water behind Magnus, its sharply-winged form rising like a mountain of black marble, nearly towering to the height of the arch's pinnacle in its undetected ascent.

A frigid mist rolled off the assassin's sharp wings, curling around the cylinder-shaped shafts of light, clouding the champion's emerald eyes with a stinging sensation.

Magnus' heart raced with surprise at the sudden stinging in his eyes, squinting at the tunnel in front of him. He held his stance, refusing to rub at the pain in his eyes as the shadows of the sewer fell like a suffocating veil in front of him, leaving only the finger hole shafts of light to see by. He'd been lulled into thinking the threat was in front of him, only to realize it was behind him.

He could see that mysterious rebel's white stare in his mind as his heart beat wildly. It was as if those insidious eyes were burning into the back of his skull even now. Yes, he thought, even now.

Magnus twirled around on the surface of the water suddenly to face his stealthy adversary, sending waves against the tunnel walls with his lightning feet. He pulled his right fist back in mid punch, surprised to find nothing but the arch and the finger hole shafts of moonlight stretching back down the tunnel.

He stood in silence as the waves rebounded off the walls of the trench, soaking the tops of his boots, his mind racing to figure out what was happening.

Water dripped from the ceiling of the sewer behind Magnus, echoing like distant footsteps. He started to pray for guidance where he stood, but was quickly interrupted by something softly wicked in its tone.

"God's Champion."

Magnus took a quick breath of surprise through his nose as the sinister voice whispered to him from the shadows in a frigid whisk of air, bouncing off the walls around him to mask its origin. Such stealth continued to surprise him. All he could do was wait for the first blow, determined to defend his mind from the dark charms of that powerful voice.

"I can smell the wine in your blood, champion," the voice said in a near whisper, its pitch a windblown hiss. "The vintage of Heaven's vine exposes your weakness like an open sore."

Magnus stood motionless, keeping his stare straight ahead while trying to discern the position of the voice.

"I am beyond the scope of your powers, champion," the voice echoed.

Magnus set his face like flint, trying to pace his breaths with a more controlled rhythm amidst the annoying drips of water that were allowed to resume their dominance of sound throughout the tunnel.

A pair of white, blazing eyes appeared to the left of the champion high above him in the shadows, with a vampiric smile stretching beneath them. Golden locks of hair slid around the slanted orbs, with the sharp outline of a bronze-colored wingspan following in a liquid motion.

A black fist larger than the size of Magnus' head plunged from the shadows suddenly.

Magnus snapped his head to the left, finally sensing a slight motion. The shiny fist struck him square in the face before he could react, though, repelling him backwards like a bullet. He hit the wall with a thunderous crash that brought part of the ceiling down on top of him.

His shoulders and head revealed a two-foot indentation in the sewer's cobblestone wall when he ricocheted forward into the water on his knees.

"Humbling, isn't it, champion?" the assassin echoed.

Magnus stood up slowly, rotating his jaw angrily as water poured from his clothes. He lifted his gaze from where he stood on the other side of the trench in the knee deep water, eyes clearing enough for him to see the sharp outline of the golden-haired rebel, his white stare and diamond smile blistering back at him with an evil delight.

Without a word, Magnus shot towards the assassin with vengeful speed, passing unseen through the spirals of moonlight falling through the manhole cover above as though he were made of the purest glass.

The assassin was a quarter of a second faster than Magnus, closing his metallic wings around his shadowed self, pulling the

217

razor edges together tightly in a liquid motion that solidified instantly.

Magnus slammed into the center of the assassin's adamantine wall, pushing him back against the sewer's fractured stones with a lowered right shoulder. The collision rocked the tunnel, cracking its ceiling even more.

Magnus had held his ground after the initial impact, landing solidly on his feet in the water in front of the assassin.

The assassin was only moved back a few paces, appearing unaffected when he opened his wingspan again, still smiling devilishly. "Excellent execution," he replied.

The compliment had barely issued forth from the assassin's mouth before he unleashed another lightning-fast jab at Magnus' head.

This time Magnus was equally as fast, catching the giant fist with his left hand as it bore down on him, fingers barely cresting over the assassin's enormous knuckles, his hardened fingernails digging into the rebel's marble-like skin, feet sliding back a bit through the water. The blocked jab was thunderous, its aftershock coursing through Magnus' arm like a thousand bolts of lightning, eyes dancing with delirium from the absorption of the impact.

The assassin responded with a right jab that was faster than his left, racing forward like a knuckled juggernaut.

Magnus came up just as fast, catching the fist with his other hand before it could crush his face. His entire body burned with the sensation from the combined jolts of the two punches. He held the assassin's fists as though they were small boulders, amazed at his own wide-eyed reaction to blocking another jab. Even before his induction into the Shekinah Legacy, Magnus had never lost a one-on-one battle with any adversary.

The assassin's fanged smile broadened even more. "Again I am impressed," he replied, his voice a sly whisk of coldness. "Your strength has served you well over the ages. But it is your greatest weakness."

Magnus squinted with bewilderment, watching as bolts of blue, preternatural flames sparked up from the assassin's thick forearms in spirals, forming small rings that orbited on a single larger ring around each forearm. He couldn't let go of the assassin's fists in time as the two larger rings spun around his forearms quickly, shooting stiletto-shaped projectiles of silver flame at him from the smaller rings like bullets from the barrel rods of a motorized minigun. The speed of the stilettos was faster than both of the fists thrown at him, slamming into his body with such force he was knocked backwards off his feet across the trench, casting him against the same place in the sewer's wall as before, creating an even deeper indentation.

Magnus managed to land on his feet in his rebound off the wall as cobblestones fell from the ceiling, splashing in the water all around him. He staggered back and forth on his feet with hundreds of fiery stilettos stuck in his face, chest and arms; their lightning sting weakening him like the venom of a snake.

Throbbing with pain, Magnus acted quickly to rid himself of the projectiles before his strength waned. He threw out his chest and arms, unleashing a controlled roar that brought down more cobblestones from the ceiling in his expulsion of the stilettos from his body, redirecting them at the assassin hovering in the shadows across the trench.

The assassin snapped his wings shut again, deflecting his own stilettos to the right and left of him in a fireworks display.

He threw his wings back open in an arrogant flare as the projectiles disappeared through the walls of the tunnel, his wicked smile reappearing once more. "Well done," he mused, trails of white light creeping from the corners of his squinted eyes. "Well done."

Magnus staggered forward into the spirals of moonlight, legs sloshing through the knee deep water, blood streaming from the smoking wounds in his face, chest and arms that were already starting to heal. Heaven's wine sparkled like grains of light in his exposed blood, reflecting the lunar spirals when he lifted his weary eyes to face the assassin.

The assassin hovered near the light where Magnus stood, looming before him like a cosmic mountain, his golden hair whirling gently on the sides of his shadowed face like the split veil of a favored crown. "Ready for round two?"

Before Magnus could react, the assassin's right fist pierced the moonlight above him, crashing down on top of his head like a hammer, driving him face first into the murky water. He hit the bottom of the trench faster than the speed of sound, creating a deep crater in the tunnel's basin which brought down more cobblestones from the ceiling.

The assassin laughed softly as the champion floated back up to the surface of the water.

He reached down and grabbed him by the back of his collar, lifting him above the water's surface as he turned and walked through the arch, dragging the champion's body beside him through the dank tunnel.

Chapter Fifteen

Magnus slowly regained consciousness in the coolness of a breeze. The tops of swaying grass were the first things to emerge in his blurred vision when he opened his eyes.

As his surroundings became clearer, he realized he was suspended high in the air somehow, his wrists starting to register the nags of a biting pain. He looked up to see his arms stretched above his head, with a large black fist holding both wrists together in an iron grip. His mind was overwhelmed with a sudden fever of alarm when he looked back down between his dangling boots. The meadow where he had found April last night was some 30 feet below him.

"It's a perfect killing field, isn't it, champion?" the assassin said from behind, the frigid vapors of his wings wrapping around Magnus' face, torturing his eyes with their burning touch.

Magnus struggled to free himself from the clutches of the assassin, twisting back and forth in the air. His attempts were useless, though, his strength having been weakened beyond a point never experienced before.

"Your efforts to free yourself are futile, champion," he laughed, his white eyes gleaming with pride above Magnus' head. "I have impaled your strength. The very thing in which all your hope has been entrusted. Your mission here was doomed to failure before it even began. Such is the destiny of anyone abandoned by God."

Magnus threw back his head, the stars reflecting in the tears of his eyes. "The Lord has not abandoned me!"

"You will find, champion, that his promises are always hollow in the clutch," the assassin sneered. "You came willingly into the very heart of darkness…the shadow of his wings cannot protect you here."

Magnus' head fell forward, the tears now streaming down his face as he hung in the air in a defeated pose. The memory of his beautiful Rachel impaled before the gates of a smoldering Jerusalem came to his mind in a death march, stabbing him at the core of his spirit. Every imaginable failure since then seemed to follow, crushing his mind with an avalanche of consequences.

"Fret not, champion," he hissed. "Death has not come for you yet. You will watch with paralysis as the world comes to the door of Tower Valley. And with it, you shall see the ascension of Perdition's Son."

He tugged at Magnus' arms with a chest-wrenching jerk that snapped the champion's head backward. "But first you shall taste the fever of shadowed truths."

Magnus' head slumped forward again as the assassin unfurled his metallic wingspan, his mouth opening wide with sharp, gleaming fangs. He lunged for the right side of the champion's neck behind his ear, sinking his fangs into his hardened flesh. A black venom spurted from his fangs as he bit into the champion's neck, infecting his blood stream with a ceaseless parasite that would eat away at the heart of his mind and spirit.

Magnus rocked back and forth, twisting in the assassin's unyielding grip as the strength of his teeth sank deeper into his flesh with a fiery surge. His resistance faded quickly as the virus spread through him with a maddened drive, sapping his remaining strength.

The assassin jerked his fangs from around Magnus' throat, the champion's blood spewing through the air in a mix of his own venom.

Magnus' eyes glazed over from the fever of the assassin's bite. The world spun wildly beneath him as he was suddenly flung forward, falling toward the same spot where Tsavo had fallen the night before, arms and legs limp, his body powerless as darkness set in on impact.

Chapter Sixteen

Beads of sweat bubbled up on Magnus' brow, reflecting the rays of the noonday sun. He lay on his back, his head rocking from side to side in the meadow's tall grass, eyelids fluttering.

"No," he moaned, struggling to wake up. "Rachel...Rachel!"

Magnus' eyes jolted open suddenly, severing the visions of a terrible nightmare. He sucked in a deep breath and released it, blinking with confusion at the sun above him. He couldn't figure out where he was until the weight of a lingering soreness started to settle on him, its sting increasing his awareness with each passing moment of consciousness.

He lifted his hand behind his right ear sluggishly, wincing in surprise when he touched the gaping wounds on his neck. He lifted his hand to see what had burned his flesh. A black liquid dripped from his raw fingertips. The wounds on his neck had not healed. It looked as though he had been poisoned with some sort of venom.

Magnus stared at the black crude, his mind reacting to the sight of it. "No...she's not there," he whispered to himself, the crude's viral nightmare exhausting his thoughts.

He sat up slowly, struggling to push back the chaos in his mind. He could tell his strength had been drained tremendously when he sat up. His sight and heightened senses, he noticed with a wandering stare, were dimmer than usual even in the brightness of the sun.

"Who are you?" he asked, as if his taunting adversary was the sun itself.

A line of vehicles started to move down the valley's southern road through the woods to his left as he sat there talking to himself in his weakened state.

Magnus cut his eyes to the thin patch of pines separating the meadow from the road. He struggled to make it to one knee, the tips of the tall grass brushing against his chest.

A fleet of nine black limousines, with three Suburbans at the front and rear of the procession, were making their way down the valley road on the other side of the trees in front of him. The caravan held a moderate pace as it passed by the partially-veiled meadow where he was kneeling.

Magnus managed to remember through his fever-ridden mind what April had told him about the conference of world leaders to be held in the town this week.

He wobbled to his feet as the rear Suburban passed the meadow, watching the tail end of the caravan until it disappeared around another bend of trees.

The champion stood in a swaying silence, hair and coat tossed by a wind sweeping down over him in gentle currents from the mountain. His eyes fell toward his feet with a look of finality, the assassin's venom dripping from the wounds in his neck, pelting the tips of the darnel grass with a soft thunder.

Magnus clenched the sides of his head, turning to the mountain in a stooped posture. His thoughts swirled with images of the assassin's shadow-covered face again. The rebel's white eyes glared at him brightly from the field of nightmares in his mind as he limped through the grass, shoulders sagging, knees buckling with each step from the fire of the monster's teeth that sank into the flesh of his mind over and over, numbing his resistance with each puncture, draining the fight from his warrior spirit with a rush of hellish images.

"Forgive me, Rachel," he moaned. "Forgive me...."

Chapter Seventeen

Some of the world's most powerful leaders were gathered together in the French chateau located in the foothills of the valley's northern mountain range. The power brokers were assembled in a grand dining hall decorated with dark panels of wood on the left side of the room, with the right side showcasing 12 windows reaching from the floor to the base of the coffered ceiling's vaulted arch. French doors on the right side of the dining hall led out to a placid balcony overlooking the chateau's vineyards. A 30 foot long table of polished cedar was positioned in the center of the room, with a crystal chandelier hanging above it, reflecting the afternoon sunlight pouring through the room's tall windows

The leaders were all seated in leather chairs, with most dressed in handsome power suits of various designs and dark-hued colors. Their chairs were positioned near the far end of the table that was facing the rear wall where an enormous mirror trimmed in gold filled much of its center. Seated at the head of the table, with the room's honeycomb-shaped doors of oak facing him, was Cardinal Simon Menelaus.

To Simon's immediate left was Joseph Shamur, Prime Minister of Israel; a handsome, dark-haired young man who was a 33rd degree Mason like most of the others seated around him. To his left sat William Wessex, Prime Minister of England; a relatively tall man with salt and pepper hair and a smile that was deceptively polite. To his left sat His Majesty King Marcelo Varela the First of Spain; a lightly-tanned man with black hair and subtle eyes. Beside him sat Angelo Martini, Prime Minister of Italy; a heavy-set man with thinning black hair. To Martini's left sat Adrianus Willebrands, Prime Minister of the Netherlands; a tall man with a stern mouth and graying hair.

Across the table, directly in front of Willebrands, sat Jean-Marie Kober, President of France; a man with receding black hair and a tanned face which seemed to carry a permanent scowl. To his left sat His Majesty King Haji Al-Saud of Saudi Arabia; a man with dark eyes and a black goatee peeking through the sides of his white headdress. To Al-Saud's left sat Hotep Abydos, President of the Arab Republic of Egypt; a husky, olive-skinned man with dark hair and impatient eyes. And next to him sat Hans Heidelman, Chancellor of Germany; a thin man with white hair and glasses.

Simon leaned forward and placed his hands on the table beside a small petri dish, his hardened features reflected in the table's glossy surface. "Gentlemen, let me be the first to officially welcome you to Tower Valley," he smiled. "As you were informed while enroute, Mr. Tsavo has met with an untimely death…and due to such a tragedy, I have been asked by the Omega Group to assume his responsibilities of overseeing the first day of events at our summit."

President Abydos leaned forward on the table with his thick arms, staring coldly at the strong-featured cardinal seated at the head of the table. "Who are you, sir, if I may ask?" Abydos in a broken accent.

Simon leaned back in his chair, answering with only a steely grin as he reached out and touched his black-scaled staff positioned to the right of him, the golden sphere on the bottom of the *Oracle* being perfectly balanced on the room's marble floor by the power of the Dragon Lord's alchemized blood flowing through it in a tireless circuit. The energy emanating from the staff ignited the flecks of silver on the rims of his brown irises with an eerie light which caught the Egyptian leader and the others at the table by surprise. But not totally. For they had each seen strange things in the dark rituals and varying forms of Masonry practiced at the highest levels of all their governments.

Simon lowered his hand slowly from the *Oracle* in a slow manner, seeing he had made his point of who held the real power in the room despite his identity.

Prime Minister Wessex leaned forward, cautiously offering a word to ease the quiet tension that had suddenly seized the room. "You needn't worry, Mr. President," he replied, his British accent managing to attract Abydos' polarized attention in his effort to explain Simon's presence. "I don't know the cardinal very well. But I do know that he is a trusted confidant of both the Omega Group and Mr. Alchemy."

Abydos pressed his concerns as he glanced back at Simon. "And just what does the Vatican have to do with the Omega Group's project here in this valley?" he asked in a more measured tone.

"Nothing," the sorcerer answered. "I am only here to oversee the first day of this summit as a result of Tsavo's untimely demise."

"And what was the nature of Mr. Tsavo's untimely demise?" Abydos prodded.

Simon mastered a sigh of seeming regret when he answered. "I'm afraid, Mr. President," he said, "that Mr. Tsavo was found to be a traitor to the Omega Group and its allies."

A frigid silence swept through the hall like a ghostly wind as most of the leaders were visibly stunned by the revelation. All except for Abydos. His expression was one of restrained suspicion as he quietly reclined into his chair, choosing not to press the issue any further, sensing he and his friend King Al-Saud were among unfamiliar wolves.

Simon spoke quickly. "Gentlemen," he said, his voice echoing in the acoustics of the dining hall, "we all here have certain public masks we wear to protect our places of authority. Tsavo wore the wrong kind of mask. However, you need not concern yourselves with the details of the matter. The past is not a priority. The future is. Which is why I remind everyone here of the secrecy of this project. The Omega Group has gone to great lengths to make your presence here unknown to the rest of the world, except for our friends among the International Bankers and those who live here in the town. We have also made sure that your tracks will be covered on your trips back home with the false itineraries we have created for each of you."

The leaders said nothing as they were reminded of their allegiance to the secret covenants they had agreed to.

"And with that reminder, I now show you the future," Simon continued, pointing to the small petri dish on the table before him. "If you will, gentlemen, please direct your attention to the containers in front of you."

They each looked down at the petri dishes in front of them.

Simon reached for a pair of surgical tweezers sitting on the table to the left of his own dish. With the tweezers, he picked up the black, grain-like object in his dish and held it out in front of him for all to see. "This, gentlemen, is the A-6 Mark." The leaders looked up from their dishes as the sorcerer lifted the chip. "No larger than the size of an uncooked grain of rice, the A-6 Mark is the single greatest achievement in Quantum and nanotechnology. With it, we have managed to step thirty years into the future."

"The transition has gone smoothly, then?" Prime Minister Wessex asked.

Simon placed the nanochip back in the dish in front of him, setting the tweezers down as he answered. "Yes, Mr. Prime Minister. The transition was received with more enthusiasm than we anticipated. And because of it, the citizens of the town have grown closer together. They work and worship side by side like the parts of one body. Crime is nonexistent. And those who have increased their wealth and importance have earned it on the level playing field of performance and loyalty within the group's infrastructure."

King Al-Saud looked over at Simon "All of what you say sounds very compelling," he remarked, speaking in the same broken accent as Abydos. "But will the experiment be as successful in the fractured Middle East?"

Simon turned to his right with a convicting stare. "Success is inevitable, your majesty," he answered. "As you have noted, the Middle East, as well as the rest of the world, has already seen some major changes in every sphere of life. And the storm to come will not adhere to our borders of political, economic and social differ-ences." The sorcerer glanced around the table. "But the group will be ready."

"The government of Israel will remain at the group's side as this bold campaign continues to unfold," Shamur replied, his dark eyes meeting with Simon's. "And as Prime Minister, I can guaran-tee you the full support of the Israel Defense Force during this hectic time of transition in the Middle East."

"Thank you, Mr. Prime Minister," Simon nodded. "Your words of fidelity are most comforting."

Shamur shook his head, knowing that he was but a knight in the game. "I owe Mr. Alchemy and the Omega Group everything," he said, eyes wide with a sheep-like adoration. "Both he and the group will always have my loyalty."

Kober leaned into the conversation suddenly. "I take it that Monsieur Alchemy will be arriving for the rest of the summit as scheduled?"

Simon turned his gaze to the French President, propping his elbows on the arms of the chair and pressing his fingers together into a triangle. "Yes, Mr. President," he answered. "Mr. Alchemy will be arriving tomorrow morning for the second day of our summit. He will bring us up to speed on the global implementa-tion of Project Palladium. And he will also alleviate any reserva-tions you may have about the next phase of our current campaign unfolding in the Middle East…Operation Assyria."

The large honeycomb doors at the other end of the dining hall opened as Simon finished. Specter stepped through the slen-der crack in the huge doors, holding a leather brief in his hands, his image reflected in the mirror behind the cardinal at the oppo-site end of the hall. "Excuse me, your eminence," he said, his voice carrying across the expanse of the room. "The Sentinel Corps is ready for your tour of the town."

"Excellent," the sorcerer replied. "We will meet your team in the courtyard."

Specter nodded, closing the doors quietly behind him.

Simon leaned forward proudly. "Shall we see our dreams in action, gentlemen?"

Sodom watched as the leaders left the room with the sorcerer. But he would not be idle for long.

"It is time, Sodom."

The rebel prince shot up from the chandelier at the sound of the frigid voice behind him, spinning around in the air while clinging to the chandelier's chain. He dropped to the table in front of the chair where Simon had been sitting, facing the enormous mirror covering a sizeable section of the room's rear wall that reflected the hall behind him.

The atmosphere of the room became increasingly frigid as Sodom stared at the mirror, waiting, anticipating that familiar voice to pierce the air again. The mirror began to ripple like water at its center, its glass rolling in continuous waves that spread to the frame's four corners. A pair of white, slanted eyes appeared in the ripples, followed by a sharply-winged form with a mountainous build that stopped just short of penetrating the mirror's glassy border.

Sodom fell to one knee at the assassin's appearance, keeping his head up for the first time when facing him. The mirror's ripples circled around the muscled outline of the assassin's form, the structure of his face being distorted with a wavy mask that reflected the hall's interior in stretched images, his hair swimming through the waves like snakes.

"All is in place, Sullier," the assassin told him, eyes blazing through the mirror. "No obstacles remain…see to the safe passage of the Alchemy King."

Sodom was wordless, amazed at how the assassin revealed himself in such poetic fashion, his distorted face remaining cloaked as it pressed through the glass in ripples without breaking its seal.

"Hurry, Sodom," he said, his form starting to sink back into the mirror again. "The Imperial Fortress is coming."

The glassy ripples rolled flat with a quick bounce from the center as the assassin disappeared from sight, his words still echoing throughout the dining hall in frigid whispers.

Sodom's voice was almost a murmur at first. "Dragylon...."

He jumped to his taloned feet, drawing his blade with a proud roar. "DRAGYLON!!"

Sodom shot sideways, sifting through the French doors to his left and exploding upward into the afternoon sky.

231

Chapter Eighteen

The sun was in its four o'clock descent over the valley as the fleet of limousines slowly toured the streets of Tower Valley, stopping at different storefronts and places of business to witness the Omega Group's experiment in action.

Above the town, Sodom's elite 24 were in a bustle of activity, circling the tower with an energy of great anticipation.

Bastion hovered 50 feet above them, his false wings spread wide as he scanned the four corners of the heavens. Clutched in his right hand was a black, corkscrew-shaped ram's horn known as the *Herald of Thunders*, an instrument used only by the Dominium Gate Master of Dragylon.

He twisted around in the air, rotating slowly, wings stretching wider, tightening his stone fist on the glossy surface of the horn. His black and red eyes began to bulge even more from their sockets, glittering in the rays of the setting sun, body tingling with the electricity of an approaching power so immense it felt like he was being raptured into Heaven itself by its draw. He searched the sky, mouth gaping as if to savor the sensation like rain from above. Still there was nothing but miles of blue sky and puffy white clouds stretching from the mountains to the Pacific.

But that was about to change.

Bastion's granite body suddenly exploded with rings of blue electricity, pulsing from head to foot, circling his muscled arms and legs, eyes vibrating wildly. He threw his head straight back, locking his gaze on a large formation of cumulus clouds above him, fangs bared in a wicked smile.

The cumulus formation began to breathe with motion, sucking in and out slowly, swirling. The clouds parted suddenly, twisting open in a counterclockwise spin. The warriors circling the tower beneath Bastion stopped their orbiting conference when the phenomenon began, forming a complete ring of salute as they connected the tips of their black wings and held their weapons high.

Bastion moaned with delight, fangs opening wider as a round portal to the Outer Realm appeared at the center of the parted clouds, stretching the veil of the blue sky to the boundaries of the valley's mountain ranges, stars teeming brightly against the velvet backdrop of space. Then, like a royal flagship, a colossal sphere crested the southern lip of the circular opening in the clouds. The sphere itself was a forcefield of golden light surrounding an inner court. It shimmered as brightly as the sun, rolling with thunder in its descent through the opening, the clouds and the Earth's blue field closing in around it as it stopped halfway down through the portal.

Bastion pursed his lips of fluid stone together and lifted the ram's horn to his mouth. The heavens trembled from the blast of the horn, ripping through the air with such force the valley floor below vibrated with a seismic tremor.

Bastion lowered the horn, bringing both arms out to his sides, rising higher above the town's ivory tower, twisting around slowly to survey the ring of tribute below him. "BEHOLD, YE POWERS OF THE AIR!!" he roared, his black wings spreading to an even more impossible width. "DRAGYLON, THE IMPERIAL FORTRESS, IS AMONG US!!!!!!"

The ring of warriors exploded in a unified roar. "DRAGYLON! DRAGYLON!!! DRAGYLON!!!!!" they all shouted, weapons held high in the gleam of the sphere's golden glow.

Bastion lifted the black horn back to his mouth again, unleashing another thunderous blast from the *Herald of Thunders*, waving to the warriors to follow his lead into Dragylon.

234

Sodom's warriors broke formation and raced toward the sphere for their first invitation to lay eyes on the master's mythic citadel.

Chapter Nineteen

The assassin sat perched on intersecting limbs at the top of two neighboring pine trees near the peak of the northern mount, wings curling in front of him, wrapping around the more tapered portions of each tree.

Dragylon hovered brightly above him in the night sky next to the Earth's moon.

In the distance, the town of Tower Valley had settled in for the evening. Spotlights beamed upward from the interior courtyard of the Westminster-style courthouse, illuminating the clock tower rising up from its center. There was no civilian traffic in the streets, only the roving Suburbans of the Omega Group enforcing the town's curfew.

The assassin kept his gaze just above the treetops in front of him, scanning the starry horizon of the valley's other mountain ranges. He alone kept the town's spirit watch. Sodom had been dispatched to San Francisco to escort Alchemy to the valley, with his warriors and Bastion having ascended into Dragylon to prepare their lines of tribute for the master's imminent arrival from Heaven.

He cast his white gaze to the left to focus on the eastern mount. "Is he who knew no fear now fearful?" he mocked.

"Rest if you can, my wounded champion. I am coming… soon."

Magnus struggled to climb the old sanctuary's closed-in stairway leading up to the balcony. His breaths were labored with each shuffle up the debris-covered steps. He stumbled around the corner of the spiral stairway, strength exhausted, polluted by the assassin's venom coursing through his veins like a raging fire. With his strength spent, it had taken him the entire day to climb back up the mountain.

He finally reached the top of the stairwell, his sweat-covered face awash in the moonlight flooding the center of the balcony. He staggered for a moment, glancing at the back wall where April lay curled up in one his sleeping bags, with another one rolled out beside her.

Magnus shuffled towards the empty bag, his entire body drenched in sweat from the fever of the assassin's venom. His vision blurred without warning, knees buckling completely with the ebbing of his last vestige of strength. He crashed to the sleeping bag beside April, creating plumes of dust on each side of him from the impact against the balcony's old plank floor.

April jumped up from where she lay, falling back against the wall at the sudden thud beside her. She cradled her broken arm defensively, her vision slow to clear in the dust-mixed shadows of the balcony.

She looked to her left at the body lying face down beside her. "Magnus!" she cried. "Where have you been?!"

He gave no answer.

"Magnus?"

April crawled to him, pulling him over on his back by his shoulder. "Magnus!" she gasped, noticing the two large holes on the right side of his neck that were bubbling with a black liquid. "What happened?!"

The champion didn't move, looking more dead than alive.

April's hand trembled as she wiped away at the sweat on his face. "You're burning up," she cried, her voice frantic as she looked around the balcony for something to wipe away the sweat that kept beading up on his face.

She looked back to her right, remembering the towel and the half empty water bottle she'd brought up earlier from one of the crates downstairs.

April grabbed the towel, folding it the best she could with her one hand, wetting it with the bottle of water. She began dabbing his face with the wet towel. "What did they do to you?"

Magnus still did not answer.

"Magnus, please! Please wake up!"

April took his pulse, noting his rapid heartbeats. She dabbed at the wounds on his neck in attempt to stop the strange bleeding, only to watch as the black liquid bubbled up even more, staining the white towel. "Magnus, please," she begged. "Wake up!"

April began to cry softly as the confusion and fear of the moment overwhelmed her. "You can't be hurt," she sobbed. "You're not like other men...I have seen what you can do... please, Magnus. Please wake up."

Her pleas fell on deaf ears as Magnus sank deeper into the venom-induced coma, the sweat rolling down the sides of his face and chest.

•••—◄○►—•••

The fever of the assassin's bite transported Magnus' mind to the deepest well of his imagination.

He found himself standing in the middle of a wide path of phosphorous ash hemmed in on each side by thick forests, the odor of brimstone rushing into his nose. The trees along the pathway towered hundreds of feet into the air. The bark of each tree was razor sharp and as black as coal from what he could see. The tops of the trees were shaped like pines, with needles resembling blackened bones.

Directly in front of him, some distance away, he could see a gated arch stretching across the end of the path. A wall of jagged granite could be seen towering to the height of the black and gray clouds on the other side of the arch, with a vast plain covered in phosphorous ash filling the distance between them. He could see neither the beginning nor the end of the wall's immeasurable width. Another archway of galactic proportions was cut into the wall's center, filled by a deeply-set gate having segmented bars pulsating with a hot, orange glow. Plumes of black smoke rose through the top of the bars, polluting the gray skies overhead with an eternal stream of misery. A small mountain of stone steps protruded from the wall's center, descending to the plain from the bottom of the enormous archway.

He noticed that he was wearing the armaments and *lorica* tunic he once wore as a young cavalryman in the *Alae Milliariae*, with a familiar, purple cloak draped over his shoulders.

Magnus started forward hesitantly, glancing into the shadowy forests on each side of the path, ash melting like snow against his cloak and the scales of his armored tunic as it rained down from above, with the faint groans of tormented souls whispering in his ears as each flake pelted his body. His breaths quickened, sensing the sudden approach of threat while listening to the melting flakes of misery. He could see star-shaped irises of red and yellow fires burning into view in the shadows of the surrounding trees, followed by long, soft howls and angelic murmurings that merged with the whispers of torment falling from above.

His left hand instinctively fell upon the hilt of his spatha blade as the hovering eyes swelled in number, not fully realizing that the unvoiced threats of the hidden goblins were pushing him forward.

He reached the smaller archway without incident. But he kept his peripheral senses trained on the movements of the rebels lingering behind while he inspected the gateway. The space above the arch's crest rolled like water with translucent flames every few seconds, warning of some sort of force field obviously meant to prevent anyone from leaping or climbing over.

The gateway's arch was shaped like a rainbow that spanned the flat tops of the tall pillars on either side of the path. Both the arch and the two pillars were constructed from smooth blocks of galactically-heavy stone constantly pelted by the flakes of ash from above. A black, wrought-iron gate of adamantine filled the expanse between the pillars and the arch, its spire-shaped tips as sharp as the bark covering the trees of the path. A square lock was fixed in the middle of the gate.

The most outstanding element of the gateway, though, was the epitaph carved into the arch's central block. The word *Hell* was inscribed with golden symbols in every language of mankind. But the predominant symbols were angelic and cherubic script.

Beneath it was another phrase recorded in the Book of Matthew, which read, *Prepared for the Devil and his angels.*

"*Hear me, my son,*" the Lord said, invading his dream in the form of a brisk wind.

Magnus stiffened as the wind orbited around him, stirring the ashes of the path beneath his feet. The rebel hosts hiding in the shadows of the forests fled into the darkness with retreating howls, frightened by the sudden intrusion of the divine.

" '*Believe not every spirit,*' " said the Lord.

Magnus bowed his head as the voice of the Lord receded as quickly as it had come, the ashes still falling like snow in front of him. "My King," he whispered.

Magnus lifted his head again. The sound of distant hoofbeats suddenly filled his ears. He turned to see a black, spectral horse and rider barreling down the path toward him. The mythic-size steed was a high-necked, short-bellied breed similar to the ones used by the Moorish Cavalry of old, snorting small flames of fire through his rounded nose in his charge down the wide path of ash, kicking up clouds of dust with his silver, dragon-marked horseshoes, covering 10 yards of ground per stride. The steed's head was shielded by a metallic, crimson-colored chamfron like the horses he used to ride during his days in the *hippika gymnasia*, with a golden medallion depicting a black and red dragon with two heads fixed in the center of the breast strap that was tacked around the horse's thick chest.

The rider was massively built, towering in the saddle even while hunched forward toward the horse's armored head. He was clothed in a long golden cloak flapping with a ghostly beat in the wind of his charging steed, his head covered by a large, fold-layered hood. His thickly-cut forearms shimmered like black marble as they protruded through the oversized sleeves of his billowing cloak, controlling the reins with little motion, as if guiding the steed with his thoughts rather than his hands.

Magnus prepared for battle, hardening his stance as the spectral horse and rider drew closer in a thundering rumble like

241

one of the *Four Horsemen of the Apocalypse.* The rider held no weapon from what he could see. He was a bow without arrows it seemed.

Magnus waited until he could feel the heat of the flames exploding through the steed's large nostrils. He pivoted back to his right on one foot just as the steed was about to trample him, letting the horse and rider pass mere inches from him. The entire moment of the horse's passing seemed in slow motion when he stepped to the side, with the rider turning his head to look down at him. He recognized the white eyes glaring down at him through the shadow inside the rider's large hood, invoking the image of the hooded-serpent god of Egypt Basiliscus. The rider's large-knuckled hands and muscular forearms were painfully familiar as well.

A portion of the rider's golden cloak brushed across Magnus' face in that moment, embracing his mind with its velvet touch, allowing him to see the figure of a dark-haired woman who lay straddled over the horse behind the rider, wrapped in heavy chains from the neck down.

Magnus gasped for the strength to speak as the woman slowly lifted her head from where she lay bound on the horse. He recognized her face with great horror, reaching out for her as she cried out his name in what was nothing more than a shouted whisper.

The rider's cloak fell away from his face as the steed exploded with speed once more, leaving the champion in a kicked up cloud of ash.

The wrought iron gate in the archway exploded inward with a gust of wind with the approach of the horse and rider.

Magnus spun around toward the stone archway, watching the horse and its rider race across the plain of ash toward the granite wall in the distance. "Ra...Rachel," he gasped, struggling to speak.

The champion burst forward as the black gate began to close, running through the archway in a desperate pursuit. The granite wall with the glowing gate in the middle loomed above the desolate plain before him like a rectangular moon cresting over a distant horizon, the horse and rider closing in fast on its basin.

Magnus was less than 30 yards from catching the horse when the rider stopped the beast dead in its tracks, reigning the black steed around in a hellish fury.

He leaped forward through the air towards the rider, covering the distance in less than a second, only to be knocked flat on his back when the rider reared the front legs of his large steed high into the air, catching him square in the chest with both hoofs in a thunderous jolt.

Magnus fell with a loud thud, plumes of ash mushrooming around him on impact.

The rider reached beneath his billowing cloak while the champion lay stunned below him, pulling out an enormous sword.

Magnus peered up at the rider, the folds of his golden hood shining like the rays of the sun against the black and gray clouds above, his slanted eyes burning with white fire in the shadow masking his face.

The rider pointed his shiny, black-scaled blade at the champion, his large knuckles bulging like rounded nails from his fierce grip on the sword's rectangular hilt of silver that was inscribed with an archaic scrollwork. A golden, two-headed dragon spiraled up from the hilt's hand guard, its winged heads forming a pommel of broken infinity. Lightning grain patterns of sparkling gold had been hammered and shaped into the sword's razor edges with a diabolical craftsmanship.

Magnus recognized the sword with great surprise. It was the same one he had found in King Og's iron sarcophagus long ago. It was a blade known by the esoteric mystics of the Ancient World as *Dragaduceus*; a staff-length sword of immense power. He had pursued it across the world when he found out it had been removed from Og's tomb centuries after his initial discovery of it. But he had never been able to pick up its trail, following many false leads throughout the course of the Crusades.

"Behold the wages of power," said the rider, his voice echoing with cold pestilence, vexing the champion's soul with a leanness of truth. "Judgment always has its price…even for those who administer it, son of my heritage."

The rider was the picture of *Death* himself it seemed, curling the large sword in front of his chest. He spurred his steed in the side, turning him in a fury of snorting flames to resume his course for the wall.

The words of the Lord that had invaded his dream earlier echoed in Magnus' mind while he still lay stunned on the plain of ash. " *'Believe not every spirit.'* "

Magnus pulled himself to his feet as the voice of the Lord helped battle his confusion and feelings of guilt. He looked into the distance. The cloaked rider was dismounting from his steed, yanking Rachel by her chains off the horse with his left hand while holding the ancient blade in the other. The rider skipped up the stairway descending from the bottom of the wall's galactic archway in leaps and bounds, Magnus' precious Rachel in tow beneath the train of his fluttering cloak.

Magnus took several quick strides forward, throwing his arms behind him as he soared determinedly through the flake-filled atmosphere, only to be slowly pushed down by the atmosphere's weight of death. He landed back down on the plain of ash in front of the first step of the stone stairway where the rider had left his steed, but recovered quickly to take the steps in the same leaping manner as the cloaked power had done before him. He vaulted upward through the heavy atmosphere again when he reached the middle step of the stairway, calling out to his wife as he flew through the storm of ash and heat-filled wind coming from the galactic archway above.

He landed in a crouching posture on the archway's flat ledge, sinking into ankle-high layers of ash that was constantly being blown over the edge from the heated drafts of wind howling through the gate's glowing bars.

The rider stood in front of the gate that was set 20 feet into the granite from the wall's jagged exterior. The bust of a basaltic angel protruded from the flat bars of the gate's lower center, its sharply-tipped wings spreading high above its head, with a glowing lock in the shape of a broken symbol of infinity with winged dragon heads carved in its chest. The black clouds rolled through the top of the gate, showering ash on the wings of the towering bust shown holding the blackened skull of a man just beneath the bright lock nestled in the center of its wide chest. The stone eyes of the basaltic angel stared down at the object cradled in its hands, frozen in a look that demanded worshipful obedience.

The rider hoisted Rachel in front of him like a puppet on its strings, dangling her in front of the gate's center with a sharp glare at Magnus. "Do not interfere again, champion!" he warned. "She cannot escape her punishment!"

A flash of red fire exploded through the lock as the rider made his declaration of judgment, splitting the basaltic angel and the blackened skull it held down the middle. The fire roared with the grinding clatter of indestructible metals as both sections of the gate were pulled open by boulder-size chains inside the right and left side walls of the galactic archway.

The gate's monolithic sections stopped as suddenly as they had parted, leaving an opening about six feet wide between its central bars; a proverbial crack if gazed at from a distance. The cries of the damned rose through the wider opening in a larger tumult of black smoke, racing toward the gray clouds above like a funeral pyre begging to be quenched with rains of mercy.

Magnus stood upright as the rider dangled his precious Rachel in front of the opening. He took a cautious step forward. "She is a child of God!" he declared, his voice unable to ring with its usual power above the cries of the damned. "I knew her better than anyone in the days of my mortal life! She was chosen by the Master before the foundations of the world were laid! And I know that she loved him more than anything! Even me! You have no authority to do this!!"

The rider laughed hideously.

The Lord's previous command to not believe every spirit continued to prompt Magnus with the truth. "Wait!" he said, pointing at the rider defiantly. "Is this Hell?"

"Yessss," the rider hissed.

"You're a liar!" he replied. "All of this is a lie! Hades and the Abyss are not the same as Hell! The Word of God is clear! The Beast and his False Prophet will be the first to be cast into Hell!"

"You should have read the alternate ending, champion."

"He who adds to the Apocalypse shall suffer an added curse of its plagues!"

"Judgment has been passed!" the rider proclaimed. "She was a whore among men!"

The rider's decree brought forth a swirling mass of black smoke through the opening. Rachel looked up for the first time as the smoky tentacle wrapped itself around her chained body. She screamed in terror as she was jerked from the rider's grip.

"No!" Magnus cried, jumping toward the gate as the rider vanished in a whirling explosion of shadows and light.

Rachel was pulled through the opening before Magnus could reach her.

He landed between the split sections of the gate's basaltic angel as it started to close together again, clasping his hands flat against both sides of the interior walls that glowed hotly. The full heat of the flames warred against the preternatural flesh of his dreams, boiling the very marrow of his divinely-hardened bones, its tortured winds scrambling his thoughts of what he knew to be true with innumerable slashes of razor sharp insanity. He tried with all his might to hold the gates at bay, shoulders trembling, flesh burning and healing at the same time.

"Rachel!" he called, staring hopelessly into total darkness, grunting with guttural heaves as swirling flakes of ash and the cries of the damned pelted him in the face with torrential force.

Just as Magnus' unhindered rage seemed it would prevail against the gates in his assault, an enormous cloud of black smoke in the shape of a dragon's head thundered through the swirling ashes with a roar, striking him squarely in the chest, knocking him from his stance with ease. He was launched backward in slow motion, tears forming in his eyes as he watched the gate's basaltic angel become one again, slamming together with a thunderous finality.

Magnus tumbled head over heels, falling downward in despair, the cries of his wife filling his ears as he fell.

<hr />

Magnus exploded from the floor of the balcony, willing himself off the old planks, vaulting forward on instinct to recover from his nightmarish fall.

April crashed backward from his sudden flight, having fallen asleep several hours ago. She rolled over cradling her arm as Magnus landed on one of the post heads of the balcony's rail, teetering forward from the push of his subconscious reaction, rocking back at the last moment to balance himself before going over the edge.

Magnus rubbed at his eyes, sweat dripping from his face. He lowered his hands, looking confused when he took a bleary-eyed note of his unfamiliar perch. He could barely make out his shadow on the far wall above the pulpit's arch.

He squatted down on the head of the rail's post, burying his face in his hands, the images of his tortured wife refusing to go away.

He lunged backward, arms falling away from his body. "Father!" he cried, the level of his voice muffled in his weakness, destroying only a portion of the ceiling above him.

A curtain of moonlight engulfed Magnus along with a shower of splintered wood that pelted him from the hole his weakened voice had blown in the roof.

April curled up against the balcony's back wall, frightened as the shattered wood fell from the ceiling in front of her.

Magnus collapsed to his back on the balcony's floor. He lay stunned, murmuring through clouded vision. "Father," he whispered. "Father...."

April waited a moment, not sure what to do. She looked at her good hand that was still clenching the towel. It was completely black now.

She turned to Magnus, pushing the roof debris aside in her shuffle to his side. "Magnus," she said softly, throwing the blackened towel behind her. "Magnus!"

There was no reply. His mind had slipped away into darkness again.

She stroked the sides of his face gently. "Magnus," she pleaded. "What's the matter with you? Wake up."

———— ✦◯✦ ————

A tall figure of a man hovered unseen in the rafters above the balcony's rail, squatting on one of the crisscrossing beams, eyes burning like silver pyres.

Scriptos wrote in blood-red ink along the vellum pages of his book, dipping his pen in the ivory inkhorn on his belt every few lines while listening to April lament over Magnus.

He closed the book slowly, securing it back inside the square holster on the right side of his belt. He leaned forward from his perch, hovering down just beneath the rafters as he floated into the curtain of moonlight coming through the hole in the ceiling, his long coat fluttering around his powerful legs. He stared at Magnus, peering into the nightmare plaguing his mind. The desperation in his face was a pinnacle of suffering in his repeated efforts to save his wife from torment.

He looked at April. She was tearfully desperate to keep from letting the only true light that remained in her dark world from being snuffed out. But fear had conquered both of their worlds now. They had been successfully taken out of the battle before it had even begun.

Scriptos snapped the sides of his coat around him tightly, knowing what he had to do as he looked up through the shaft of light he was hovering in. He shot up through the hole in the roof with a quick thought, disappearing in a silver flash across the night sky.

Chapter Twenty

Sodom was in a squatting position on the slim obelisk of the Transamerica building that was located in the heart of San Francisco's Financial District, its white, precast-quartz aggregate panels shining brightly against the midnight sky. He probed the sleepless acropolis below. Down to his right, rising high above the ferry complex of Justin Herman Plaza, was the great San Francisco clock tower. Behind him loomed the bland Oakland Bay Bridge. To his left were the swank hotels of Nob Hill which overlooked the gateway to Chinatown and the chic restaurants and upscale department stores of Union Square, the air around them sounding the sporadic bells that rang from the street cars of the Powell-Mason&Powell-Hyde Cable Car Line. Before him loomed the famous Coit Tower and Fisherman's Wharf; a circus of curious confections from which the powers of darkness often chose the annual Samhain sacrifice to celebrate the city's beloved Halloween festivities. It was a holiday the city seemed to cherish as much as Christmas, with its grand climax taking place in the Castro District; the dung heap of drag queen sodomites and filth-minded revelers who often dressed as mythical characters and even fire itself while participating in the district's raunchy parade.

Sodom's eyes swelled with a black and yellow pride as he surveyed the boundaries of his greatest stronghold. All was secure in his city. His legions consumed much of the atmosphere above his position on top of the 48-story Tansamerica building, leaving a large empty circle of Dominium Gate Masters directly above him to serve as an epicenter of 11 other larger circles extending outward from that point in the sky, rotating slowly with the glow of millions of fiery eyes spanning the entire the city. But a select number of the demon spirits under his command walked stealthily beneath the ceaseless canopy of lights below, feeding off the city's wickedness that always increased greatly as Halloween approached, taking great care to mark their chosen victims as they prepared the way for the High Grand Climax of the Winter Solstice sacrifices celebrated on December 24th. Not much had changed since the reign of the demigod gangster Jerome Bassity. Buildings could rise and fall, but the hearts of mankind remained the same. For history had proven that even the greatest cataclysms of judgment, such as the one that struck the Bay City in 1906, were easily forgotten with the passage of time.

Sodom turned his head to the left, fixing his stare on the cable-connected towers of the Golden Gate Bridge stretching across the moonlit waters of the bay just beyond the Palace of Fine Arts. His gaze drifted to the starry horizon arcing above the tops of the Golden Gate's streamlined towers, eagerly anticipating the arrival of a god more wicked than his puppet Jerome Bassity could have ever dreamed to be.

A black Learjet streaked across the starlit dome stretching over the dark waters of the Pacific. A golden symbol of broken infinity with winged dragon heads was painted on each side of the plane's tail section, with flashing red lights holding a steady beacon beneath the jet's silver belly as it sliced acros the night sky.

Inside the jet, at the rear of the customized cabin behind a set of intricately carved doors, was a lavish, dimly-lit stateroom.

Iscarius Alchemy lay sleeping on top of a wood frame bed that extended from the stateroom's left side wall, fully clothed in a black Armani suit. He lay motionless on his back, hands crossed over his chest as if he were a corpse lying in a casket. His head was partially submerged in a silk pillow.

Alchemy's eyes moved back and forth beneath their closed lids, his mind sinking slowly into a dreamworld of ancient memories, transporting him to the land of his youth. The great walls of the ancient city of Jerusalem appeared beneath him as his black-robed dreamself swooped down across the night sky like a carrion bird.

He was immediately drawn to the House of Caiaphas on Mount Zion, following the columned pathway leading to the large structure. As he approached the house's open courtyard, a silver flash of light engulfed him.

When the light faded, he found himself standing in a chamber on the second floor of the opulent house that was filled with muffled voices. He lingered at the center of the spacious room, surrounded by two split-level rows of limestone benches. On the back wall, fixed in the middle of the semicircle rows, was a throne-like seat, also of limestone.

Aged men with educated stares filled the benches of the chamber. Seated on the throne-like seat was Caiaphas, Israel's high priest. His face was wrinkled and sour, with a long white beard flowing to his robe. His vestment and place of seating clearly showed his rank above the others, the long sleeves of his mantle draping over the front of each armrest of his exalted seat.

The assembly mumbled together while Alchemy stood as an invisible witness to their illegal gathering. There was an urgency in the atmosphere of the drafty chamber due to the fact that Jewish law prohibited the Sanhedrin from holding court proceedings at night or in secret. Familiar, falsely-winged shapes hovered in the shadows cast by the room's torch-lit corners, their gleaming eyes seemingly unaware of Alchemy's presence.

Alchemy turned completely around at the sound of a great commotion coming from just outside the chamber's only entrance. The sound of clanging armor could be heard in the chamber's lower courtyard where the house servants of the high priest were preparing to build a small fire.

The Captain of the Temple Guard stepped through the doorway suddenly, carrying a torch while escorting a bound prisoner into the chamber, marching him to the center of the room and making him face the throne on the back wall. The prisoner was silent as he stopped near Alchemy, shoulders stretching the neck of his multi-layered vestment from the wrench of his arms that were bound behind him.

Alchemy stood motionless in front of the prisoner as Caiaphas and the other priests and scribes questioned some conveniently drummed-up witnesses standing nearby. He slowly recognized the bull-shouldered man before him as the witnesses testified to the prisoner's crimes, remembering how he had once carried his formidable frame with immeasurable grace. His bearded face and his garments were stained with hundreds of droplets of blood that had sweated through the pores of his body, making his skin hematidrosivley sensitive to the slightest of touches; a condition to be exploited later by *flagrum* whip masters who would peel his flesh like strips of cloth.

Caiaphas dismissed the contradicting witnesses and focused on the tall prisoner. "Bring him closer," he said to the Captain of the Temple Guard.

The captain complied instantly, shoving his prisoner forward several more steps.

Caiaphas stroked his white beard as the prisoner shuffled to a stop in front of him with a grunt of pain, besetting him with questions of his identity. " 'Tell us, rabbi,' " he sneered. " 'Whom do you say that you are?' "

Jesus remained quiet as his skin ached from the fire of the captain's shoving hand, a virtual calm in the midst of a stormy and merciless assembly of malefactors. His silence was the very essence of humility.

Alchemy watched what was transpiring with great interest, absorbing every moment of this strange and inviting experience. Though he had not been present at this secret trial, he knew what was about to happen. Even with the supernatural knowledge given to him through the Dragon Lord's alchemized blood, and the message of victory proclaimed to the wicked spirits in prison at the Lord's descent into the lower parts of the Earth, he still had read the story many times since his resurrection.

Caiaphas rose from his throne as he spoke again, pointing a long, bony finger at the prisoner. " 'I adjure you by the living God!' " he said. " 'Tell us if you are the Christ, the Son of God!' "

Jesus was powerfully articulate and unwavering even in his weakened state when he spoke. " 'It is as you said,' he answered calmly, his reply echoing in the minds of the Sanhedrin with a soul-piercing pitch. 'Nevertheless, I say to you, hereafter you will see the Son of Man sitting at the right hand of the Power, and coming on the clouds of Heaven.' "

Caiaphas lifted his rage-filled gaze to the ceiling as the prisoner gave himself the exalted title *Son of Man* recorded in the Old Testament prophecies of Daniel. " 'He has spoken blasphemy!' " the high priest shouted, ripping his tunic in half to his stomach, appealing to the rest of the Sanhedrin in a maddened fervor. " 'What further need do we have of witnesses? Look, now you have heard his blasphemy! What do you think?' "

The Sanhedrin rumbled with a similar outrage, demanding the prisoner's death.

Alchemy moved closer to the Lord. He stared at Jesus with a look of awe, listening to the rumblings from the gallery crying out for his blood.

Caiaphas threw up his hands at his surrounding priests to calm them. He stepped forward a pace from his throne, eyes vibrating with an unquenchable hate as he stared at the prisoner before him. "You will suffer the tree for this, blasphemer!" he vowed.

The rebel angels lingering in the shadows along the wall stirred fearfully at the priest's vow, moving through the light of the torches like windblown wraiths on a desperate mission. Their red and yellow eyes gleamed in terror as they circled the heads of the Sanhedrin, trying to clear their minds of their desires to have him executed on the tree of death, lest the prophecy of their doom be fulfilled.

A mountainous rebel with golden hair and sharpened wings sifted through the wall behind Caiaphas. "Stone him!" he growled, curving his metallic wings down around the sides of the high priest in a liquid motion. "KILL HIM NOW!!!"

❖

Alchemy's blue eyes opened suddenly as he lay on the bed in the rear cabin of the Learjet, his journey into the past having been severed with the assassin's unheeded command. His expression was cold and calculating as the drumbeats of war thundered in his mind.

Chapter Twenty-one

Dragylon, the Imperial Fortress of the evil one, filled much of the morning air over Tower Valley. Though its enormity would fill the gaze of spiritual eyes, both the sky and its newly risen sun appeared in their normal positions in the mortal realm; the sphere remaining as invisible as the evil agents inhabiting it.

The very name of the hovering fortress was of great renown in the Ancient World. Some of the structures inside the sphere had even served as models for temples and palaces of empires past and present, with one of the more notable being the ancient acropolis of Pergamos built in the Caicus Valley of Asia Minor. It was there the words of men were first recorded on scrolls of parchment, destroying the monopoly of Egypt's papyrus trade. It was also the site where the first temple of the Caesar cult was erected, joining the throne-like altar of the serpent god Zeus once positioned on a crag above the city of Pergamos. But its darkest fame was yet future when Satan's earthly throne would rise from the shadows of Pergamos' underworld of secret societies, reestablished on that same crag in greater glory and might than ever before.

Inside, at the very heart of the sphere, was a golden, craggily-crafted mountain range covered with emerald pines. The mountain formed a semicircle around a vast, circular plain of diamond tile. Ivory palaces, colonnaded council buildings and sleek towers filled the plateaus and peaks of the mountain range. Wide, arch-shaped harbors were forged deep into the mountain's sprawling cliffs and smooth faces. Marble-style fittings and tall pillars lined the mouths of the arches, with armor-clad rebels standing guard in the wide expanses between each pillar that served as launch bays for the siege ships and other rebel vessels of war designed for the final assault on the splendid shores of Heaven.

Behind the plain of blazing tile below stood an array of towering, roof-covered columns of black marble reaching as high and as wide as the mountain range itself. They were built on two rectangular foundations of pearl-colored strata separated in the center, with gilded friezes of cosmic battles carved into the smooth facades of each foundation. The rolled tops of each column spread out against the gilded trim of each roof's spire-crowned overhang.

At the center of the space between the two roof-covered colonnades was a grand arch surpassing the largest of the great archways of Europe in size. A galactic pane of blue crystal filled the space between the archway's intricately carved borders. Carved in its center was a broken, diamond-encrusted sign of infinity with winged dragon heads extending from its severed ends.

A colossal mound of diamond steps was positioned at the base of the wall's grand arch, with 24 rebel angels formed in two lines of tribute on the corners of the mound's trapezoid-shaped stairway. A throne of black marble with an arced backrest and a wide seat of padded silver filled the center of the mound's platform, trimmed in a gilded pageantry of pagan reliefs. A large tree sprouted up from the mound on each side of the throne, rising halfway up against the backdrop of the crystal-filled arch. Each tree had a thickly twisted trunk dressed with crimson-colored bark similar to the armored scales of a dragon, both gnarled with blackened scripts of cherubic cuneiform, with the one on the right side of the throne detailing the rise of the Great Tree and the one on the left recording the growth of apostasy sprouting from Israel and the Church over the ages. Their branches were spread wide in a circular fashion, with flat tops resembling acacia trees. Thistled acanthus leaves bloomed sharply from their limbs, with large, blackened fruits of pride and every other imaginable sin and pernicious power dangling between the thistles of each leaf.

Sodom's warriors, along with millions of other rebels from around the globe, filled the treetops of the mountain range's emerald pines. Their false wings connected their ranks from treetop to treetop.

The Council of Thrones, minus Sodom, was assembled in front of two walls of black marble that formed a covered library stretching a quarter of a mile to the diamond mound's three-sided steps, with the tops of each wall reaching to the middle step of the mound. Separate sets of steps angled down from the flat, banister-lined walkways on top of the walls, meeting with the tile on each side of the library's entranceway that could only be entered by the master and his personal scribe. A-shaped frames of gold connected by black panels extended from the inner sides of the walkways to form an ark-like roof over the library, with circular Zodiacs and other cosmic friezes carved on the facades of each golden frame.

The council members were divided into two groups, facing one another silently, leaving a wide path between them leading to the library's doorless entryway. Their multicolored wings were arced high above their heads. The majority of their faces were beastly in shape, with the rest having more humanoid features.

The Shadow Kings in the Council of Thrones ranged from every corner of the globe; Africa, Asia, Europe and the Middle East, each summoned to Dragylon to witness the events in the valley below.

Bastion stood on the mound's platform in front of the throne high above the assembled court below, wings arcing high above his head in a sharp display of ribbed flames. A black-scaled pole was clutched in his right hand, with a gold, serpentine standard of broken infinity framed in a silver victor's wreath positioned on top.

Two warriors were posted nearby, one on each side of the throne behind Bastion. Both were over eight feet tall, their bodies shaped and colored like chiseled granite, their disfigured faces and heads masked with blue pyres that matched the color of their fiery, holographic wings, with shotel-style swords hanging by their sides.

A blackened tree stump in the shape of a lectern stood several feet ahead and to the right of the mound's ruling throne, sprouting from the serpentine roots of both trees that ran beneath the plateau of the diamond mound. Its black, twisted exterior of shimmering scales was gnarled with golden symbols similar to the blackened script etched into the crimson scales of the twin trees.

A black-robed angel loomed over the lectern, holding a quill pen in his marble-white hand, the pen's fiery tip poised over an ivory-colored scroll. His eyes burned with orange fire in the shadow of his hood. Medius, Lucifer's personal scribe since the Fall, recorded all that was spoken by the Archrebel when the Imperial Court was in session, filling the Imperial Library below with countless scrolls of evidence and wisdom that would, in strange effect, be used as part of his master's defense in the final judgment. And it was that same tainted wisdom which gave off enough alchemizing energy to mask the all of Dragylon in a heavenly illusion of jeweled structures that were much darker beneath their exteriors.

Dragylon's cosmic audience remained silent and perfectly still for what seemed like centuries, waiting in their assembled positions for their master's imminent arrival.

Suddenly, in perfect symmetry, every angelic head throughout Dragylon tilted upward at the silver clouds of the sphere's sky-blue atmosphere as they pitched and rolled with a distant thunder. They watched as the clouds began to swirl in a counterclockwise formation above the plain of diamond tile where the Shadow Kings were gathered.

A bolt of lightning struck through the middle of the circling clouds, tearing a craterous hole in its center to reveal another opening in the sphere's rounded roof. The morning sky outside the sphere had given way to a field of stars and various constellations stretched out across the Outer Realm.

Bastion lifted the *Herald of Thunders* from his belt, blasting note of declaration from the horn's wide muzzle, its tubular resonance electrifying every inch of the Imperial Fortress.

A metallic shear roared from the emerald treetops of the mountain range as the assembled legions drew their array of weapons in unison.

A hush fell over Dragylon's assembled masses when the sounds of a tranquil music started to emanate from above, its source distant, building with each passing second as if it rode upon a rejected tide from the eternal shore.

Every rotating iris of fire below was fixed on the stars in the portal hovering above the Imperial Court. They all watched as a small beacon of golden light streaked across the northern reaches of the cosmos, trailing through the heavens like a comet.

The music grew louder as the light fell towards Dragylon, its texture resonating with the more distinguishable sound of a violin being played with masterful strokes.

The comet-like beacon quickly crossed the spaciousness of the galaxy, growing brighter as it finally entered the Earth's atmosphere.

With a clap of thunder, the comet's engulfing light exploded outward from its core, revealing four armored steeds, shimmering like black marble in the glow of the sphere's bright interior, pulling an enormous ivory chariot with golden emblems and fiery wheels spitting flames in every direction. The team was harnessed side by side with crimson reins flapping about wildly as they streaked across the sky, their silver, dragon-marked horseshoes expelling electromagnetic hoofbeats that charged the different elements in the atmosphere, briefly pulling them together in a broad road of jeweled cobblestones which slowly vanished from sight with an oscillating fire after the rig passed over them.

At the helm of the chariot, his back facing the team, was the Scourge of the Ages, the Prince of Pain. Lucifer's reflective locks of black hair flailed wildly in the wind, slapping at the sides of his man-shaped face. Every enormous muscle on his galactic body shimmered like translucent gold, outshining the glow of the sphere itself. His crimson, feather-lined wings were encrusted with eye-shaped scales of glass, with nine different types of jewels shining from beneath their transparent surfaces. The velvet edges of each wing rustled wildly around the sides of his thick legs, each side rippling with dual motions as if his wingspan was two sets in one. A jewel-encrusted apron of cut strips matching the color of his wings was held in place by a diamond, chainlink belt sagging around his tapered waist. An empty black scabbard with runic emblems of gold carved down its center hung from the belt as well, resting against his left thigh.

A crimson mark of broken infinity with winged dragon heads was animate with life as Lucifer's enormous chest flexed back and forth from the motion of his right arm, fingers guiding a fiery-stringed bow across the crystal strings of a black violin tucked beneath his chin. The violin's charge was building with the beating rhythm emanating from the ruby, horizontally-shaped vents protruding three inches from the muscular mid-section of his translucent torso. Each vent was seven inches long, segmented into three stacked rows, with three vents in each segment.

Lucifer turned to his right as he slowed his *quadriga* chariot by telepathy, making a ceremonial pass in front of the warriors posted in the emerald pines on the mountain range. The vents in his midsection resonated with a quick, methodic drum beat as they pumped back and forth, flowing with the rhythm of his violin. His dragon eyes glowed like crimson suns as a column of nine star-shaped pupils with six points rotated counterclockwise in the center of each golden iris.

His diamond fangs emerged through a sly smile, his left wing rustling out away from his body like a cape in the pull of the music as he mastered the strings of his black instrument with an ethereal ease that only the concert halls of Vienna could envy.

Lucifer crouched forward as the chariot slowed even more, the pace of his music increasing with even more energy, hair flying wildly around his golden face as he pivoted back and forth, strumming his fiery-stringed bow to the chords of a symphonic piece recorded in the vibrations of his body; an effect achieved after millenniums of being saturated in countless human sound bytes permeating the Earth's atmosphere and beyond.

The chariot exploded with speed once more as Lucifer approached his destination, roaring past the warriors posted in the treetops who were chanting like obsessed fans at a rock concert as he finished his modified gamut.

Lucifer lowered the violin as the music in his vents faded, narrowing his dragon eyes as he turned toward the team. With a telepathic whisper in a language known only in the throne room of Heaven, he commanded the team to land, hands never once touching the reins.

The team threw their heads back at the command, snorting bursts of fire from their nostrils as they descended toward the diamond-laid court. They landed with the clatter of a distant storm, the wheels of the chariot turning gold the instant they touched down on the tile, stopping short of the aisle separating the monarchs.

Lucifer propped the violin against the chariot's helm. Thunder rolled throughout Dragylon when the Archrebel stepped down from his opulent vessel, wings swishing with cape-like motion over his shoulders and arms as he swaggered around the team toward the aisle prepared by his Shadow Kings. The vents in his midsection pumped back and forth with an ominous march of drumbeats, his glassy hair swirling like tentacles, reflecting Dragylon's false light. His diamond fangs almost outshone the glow of his sharp face that was already melting into a more business-like scowl.

A metallic thunder exploded around him when the Council of Thrones drew their blades, each dropping to one knee, placing their enormous swords at the master's cleft-shaped feet when he started to pass between them.

The council rose again with a quick jolt as Lucifer melted into the shadowy entranceway of the Imperial Library, both lines turning toward the gothic wall in the distance.

Lucifer walked slowly along the surface of the library's dark aisle of ethereal water that was connected to cosmic engines located at Dragylon's core. His jewel-encrusted wings fluttered behind him like the robes of a scholar while he glanced at the towering bookcases to the left and right of him. He strode through shafts of light descending down from the sphere's atmosphere through certain panels that were open on each side of the library's vaulted roof, eyes flashing brightly each time he passed through the pockets of thick shadows, the darkness consuming all but the muscled outline of his golden form like a solar eclipse.

The library consisted of rolled scrolls of ivory parchment stuffed into open sleeves, with each sleeve stacked on top of one another on the shelves. Small flaming symbols of angelic and cherubic origin hovered in the space of each sleeve's open circle, serving as a coded filing system created by his scribe Medius. Lucifer's own voice whispered at him from behind the scrolls' fiery symbols as he walked past them, swirling around him in cosmic drafts of devilish diatribes and prideful proclamations.

The Archfiend stopped at the end of the aisle of water where the roof opened in a triangular fashion at the mound's middle step, standing in a veil of shadows that defied the light of the starry steps. He focused on a particular scroll at eye level in the towering bookcase to his left. A flame-cast symbol of a human DNA strand hovered brightly in the scroll's open circle, rotating in place between two angelic icons. He studied the symbol with a careful hate just as he had always done when proceeding to his throne. The story logged behind the flaming symbol told the tale of his attempt to contaminate the human race after the Proto-Evangelum prophecy of his future doom was issued in Eden. But he, the great Ha-Seraph, would not be brought to his belly in prostration without a fight. He would choose a select number of his fallen angels to spawn a race of demonic giants through intercourse with mortal women to corrupt the bloodline of the Christos Champion who would come and redeem the elect. Noah and his family would be the only ones left on Earth who weren't genetically soiled by such unions and cross-breeding that reached its peak at the time of the Second Great Deluge. But a new seed of the *Gegenes Gibborim* would be sown after the Flood, a lineage largely destroyed by Joshua and his Israelite Army during their invasion of Canaan, with the remnants fading away throughout history by victorious champions and other rods of divine retribution. A retribution which would be unleashed on a third wave of giants still to come.

Lucifer hissed softly as those first millenniums of pride and defeated schemes burned brightly at the core of his eternally insulted intellect. He took the starry steps in a slow and powerful stride, ascending from the shadows of his library through the roof's triangular opening, wings billowing out behind him regally. He walked between the stone-colored rebels formed in an aisle of tribute on the starry corners of the three-sided steps, their fiery-blue wings arcing high above their flaming heads. They each carried a round black shield on their left arms bearing a silver ensign in the shape of their master's broken mark of infinity.

The priestly warriors bowed to one knee as Lucifer passed through their lines, lowering their shields while, with their right hands, lifting a golden bowl above their heads. Black clouds of incense harvested from the molecules of the Earth's atmosphere ascended from the bowls. They were the vapors of genocide and war permeating the air around abortion clinics and battlefields of the world's industrialized and Third World nations; sacrifices slain on the altars of mankind's Adamic nature. But it was this time of the year, the time of the Hunter's moon, that such harvests were specially gathered for his consumption and regurgitation in honor of the Samhain celebrations already in full swing on the other side of the world.

Lucifer stopped between the last two warriors who were kneeling several steps down from the mound's flat platform. He spread his crimson wings toward the bowls on each side of him, watching their black clouds swirl around him for several seconds like ghostly apparitions, shooting forward and backward through his wings in a torrent of scream-filled wind. The Archfiend shimmered with delight as the black smoke sifted back and forth through his wings, funneling down through his vents, his golden muscles brightening even more. "I am the god of this *cosmos!*" he roared, his voice echoing throughout the whole of the Imperial Fortress. "Prophet, priest and king!!!"

Dragylon exploded with a clap of thunder as Lucifer snapped his wings back down, scattering the black smoke of human remains in different directions. He continued up the steps as residual smoke and dark harmonies filtered from his vents.

263

Bastion fell to his knees when Lucifer reached the mound's plateau, holding the Imperial Standard by his side as he passed. Medius and the two rebels standing on the mound's plateau also dropped to their knees.

Lucifer turned toward the court below, with the trees beside his throne and the crystal blue pane in the wall's background arch looming high behind him. He paused for a moment before slowly sitting down in the throne's wide seat, the razor tips of his emerald fingernails falling on top of a pair of silver dragon heads protruding from the end of each armrest. He rested his head against the throne's arced back, positioning his feet so that they appeared to rest on top of the library's long, A-shaped roof, mimicking the posture of the invisible God who once used the Ark of the Covenant as a footstool while seated on his earthly dispensational throne in Solomon's Temple; a tradition carried on in the Ancient World by the kings of the east who kept their covenants and treaties in a chest at the foot of their thrones in like manner.

Both warriors kneeling on each side of the throne stood after Lucifer sat down, turning toward one another. They started to rise above the throne, their taloned feet stopping just above its backrest, wings spreading over Lucifer's head in plumes of blue fire. The flaming tips of their holographic wingspans touched as they hovered beneath the lowest branches of the tall trees behind them, melting together in a perfect canopy just as Lucifer did many times when protecting the throne of God.

Lucifer lifted his eyes for a moment, enjoying the bright shadow of the fiery wings hovering above his head.

The Archlord looked back down at Bastion where he was kneeling. "Report," he said, his voice echoing with a mixture of tenor and bass.

Medius stood up behind the twisted lectern as Lucifer spoke, quietly pushing his fiery-tipped pen against the parchment sprawled out across the dragon's mouth desktop.

Bastion stood and walked over in front of the throne, clinging to the black-scaled pole in his right hand while prostrating himself again to properly address the master. "The dust leaders that have gathered in the valley below are greatly pleased with the

Mark's progress and its binding effect on the town's community," he reported.

"Excellent," Lucifer replied. "And what of Operation Assyria?"

"All is going as scheduled, my lord," Bastion answered. "The Red Horse Units of the Omega Group's Alpha Corps Army have struck Lebanon with a lightning push deep into the heart of its territory."

"And the fallout?"

"With the intelligence blackout propagated by the group, news of the invasion has been kept from hitting the world's major wire services. However, such news cannot be contained for long…and we can count on the remaining dust armies of the fractured Arab League to be the first to take an immediate course of action against Apostate Israel and the coalition forces that will seize control of the territory."

Lucifer rested his head against the back of the throne again. "All seems to be going well," he remarked. "And without a single case of interference, correct?"

Bastion was slow to answer. "Not exactly, my lord."

"Not exactly?"

"Yes, my lord," he said, bowing his head with embarrassment.

"Yes, indeed," Lucifer replied, looking back down at the gate master. "Not only did Tsavo finally take his last step into betrayal, but now we have a force from the other side working against us as well…the Shekinah Champion himself."

Bastion lifted his head in surprise, his hair falling away from his gargoyle face in a chimed clatter from the golden rings looped around the curled tips of his dark hair. "How do you know these things already, my lord?" he asked. "You have only just returned from the assembly in Heaven…."

Lucifer leaned forward in his throne, clutching the dragon head busts of his armrests. "I know everything that takes place within my kingdom," he smiled brightly.

Bastion bowed his head in a fearful silence.

"Now," Lucifer continued, "what of Sodom?"

"His arrival with the Alchemy King is imminent, my lord."

"As is the storm of change."

Bastion managed enough strength to lift his gaze again, looking upon the master's frightening and alluring face that still glowed from having been in the presence of the Ancient of Days. "Shall I inform Sodom to take extra measures against the champion?"

Lucifer said nothing. He gazed up through the fiery canopy above him, eyeing a shiny black fruit hanging from one of the lower limbs of the tree to the right of his throne. He plucked it from the limb with a thought, causing it to fall through the fiery wings of his covering guards. He turned the fingers of his right hand upward, catching the flambee`d fruit on the tips of his razor sharp fingernails.

Lucifer lifted the fruit toward his mouth, quenching its flames with a frigid vapor as he sunk his diamond fangs into its roasted skin. The crisp swishes of the fruit's juice-filled skin rushed through his mouth like the blood of a fatling's flesh.

Bastion hesitated to repeat himself. "My lord? Shall I inform Sodom to take extra measures against the champion?"

"No," Lucifer answered, smiling devilishly as he glanced back down at his subject. "That problem is being handled by the most capable of powers."

Chapter Twenty-two

Alchemy sat alone in the rear section of a black Mercedes limousine making its way down Tower Valley's southern road. He peered out the right side window meditatively. His stylishly-tossed hair brushed the collar of his dark blue Savile Row suit. A shadow of growth dressed his square jaw line, giving him a rugged, messianic appeal.

Alchemy leaned closer to the tinted window to view the town's ivory clock tower cresting above the pines in the distance.

He turned his attention to the sky above the clock tower. Needle-like shafts of light appeared on the surface of his blue eyes, pulsing up and down for several seconds before dissolving away into the corners of each eye as a portion of the sky's electro-magnetic canopy was torn away. He grinned when Dragylon's great golden belly came into view above the treetops, sensing with greater force the powers hovering within the sphere, melding with the energy of the rebel host following behind the limo.

Alchemy closed his eyes with triumph, reclining into the limo's leather seat. His skin tingled with a shared power from the master's presence in the Imperial Fortress above the valley.

—•··—≖◯≖—··•—

The sun's morning rays poured in through the arched window of the church's choir balcony, its pane-shaped shafts cutting a tunnel through the church's gray shadows.

Beads of fever-filled sweat covered Magnus' face. His eyes were closed in a fearful sleep, mind and spirit still locked in the nightmare of his wife's torment. He clawed at the planks of the choir balcony with his diamond-hard nails, splintering the wood with the weakened strength of his fingers, reaching out in his mind to pull his precious Rachel to safety.

He mumbled under his heavy breaths while scratching at the floor. "Help her," he begged. "Lord Jesus, help her!"

April, huddled against the wall beside him, dabbed his forehead with another wet towel, listening as Magnus prayed in his state of delirium. She was tired and ragged from the long night, drifting in and out of sleep.

━━━━━◆◆◆━━━━━

Halfway around the world, far from the sun-splashed forests of Tower Valley, the hoofbeats of war were thundering across the night sky of Palmyra; an oasis of ancient ruins in the middle of the Syrian Desert. Known as Tadmor by the locals since the 19th century B.C., Palmyra had once been an important stop for traders and caravans traveling on the Silk Road that ran from the Far East to Europe. It became an even more important commercial stop when other trade routes of the Old World were rerouted through Syria after the merchant empire of the Nabataeans was defeated by the Romans and absorbed into its Arabian province. But that prosperity began to fade when Odenathus, a brilliant military commander allied to the Roman Empire, was supposedly assassinated by his wife Zenobia during an internal struggle to make Palmyra a totally independent power in the region; a rebellion that would seemingly enjoy great success as Palmyra's new queen eventually conquered all of Syria, Palestine and part of Egypt. Defeat came in 272 A.D. when the bold queen who claimed to be a descendant of Cleopatra was captured by the forces of Emperor Aurelian and taken prisoner to Rome, leaving Palmyra behind to be completely destroyed a year later in one final rebellion.

The city, however, still held great economic value to the citizens of New Palmyra, a prosperous town which had grown up around the ruins. Though free of its usual human traffic for the moment, Old Palmyra was the premier attraction for tourists and archaeologists visiting Syria.

The expansive ruins were not completely abandoned. A tall, platinum-haired figure of a man dressed in a hooded-robe of sky-blue flax stood on top of a crumbling stone wall on a hill overlooking the famous funerary towers of Palmyra's Valley of the Tombs. This vantage point gave him a bird's eye view of the main sprawl of ruins on the desert basin below.

Gabriel stood on the highest point of the old wall that extended down the steep slope some 20 feet, with adjacent walls and crumbling columns extending to the left and right of him. He magnified his bright focus on the moonlit ruins below. The columned street of the Great Colonnade and the Temple of Bel-Shamin stood out the most amongst the other fragments, friezes and hypogeum tombs spread out across the basin below. But the real attractions were the armored rebels posted atop some of the columns below, each looking to the west of the ruins in the direction of the Orontes River and the Anti-Lebanon mountain range where an air force base once operated by Syria's fallen regime, was located. The base, was now operated by the armed forces of the Illuminati who also controlled a high security prison located nearby.

Gabriel turned his focus to the west. Trails of tracer fire lit up the night landscape on the other side of the peaks of the Anti-Lebanon mountain range. The air force base below had grounded all of its usual patrols of the border between Syria and Lebanon, ignoring the rumbles and flashes of intense fighting taking place on the other side of the mountain range. Even the squadrons which would normally be patrolling above the main highway to Homs and Damascus had been grounded.

"It seems we share grim tidings, my prince."

Gabriel looked back to his right when a familiar voice spoke to him out of the shadows. A towering, wraith-like figure of a man stood about 10 feet away on top of a jagged pedestal of stone positioned on the wall adjacent to his. The figure's hands were tucked into the pockets of a long, velveteen coat of royal blue flax that flowed with a silken motion in the drafts of the night air, his shoulders spanning past the width of the cracked column rising up behind him, spirals of silver light rolling from the corners of his solid eyes.

"What news do you bring from Tower Valley, Scriptos?"

Scriptos was hawkish and to the point with his reply. "The champion has fallen prey to a venomous attack from the enemy, my prince."

Gabriel was silent for a moment. He offered no looks of surprise or disapproval at the news his faithful Book Master had brought him. He looked back down at the ruins below, scanning the faces of the rebel hosts perched on top of the columns of the Great Colonnade. He was reminded of a difficult mission given to him in the past. He had been dispatched with an important message to be delivered to the Prophet Daniel who was living in exile in the courts of Babylon at the time. But he was delayed by the evil Prince of Persia for 21 days. It wasn't until the Archangel Michael came to his assistance that he was able to break through the enemy's defenses and deliver the message. It was a lesson about teamwork and trust for both man and angel.

"What are your orders, my prince?" Scriptos asked.

Gabriel kept his gaze on the rebels below as the Spirit of the Lord whispered the answer into his cosmic consciousness.

He quickly turned his attention back to Scriptos, relaying the answer in almost the same instant it was given to him. "Go to Venice," he told him. "Tell the great prince all that is transpiring in the valley. The Lord will then instruct you both on what to do next."

"Yes, my prince."

"Hurry, Scriptos," Gabriel urged. "The shadow of things to come is upon us."

Scriptos immediately eschewed the offerings of protocol and vaulted upward from the jagged pedestal, leaping above the cracked column behind him before vanishing in a flash of silver light.

Chapter Twenty-three

Alchemy stepped from the limousine as the driver opened his door, casually weaving the buttons of his double-breasted suit into the narrow slits of his coat. The thin strands of gold, translucent highlights that were mixed with his black hair caught the sun's rays, causing 10, horn-like beams of golden light to rise up from his regal head, resembling the Zoroastrian halos depicted in some of the world's most famous works of religious art.

The Omega Group's southern building towered in front of him as Alchemy stepped forward from the limo's open door. A statue of a large, Taurus bull with a Virgoan goddess riding on its back was positioned in front of the building's mirror-like panels of glass, a torch raised in one hand and an ancient ephah uplifted in the other. Behind the statue stood a towering cedar tree transplanted from the mountains of Lebanon, its expansive boughs casting a long shadow over the bronze sculpture.

Specter was standing near the statue, dressed in a black suit that had a gold and red insignia of Greek and serpentine design stitched on the left breast of the coat. The wire rim glasses he wore were pressed snugly against his face, his red hair parted to the side with great care.

He moved forward a step as Alchemy walked toward him, shoulders slumping a bit as if he wanted to bow his head. Alchemy's ethereal presence almost pushed him back on his heels the closer he came, mixing with the force of his darkly-fabled celebrity preceding him like a telekinetic wind.

Alchemy stopped within an arm's length of him, lessening the power flowing out of him with a mere thought when he noticed Specter's disorientation. "Salutations, Mr. Specter," he smiled, the power of his eloquent voice wrapping around him like a serpent's tail to steady him on his feet.

Specter blinked rapidly several times. He was immediately sucked into Alchemy's piercing stare, a power that always bewitched the weak of mind.

"Mr. Specter," Alchemy repeated, using his voice to break the spell of enchantment.

Specter, embarrassed, stumbled his words. "I…I'm sorry, Mr. Alchemy," he said. "Welcome to Tower Valley. The dignitaries have already gathered in Mr. Tsavo's conference room."

"Very well," he said. "Tis tragic, though, that Mr. Tsavo will not be joining us for this momentous event."

Specter nodded warily.

"Have you disposed of his body yet?"

"Cardinal Menelaus instructed me to wait for your orders on what to do with it. The R&D techs in the Project Nietzsche program wanted to preserve it for research."

"Project Nietzsche has been terminated," he said. "All materials and research that have been developed for the program, including Mr. Tsavo's body, are to be destroyed. It has been replaced with a new program…Project Gegenes."

Specter stammered in his reply, unnerved by Alchemy's peculiar forcefulness toward the giant. "Y…yes sir."

Specter hesitated for a moment before he spoke again, wondering what the giant had done to cause the cancellation of such a highly-funded program like Project Nietzsche. "What about the prototype, sir?"

Alchemy drew closer to Specter's face, barreling down on him with his bright blue eyes. "What prototype?"

Specter stammered in surprise. "The…prototype agent that was injected with the program's experimental serum," he answered. "I assumed that you and the rest of the group's top brass had been briefed about him by Mr. Tsavo."

"No, Mr. Specter…we were not briefed."

Alchemy continued to hover close to him with his powerful stare, intimidating him beyond anything he had ever experienced with the giant, just as Commander Kane's taunting had indicated would happen.

"This…prototype agent…. Where is he at the moment?"

"I don't know, sir. Mr. Tsavo dispatched him on a very secretive mission months ago. As far as I know, he was the only one that knew anything about the agent's mission."

"Does he have any tracking implants?"

"Mr. Tsavo gave explicit instructions that he was not to be fitted with any such devices."

Alchemy stared at Specter for a moment, smirking at the giant's determination that continued even in the wake of his demise.

Specter fidgeted in place. "I can start an immediate hunt for the prototype agent," he suggested. "We do know that he was Mr. Tsavo's top recruit for the Wolf Pack units."

"No," Alchemy replied. "I will have a unit of the Harness Magi track him down. They have quite a unique history when it comes to hunting rogue wolves."

Specter nodded dazedly when he made mention of the infamous Harness Magi.

"Now," said Alchemy, "I trust that everything else within the sphere of your responsibilities has been taken care of?"

Specter cleared his throat. "I stepped up the security measures throughout the valley before the dignitaries arrived, sir. And I was assured by Cardinal Menelaus that our infiltration problem was being taken care of…I remain uninformed, however, by what means this problem is being solved, and by whom."

"Not to worry, Mr. Specter," he grinned, glancing upward. "The problem is being handled by the most…capable of powers."

Chapter Twenty-four

Specter escorted Alchemy down a dimly lit hallway made of dark panels carved with more of the town's familiar Virgoan and Taurus imagery, walking for almost a full minute before they reached a set of oak doors covered in a honeycomb-style exterior, the design concealing another set of doors beneath the wood as dense in their durability as a bank vault. There were no handles on the hallway side of the doors. But there was a computer terminal built into the wall at eye level on the right side of the enormous doorway.

Specter stepped aside, allowing Alchemy to pass in front of him. Specter turned to the square panel of glass-covered buttons on the wall beside him. He waved his hand in front of a large sensor in the middle of the panel. A pulse of red light illuminated the entire terminal, activating a digitally-recorded voice. "Step forward for identification," said the automated voice.

Alchemy played along with the formalities, stepping toward the terminal as the blank screen above the glass buttons slid down into a groove, revealing a facial unit similar to the eye fittings from a pair of binoculars that rolled outward on an electronic track. He placed his eyes into the slots of the unit, the device wrapping snugly around the top portion of his face. Though the device appeared to be a sophisticated retinal scan, it was, however, something much more. The terminal, using positron emission tomography, was a cerebral scan capable of registering the uptake of blood sugar in his brain cells, measuring the very core activity of his IQ that was stored like a classified signature in the Omega Group's interconnected mainframes throughout the world. It was a security clearance that didn't have any real binding or empowering effect upon him. As long as the Dragon Lord's blood coursed through his veins, he could come and go anywhere on the planet he pleased without hindrance.

Specter waited quietly beside him, looking puzzled. The scan was taking longer than usual to download the activity of Alchemy's brain.

"Thank you, Iscarius Alchemy," the digital voice said finally. "You may enter."

With that command, the doors to his left opened inward with a rush of air, allowing the rays of the morning sun to flood into the hallway from the conference room.

Alchemy pulled back from the facial unit and stepped into the light, leaving Specter behind as the roar of applause filtered into the hallway for a brief moment before the soundproof doors locked shut once more.

Specter stood silent in the hallway, gazing at the terminal with a gaping mouth. A small readout monitor on the left side of the terminal's glass buttons was showing Alchemy's wicked IQ. The bright red figure that had left him stunned was the number 666.

A touch on his shoulder from behind surprised Specter while he stood there staring at the terminal's three digits. He turned around to see a dark-haired agent standing before him, dressed in a black suit like his own to signify his position with Shadow Corps Intelligence.

"I didn't mean to startle you, sir," the agent said in a low voice.

Specter tugged at the knot of his tie. "Never mind," he said in a haunted tone, glancing back over his shoulder as the number disappeared from the screen.

Specter turned his head back around again, wondering if what he had seen was real. "You're just the man I need, Mr. Grimes," he said.

Grimes stood at quiet attention, holding a leather brief by his side.

"A new protocol has been initiated by Mr. Alchemy," Specter told him. "Effective immediately, all research and materials developed for Project Nietzsche are to be destroyed, including Mr. Tsavo's body. And all nonessential personnel within the R&D labs are hereby terminated from their current positions. Make sure the necessary security changes are completed before the end of the day."

"Yes sir."

"And have Special Services check out the identification terminal for this conference room for any glitches as well."

"Yes sir."

Specter took a quick breath, exhaling with an exhausted sigh. "Now, I take it you have something for me?"

"Yes sir," he answered. "We used our uplinks with ECHELON and MILSTAR to track down that SATCOM signal bouncing all over the valley the other day." Grimes pulled out a satellite photo from the leather brief he was holding, pointing to a magnified image on the print. "The signal originated from here…. An old abandoned church building built on a plateau on the western face of the valley's eastern mountain range."

Specter leaned forward for a closer look at the magnified images in the photo.

"It's the only piece of property not listed in the town's registry of deeds," he replied. "We would've never spotted it as quickly with a chopper as we did with the satellite. It's almost virtually invisible to the eye since the building was built on the northern side of the arid plateau where there's an overgrowth of pines shading much of it."

"Our intruder is there," Specter pointed, eyes widening. "And I'm willing to bet that Dr. Wedding is with him. Our agents would have picked her up on the Pacific Coast Highway by now had she left the valley."

"I agree, sir. But we were told they were both being taken care of?"

Specter paused for a moment as he glanced back over his left shoulder again, his eyes falling on the closed doors of the conference room this time.

He looked back at Grimes with a hint of reservation in his stare, trying not to show his nervousness for the decision he was about to make. "We have the future of the world meeting on the other side of those doors, Mr. Grimes," he noted. "And I'm not going to take any more chances of something going wrong again. All the dignitaries, except for Mr. Alchemy, will be leaving after the meeting later today. I want you to prep the Apache and assemble the Wolf Pack. I need to know that this problem has been resolved."

"Yes sir."

"But don't move against the target until three hours before dawn," he ordered. "I want to make sure the town's normal activities aren't disrupted in any way. Secrecy is vital…I'll be monitoring the operation from the situation room."

"What about your orders for Project Nietzsche?"

Specter hesitated, giving another quick glance over his shoulder at the conference room doors. "See to the security changes first. We'll take care of the other termination procedures for the project's materials and Mr. Tsavo's body once this mission is complete."

"Yes sir."

"Make ready your crew, Mr. Grimes…we have some moles to burn."

Chapter Twenty-five

Alchemy glided slowly across the floor of the conference room, mentally controlling the energy outflow of the Dragon Lord's blood pumping through him.

The dignitaries were standing in front of wingback chairs positioned on the right and left sides of the room's trapezoid-shaped table, each one clapping loudly for the princely figure strutting before them; someone only a select few in the room had ever seen with their own eyes before. Though he was only known as a private consultant who held no official title within the group's infrastructure, everyone there knew that it was he who stood in the shadows mastering the strings of the Omega Group instead of its publicly recognized CEO's and board of directors. And his legend went far beyond the dark fame of his consultant capacity with the group. Rumors abounded about his skills as a world-class violinist, swordsman and archer. Fantastic tales were told of his hands-on leadership during some of the group's covert military OPS in Africa and the Middle East. But the grandest tales were those linked to his name. Some thought he was the Fisher King of the Masonic Grail Feast who was known by the Welsh as Pwyll, a name which meant *Master of the Abyss*, tying it to the lapis elixir Arabic term for alchemy used in describing the Philosopher's Stone. The stone was a fictional emerald that supposedly fell from Lucifer's head during his rebellion and was used in the formation of the multifaceted Grail. These stories and the many others in Arthurian lore were some of the most famous Antichrist treatises ever perpetrated on the world, mimicking the tales of Nectanebus the Wizard and Alexander the Great that were fictionalized in the same vein as those told about Semiramis and Tammuz, with each serving to parallel and distort the Proto-Evangelum prophecy in the Genesis account that predicted the birth, death and resurrection of the Messiah.

Alchemy passed by the enormous statue of Goliath that loomed over him in a foreshadowing glory of triumvirate sixes expressed in his stature and armaments. His gaze was respectful as he thought about the recent demise of another giant who had not been as loyal as the Philistine had been. He knew Tsavo's ambition for the *Covenant Harness* would not allow him to sit idly by while another ascended as the master's chosen messiah. And it had cost him damnation sooner than anticipated.

Alchemy focused on Tsavo's granite throne situated at the head of the table, the applause from the leaders building progressively in his approach to the enormous seat.

He stepped in front of the throne, allowing the leaders to admire him fully. He was, to those in the room who had actually met him in person before now, an enigma of unknown birth with seemingly ageless beauty who had promised them even more than the prosperity of politics. Infinitely more.

Alchemy sat down in the granite throne, motioning for the leaders to take their seats, carefully surveying each of them as they sat down. He worked the atmosphere of the room with his silent and masterful inspection of the gallery, creating a hunger for the wisdom of his first words in those who worshiped his mysterious power.

He nodded to Cardinal Menelaus sitting the closest to him.

◆━┅━▆◦▆━┅━◆

Sodom was perched on the throne's high back behind Alchemy, arms folded imposingly across the chest of his muscled cuirass. This would be one of his greatest moments of achievement.

◆━┅━▆◦▆━┅━◆

Alchemy checked the gold Rolex on his left wrist, noting the start of the morning's last hour. He glanced back at the leaders in waiting, speaking to them in a masterful voice that defied all traces of any accent. "Gentlemen, I bid you both grace and peace for such a warm and heartfelt reception…. I am truly honored to be esteemed so highly by each of you. Thank you," he smiled.

Alchemy paused for a moment, checking his watch again. "Now," he continued, "let us attend to the business which has brought us together today."

He leaned forward and pressed a button on a small computerized panel near the end of the table. The button flashed red for a moment, activating the 36 inch computer projection screen flatly embedded in the center of the polished table. A square shaft of light shot up to the coffered ceiling in front of the leaders gathered around the table, its image flickering with a brief picture of static snow as the satellite feed took several seconds to link up with its receiver.

A darkened landscape of desert terrain soon appeared before them, filled with the sight of Stryker armored vehicles and black-clad mercenaries riding high on groups of fast-moving horses. An imposing figure with a bullish, unmerciful face quickly appeared in the center of the picture, barking a sharp command to the soldier who was holding the camera that was transmitting the satellite feed back to the conference room, ordering him to hold still as two RAH-66 Comanche assault choppers buzzed them from above.

Alchemy settled back into the throne as the sight of the large mercenary was steadied in front of them. "Status report, Commander Kane," he ordered, every eye focusing on the digitally-enhanced merc standing in the center of the table.

Kane secured his OIC smart gun on his shoulder as a sizeable spray of tracer fire lit up the night sky behind him, followed by more images of electromagnetic resistant Comanches flying low to lay suppression fire on a crumbling position of Hezbollah guerrillas near the Israeli border. "We've already destroyed the major tactical infrastructures of military and political significance from Tripoli to Tyre," Kane replied, placing a finger on the earphone of his SATCOM headset in an attempt to drown out the sounds of war behind him.

"And the resistance factor so far?" Alchemy asked.

"Minimal at best, sir," he answered. "The element of surprise for such a full-scale attack worked well in our favor. The blackout at CENTCOM and the other intelligence, surveillance and reconnaissance agencies monitoring the area, along with Shadow Corps' topographical layout of the region, made it relatively easy to destroy most of the military sites. The Syrian battle groups were a little harder to deal with in the first few hours of our multiple, rapidly-moving fronts. But their disorientation and their inferior Soviet-era armaments couldn't stand up to the firepower of our Comanches and Apache Longbows. Disabling the remnants of the Syrian Air Force before they could scramble to a coherent defense only made it easier. They won't be able to offer any sustained resistance once the main forces of our allies invade the land."

"And how have your men performed with the special armaments they were issued?"

"Better than expected, sir," he replied, resting his hand on the wooden hilt of a gladius-style sword strapped to the belt of his bandolier. "We used EMP charges on several strongholds to give us close quarter practice with our CT-20 blades and crossbows. Our mounted units were especially impressive when they came under fire."

"Any KIA or fratricied incidents within your ranks?"

"Negative, sir.

"Excellent, commander," Alchemy remarked. "Make sure your men are properly debriefed on the secrecy protocol for this mission during the evacs to Macedonia and Italy."

"Roger that, sir."

"The Alpha Corps' Red Horse Units have performed to all my expectations, Commander Kane. I salute you."

"Aye, sir," he barked. "Kane out."

Alchemy pressed the button on the panel to his right, extinguishing the image projected in front of them. "Gentlemen," he said, scanning the faces around the table, "it looks as though the next phase of our campaign for the restructuring of the Middle East is well in hand."

A round of applause erupted in the room as Alchemy basked in the glow of his success.

Chapter Twenty-six

Alchemy motioned graciously in an appeal for quiet. The applause eventually faded at his request, allowing order to be restored to the room once more.

Prime Minister Wessex was the first to speak, leaning forward beside Shamur to look at Alchemy. "First of all let me say that it is a pleasure to meet with you face-to-face again," he said. "Your presence, as I remember it to be the first time we met, is the very essence of inspiration. But I do have one question about the theater of operations in Lebanon."

Alchemy nodded with a knowing smile. "The sword and horse-mounted legions?"

"Yes," he replied, careful to keep his tone respectful. "Such means of war are considerably outdated for our present age, are they not?"

"We live in a world of Trojan horses, logic bombs and computer mercs with zombie mainframes that can wreak havoc on our CNO technologies almost at will, Mr. Prime Minister," Alchemy answered. "Total reliance on computers and technological advances will prove to be the paper shields of the foolish. As Commander Kane and his Red Horse Units have shown, EMP charges can render much of the technology of any army useless. But those who are skilled in the arts of both the Ancient World and the new will be the ones left standing when the smoke clears. For there may come a day when we will have to literally beat our plowshares into swords to make peace when the age of *magick* dawns upon this world again."

The leaders around the table looked back and forth at one another, chattering in hushed tones of amazement at the boldness of Alchemy's tactics.

Alchemy cut his eyes to his immediate left, garnering the attention of the Israeli leader, his voice immediately quieting the other leaders as he spoke. "Mr. Prime Minister, I would like to continue along this line of discussion to address the concerns that I know you have now that Lebanon, as we knew it, has passed into history."

The youthful, dark-haired leader's stare of enchantment didn't waver as he nodded his head in agreement with Alchemy's insight. "Though I fear a considerable amount of backlash from the invasion of Lebanon," he said, "I still support both you and the Omega Group wholeheartedly. With your help, I know we will be able to weather the storm to come."

Alchemy responded with a crooked grin. "I'm afraid, Mr. Prime Minister, that the backlash will be far greater than you and many of your peers here anticipate," he noted. "Once the world finds out that a supposed American force invaded Lebanon with help from your nation, other hardliner nations in the region will cry out for the blood of your people like never before. But fear not. We will bring *order out of chaos.*"

Shamur glanced over at Abydos, but quickly turned his attention back to Alchemy as the thick-faced Egyptian gave him a cold stare. "I know there are great threats on the horizon," he said, "but I have every confidence that you will help bring us real peace."

Prime Minister Wessex leaned forward beside Shamur again. "I think I can speak for everyone gathered here, Mr. Prime Minister," he said crisply, "in that not only will you have the support and protection of the European Military Union, but that of the entire coalition force in the Middle East. And I'm sure that same sentiment will be offered by our allies in the Arab League."

Wessex peered over at Abydos and Al-Saud. Both nodded hesitantly.

Alchemy took note of the reactions from Abydos and the Arabian King. "We are in this together, gentlemen," he interjected. "We

284

all know that it is a great risk for the both of you to be involved in this campaign. The history of antagonism between Israel and the Arab world needs little elaboration for those of us who are gathered here today. But it is only by the boldness of your combined participation that the current world system will be changed…and we have started that change right here in this valley."

"Do not think that I am unappreciative of being a part of this alliance," Abydos replied. "But I do have other concerns than just that of the plight of Israel. Iraq and Syria have already become state satellites of the Omega Group and its allies among the International Bankers. And it is only because the terrorist factions in Lebanon posed a threat to the other nations of the Arab League, like Iraq and Syria did in the past, that I pledged my support to this brinkmanship phase of Operation Assyria. But what assurances do you offer us that OPEC and the members of the Arab League will maintain a balance of power with the coalition forces once they gain even more control of the Levant land bridge? The U.N. has already allowed Europe and the other Jewish capitalists of the United States to control the world's second largest oil reserve in Iraq thanks to the success of Operation Assyria's first phase, not to mention the water supplies of the Tigris and Euprhates rivers."

Alchemy nodded like a patient statesman. "I understand your reservations, Mr. President," he said. "But look at how Iraq has progressed since the first phase of Operation Assyria. Take Al-Hillah, the city we have all come to know as the new Babylon, for instance. It has become one of the Middle East's most prominent cities, expanding to greater heights with new construction every day. And need I remind you of the mutual cooperation that we have all enjoyed already in this valley experiment? Our success is your success. But future success, especially in the coming days of transition, depends greatly on the unified commitment of you and your friends in the Arab League, Mr. President."

Alchemy cast his gaze around the table. "That goes for all who are gathered here."

"I agree," the King of Spain said, leaning into Alchemy's view. "I have seen the tremendous inner workings of this town.

The technology of the A-6 Mark has made this community one vibrant body. But I am curious about something that I saw among the townspeople?"

Alchemy nodded with another insightful smile. "The visual marks?"

"Yes," Varela answered. "What are they?"

"You're not familiar with that bright and shining serpent of old? That winged Nehushtan who heals the chosen ones as they are led out of the wilderness of this world? The great Seraph himself?"

"I am more than familiar with the histories of other similar images," the king answered. "But what is the purpose?"

"They serve as visual identification in case the computer network operation systems that link the nanochips suffer an electromagnetic or cyber attack. The ink cannot be removed, and there is a secret three-digit nanite numerical code incorporated into the visual marks so that they can't be reproduced outside of the valley. A code which can only be deciphered by a special black light that scientists working for the group developed especially for this project."

Alchemy paused for a second before continuing, knotting his fingers together as his elbows rested on the armrests of the throne. "From the daily reports I have been receiving on Project Palladium, and from what you have no doubt learned first-hand, it would appear that the townspeople have embraced the marks. The marks, along with the spiritual conditioning provided by the group in conjunction with our Masonic brethren, have unified the townspeople. They have given them a sense of purpose above just collecting on the prices they were promised for their homes and properties. A unity surpassing the original brotherhood of the Masonic Order first established in this town over a hundred years ago. And this is exactly what we had predicted would grow out of our overall control of their society."

There was a brief moment of silence around the table as the leaders looked around at one another, most nodding their heads in seeming agreement.

"Tell us more about the implications this mark will have on the world's economic systems," Kober interjected, leaning forward.

"Gradualism, as perfected by the Roman General Quintus Fabius Maximus, will soon reach its synthesis in all its varying forms of usury lending and land grabbing," Alchemy told him. "Only the beasts with teeth of intrinsic value will emerge victorious atop the heaps of ruin. The roars of the rest will prove to be nothing more than that of paper tigers meant to be mastered. And when this comes about, it is then that the Ancient World will inherit the *Palladium Torch* of societal leadership once more, with the A-6 Mark serving as the birthroot of the Great Tree that will shadow all nations."

"The strategy for the passing of the torch has been perfect in its execution over the last few years," Wessex noted. "But how long can the experiment in this valley continue before it is exposed by one of the enemies of our grand campaign."

"You need not worry, Mr. Prime Minister," Alchemy answered. "This was all done with the tightest of security to prevent exposure by the few enemies that we have.... Nicholas Forrestal being one of the greatest threats we've encountered so far."

"Yes," Wessex replied. "I know this man of whom you speak. He's a newly-crowned media baron."

"To put it mildly," Alchemy replied. "His father, a one-time ally of ours who passed away in a most unfortunate manner earlier this year, made the mistake of leaving his newspaper conglomerate to this maverick son of his. And he's been using the power of his father's paper to investigate some of the group's subsidiary companies and their private projects. The NGO's of our allies in this country have been his primary targets for the last six months. He's hounded Book&Snake, Skull&Bones, the Council for National Policy, and the Carlyle Group. He's even been so bold as to investigate Jupiter Island. However, though he is dogged in his conspiracy witch hunt, he still remains in the dark about where the true power base lies...and we have taken measures to ensure that he never finds out."

There was a brief pause of silence among the leaders, each taking the time to digest what had been discussed.

The British prime minister was the first to speak, shaking his head as he looked at Alchemy. "It sounds as though all the bases are covered," said Wessex. "But can this project continue without eventually drawing some sort of outside attention?"

"You seem to be the conscience of concern for everyone here, Mr. Prime Minister."

Wessex leaned back in his chair with a grin as the other European leaders laughed softly at the remark.

"But you're right, though," Alchemy said. "If the project continued here in this valley much longer it would definitely run the risk of exposure. That's why everyone involved with this project is being reassigned to another secluded province in Canada for the next stage of the experiment."

"When will the move take place?" Wessex prodded.

"Each citizen of Tower Valley will be moved out of this town one week from today," he answered. "The town will then be gutted and destroyed. And neither a single fingerprint nor a traceable paper trail will be left behind to incriminate the group."

Sodom listened to the leaders as they continued their conference for a while longer, remaining perched on the high back of the granite throne.

Ushers were finally called into the room to escort the leaders to a small fleet of limousines waiting for them in the courthouse square below.

Alchemy and Simon stood near the large doorway on the other end of the conference room, *striking* hands with the Israeli prime minister first as he exited the room, the other leaders following.

Alchemy and Simon turned toward the other end of the room as the doors locked behind the leaders. The winged mountain of scarlet muscle standing on top of Tsavo's granite throne was visible to them both.

"You have done well, anointed one," Sodom remarked to Alchemy.

"The stage is set," Alchemy replied.

"All of Dragylon will praise you when I present my report."

Sodom shot backward in a windswept blur of wings with that final word of praise, sifting through the glass wall in an eager flight toward Dragylon's golden belly.

Chapter Twenty-seven

Scriptos was posted high above the city of Venice, squatting on the ledge of an ancient column towering high into the star-strewn sky at the city's famous Bacino entranceway of the Piazza San Marco; an arid harbor once used by diplomats of old during the Renaissance when crossing the vast lagoon separating San Marco from the baroque island of San Giorgio Maggiore. A stone statue of a winged lion lurked behind him on the column's squared crown, its fanged mouth fixed in an open snarl just above his head from where he was balanced.

The city the lion statue stood guard over was renowned for many other similar statues. Preaching lions adorned St. Mark's Basilica at the other end of the piazza's rectangular street of arched balconies and the column-lined walkways of the Doge's Palace. The city was practically overrun with lions.

Scriptos wrapped his thick arms around his knees as the train of his royal blue coat swayed gently in the breezes sweeping up from the gondola harbor below. He watched the crowds below stroll back and forth beneath the piazza's wrought iron lamp-posts, migrating with soft revelry from the yellow tables of one campanile cafe` to another. Their laughter and words of desire filled the air, mixing with the intoxicating aromas of wine and Venetian-flavored delicacies flowing through the loggia arches of the Doge's Palace where an elaborate masquerade ball was taking place to celebrate Halloween.

Scriptos slowly turned his attention to the landing steps at the edge of the piazza's harbor entranceway. As he did, he saw a sleekly built man in a pale-colored suit emerging from one of the many gondola boats tied to the harbor's mooring posts, his head covered with a brown, safari-style hat like those worn by British officers stationed in Africa in the late 19th century. His face was covered in a black and gold masque of Venetian design, shaped like the veneer of a wolf.

A harbor breeze, casting an old and familiar scent across Scriptos' face, drew his attention to the man. He watched him negotiate the moss-covered landing steps with an unnatural grace, his right hand clinging powerfully to the thick strap of a long case hanging over his shoulder. The scent seemed impossible to be true since he knew there was only one other abomination who still had a living connection to that particular bloodline. It could be an ungodly mixture of the vampire demoniacs of old, he thought. These were men and women endowed with great powers through generational possession by demons; an elite number organized into powerful covens at the onset of the Dark Ages.

He noticed how the man appeared to move of his own accord, though, instead of on the strings of another power he couldn't readily detect within him. But the traveler's senses were as sharp as a wolf on the run it seemed as he looked back over his shoulder in a wary manner, quickly turning his concern upward as if he could see the sporadic patrols of fallen angels winging back and forth over the many steeples, domes and lion-crowned columns and gables of the floating city.

Scriptos turned his head to the right as the dark traveler walked into the piazza guardedly, wondering what he was running from. His attention was drawn to a layer of fog drifting across the lagoon separating San Marco from San Giorgio Maggiore. The fog was thick, appearing out of nowhere as it rolled against the facades of Maggiore's ancient structures, eclipsing the demigod saints standing on the arches and gables of its fabled cloisters. The moon started to turn blood red for a moment as the fog passed in front of a steeple-crowned bell tower near Maggiore's waterfront, casting a forbidding glow on the lagoon as the fog's shroud rolled slowly across its surface.

A black gondola with polished fittings emerged through the fog from the direction of San Giorgio Maggiore, sifting through the lagoon's mist like a ghost ship from the past. A dark-skinned gondolier stood near the curved stern of the elongated craft, steering it with a pole-length paddle while another man sat in a plush seat in the middle of the narrow boat staring straight ahead at the Piazza San Marco.

The man in the middle of the boat rose slowly as the gondola neared the piazza's landing steps. He stood with perfect balance against the boat's forward motion. He was arrayed in blue jeans and a leather, knee-length coat that had an arced collar and rolled back lapels of shearling fabric, with a thin layer of powdery sand clinging to the weather-beaten wrinkles of its sleeves. A head scarf of smooth camel's-hair masked his face in a hood-like fashion, its thick folds tucked beneath the rolled back lapels of his coat.

The man in the middle stepped out of the gondola when it pulled up next to a mooring post, the lagoon's water splashing against the heels of his hiking boots as he touched down on the harbor's moss-covered landing steps. The grandeur of the Piazza San Marco opened before him in all its pagan majesty when he reached the top of the steps. The Doge's Palace and its loggia balcony of limestone-colored arches loomed to the right of him, with a baroque bell tower rising high into the air to his left on the other side of the piazza's campo of red pavement. Wrought iron lampposts stood like sentries throughout the piazza, with only a moderate number of pedestrians moving back and forth between them and the Bacino entranceway's two famous columns.

His distant pursuit of the dark traveler had spanned two continents and several bodies of water, starting from Egypt's famous port city of Alexandria where an artifact of apocalyptic design predating the Antediluvian World had been stolen from the secret hypogeum tomb of Alexander the Great.

The hooded man picked up his pace when he spotted the dark traveler weaving through the small crowds of people, heading toward the famous corner arch near the Porta della Carta entrance of the Doge's Palace where a Gothic and sinuous portrayal of the *Judgment of Solomon* was carved into its angle,

293

depicting the king on his throne as two women stood by while a military executioner was holding a baby by its hair in one hand and an *invisible* sword in the other.

The hooded man stopped suddenly in his pursuit, halting near the base of the right-side column of the piazza's arid entranceway. He lifted his head, sensing the presence of a hidden purity, his masked gaze trailing up the surface of the column. A colossal figure dressed in royal-blue garments burned into view on the column's flat capital, perched on top like a hawk as vaporous streams of silver light seeped from the smooth sockets of his burnished face. He stared at the Book Master as a patrol of rebel hosts flew across the night's jeweled sky high above the column's winged lion, unaware that their glorious city had been infiltrated.

Scriptos dropped from the top of the column as the rebels flew by above him, the train of his coat flapping over his head.

The hooded man was unafraid as the angelic figure landed in front of the column's fenced off foundation and started walking toward him, stepping into the light of one of the piazza's wrought iron lampposts, his head reaching close to one of its polygonal lanterns, face and eyes shining even brighter in its glow.

Scriptos peered through the shadowy veil of the man's camel's-hair hood to see a youthful face with an aged stare of subdued brightness. "You are needed most urgently, great prince," he said to the man. "A son of *The Way* has fallen into darkness...."

The hooded man's rigid focus softened at the unexpected news, glancing around the tall Book Master to see the dark traveler disappear into the shadows of the loggia archways of the Doge's Palace.

He looked back up into Scriptos' bright face, turning his attention fully to the grim tidings. "Tell me what has happened," he said, knowing that the dark conspiracy of the traveler and his handlers would not alter the course of the future.

Chapter Twenty-eight

Sodom knelt before Lucifer's throne on the top step of Dragylon's diamond mound, head bowed low, his false wings bending forward in front of him, their prickly tips resting flat at the master's cleft feet.

Bastion stood on the top step several feet away from the Shadow King. He pounded the step with the golden sphere on the bottom of the Imperial Standard's black-scaled pole he was holding. "You may address the master with your report, Sodom."

Sodom lifted his head, eyes swelling with silent desire as they fell upon the master's translucent face of gold.

Lucifer leaned forward in his black throne, his fang-shaped irises flashing with golden light as he spoke. "You have news for me?"

Sodom drew back some from the master's leaning presence. "The conference was a success, my lord," he answered. "The dust leaders were greatly impressed by Project Palladium and the current phase of Operation Assyria unfolding in Lebanon. The stage is set. You may put your blockade in motion, great one."

Lucifer reclined in his throne with a diamond-filled smirk, his star-shaped pupils ever in motion as all eighteen of them spun slowly in retrograde patterns. "The blockade of the Parade Route in the Outer Realm was set by the Dominium Gate Masters long ago, Sullier," he said snidely. "And it will take more than that to prevent the Ascension of the Church. But this is not your concern.... Return to your town below, and see to your remaining duties there."

"I will not fail you, my lord," Sodom vowed.

"See to it that you don't," he hissed. "And make sure your warriors are aware of the seriousness of protecting this town over the next week. If the enemy can penetrate your defenses with one, then they can penetrate with many."

Sodom paused, his gaze falling. "I was told, my lord," he said, "that the champion had been taken care of."

"The problem has been handled," Lucifer replied coldly. "But when you think you're at your strongest, it is then that sudden destruction comes. Beware."

"Yes, my lord."

"Go, then," Lucifer waved. "Make straight the way for the kingdom of my anointed one."

Sodom stood, bowing at the waist before shooting backward in flight, wings exploding wide. He spun around and soared over the assembled court below, calling to his elite twenty-four when he passed over the golden mountain range. The warriors he singled out shot up from the tops of the emerald trees on the mountain and followed him out of the fortress.

Bastion turned and stepped in front of the throne, kneeling to one knee before Lucifer. "What are your orders, my lord?"

"Pergamos," he answered. "Set a course for Pergamos."

Bastion stood back up and whirled around in a torrent of speed, leaping from the top of the diamond mound, holding the Imperial Standard out to the side while he glided toward the roof of the Imperial Library. He landed on a circular pilot balcony connected to the middle A-shaped frame of gold rising above the other golden frames segmented between the roof's black panels. He stood before an enormous, wheel-shaped mosaic that was carved into the golden frame. Silver icons of the Zodiac struck their poses against backgrounds of scale-shaped rubies, each segmented from one another by shimmering lines of blue feeding into a circular line that enclosed the wheel. Diamond stars were speckled throughout the Zodiac's blue, inner wheel, surrounding a jeweled depiction of the multi-named sun god riding in his *quadriga* chariot.

Bastion reached out with one of his black-nailed fingers, touching the Scorpio icon to program the desired trajectory into the wheel. The image glowed even brighter from his touch, causing the Zodiac's outer wheel of segmented icons to turn slowly around the stationary images at its center.

The outer wheel's motion sparked activity in the shadowy library beneath the vaulted roof, causing the flaming symbols hovering in the open circles of the countless stacked scrolls burn even brighter. The increased brightness of the flaming symbols continued the chain reaction, centralizing the movements of the devilish whispers spiriting back and forth between the rolled books. The dark shapes of sound dove into the aisle of crystalline water running through the middle of the library, creating nine whirlpools that activated the cosmic engines at Dragylon's core.

The whole of Dragylon shifted with thunder and an even brighter alchemized glow as the power of the Imperial Library and the cosmic engines beneath it struck the invisible mooring lines of the hovering fortress, lifting it to its programmed trajectory.

———⋯•⋯≡◇≡⋯•⋯———

Alchemy stood facing the glass wall of Tsavo's conference room in meditation, watching Dragylon's golden sphere fade away over the horizon where the sun was setting.

A rush of air pressed against his back suddenly. He turned to see Simon standing before him, his purple cape rustling to rest around the sides of his black cassock, its hem brushing the golden buckles of his Pilgrim-style shoes.

"Have the leaders arrived at the airport?" Alchemy asked.

"Yes, my lord," Simon answered, positioning the *Oracle of the Dragon Lord* in front of him with a quick bow of his head. "Mr. Specter confirmed their arrival at the group's private terminal thirty minutes ago. They should be in the air by now."

"And Mr. Shamur's plane?"

"My Magi are in place. They'll rig it to detonate after his stop in Rome. News of the incursion into Lebanon will have broken by then."

"And what about President Abydos and King Al-Suad?"

"We have operatives placed in the security details of both leaders. They'll carry out the assassinations simultaneously a week after Shamur's death. The timing will be perfect. We can make it look as though the Duvdevan Units of the IDF carried out the assassinations of the two leaders in response to Shamur's death."

"And our allies from Europe?"

"My Magi will take them out once they have given their independent reports of what they have seen here in this valley to our supporters in Brussels and our other allies among the International Bankers. They will make their assassinations look like the work of Arab terrorists as a response to the assassinations of Abydos and Al-Saud. It will serve as excellent propaganda for our allies as they invade Lebanon from Syria and maintain control of both countries in the midst of the chaos. All as you have planned, great king."

"Good," Alchemy said softly. "The counter response of the remaining hardliners in the fractured Arab League and its allies will pose just the right threat to Israel."

Simon bowed his head slightly, mulling over the ultimate consequences of their actions prophesied in the Scriptures of their enemy. "Lebanon, like Syria and Iraq, will be difficult to control in the beginning," he said respectfully, lifting his head. "We could bypass it for now, and possibly even change prophecy as a result."

"No," Alchemy insisted. "Lebanon is crucial in controlling the Levant land bridge and its ports along the shores of the Mediterranean. Plus, there are things we must allow if we are to achieve our ultimate ends. We must play along with the grand scale set before us. We must plow our hope in the obscure as we wage our war for the universe. Details, Magi…. The *Devil* is always in the details."

"But what about the prophecy of Egypt's greater empire to come, my lord?"

Alchemy shook his head dismissively. "Though the empire of the south may span to the Horn of Africa in days to come, I assure you by the vow of Holy Writ itself that Egypt and its forces will not prevail against me. I will establish a new dynasty in Egypt just as the Assyrians of old did when they dispossessed the royal families of Egypt after the rule of Jacob's beloved son Joseph. But I will not make the same mistakes as the Assyrian Pharaohs did when they allowed the Hebrew slaves to become their masters. I will slay their prophets and lead them astray. I will show them wonders greater than the plagues that Moses struck Egypt with. I will be as God, and the Simonian Beast to come will be my prophet."

The sorcerer stood in silent amazement at Alchemy's ability to navigate the prophetic Scriptures of their enemy.

Alchemy paused for a moment, still dwelling on his designs for Israel. "Now," he said, "what about Project Samson? Are our containment contingencies in place?"

"Our operatives in the Knesset's foreign affairs and defense committees have assured us that all nuclear options at Dimona will be secured in the wake of Shamur's assassination and the world's reaction to the fall of Lebanon and the Syrian factions that retreated to that region when Damascus fell."

Alchemy nodded his approval at the sorcerer's assurance.

"I do have one other piece of news for you, my lord."

"The bloodline confirmation?" he replied, reading the sorcerer's thoughts that were psychically discernable to him at will through the Dragon Lord's alchemized blood that linked him to the power flowing through the staff in Simon's hand.

"Yes, my lord," he answered. "The Presidential Attaché to Europe's Idumaean Council of Princes has confirmed your Danite descendancy that was captively integrated into the Assyrian Empire during the reign of Tiglath Pileser III. You will have the official endorsement of the Illuminati to be the military and political governor of the capital cities of Babylon and Tyre in the restructured Levant land bridge. But they refuse to give you Godfrey de Bouillon's crusader title as *King of the Jews* until you reveal the full depth of your origins to them. They want to know if you're real, or if you're some sort of elaborate hoax being perpetrated on them by one of the other elite orders in a power play to upset the current balance of rule. They want to know if you're the one that was prophesied to come."

Alchemy sneered at the demands of his future vassals. "The Illuminati are nothing more than a *carcass* regime. Shells of their former glory," he remarked. "All those in places of power who have seen my face before the time of my public unveiling are dead. And those who aren't, soon will be."

Alchemy turned toward the sorcerer, his blue eyes burning with a hate tempered by the preparatory flames of the *well*. "These small men think they can manipulate me with their vast wealth of promised support for the A-6 Mark," he said sharply. "They have forgotten that their kingdoms belong to my father. And his delight is to give them to me."

A pressurized rush of air spewed through the air from the other end of the room suddenly as Alchemy discussed the future.

Specter appeared in the doorway of the conference room, waiting for permission to speak.

Alchemy focused on Specter as he stood across the room. "Yes, Mr. Specter?"

"The car is here to take you to the chateau for the evening, Mr. Alchemy."

"Thank you, Mr. Specter," he said, his fiery demeanor cooling. "I'll be down in a few moments."

"Yes, sir"

Specter hovered in the doorway. "I noticed that your P2 guard detail have left without you, your eminence," he said to the sorcerer. "Shall I inform the staff at the chateau that you will be prolonging your stay?"

"No," Simon answered. "I won't be staying."

Specter started to question how he would leave, but quickly thought better of it. "As you wish, your eminence. I will have a team from the Sentinel Corps escort you to the airport at your leisure."

"That won't be necessary, Mr. Specter."

Specter looked at him in confusion.

"Thank you, Mr. Specter," Alchemy interjected. "We will notify you if we have further need of your services."

"Yes, sir."

Specter turned and left the room, sealing the doors behind him.

"You enjoy tormenting his intellect, don't you?" Alchemy remarked.

"There's great power in torment, my lord," he answered. "I have learned that lesson well during my mastery of the Harness Magi."

"Yes, I'm sure you did," Alchemy mused.

Alchemy paused for a moment before speaking again. "Tell me something, Magi," he said with a sly grin. "You have protected the *Covenant Harness* for a great deal of time, correct?"

"Of course, my lord," he answered, his brow crinkling with question.

"Yes, of course…then tell me, how is it that others fell prey to the allure of the armor of promise, and not you? Surely it graced your head and shoulders at least once in all the years it has been in your possession?"

Simon turned to the side and quickly dropped to his knees before Alchemy. "Never, my lord!" he declared, laying his staff at Alchemy's feet.

"Are you sure?"

"I speak the truth, my lord."

Alchemy held a suspicious look with a certain gleam of playfulness.

Simon stood up again with a slow reverence. "I know my place in the scheme of things, my lord," he continued. "Every two hundred years the stewardship of the *Covenant Harness* and the *Oracle of the Dragon Lord* are passed to the next in line. And when the time comes for the final Simonian Magi Master to *come up out of the Earth* to claim what is his, I will humbly fade away as one of the flowers of the field, awaiting my resurrection at your triumph with my other brethren who've gone before me."

"Rest easy, my loyal Magi," he said. "I believe you."

"Then why the scrutiny, my lord?"

Alchemy cracked a wicked smile. "Why not? 'There's great power in torment.'"

Simon stared momentarily as Alchemy hit him with his own words. He bowed his head with a chuckling breath. "As always, my lord, your are the mate to my check."

"But victory is never achieved without the combination of the two."

"Indeed, my lord…. Indeed."

Simon took a couple of steps back toward Tsavo's granite throne. "I must tend to our next move, then, if we are to have that victory, my lord."

"With all haste, Magi. Make straight the way for my kingdom."

Simon grinned with an evil pride, stretching out the left side of his cape. He pounded the floor with the golden sphere of his staff, expelling three demonic shadows. They swirled around him like black smoke from the mouths of the lion and the two-headed dragon posted on top of the *Oracle*. He snapped his cape in front of him as serpentine shadows swirled around him in a quick wind from head to toe, disappearing a second later as the spinning shapes exploded outward in flakes of frigid light.

Alchemy started to turn back to the glass wall after the sorcerer disappeared from the room, only to have a small gleam of light catch the corner of his eye, giving him reason to pause. He walked over to the room's right side wall where the life size statues were lined up, drawn to the gilded skeleton positioned near the corner as one of the Dragon Lord's ancient memories seized his thoughts.

Alchemy stared at the skeleton's elaborate helmet, peeking into the large and protruding eye holes of its rounded face mask. His gaze eventually roamed to the left side of the bronze-colored helmet where the golden emblem of the fierce lion's head was etched into the metal, its inanimate jaws clenching a ring of keys leading to death and punishment.

The sight of the Christaloy emblem invoked a sudden and hateful response from him. "So bold looking," he said, staring into the lion's emerald eyes. "But are you bold enough to face me at the end as the chiefs of old did when they went sword to sword in the middle of the field? Will you dare such conflict when we meet?"

Alchemy nodded his head proudly. "Yes…yes you will. And I will be ready. That is, of course, if I haven't defeated you before then."

A rush of air blew open the closed doorway at the other end of the room while Alchemy boasted, exploding against the glass wall with a frigid blast, the heavy drapes in the corners whipping around wildly from the impact.

Alchemy snapped his head toward the wall of frozen glass. He took a step back as an invisible hand, one that even he could not render into focus, began to write along the frozen surface. A familiar curse in ancient Aramaic was scrawled out before him, almost paralyzing the rhythm of his proud heart as he read it.

MENE,
MENE, TEKEL.
GOD HAS NUMBERED YOUR
KINGDOM AND FINISHED IT; YOU HAVE
BEEN WEIGHED IN THE BALANCES, AND FOUND WANTING.

303

Chapter Twenty-nine

Night shrouded the sky over Tower Valley. Beneath it, standing in a curved section of the valley's southern road several miles from the town limits, was a lone figure dressed in blue jeans and a knee-length coat of dark leather. His face and head were masked by the heavy folds of a camel's-hair scarf draped over his head like a hood.

His masked gaze was set on the distant clock tower, its ornate belfry rising high above the pines, reflecting the glow of a large Hunter's moon. But he saw much more than just the tower. He could see a small, but formidable, band of falsely-winged rebels circling the starry scape above the ancient landmark, with one standing above them on the tower's obelisk.

Having surveyed the visible strengths of the enemy, he then turned and started down the steep slope on the right side of the road, vanishing into the wooded foothills of the eastern mount before drawing any attention from the rebel eyes circling the clock tower.

April cradled Magnus' head in her lap, the moonlight showering them both as it fell through the balcony's window. She watched him struggle in his sleep, dabbing at the wounds on his neck that continued to bubble up with the black liquid. She had already accumulated a small pile of stained towels, doing what she could to stop the strange bleeding. Her one good hand had grown tired from keeping the pressure on his wounds. She'd had very little sleep in the last day or so. It all seemed hopeless.

Magnus hadn't woken up once the entire day. His fever only seemed to worsen with each passing moment.

April leaned back against the wall exhausted, grabbing another fresh towel from a stack she had made beside her She pressed it gently against his forehead, stroking the sides of his face. "So handsome," she whispered, setting the towel back down on the floor.

She stroked his wet hair back away from his face, fingers sliding gently along the contours of his cheeks. "Why did you help me?" she whispered, knowing he couldn't hear her. "You didn't even know me...."

She glanced around the moonlit balcony, fighting back relentless tears.

"Men like you aren't supposed to exist," she insisted, looking back down at him. "I can't make sense of anything any more...your abilities...your motives. Nothing."

April sighed softly, silently questioning the validity of everything she had seen and heard over the last few days. But the proof was overwhelming, unexplainable by contemporary means.

"Your wife was a very lucky woman," she continued, gently stroking his head. "I imagine that's who you're dreaming about. I know you would probably never tell me, but you must have lost her to something tragic the way you're calling out to her. She must have been devoted to you.... I used to think it was a woman's duty to excel in this world no matter what the cost. 'Who cares about relationships,' I used to say. My career, along with bringing up my daughter in my own image, was all that mattered to me. Sure I had my flings with other men, but none of them meant anything to me. They were as full of themselves as I was...a perfect match at the time, I guess."

April pulled her legs up, lifting Magnus' head. "But you're different," she went on. "You risked your life for no reason. I insulted you. I called you a liar, but still you helped me. Heroes aren't supposed to be real. Don't you know that? They don't fit into this world any more."

She leaned down close to his face. "Thank you for everything you tried to do, Magnus," she whispered, her tears pelting his face as she kissed him softly on the forehead.

April glanced up at the hole Magnus had blasted in the roof the previous night, looking through the ceiling's crisscrossing beams at the stars visible through the jagged opening. "God, I have no clue what to say to…."

She stopped suddenly, burying her face into her one good hand.

A sudden pressure began to constrict a part of her spirit, urging her to forge ahead with her plea. She looked up through the hole again. "Why am I nervous?" she asked herself out loud, glancing at her trembling hand.

April looked at Magnus' face, remembering the passion that burned so brightly in his eyes. "I believe you…."

She placed her hand on his forehead to keep it from shaking as she looked back up through the hole again. "God,…may I talk to you?" she asked, pausing for a second as if she expected to hear an audible reply. "As a scientist, I have seen how life works inside and out…I came to the conclusion some time ago that life didn't just happen. But I let it go at that rather than pursue it. Magnus was right about me. I just didn't want to face it. To consider your existence in any form would have been fatal to my career…."

April stopped for a second, huffing with a look of frustration. "I know nothing about you," she continued. "I have never read the Bible. Sure, I've heard the basics like most people, but that was as far as I ever went with it. I have always despised those people who used to give out those religious tracts at airports years ago. I didn't like my explanations for the origins of life being questioned by someone who probably just barely graduated from high school."

She stopped again, biting on her lower lip. "I don't understand all that Magnus is," she continued. "I doubt there are any more like him. But he talks like a few Christians I have encountered before. And as strange as this sounds, I believe him…. I do."

"I have seen a lot of fake people in my life," she replied, "and I'm one of them. But Magnus is right. You can't fake the truth.

And I believe he's telling me the truth. And there's something else." The tears started to flow again as she tugged at her white blouse. "There's something pulling at me. I can't explain it. I have never talked like this before. I'm not sure how to make it audible."

She bowed her head. "I don't want to be alone any more," she said in a sobbing voice. "I want to be forgiven of my sins. I don't want to die. I want what he has, God. I believe Jesus died for my sins. I believe he rose again. I want to know you the way Magnus does. Please forgive me."

"Fear not," said a voice in front of her.

April jerked her head up with a look of surprise, gasping at the sight of a hooded man standing in the shaft of moonlight shining down through the hole in the roof, thin streams of smoke rolling off the shoulders of his long coat.

April stretched her good arm across Magnus' chest in an attempt to protect him from any more harm. "Who are you?" she asked in a trembling voice. "What do you want?"

"I am one of Magnus' friends," he answered, pulling back his camel's-hair hood to reveal a youthful face with a black beard and a head of wavy hair, his blue eyes tinted with faint rays of gold and diamond light. "I have come to help."

"Are you an angel?"

"I have come to help…that's all that matters right now."

"Can you tell me how to know Jesus like Magnus does?"

The youthful man walked over and squatted in front of her. "I tell you a mystery. Election determines conformity to Christ. But know this more simply. The Lamb of God, the Living One, has forgiven you of all your sins. It is a gift first pledged in eternity past, which was to be granted and realized only at the appointed time, April."

Her eyes swelled with great surprise. "How did you know my name?"

His silent smile was more than enough of an answer.

April stared at him with tears in her eyes, not understanding who he really was. But that didn't matter. She had heard the truth and sincerity in the power of his words. It was the same truth and sincerity she had heard and seen from Magnus, and that was all that mattered. She had been equipped from on high to ask for forgiveness of her sins without even knowing it, the chains of her pride and arrogance which had held her captive for so long having been shattered in that simple moment when she struggled to find the right words to say.

"What now?" she asked sheepishly.

"Do you believe that the Lord Jesus has saved you, and that he has forgiven you of all your sins?"

"Yes…yes, I do. I don't know how I know that, but I do."

"It's not a magic trick, April. Salvation does not come by singing a hymn or the pricked emotions of an altar call. No one *can* come to the Lord unless the Father, through the working of his Holy Spirit, draws them," he noted. "He was the tugging that you felt earlier. And he is with you now, forever your seal for the Day of Redemption. Remember that, you beloved daughter of *The Way*."

April wiped the tears from her eyes with a thankful nod.

He glanced down at Magnus as he lay in April's lap. "There is much more I would like to tell you," he said, looking back up, "but our time is short."

The stranger reached out to touch April's broken arm. April wasn't sure what was happening, but she began to feel a surge of energy pass from his gentle hand and into her arm, the pain of her broken bones and her other smaller injuries disappearing instantly.

April inhaled deeply when he removed his hand. She pulled her arm from the sling Magnus had made for her, extending it back and forth with a look of utter amazement. She touched the top of her head where a large knot used to be. Even the pain in her feet was gone.

"Is this real?"

"Yes," he answered. "But do not confuse the mercy of God with the acts of those false prophets who parade around on that device you call a television."

She gave a half smile at his comment.

"Time is short," he repeated. "Help me get him to his knees."

They both grabbed Magnus beneath his shapely arms, pulling him to his knees beneath the arched window.

The youthful man held him steady by his shoulders, the champion's head falling backwards in April's hands.

"Is he going to be okay?" she asked wistfully.

"Yes, but I need some time alone with him."

April appeared reluctant to relinquish her care of him, peeling back the wet strands of hair stuck to the sides of his fever-ridden face like before. "You're going to be okay," she said in a hushing voice, kissing him softly on the forehead again.

She looked back at the youthful man as he waited patiently, lowering Magnus' head the rest of the way. "I'll be outside," she told him.

She walked to the balcony's stairwell, hesitating at the top step.

"I'll take care of him," he assured her.

"I know," she said with a smile.

April turned and walked down into the shadows of the stairwell.

The stranger turned his attention to Magnus once more, gripping his shoulders tighter. "Magnus," he said, his voice altering into a soft echo of another dialect." Wake up. The darkness cannot last forever."

Magnus' eyes fluttered with more activity than before as the man's familiar voice penetrated his mind with a strange power, echoing across the reaches of his dreamworld.

"That's it," the man replied, watching the activity of the champion's closed eyelids. "Wake up...."

Magnus started to lift his head as the voice got louder in his mind, its power pulling him away from the ceaseless images of his wife being dragged into a false Hell.

"I command you in the name of the Lord.... Wake up!"

Magnus lifted his head fully, eyes opening slowly as his mind finally broke free of his captive dreams. His vision was blurred with sweat and tears. He could barely discern the outline of the figure standing over him. "Who's there?" he asked weakly.

"One who is a friend to all the beloved sons of *The Way*," the man answered.

A certain familiarity rose up through the Paradisal texture of the man's voice, defying the bonds of time and separation.

Magnus tried to focus harder on the blurred figure before him, unsure if the voice he was hearing was real. "M…Michael?"

"Yes, brave one. It is I."

"Michael!" he cried out in exhaustion, embracing him around the tops of his hiking boots with all the strength he could muster with those confirming words of endearment.

"Do not fall at my feet, Magnus. Rise," he said, touching him on the head to give him enough strength to comply to his command.

Magnus struggled for his breath, looking back up in his weakened state with a clearer vision. "Please tell me that I'm not still dreaming," he pleaded, the fever in his mind causing him to teeter with uncertainty at the Archangel's unfamiliar appearance.

"You are not dreaming," he told him. "I am Michael, one of the seven spirits who stands before the throne of the Living God, a servant of the Lord Jesus, the risen Christ…. Hear me with quick submission, for the shadow of things to come surrounds us."

Magnus struggled against the fever in his mind. "The shadow of things to come?"

Michael shook his head. "We both hear the *snorting of the swift horses* from the Serpent Tribe of Dan. But the *sunteleia* consummation and the *telos* reckoning is not yet."

Magnus grabbed Michael's arm with a sudden urgency at the imagery of his words, eyes widening with tears. "I've lost her, Michael!" he said, his mouth quivering as the visions of his precious Rachel in torment flashed back into his mind.

"Lost who?"

"Rachel," Magnus gasped. "She's in torment! I have seen her. I don't understand, Michael! Please help me to understand!"

The Archangel stared straight into the champion's eyes, piercing his soul with the honesty of his gaze that flashed with bursts of blue and gold light. "Rachel is not in torment, Magnus," he said with confidence, his voice deep with ancient wisdom.

"The Lion of the Tribe of Judah holds the keys of Death and Hades."

"But the visions are so real," he said softly. "I can literally smell the brimstone of that torturous place."

"I know…Scriptos told me you were besieged by a crippling nightmare. But were the lie not convincing to the point of death, what use would it be to the enemy?"

Magnus stared at Michael's bright eyes. "I could hear the Lord's voice in my spirit as the nightmare played through my mind," he replied.

"What did he say?"

"He told me not to believe every spirit…. But it's difficult to rest in those words because the nightmare is so real. It plagues me no matter what the truth is."

"Show me where the enemy has wounded you."

Magnus turned his head to the left. "A power," he said, eyes jolting back and forth, "held me as if I were a child. He bit me like one of the vampire demoniacs of old. His strength…was incredible."

Michael inspected the two gaping holes on the right side of the champion's neck, with black, ring-shaped scabs bordering the outside of each wound.

He touched the top of Magnus' head, gently lowering it in front of him. "I will help you," he pledged. "By the grace of the Living One, I will help you."

Magnus closed his eyes with a sigh of relief, still trembling from the effects of the fever raging through his weakened body.

Michael touched him on the shoulders. Small plumes of fire danced from his fingertips, creating countless sparks along the fibers of his soiled coat and sweater. The leather and cotton fibers were instantly consumed by the sparks, withering off his arms and torso in flakes of ash.

After disposing of the champion's soiled coat and sweater, Michael brought his hands together in a large cup formation above Magnus' head, separating his palms as soon as they touched, letting a crystalline water pour from the empty space between them.

The water splashed wildly over Magnus' head, beads of light swishing back and forth in the sparkling water washing down over him. The scab rings of the two wounds on the back of his neck bubbled over with a black, fizzling foam as the water and the beads of light poured into the gaping holes, pulling the fever from the champion's body with its power.

The brilliant fall of healing water continued until all the fever had been extracted to the surface of the wounds, its black foam washing away by the force of the water and the beads of light mixed within it.

Magnus lifted his head as the last of the water rolled off his back, his freshly washed hair clinging loosely to the sides of his head. He stared up at the Archangel, eyes bright with a renewed strength. "It's gone," he said, bringing the fingertips of his hands to the sides of his temples, running them down the contours of his face. "The nightmare is gone."

"Rise," Michael commanded.

Magnus stood immediately, looking at his hands as he flexed his fingers back and forth, feeling the fullness of his Shekinah Strength coursing through him unhindered once more.

Magnus glanced around the balcony with a quick concern. "Where's April?"

"She went outside. But worry not. She is now alive more than she's ever been."

"Did you talk to her?"

"Yes…. She has been sealed for the Day of Redemption."

Magnus bowed his head. "Thank you, Father," he prayed, raising his head again. "And thank you."

"I did nothing but assure her of what had already been given the moment she repented."

"Of course."

Michael crossed his arms over his chest. "Now," he said, "tell me about this rebel who infected you with his poison."

Magnus' stare went blank almost immediately at the mention of the mysterious rebel.

"Magnus?"

The champion shook his head. "I'm sorry," he said. "My battle with him in the sewers still has me shaken up."

"Tell me about him."

Magnus looked at him with a sigh. "He's not like the others," he replied. "He holds a considerable place of rank amongst the enemy. Higher than any I have ever encountered before I would suspect."

"What does this rebel look like?" he asked.

"He's built like a mountain," said Magnus. "He is as black as the night itself. His hair is the purest color of gold. And his wings are as vicious as his wicked smile. He reminds me of another rebel that I encountered when I removed Rachel from that rood. His eyes of white fire and his shadowy movements fill me with a fear I haven't known since I was a boy. I think I've seen him in dreams and visions throughout the centuries as well. And I know he was there that night of the unholy nativity when Judas rose from the *well* of the Abyss."

Michael nodded. "Indeed, he is a most formidable foe," said the Archangel.

"Then you know of him?"

He paused for a moment before answering. "He's a ruthless assassin. He moves like a shadow across the face of the Earth. There is not a sphere of life on this planet that hasn't been touched by him. One of his main objectives has been to destroy the Shekinah Legacy, and all who were predestined to inherit it. His goal has been to destroy you and all that you love. Those in your life who were allowed to die a peaceful death, like your mother, are the only ones who have escaped his wrath toward you."

A glaze of deep pain resurfaced in Magnus' heart and eyes with that revelation. "My father and brother?" he replied in a breathlessly. "Rachel?!"

"Yes," he answered softly. "Herod and Titus were mere arrows in his quiver."

A mournful silence fell between them.

Magnus set his jaw, driving back the glaze of tears in his eyes. "You know who he is, don't you?"

Michael gave a nod of his head.

"Who is he, then?"

"The Holy Spirit restrains me from revealing any more knowledge about this particular adversary than is already known."

"But why?"

"You will know all that you need to know in the fullness of time, Magnus."

The champion turned and walked toward the back wall of the balcony, crossing his arms over his chest, his back muscles hardening wrathfully as he stood in the light of the window. "What is my mission here, Michael?"

"What has always been your mission from the start?"

Magnus shook his head. "It's hard to remember sometimes," he answered. "The ashes of the Dark Ages still hang heavily in my mind."

"Outward health and the firm station of form only mask the haggard and battle-worn spirit within...but such is the mantle that you are called to bear, Magnus. And now is not the season for lamentations. You must persevere."

Magnus turned around slowly, his expression one of pain and great desire.

Michael looked at him with a patient resolve as the champion's anguish spoke what his mouth could not. "I know this is not easy for you," he said. "But you have work to do...."

Scriptos told me all that has been transpiring in this valley. He said that the technology for Judas' mark has been perfected."

"Yes," Magnus said somberly. "April helped the Omega Group create a Quantum nanochip called the A-6 Mark. She told me that the group had started administering permanent marks on the skin of the townspeople to coincide with the placement of the implants as well."

"Then you already know your mission."

Magnus grew quiet as the Archangel stared at him with conviction, sensing the descent of a dreaded and familiar decree that had come so many times before through the Holy Spirit.

Michael took a step toward him, seeing the struggle in his eyes. "I come with a message from the Lord, Magnus," he said.

"You are to destroy the town in this valley. If it is to be Judas' model for stepping up the timetable, then there is no other option. This is not his time. The Zoa have not commanded him to go forth yet…. You must destroy them all."

"The whole town?"

"Everyone but the *Abominable Branch*, that is."

Magnus' countenance fell. The news couldn't have been any worse. He wanted to show mercy to anyone but Judas.

He spoke heavily, staring at the floor. "I have long desired for my tenure on Earth to come to an end before I was forced to act on this decree again."

"There is no other way, Magnus. Judas is trying to step up the timetable for his unveiling."

Michael stepped closer, his expression hardening. "Do not fear for the people of this town," he said in an attempt to comfort him. "They were branded with the *Ichabod* curse a long time ago from what I have learned. This town's cup of wickedness is full. The people have taken Judas' permanent mark of allegiance. The only result for such sin is the wrath of God. Wrath that is not to be masked in the Earth's fault lines as you have done in the past."

Magnus lifted his face again, speaking pleadingly. "It's not easy to bring such judgment on an entire town of people."

"Yes, but God's ministers of authority do not bear the sword in vain. And you must steel yourself against your emotions if you are to wield that sword properly. For the enemy is strong here in this valley. Their leader is a most potent foe from what I know of this part of the world, not to mention…."

"I know," said the champion, his tone growing cold. "The assassin."

"He is the most potent of them all," Michael warned.

Magnus' eyes started to glow vengefully. "Can I defeat him?"

"No…. But the Lord can."

Magnus turned his head in the direction of his war-cabinet sitting against the wall to his left. Though the Archangel had a more humbled appearance than when he first encountered him on the slopes of Mount Scopus, the power of his convicting gaze remained the same.

Michael gripped the champion's shoulders. "It's a trap that easily ensnares one in your position," he said, reading the hatred which had set into his face.

Magnus' focus on the war-cabinet was cold and indignant, the pride of his fleshly convictions for vengeance swelling around his heart like a cancer. "This assassin deserves the stoniest depths of the Abyss."

"In time he will inherit the dark abode," Michael reminded him. "But to defeat him in this battle, you must be focused. Remember…'Vengeance is mine, I will repay, saith the Lord.'"

Magnus searched the rafters above as if to escape the truth he already knew. His mother had taught him the dangers of personal vengeance a long time ago when he was a young and fatherless prince. But it was a lesson, with history as his antagonist, which had proven difficult to master.

"The feelings I have for Rachel still run deep," he said as he looked back at the bearded Archangel. "But I don't want those feelings to be a weakness. Tell me how to face him."

"Pray," he answered. "And after you have prayed, meditate upon all you have learned about the dream you had in the belly of that Roman slave galley."

"I don't understand."

"Bring me the pouch that Gabriel gave you on Patmos," he told him.

Magnus' stare narrowed. "I didn't bring it with me. It's in a vault I built beneath a hill in the Cotswolds of England."

"Check your trunk, Magnus…and bring me the tainted silver also."

Magnus hesitated for a second before turning and walking toward the back wall where his trunk was sitting, kneeling in front of it. He placed his hand on the trunk's treated wood, letting it slide down over the golden lock face designed in the form of a lion's veneer. His hand continued to slide down along trunk's gold trim, stopping on a rivet close to the floor. He pressed the round protrusion with his thumb, engaging a secret latch system which popped the lock face without the aid of a key. The trunk's lid started to open by the aid of mechanical hinges, creaking with a soulful invitation to the history that lay inside. The sweetest aroma of aged oil ascended through the opening, the moon's peripheral light casting a dense illumination on the trunk's contents. Inside were several sectioned levels lined with soft, cream-colored canvas. In the different sections lay beautifully-bound books of polished leather stacked on top of one another, each etched with different types of silver and gold lettering in many different languages, with a rare copy of *The Noble Lesson* holding a special place of prominence on top of one of the stacks. Vellum scrolls of Holy Writ and a folded document with signet seals of red clay were nestled between the stacks of rare books, with each parchment being vacuum sealed in sleeves of a hybrid polymer to protect against corruption.

In the middle of the trunk floor, between the levels of books and scrolls, was the old soft leather case given to him over a millennium ago. He wasn't really all that surprised to see it sitting there. Michael's words more than indicated that it had been placed there without his prior knowledge.

He stared at the *flagrum taxillatum* mark of the Roman whip master it used to belong to that was branded on the flap just above a gold button depicting Tiberius Caesar's profile. He had studied it many times in the past, always holding the case in his hands when he did to feel its weight, never once opening it, though, just as Gabriel had instructed. The desire to know what was inside had always been outweighed by the angel's firm decree. But he had an idea of what possibly lay inside, for he was more than familiar with such equipment.

Tucked beside it, in their usual places, was the copper scroll Gabriel had given him and the small leather pouch containing the thirty shekels of Tyrian silver Judas had been paid to betray the Master.

Magnus reached to the bottom of the trunk and picked up the *flagrum* case and the pouch of shekels. He held the silver in his left hand, taking note of their weight. They seemed heavier than when he last held them, as if the burden of one man's eternal guilt had literally possessed the pieces of silver over the centuries.

Magnus rose to his feet and walked back to where the Archangel was waiting. "I managed to keep these artifacts from falling into other hands over the centuries," he commented. "But I'm afraid I wasn't able to do the same with the *Dragaduceus* blade. I found out that someone had taken it from Og's tomb during the First Crusade. I spent hundreds of years looking for it, but I could never find it again."

Michael shook his head. "You did not fail in your duty concerning that wicked instrument of war," he replied. "It was I who removed the sword."

Magnus looked at him, astonished. "You took it?" he asked. "But why?"

"It was about to fall into the right hands at the wrong time," he answered. "I took it to Egypt and hid it in the secret hypogeum tomb of the Macedonian heir. Only the Watchers were to know of its new resting place. But now there are others who know. For it has been found once again."

"By who?"

"That doesn't matter right now," he said, reaching out for the pouch of shekels in Magnus' left hand. "The Lord will take care of it at the appointed time. We are to focus on the tasks that are currently set before us. For they are more than sufficient in their troubles."

"Indeed," said Magnus, placing the pouch of silver in the Archangel's outstretched hand.

Michael tucked the pouch of silver into the left pocket of his coat.

"What are you going to do with the silver?" Magnus asked him.

"What must be done," he answered. "But the case is for you. Open it."

"Open it?"

"Yes."

Magnus looked down at the case, its strap hanging down between his cradling hands. The command to open it was strange to hear after all the time that had passed, the years marked by Gabriel's decree to keep it sealed.

"Open it, Magnus."

Magnus touched the flap's leather string that was wrapped around the case's fastening toggle, its texture having the feel of hardened paint. His fingers trembled slightly as he started to peel the string back away from the gold button. The string fell to the side after he unwound it. He opened the flap and reached inside slowly, clutching three objects stacked on top of one another at the bottom.

The champion's emerald eyes filled with awe as he pulled out three iron spikes. He needed no one to tell him of their particular value. It was what he had suspected all along. The most precious Blood to ever course through a human vein stained the rough exterior of each spike, with the moonlight making it look as though they had each just been pulled from the wounds of a tortured body. Small symbols were cut deep into their squared sides, resembling the writings he had discovered in the tunnels beneath Jerusalem when he was retrieving the treasures of his inheritance almost two millenniums ago. The structuring of the symbols was arranged in what appeared to be the squared prose of Hebrew poetry, compressed into perfect form over the ages with stylus skill by the Blood itself it seemed.

He looked back up at the Archangel, confused. "What are these symbols?" he asked in wonder. "I can barely decipher their structure."

"They represent the name of God known only by the Almighty himself."

Magnus squeezed the spikes in his hand, flesh burning with memory as a trio of mallet-heavy thrusts nailed Perfection to a rugged tree, pitted iron grinding against princely bone. The mauled face of his Savior was shrouded in a planetary darkness, his thorn-scarred head teetering forward, pouring out its offering like a cup that had run over with the fullness of sin. But three days would pass as foretold. The Lord would rise in triumph after the setting of the sun on the eighteenth day of Nisan, only to descend into the bottomless pit in his resurrection body to proclaim his victory to the Nephilimite angels. He would appear to many for 40 days before ascending on high to the Father's right hand, taking his rightful seat in glory until all his enemies were made his footstool.

Magnus shook his head. "I can't take these," he said, his voice almost a tremor as he extended the spikes toward Michael.

Michael took Magnus' hand and gently closed his fingers back over the spikes. "You must," he said. "They are tools meant to be used. They are not icons to be worshiped."

Magnus stared at the priceless artifacts for a moment, his mind still reeling from his touch of the heroically-stained spikes.

He lifted his gaze from the precious artifacts. "These spikes have already been used as the grossest and loveliest of tools," he noted. "What else can be done with them?"

"You will know when the time is right. But for now, roll out your war-cabinet. Focus on the task at hand. Face the enemy as you once did before the trials of the *Wayfarer Call* clouded your hope. You are a prince in the House of Sheshbazzar, a Shekinah Champion."

The Archangel's words stirred deep within Magnus, reminding him of an earlier time when he rushed headlong into the fray wherever he was led, the days when he taunted the enemy with the flair of a brash upstart who knew the favor of God's heart.

Michael drew close to the champion again, gripping his shoulders with a fiery stare. "Show them who you really are, Magnus! Show them! And remember the first and greatest of all God's prophecies," he said, slicing softly across Magnus' forehead with the back of his fingers on his right hand. "Always strike for the head."

Magnus nodded as though he knew the totality of what he was trying to tell him.

With that final instruction, Michael moved backward into the moonlight pouring down through the hole in the roof, preparing to him leave him again, just as he had done on the slopes of Mount Scopus.

"Wait," Magnus pleaded. "I haven't seen you in almost two thousand years…there is much I would like to tell you."

Michael grinned with an insightful expression. "Am I not one of the seven eyes of the Lamb that goes to and fro throughout the Earth? I know it hasn't been easy for you to fulfill some of the things you've been asked to do over the course of your expanded life. But know this…all of Heaven has been honored by the faith of your walk in this world. Never forget that."

Magnus looked at him standing in the moonlight, his bearded appearance sparking a memory he had long since forgotten, reminding him of a man he had seen once sitting in an outdoor café in Portugal's capital city of Lisbon in the 18th century. He had noticed the man was watching him with great interest while he dined with an old friend whom he was warning to leave the city before disaster struck.

"Lisbon," Magnus replied softly. "You were there that day, weren't you?"

Michael gave a silent and confirming nod.

"That was a tough day for me," he said.

"I know."

"I tried to figure out who you were," he noted. "But I made the mistake of taking my eyes off you before magnifying your appearance. When I looked back you were already gone."

Michael pulled the camel's-hair scarf back over his head. "You're not the only one who knows how to make a swift exit, wayfarer."

"I know," he said. "I learned from the best."

The Archangel lifted his hand in a brotherly gesture. "Farewell, you beloved son of *The Way*," he said, his voice echoing across the balcony as he started to flat up into the air. " 'The Lord is with you always, even unto the end of the age.' "

Magnus stepped to the balcony's rail as the Archangel cleared the hole in the roof, disappearing in a quick flash of light that arced across the night's field of stars.

Magnus gripped the balcony's rail with a splintering strength, its posts creaking all the way across as he knelt in front of it and started to pray.

Chapter Thirty

Alchemy sat in a wingback chair of dark leather angled toward a corner in the chateau's spacious library. He was dressed in a fresh black suit, accented by a blue shirt and gold tie.

To his left was a small table on which sat a cup and saucer. The bronze helmet that once adorned the skull of the skeleton in Tsavo's conference room was sitting on the table beside them.

Alchemy was surrounded by bookcases built into the walls of the library. Exposed beams made of darkly-treated wood criss-crossed with one another across the expanse of the cream-colored ceiling, hovering several feet above the bookcases. Rustic lamps dangled between the beams, their angled and unlit globes hanging by copper chains in successive rows.

A crackling fire danced with perfect form in the belly of an enormous stone fireplace off to his left, whispering and spitting with warmth as its flames cast their yellow glow on the library's hardwood floor.

Though the library's fireplace gave a small offering of light, the room's main source of illumination came from the moon as it beamed brightly through the French doors behind Alchemy's right shoulder, its rays chasing the shadows into the corners of the room. Both doors were left open, leading out to a large patio overlooking the chateau's vineyards.

Alchemy sat motionless in the brooding atmosphere of the library, holding a leather bound version of the Harklean Syriac translation of the New Testament Scriptures in his hands. His blue eyes devoured the Aramaic words from the 18th chapter of the Book of John, forcing himself to relive his first military defeat as if to probe for weakness in his adversary. The visions of that fateful night of betrayal in the Garden of Gethsemane were wildly vivid as he read the account. He could still taste the perspired streaks of blood on the Carpenter's face as he kissed him on the cheek in the garden. The image was clear and powerful, every gesture moving in slow motion in the hovering light of lanterns, the sound of clanging armor swirling around him as the Captain of the Temple Guard moved in beside him. Words and gestures were exchanged in muffled tones in his mind, crowned with a reply from the Carpenter when he was told they were looking for Jesus of Nazareth. His words, "*I am He*," exploded through the slow moving visions in his mind, shaking the ground of his memory as he and his three hundred strong detachment of troops were flattened by the power of his voice. It was at that moment when he was lying on his back that he first felt something dark and powerfully familiar explode from his chest, its muscled form rolling like liquid fire across the field of stars above before disappearing; a force that had seemed to be following him since his earliest childhood memories, guiding him with merciless determination in all of his ambitions.

A soft breeze swept into the library suddenly as Alchemy stared at the Syriac Scriptures in his lap, rustling his dark hair. He remained unaffected by the breeze, though, still locked in the embrace of his memories, weighing the warning he had received in Tsavo's conference room against the power that had put him on his back in Gethsemane.

A hooded figure of a man stood in the moonlight of the balcony's open doorway as Alchemy sat unaware in his chair. "It's not the last time you will feel the ground against your back," he said, glancing over at the passage Judas' Syriac was open to.

Alchemy's eyes widened slowly as the memories stored in the Dragon Lord's cosmic blood brought immediate recognition of the voice behind his shoulder. He stared at the vellum pages opened in front of him, his usual, steel-like veneer bending in one haunted moment.

He closed the Bible slowly, lifting his gaze toward the fireplace, the flames dancing in the shadows. He concentrated on the middle portion of the fire, honing his stare with such devilish power he was able to alter the flames with his mind, making them reflect the appearance of the hooded figure standing in the doorway.

Alchemy crossed his legs, pulling the Bible down beside him. He reached over to the table to the left of his chair, picking up the porcelain cup that was filled with hot tea, eyes remaining fixed on the fire. "What brings you to my door on this Halloween night, Archangel?" he asked, taking a sip of the smoldering liquid. "Have you come to rebuke me?"

Michael focused on the right side of Alchemy's face. "The curse of Jotham is upon you, Assyrian."

"So you have come to rebuke me."

"I have come to bear warning," he told him. "The Church Age is not finished. The champion will bring you great distress before the *Trumpet of the Lord* is blown."

Alchemy placed the cup back down on the table. "You're wrong, watcher. This is my time. I will be delayed no longer," he vowed, his stare hardening on the fire. "I will be the messiah my people wanted the Master to be in the days of old. I have the power...and the will to use it."

"The storm of the *latter days* will come soon enough. But know this...*the Covenant Harness* will not make you its master."

"Oh, but it will," he replied. "I know what is in the darkness. And once I have *Dragaduceus* as my iron scepter, and the *well* of the Abyss is opened once more, no force in Heaven or on Earth will be able to stand against my armies of the Locust Cherubim and the Brimstone Cavalry."

"Yes, you understand dark invocations, and are wiser than the Prophet Daniel," Michael remarked, paraphrasing the prophets of old. "But the restraint of the Holy Spirit still hinders you. You will not be allowed to reveal yourself until the appointed time. This decree comes from Zoa."

"This is my time," Alchemy repeated, eyes softening with a more wily stare. "I will not be denied any longer."

"The Shekinah Champion will prove other wise, just as the Angel of the Lord did when he slew the Assyrians in the days of Hezekiah."

Alchemy glanced at the helmet sitting beside his cup of tea on the table to his left. "Your champion, though formidable from what I know of him, is no match for the master," he sneered. "For our power will not ring hollow as the voice of Sennacherib's Rab-shakeh did in the past."

"You're going to regret the day you were born when all this is done," Michael told him.

"Regret?!" Alchemy replied angrily. "I was unfairly chosen for this role! But I have accepted it. No! I have embraced it!"

Michael hardened his stance in the doorway. "The perfect sacrifice for the sins of those called by his name has been offered. There is nothing that will change that. You will be a rod of judgment in the hands of the Coming One, and nothing more."

Alchemy reclined his head against the chair's high back. "You who could not even bring a single accusation against my father dare to assign to me what my portion will be?" he said sharply, reminding the Archangel of his war of words with the Archrebel when contending for the body of Moses as recorded in the Book of Jude. "You forget your place, Michael. Such untidiness will cost you when this war for our rightful inheritance reaches the shores of your home."

"You will lose," Michael assured him, reaching into his coat pocket for the leather pouch Magnus had given to him earlier. "Your only lasting inheritance will be that of Quicksilver consequences."

The Archangel pulled the pouch from his coat pocket and tossed it forward with that decree. It hit the floor in front of Alchemy's right shoe, its impact echoing like a gunshot as it slapped the hardwood forcefully.

Alchemy snapped his head to the right, visibly shaken by the sudden noise. He looked down just as one of the silver shekels was thrust through the opening at the top of the pouch, twirling around in place at the toe of his shoe for several seconds.

The shekel quickly faltered in its wicked twisting, its motion slow and torturous as the shekel's face slowly came into focus.

Alchemy's gaze was that of a man suddenly haunted by a vision from the past as the shekel the size of a half dollar finally landed flat on the floor. There before him, awash in the moonlight, was the curly-haired image of the Phoenician god Melkart, his familiar profile appearing as though it had just recently been hammered, punched and stamped with the die tools of old.

Alchemy stared at the Tyrian shekel for a moment, hesitating before reaching down to pick it up. An electric current shot through his hand the moment he touched the ancient coinage, its energy coursing from his arm to his mind, eyes slamming shut in a tortured grimace. His mind was overwhelmed by a rush of nightmares. The garden. The kiss. Devilish separation. Silver falling. Fire raging around his neck. Darkness embracing him.

"No!" he shouted, jumping to his feet.

Alchemy opened his eyes, the sound of his voice driving the visions away. He was speechless, his breaths coming rigidly as the taste of the *well's* flames rose with a familiar flavor in his mouth.

He whipped around toward the French doors to find himself alone in the library.

Alchemy hurried to the open doorway, gazing toward the vineyards beyond the patio's stone rail harvested earlier in the day by the chateau's migrant work force. His entire veneer of indestructibility had been disarmed in one single reminder of his past weaknesses, shrouding him in a disheveled cloak of fear as he stood their staring at the bare vines in the distance, their twisted and naked poses reminding him of the grapes of wrath already stored up against him.

Alchemy slowly emerged from the spell of doom cast over him, setting his jaw in an angry manner as the Dragon Lord's cosmic blood quickened his wicked spirit with a renewed stance of invincibility. He lifted the shekel in front of him, his reflection staring back at him in the shiny surface of Melkart's chiseled face. "Your challenge is taken, Archangel," he said. "I will prove my might. I will be the crucified superman this world has longed for...no matter how many lives it may cost."

Chapter Thirty-one

The waning hours of the previous night's starry canopy hung over the valley like the calm before a storm. With the exception of some unusual traffic patterns from group helicopters, all seemed peaceful and secure. Most of the town's resident adults and their children had turned in long ago after an evening of trick or treating and Halloween celebrations made to end at the stroke of the town's curfew.

But there was still a bustle of activity near the center of town. Sodom held his usual position atop the clock tower's obelisk, taking note of the unusual patterns from some of the Omega Group's security forces. His 24 elite warriors were posted in the tops of the redwood trees sprouting up through the roof's corners of the town's Masonic Temple, giving little heed to the changes in the group's security patterns. They were absorbed in the music coming from a group of demon possessed men dressed in Druidic garb who were dancing around the stone altar in the center of the temple's expansive roof. They had watched with pleasure only hours ago as the mayor of the town sacrificed his youngest daughter in the flames still rising with a hellish glow through the square opening of the dragon-marked altar, reminding them of how the Israelite parents sacrificed their children on altars dedicated to the Ammonite deity Molech in the Valley of Hinnom. Similar sacrifices were made to the Moabite deity Chemosh on the Mount of Olives, abominable acts to be magnified with a cruel hypocrisy as the parents would later enter the House of the Lord to worship him. It was an era of great triumph for the powers of darkness, a time they relived with great zeal over and over on the night of Samhain and the predawn hours of the Babylonian festival of All Saints Day.

◄•┈•══○══•┈•►

Twelve shadowy figures moved through the trees along the dirt road leading up the eastern mountain range. They were split in two groups of six on each side of the road, outfitted in black, swat-like uniforms. Smooth, ninja-shaped hoods were pulled tightly over their heads. Hi Power night vision goggles filled the openings of their masks that stretched wide across the upper portions of their faces, equipping them with the ability to move with ease through the shadows. They were each armed with Heckler&Koch G36 Carbines cut down almost to the size of PDWs, loaded with 5.56 caliber rounds. Magazine-stuffed bandoliers were strapped over their shoulders and around their waists, each stocked with extra tape and turn clips and phosphorous grenades.

Both units were a panoply of professional soldiers recruited by the Omega Group from some of the elite military units of the world's most powerful nations. Most were former Delta Force operatives from Fort Bragg, while others hailed from the camps of the British SAS and the Israeli special forces of Sayeret Matkal.

The shortest of the 12 shadowy figures led the group of six on the left side of the road. He stood only 5 feet 7 inches, but was built like a small gorilla.

The short leader stepped from the shadows, throwing up his right fist to give the signal for the rest of them to stop. He slid his night vision goggles to the top of his head to study the ground in front of him, spotting shards of glass in the dirt that were reflecting the moonlight, with pieces of metal mixed in among the rocks. He covered a larger area of the road with his eyes, noting the unusual makeup of the dirt. It looked as though it had been disturbed.

He turned back around and motioned for his split team to approach. His men stepped from the shadows of the trees like ghosts, maintaining muzzle discipline so as not to sweep one another when they squatted to one knee to form two lines behind their leader. They turned their heads back toward the trees from whence they had emerged, cocking the foldable stocks of their HKs against their shoulders, barrels pointing down as they kept a careful watch on the pines with their night vision gear.

The leader shouldered his weapon, pulling part of his mask down beneath his chin at the same time, adjusting a small microphone extending around the right side of his mouth from an earpiece connected to a SATCOM computer in his rucksack. He spoke into the black mouthpiece with a disciplined softness. "Hawkeye One, this is Pack Leader, do you copy?"

Grimes' gruff voice rang back with clarity through the leader's headset. "This is Hawkeye One, Pack Leader. I read you loud and clear…. What's your position?"

The Pack Leader pulled back a patch on his right arm to look at a small map attached underneath. "According to topographic intel, we should be less than two klicks from the target," he reported.

"Copy that, Pack Leader," Grimes replied. "Be aware that mission status has been moved up. Shadow Corps just picked up on another outgoing call from the suspected target. They couldn't track it down or listen in on the whole transmission for some reason, but they believe the target is still holed up in the old sanctuary as intel indicated on the last call that pierced valley security."

The leader swivelled around towards his men, covering the map on his arm again. "Roger that, Hawkeye One," he said. "What's you're ETA?"

"Twenty minutes, Pack Leader. There's only one entrance to the old meeting hall from what satellite imagery shows. So get your men in gear and secure that sally port."

"Copy that, Hawkeye One. We'll be jacked and stacked. Pack Leader out."

The leader pulled his goggles back down over his eyes, speaking to his men in a hushed tone. "Twenty minutes. Move out."

The Wolf Pack sprang to their feet, weapons held at chest level as they made double time up the mountain road.

Chapter Thirty-two

Magnus held a ceremonial silence while standing in front of his portable war-cabinet that was positioned in front of the balcony's rail, dressed in a pair of black leather pants and a white T-shirt. A curtain of moonlight fell through the roof's hole, circling around him and the wardrobe-style cabinet. Fierce zoons rose from the four corners of the cabinet's square top in brilliantly-carved extensions of the acacia frame. A round seal of gold was nestled in the center of its rectangular doors, with a bronze lion's head protruding from the center.

Magnus ran his hand down along the cabinet's right side door just above the seal, feeling the slightly raised surface of the elaborate trim that traced the edges of both doors. The rectangular section of the trim was shaped in a pattern of stacked squares. Beneath its segmented surface was an ancient and elaborately designed lock system made of square pressure plates of steel engraved with a codex of Hebrew letters, coinciding with their duplicate counterparts carved into the squares of the cabinet's raised trim of hollowed-out wood. The lock could be opened only by rapping on the engraved pressure plates and spelling out a combination of preset words. The system, and the wardrobe-style cabinet itself, was one of two he had designed for himself. It had served as his portable ark of war for hundreds of years.

Magnus proceeded to knock on the pressure plates beneath the raised squares of wood with careful speed, spelling out the verse, "*Behold, I stand at the door and knock,*" from the third chapter of the Revelation of Jesus Christ, foreshadowing the Greek-rendered warning the Lord had given to the future Hebraic assembly of Laodicea. The sound of flat, heavily-gauged bars of steel could be heard rifling off in unison from the bottom of the cabinet's doors to the top, each sliding into square grooves on the right side door. The lion's-head seal split in the middle as the thick doors opened mechanically. A shaft of golden light exploded from the vertical opening as the doors slowly yawned to the sides.

Magnus peered at the ancient artifacts arrayed against the cabinet's interior, its walls of padded velvet having been dyed in a royal color of purple with secretion fluids extracted from bivalve mollusks found on the shores of the Mediterranean. A full-length leather coat of late-18th century French design hung on the cabinet's left wall. Gold-velvet buttons spanned down the right side of the single-breasted garment to its tapered waist, with more velvet embroidery of the same golden color stitched into the breasts of the coat's crimson-colored leather, depicting the image of a large lion's head with emerald eyes on the left side breast, a jeweled palm tree on the right. The entire coat was trimmed with the bright embroidery. But the coat's most unique quality was its calf-length train that had flexible rods sewn into the garment's thin lining. The rods would spread out the coat's split train when bloated with wind, giving it a stealthy glide when its wearer descended from great heights.

The source of the cabinet's light was a suit of sleeveless armor made of bright golden seals that was positioned on a valet stand, with Hebraic inscriptions engraved in bronze in the flat centers of each signet-like seal, sunken beneath their circular borders like pressed clay. The writing inside the seals told the stories of every champion who had preceded him in the Shekinah Legacy.

The armor itself, though thousands of years old, shimmered with an ageless luster, with a leather tunic perfectly preserved beneath it by the energy from the armor's Christaloy gold. Six square buckles of purified silver were fastened to the right side of the garment's open seam running down the middle of the armor, with small golden crowns engraved in the middle of each buckle. Triangular-shaped hooks were fastened on the left side of the seam.

A pair of black, English hunting boots sat beneath the open suit of armor. Razor-sharp claws were tied to loop holes around the top rim of each lace up boot; relics from a battle he'd had with a demon possessed lion bent on ravaging missionaries during the Boer War in South Africa in 1899.

On the rear wall of the cabinet was an ancient, single-edged blade slightly curved like the Heiman swords of the Far East, housed in a sheath decked with embossed squares of silver sheet. Its two-handed hilt was molded from pure ivory in a tubular design, with artisan scrollwork of golden images engraved on its rounded sides, detailing some of the epic battles he'd had throughout the centuries. The tales of his exploits extended down across the sheath, spanning to the last squared sheet left blank beneath its elaborate borders.

Magnus bent forward and grabbed the tall boots, pulling them up over the legs of his leather pants. He tied the laces with quick snaps, making the claws dangling from the tops of each boot clang together with monstrous chimes of the past.

Magnus stood back up and reached for the armor next, his hands absorbing a warm jolt of energy as he lifted it carefully from the valet stand by its round collar, slipping his arms through the holes of the vest-style garment, the leather tunic beneath clinging tightly to his chest, its golden hem falling to his thighs. He took the armor's top silver buckle in his right hand and the triangular hook in his left, snapping them together force-fully, igniting tiny spirals of golden light in the Hebrew words, *The Spirit of the Lord*, that were carved beneath the buckle's crown. He rifled down the line with a sly smile as the armor was brought together in a form fitting target, igniting more spirals of golden light from the Hebrew phrases engraved beneath the other buckles that sang with *The Spirit of Wisdom, The Spirit of Understanding, The Spirit of Counsel, The Spirit of Might* and *The Spirit of Knowledge.*

Though the armor had always traveled in the cabinet with his sword, he hadn't actually worn it since the 17th century. But at Michael's insistence, he would remind the enemy of who he was, defying the shadows of history and lore that had masked him for so long, rising from the ashes of absence in all the glory of his kingly heritage.

Magnus reached inside the cabinet again, grabbing his blade that hung on the back wall by a belt of round, miniature bronze shields. It had a silver buckle like those on his armor, with a bronzed lion's head etched in the center. He pulled the sword from its sheath of embossed squares, hands charged with memory as he governed his strength carefully on the hilt's elaborate scrollwork. He held it vertically in front of him, its curved blade reflecting the light coming through the roof's hole. He had forged the blade himself using Damascus steel, a metal of great tensile strength and flexibility. A thin crimson sheen of his own blood had been hammered into the lightning grain patterns of the sword's razor edge during its meticulous folding and planishing stages, giving him a weapon that could cut through both mortal and preternatural flesh.

Magnus had first learned the secret of adding his own blood to a sword's edge after finding the *Dragaduceus* war-blade in King Og's tomb. The double-edged sword had been carefully wrapped and preserved in Og's iron sarcophagus; a sepulcher hidden in a cave-like tomb of grand arches and black basaltic pillars decorated with shields and other armaments in a gorge along the Jabbok River. Its size was that of a large staff; a two-handed weapon wielded easily in one hand by a pagan warrior who had once stood well over nine feet tall. But the blade's black-scaled design and lightning grain patterns of gold clearly showed that it was a weapon of supernatural design. He learned in the process of deciphering the archaic scrollwork on the hilt, with great surprise, that the liquid used in the smelting of the sword had been alchemized from the spiritual substance of the evil one himself. While deciphering the scrollwork out loud, he would also discover the sword had a cloaking capability, making it invisible to his eyes for a brief moment before adjusting to it with his Shekinah Vision. The sword had easily cut his hardened flesh when he dislodged one of the blade's scales with an investigative touch, his blood falling to the ground for the first time since his coronation, mingling with the scale as it liquified in a reverse oxidization, splattering together on the earthen floor of the tomb in a slight tremor.

He would use the knowledge from that blade to shape his own weapons of war, employing them against all forms of evil. The Isma'ili Assassins of Mount Alamut Castle who ruled Northern Persia in 1090 A.D. would be among some of the more notable foes who fell beneath the edge of his sword; ruthless men who became possessed during dark invocations and binges of Hashish hallucinogenic wine. The European covens of the vampire demoniacs who terrorized the continent of the Old World during the reign of Vlad Dracul would suffer the same wrath centuries later.

Magnus sheathed the blade quickly, setting his mind on the present once more. He slapped the belt around the tapered waist of his thigh-length armor, snapping its silver buckle together in a divine seal, igniting one final array of golden spirals from the Hebrew phrase, *The Spirit of the Fear of the Lord*, engraved beneath the buckle's bronze lion's head. Finally, he reached back inside the war-cabinet for his coat, a leather garment such as those cherished by all true cavalrymen. He twirled the coat like a matador's cape, catching it behind his waist with both hands, forearms slowly bulging down through its tight sleeves. He snapped his arms forward with a quick jerk as his hands neared the cuffs, letting the sides of the coat slide down over the reflective seals of his armor.

Magnus closed the cabinet's doors, rapping on the coded pressure plates in the same manner as before. He spelled out the verse, '*And the door was shut,*' from the 25th chapter of the Book of Matthew, activating the lock's flat, heavily-gauged bars of steel.

Magnus turned toward the balcony's stairwell, aware of soft footsteps ascending the stairs. "It's okay, April, you can come up," he said.

April hurried up the steps, bursting into the moonlight as she ran to Magnus. "You're all right!" she cried, throwing her arms around him. "Praise God."

Magnus embraced her with equal enthusiasm. "Where were you?" he asked.

April pulled back from the embrace, letting her hands slide down his arms. "I wanted to give you and your friend plenty of time alone," she answered, bowing her head in a mournful gesture. "I went out back to the cemetery…I saw Megan's grave."

Magnus reached out and embraced her again.

She pulled back after a long moment of silence. "I'm okay. It's just difficult to still comprehend all that's happened over the last few days."

"I understand."

April looked around the balcony. "Where's your friend?" she asked softly.

"He's gone."

"Is he coming back?"

Magnus shook his head.

"Look," she remarked, extending her left arm. "He healed my arm. I've never seen anything like it before. And you…I thought you were going to die. Now look at you."

April paused in her excitement, galvanized suddenly by the halos of light reflecting off the silver buckles and the golden seals of the champion's armor. "Wow! I should've known you had a shiny suit of armor hidden away somewhere."

Magnus smiled as she reached out and touched the seals of his armor with her fingers. She jerked her hand back from the slight shock she received.

"What was that?"

"The signature of the One who made this armor for me," he answered.

"And who was that?"

"'He who made the heavens and the earth,'" he replied.

"God?"

"Yes, April. The Word made flesh himself."

"I don't understand."

"It's a passage from Isaiah. It refers to the greatest of all craftsmen. My friend who healed you was one of his greatest creations."

"Who exactly was he, anyway?"

"An old friend."

April stared at him with a raised eyebrow. "How old?"

"Trust me. It's best that you don't know."

April smiled. "It's okay. I know enough already."

"Yes, I heard."

"He told you?"

Magnus nodded.

"Jesus saved me, Magnus. I never dreamed I would say that…but he did."

Magnus embraced her again. "You are now bound to Christ Jesus forever, April Wedding. And he will never leave you nor forsake you."

She pulled back from his embrace with an endearing gaze. "Thank you for telling me the truth. I owe you my life."

"Don't thank me," he said. "Thank the Lord."

"I have. Believe me, I have."

Magnus caressed her face with his hand.

"But what now?" she asked, eyes serious with the threat still facing them. "Where do we go?"

Magnus placed his hands on her shoulders with a grim expression. "I still have business here in the valley," he answered.

"I don't understand."

Magnus sighed patiently. "I am bound by a certain calling on my life that's quite complicated to explain. In time you will understand all you have seen and heard from me. But know this: During the Old Testament era there were certain people and events that acted as living foreshadows of things to come in the future."

April looked at him with a puzzled expression. "What does that have to do with you and this valley?"

"It means, April…." He paused for a second, dreading what he was about to tell her.

"Means what?"

Magnus looked at her with uncompromising conviction. "It means that I have to destroy the entire town, and its population."

She shook her head with disbelief. "Wha…. Why? How?"

"Why? Because your former employer, Iscarius Alchemy, is trying to step-up the timetable of his unveiling…and because I am a living foreshadow of the wrath that is being stored up against the wicked."

April was more than a little unnerved by his answer. "What are you trying to tell me?"

"Alchemy is the Antichrist, April. And he is trying to change prophecy."

April stood there in a moment of stunned silence.

"I know that's shocking to hear."

April shook her head. "Yes, it is," she told him. "But it shouldn't be after everything that has happened. There were always crazy rumors circulating throughout the group about who he really was. I just thought that they were ridiculous fantasies created by some eccentric PR person who wanted to make him as dark and as mysterious as his origins were. To be honest with you, I wondered if he even truly existed since there were very few people who had actually laid eyes on him."

"Trust me," he said. "He is definitely real."

"And you have to destroy the entire town to stop him?"

"It's what God has asked me to do."

"But…God is love," she said softly. "He saved me."

Magnus cupped her face with his hands. "The last thing I want to do is to cause you to doubt God's love. But you will learn as you grow in your walk with the Lord that he is also a God of holiness and judgment. Haven't you ever wondered why the brunt of the world's worst earthquakes takes place in some of the most degenerate places on Earth? It's because God is judging sin. Usually it centers on nations, especially states located in this Masonic country, that are persecuting his children or shaking their fists in his face with their blatant promotion of sin. I know this to be true because I have been the cause of some of the world's worst quakes. The Middle East in the 4th century. China in the 16th century. I can still hear the bells in my mind that rang as far away as England during the aftershocks of the Lisbon Quake of 1755, and the cries of those who were burned alive in the cataclysm that struck San Francisco in 1906. Then there was the port of Messina in December of 1908, and the 1976 quake in China that killed over a quarter of a million people."

April pulled away from him with a mystified stare. She had seen too much to disbelieve what he was saying. The people she knew in town came to mind with that realization. She thought about her neighbors on Imperial Lane. The parents she was acquainted with in the local PTA. The children her daughter had been friends with.

She stumbled over her words, trying to grasp scientifically how he could be capable of such destruction. "H…How do you plan to create an earthquake that will destroy the entire town?"

"With a power that was given to me a long time ago."

April still couldn't fully grasp such power being harnessed within him. But she believed him regardless of the naggings of her secular education, and petitioned him for a different solution. "Can't you just destroy the group?" she asked.

Magnus shook his head. "I wish I could. But this town's cup of wickedness is full. And judgment must be poured out because of it."

"I don't understand…. What do you mean by cup of wickedness?"

"The townspeople have taken Alchemy's mark of allegiance," he said. "Because of this, I have been ordered to destroy them just as those throughout the world will be destroyed in the future who take his mark."

Magnus glanced at his war-cabinet. "That truth was something I blinded myself to when I found out what was going on in this valley," he continued. "I've been waiting for the end to come for a very long time. To see it so near at hand after all these centuries is like a sweet promise of release. But no matter how much I selfishly suppress it, I will always be a living foreshadow of the wrath to come on the *Lord's Day*."

"But what about the children?" she pleaded.

Magnus looked back at her patiently, trying not to think about the town's children who were no doubt sleeping snugly in their warm beds at that very moment. "Trust me for now when I tell you that the Lord will sort out the innocent from the guilty when this is all done…. *'God is a just judge.'*"

341

April hung her head with a look of shame. "This is my fault," she replied. "If I hadn't developed the prototypes for the A-6 Mark then none of this would be happening."

Magnus lifted her chin. "If you hadn't made the chip someone else would have," he noted. "You didn't force the townspeople to take Alchemy's mark. And from what I have learned of this place, it seems to me that God has been more than patient with their wicked ways."

April buried her face into the leather breast of his coat. "But I feel like it's my fault."

Magnus wrapped his arms around her. "Remember," he said. "He has forgiven you of all your sins. You are not under the sign of judgment as the others in the town are. You didn't take Alchemy's true mark."

He held her quietly for a minute, remembering across the centuries the people who had perished in the wake of his power. "Believe me," he went on. "I have struggled with things I should never have struggled with. I have seen more bloodshed than you can possibly imagine. I have endured the carnage of the Crusades, the depravity of the Ottoman conquerors, the rankness of Anglo-American expansionism, the infamous concentration camps of Hitler's Germany and the seemingly forgotten killing fields of the Bolsheviks. I have watched countless arrows and bullets split the skulls of men while their breath and memories of home still lingered between their teeth. I have buried the mangled corpses of brothers and sisters in Christ slain by demonic lions that still roam the Dark Continent. And I cannot even begin to count the other horrific accounts of genocide perpetrated by the Idi Amin's of this world.... Rwanda. Sudan. Somalia. They're all the same. And I have grown tired of it. But things must be fulfilled before there can be an end to all of this."

April shook her head as she looked back up at him. "How have you remained sane after all this time?"

Magnus stared blankly over her head at the peeling wall behind her. "Grace," he answered softly. "Grace and good friends."

"But they were friends you lost to time."

"Yes," he said, glancing back down at her. "But I will see them again one day. But it's the increasing depravity of humankind, coupled with my own weaknesses, that makes it difficult to endure the passing of each century that accompanies this *Wayfarer Call* upon my…."

Magnus jerked his head to the left suddenly, peering through the balcony's arched window. He could hear the sound of numerous footfalls moving swiftly toward their position. "That doesn't make any sense," he said to himself. "Why would they send them?"

"What's the matter?" she asked.

"They're coming."

"Who?"

"Soldiers for the group, no doubt. I can hear them moving in separate formations up the mountain's dirt road. They're not far away, and they're moving fast."

"You can hear all of that?"

"Yes," he answered distractedly.

April just shook her head. His abilities didn't cease to amaze her.

Magnus stared out the window, puzzled. "They must have traced one of my calls to the mountain. But it still doesn't explain why they would send them."

"What do we do?" April asked.

Magnus turned to her again. "The first thing we're going to do is to get you to safety."

"But…."

"There will be no argument about this, April," he said. "I have arranged for you to be transported out of the valley by an associate of mine."

"But I want to stay with you," she pleaded.

"You can't. I have a mission to fulfill. And you're in enough danger as it is."

"No," she refused. "I want to stay with you…I have so many questions."

Magnus took her face in his hands again. "I'm sorry. It's just too dangerous."

"I don't care," she insisted."

"No, April. Your stay in this valley is finished. It's time for you to move on."

April bowed her head with a look of defeat.

Magnus pulled her to his seal-covered chest to comfort her, watching as a fiery apparition burned into view against the peeling wall next to the stairwell. The anomaly morphed into a towering figure of a man, his eyes burning with blue fires of purity beneath the hood of his emerald robe.

Magnus pushed April back gently while still holding her arms. "It's time to go," he said.

April turned around at the sound of the balcony's floorboards creaking heavily behind her. She gasped at the tall stranger who was stepping from the shadows, vapors of blue light seeping from the corners of his fiery eyes. He was a mountain of intimidation as he walked forward and stood some 10 feet away at the edge of the circular curtain of moonlight coming through the roof. Heavy armaments could be seen bulging against the luminous flax of his emerald robe.

April grabbed Magnus' right arm as the stranger stared down at her, shielding herself behind his shoulder.

"It's okay," Magnus smiled, pulling her back around in front of him. "This is one of my associates I told you about the other night."

"This is your associate?" she remarked, marveling at the size of the quiet stranger whose face beneath the hood absorbed the moon's light like a prism.

"He and his kind have helped me on many occasions."

April looked at Magnus. "His kind?"

"Yes," he said, glancing at the towering figure. "He's an angel."

"An angel?" she remarked, looking back at the stranger. "But where are his wings?"

Magnus smiled at her. "Angels don't have wings," he told her. "Only the Zoa do."

April stared at the angel with a bewildered look. "The Zoa?"

Magnus nodded. "The Zoa are better known as the Cherubim," he explained. "They're also known as the Seraphim, which is a term that is interchangeable with the word serpent. They are supernatural creatures different from angels. It has long been a mistake of artists and writers to portray angels with wings. It's part of the enemy's deception to keep humankind from knowing the intricacies of the supernatural realm. It also speaks of the vanity of the rebel angels who aspire to stations above them."

April spoke to Magnus in a hushed tone. "He's not exactly what I would pictured an angel to look like…he scares me."

"You should see them in their full glory."

"Who is he?" she asked, her voice still hushed.

"His name is Raptos. He's one of the guardians of the elect."

"You mean a real guardian angel?"

"Yes," he answered. "God gives all of his created beings a purpose to fulfill."

April stepped in front of Magnus. "And what about me? What's my purpose if it's not to stand by your side just as you did for me?"

Magnus brushed the tresses of her auburn hair away from her face. "The Lord will show you," he answered.

"It's time," the angel interjected, his voice echoing softly across the balcony.

April glanced over her shoulder, looking back at Magnus with a frightened expression. "I don't want to leave you," she insisted.

"You have no choice. Like Enoch who escaped the judgments of the Second Great Deluge, so too must you escape. Judgment cannot be poured out on this valley until you are safe."

"But…."

"Shhh," he said, pressing his fingers gently against her mouth. "Everything's going to be all right. He's going to take you to a preacher friend of mine and his family. They're going to help disciple you in *The Way*. He will also teach you about following the Lord in baptism. You will be safe with them until another associate of mine in San Francisco finishes setting you up with a new identity. But tell them nothing of what you have seen from

345

me. They don't know the full depth of who I am yet. And that's the way the Lord wants it for now."

April looked down at the floor. "I'm never going to see you again, am I?"

"One day you will, when the time is right."

April raised her head and stared at him. She inhaled nervously as she reached out and grabbed the sides of his stubble-covered face, a single tear rolling down her left cheek as she pulled his head down toward hers. Magnus gave no resistance as she pressed her mouth softly against the left side of his rugged face.

April released him slowly. "Thank you, Magnus," she said. "For everything. I will never forget you."

Magnus gently pushed her away. "You had better go now," he said softly. "The soldiers are getting closer."

She nodded her head reluctantly, clearing her throat as she turned toward the angel. She walked awkwardly toward him, stopping halfway to glance back over her shoulder.

Magnus nodded for her to go on.

April turned and walked the rest of the way, staring up at the fiery-eyed being as she stopped in front of him, her head reaching only to the height of his armorer mid section.

She turned back around to look at Magnus one last time. "Don't forget me," she said, eyes trembling with goodbye.

"It would be impossible."

Raptos opened the folds of his emerald robe as he stepped into the shaft of moonlight, throwing them out around April while she stared at the champion. She was covered from sight in the twinkling of an eye by the heavy cocoon of luminous flax, his garment rolling in billows like water as he slowly ascended from the dusty planks of the balcony floor. They floated up through the shaft of moonlight coming through the roof, moving through the rafters in a graceful flight as they exited through the jagged hole above them. Once they cleared the roof, Raptos and April disappeared across the night sky in a sudden flash of light that quickly faded toward the horizon.

Magnus bowed his head prayerfully. "Take care of her, Father," he whispered. "Take care of her."

Chapter Thirty-three

Michael watched over the valley's dark landscape from the western mountain range, sitting on a large flat rock near the edge of a cliff some 60 feet above the ground. Beneath him was a large pond surrounded by a bevy of pines. The valley's winding road was visible through the foliage on the opposite side of the pond below. To his left, above the treetops, he could see some of the rooftops of the town's buildings, especially the glass towers and the ivory clock tower that pierced the night sky.

He sat tranquilly on the rock with the camel's-hair hood draped over his head, studying the rebel activity above the town's rooftops. Sodom still stood proudly on top of his throne-like peak, his false wings spread wide against the stars.

Michael turned away and looked down at the pond below.

It was all placidly simple. Uncomplicated. Seemingly untouched by the conspiring forces in the nearby town.

A frigid wind pressed against his back suddenly, sweeping down around him across the pond's surface in a stormy ripple. "You don't belong here, great prince," a voice said from behind.

A pair of white eyes materialized in a shadow connecting two pines behind the rock. A crown of golden hair appeared around the emerging orbs, followed by sharp wings curving outward between the two trees. "What brings you to this corner of the world, Michael?" the assassin asked.

Michael remained motionless, still staring at the water's surface that was returning to its calmer shape, eyes glowing with jeweled fires in the shadow of his hood. "As always, evil one, I bear warning," he said coldly.

"This is not your time, Archangel. Nor is it the place."

"I go where I am led."

"And what leads you here?"

"An old friend."

The assassin laughed softly. "Of course…the defeated champion."

An unseen smile filtered across the Archangel's covered face. "Not so defeated," he said, turning his head to the left to see a single helicopter that had taken off from the air base in the north, dropping down to skim over the treetops of the eastern mountain. "The tide is about to turn."

The assassin glanced to his left, focusing on the heavily-armed chopper as it darted off in an unusual and deliberate pattern. "Your knowledge pales in comparison to mine," he said, eyes narrowing as he followed the chopper's path across the eastern range for a moment before looking back down at the Archangel. "I am beyond the effects of change…I am the darkened shore."

Michael glanced down at the pond again. "I know who you are. I know the true power that you possess. And most of all, I know your weakness."

Sky-blue flames engulfed the Archangel suddenly with that reminder to the assassin, his voice echoing in the fiery remnants that fell behind him in his ascent into the night sky, showering the pond's surface below with a brilliant fall of sparks.

Chapter Thirty-four

The black-clad assault team was divided into two groups of six as before, crawling on their stomachs through the field of tall grass surrounding the old clapboard sanctuary. They were separated by the dirt road as they snaked their way slowly toward the sanctuary's sagging doorway.

The short pack leader led the way on the left side of the road, weapon cradled across his arms as he crawled.

The doorway was about 20 yards away when the leader stopped, the men behind him following suit. He held a single fist above the tips of the tall grass concealing them, signaling to his lieutenant who was leading the other group to stop.

The pack leader placed the strap of his HK around his neck, twisting the weapon around on his back. He pushed his goggles to the top of his head as did the rest of his men, their eyes quickly adjusting to the moonlight that saturated the area.

The pack leader reached to his utility belt for his square-shaped field binocular, fitted with thermal vision and a laser range finder. He lifted it to his eyes, extending his masked head just above the tips of the grass to scan for thermal patterns of body heat. He panned upward along the sanctuary's facade in the distance, quickly finding a man-shaped pattern of body heat.

The pack leader lowered the binocular for a moment, squinting with a look of disbelief. He put the MilCAM back to his eyes, fixing on the pattern again. He shook his head in confusion. The pattern was brighter than anything he had ever seen before.

The leader lowered the binocular again and secured it back on his belt, taking hold of his weapon again. He signaled to his lieutenant to move his team forward, motioning for the rest of his own men to follow him.

—•·•—✄○✄—•·•—

Magnus stood in front of the balcony's rail with his arms folded across his armored chest. He stared at the ancient spikes lying on top of the balcony's rail next to his beloved Stradivarius.

He picked up the spikes gently, tucking them one by one into his inner left coat pocket, pressing them against his heart, remembering Michael's instructions to ponder all that he had learned from his ancient dream.

Magnus reached next for the vellum parchment sitting to the right of his violin on the railing. It was thickly folded in a rectangular fashion, compacting two legal claims in one document; a deed to both the sanctuary and the valley itself the town's first settlers had drawn up prior to being forced from their homes by the enemy.

Magnus ran his fingers over the deed's folded seam that was sealed with a large, raised signet of red clay depicting the town of Tower Valley and its clock tower as they would have appeared in the early 20th century, with a large sword being thrust through its center from above. He was moved by the Holy Spirit within him to slowly crush the deed's seal, breaking it in half with the tips of his fingers, its sound igniting the buckle at the top of his armor with a silver flash of light. The first part of the document fell open to reveal the legal claim the valley's first settlers had to the land when they first filed it 11 years after the beginning of the California Gold Rush, detailing also how they had to contend with the Silver Kings and the Railroad Barons who tried to come in peaceably and take away what was theirs. He broke the seal of the deed's second fold that created the same silver flash in the next buckle on his armor, revealing the increased spiritual warfare that beset the settlers in the year 1900. The deed's third and fourth seals were broken with the same effects, telling of a boycott against resisters that led to famine and death. The breaking of the deed's fifth seal told the story of those settlers who stood firm with the Lord Jesus, while others wearied of the fight and chose to compromise with the Masons who brought a new prosperity to the settlement at the beginning of the 20th century, foreshadowing the Omega Group's takeover of the town over a hundred years later. The breaking of the deed's sixth seal told a familiar story of the Saints who felt the terrible tremors from the San Francisco Earthquake of 1906, recounting how they could see remnants of the black smoke that rose into the air from all the fires ravaging the faraway city.

When Magnus broke the deed's seventh seal the buckle on his belt exploded with a brighter flash than the rest, igniting all the golden seals and the other buckles of his armor at once in one brilliant show of light that sung with power. The final seal was a benediction that the true owner of the land was the Lord Jesus himself, and that he would do with it as he saw fit in the end. The entire deed had been written in the same vein as some of the events recorded in the Revelation of Jesus Christ, serving as a reminder of the original seven sealed books to be opened on the *Lord's Day*.

The glow of his armor subsided when he refolded the deed and placed it inside his coat next to the spikes. He bowed his head in a quiet moment of solidarity before reaching for his violin, feeling completely empowered to bring judgment on a town of people living in open rebellion against the Most High.

Chapter Thirty-five

The pack leader pressed his right hand against a plank several feet above the sanctuary's front foundation, turning his back to the structure as he stood to his feet, placing his body flat against the weather-beaten exterior. The rest of his men pulled up beside him to his right, turning their backs to the sanctuary as well. The team on the other side of the road followed their lead as they positioned themselves in the same manner.

The pack leader glanced up at the sanctuary's arched window above the sagging doorway as music started to emanate from the balcony where he had earlier seen the thermal outline of their target.

He adjusted the microphone of his SATCOM headset again as the music sifted through the planks of the old building, speaking into it with the same disciplined softness as before. "Hawkeye One, this is Pack Leader, do you copy?"

"Loud and clear, Pack Leader," Grimes answered. "What's your status?"

The pack leader glanced at his watch. "We're stacked at eighteen."

"Roger that," said Grimes. "Is target confirmed?"

"Target is confirmed, Hawkeye One. You have a rogue in a plunging fire position. Sally port is secure."

"Roger that, Pack Leader. Hold your position. ETA in two minutes. Hawkeye One is loaded for bear."

"Copy that, Hawkeye One. Pack Leader out."

The pack leader turned to his men on both sides of the road, making a silent poking gesture at his eyes before pointing to the sanctuary's sagging doorway, motioning for them to squat back down in the tall grass.

The split team disappeared beneath the tips of the grass, each pair of eyes training on the doorway through the tall husks.

Grimes sat buckled in a Kevlar armored seat of an AH-64D Apache Longbow helicopter. The lights of his instrument panels reflected off the glass of the chopper's jet-style canopy looming just above his head. A black, arm-like scope with a round, computerized eyepiece extended from the right side of his open-faced helmet, linked to the Heads Up Display in front of him that gave him readouts of his surrounding instruments.

The chopper's main pilot was positioned in the cockpit behind Grimes, elevated and sectioned off by bulletproof glass.

The chopper's pylon wings were loaded down with laser-guided Hellfire antitank missiles. A .30 millimeter chain gun was positioned beneath the Apache's nose section, fixed in a side-to-side turret that could move with the motion of the helmet of which ever pilot was in control of the chopper's weapons systems.

Grimes kept a blistering pace, flying in a nap of the earth pattern just above the treetops of the valley's eastern mountain range. He reached up and steadied the mic extending out in front of his mouth from the left side of his flight helmet, holding the chopper's fold-down control column with one hand while opening his com-link. "Wolf Den, this is Hawkeye One, do you copy?"

The reply was crisp and clear as it came through the speakers inside both pilots' flight helmets. "This is Wolf Den, Hawkeye One, go ahead."

"The target has been confirmed at the old sanctuary, Mr. Specter," Grimes reported. "The pack is stacked. The target is a rogue. I repeat. The target is a rogue."

"What about Dr. Wedding?"

"The pack made no mention of her, sir."

"Roger that, Hawkeye One," said Specter. "Proceed with your mission."

Grimes smiled with delight. "Copy that, Wolf Den," he said, "ETA in one minute. Hawkeye One out."

Grimes lowered the helmet's microphone away from his mouth, leaving the com-link open so Specter could monitor the mission transmissions.

Specter stood in the center of the Shadow Corps' situation room on the top floor of the Omega Group's glass building facing the south part of town. The room's sound-proof walls were fixed with numerous computer terminals secretly linked to the SOCRATES mainframe; a military network allowing U.S. forces instant access to detailed intelligence and satellite imagery, with additional links to the Crisis Action Center beneath MacDill Air Force Base in Florida. The terminals gave the room a multicolored glow, with several glass cabinets mixed in between the stations housing GPS databanks. On the farthest wall, reaching all the way up to the tile ceiling, was an enormous projector screen displaying live feed from the Apache's onboard cameras.

With his head tilted back, Specter watched the Apache fly incredibly close to the mountain's blurred treetops. He began to see the top of a small structure in the closing distance.

Specter stepped closer to the chair of the lone technician working the mainframe's expansive terminals. "Magnify that image," he pointed. "And then notify our agents outside the valley to be on alert for Dr. Wedding. She might be heading in their direction since there's only one target at the old meeting hall."

The technician punched several keys on the keypad fixed to the rectangular table in front of him, instantly magnifying the image the chopper's camera was filming, quickly changing tasks to make a security call to the group's agents stationed outside the valley.

Specter pushed his glasses higher on the bridge of his nose, folding his arms as the A-shaped roof of the old sanctuary was getting closer on the screen above him. He squinted impatiently, sighing with a hint of reluctance. He wanted the fireworks to be over as quickly and as quietly as possible.

Magnus stood on top of the balcony's rail, awash in the moonlight, coat swaying back and forth with the rhythm of the violin tucked under the left side of his chin, fingers falling perpendicularly along the instrument's neck that had a curved lion's head as its scroll, the bow in his right hand sliding back and forth across the strings with a virtuosos grace. Beethoven's violin concerto filtered up around him in a lavish embrace, the motion of his arms stirring the dust particles that circulated in the shaft of moonlight showering him from above.

Magnus swayed back and forth on top of the rail as he played on, fully aware of the forces skulking around outside. A divine prompting from within compelled him to continue. He chose not to question, but to simply obey the Holy Spirit.

He closed his eyes, remembering the last time he had played the concerto. It was in 1829 Europe, and Magnus had challenged Nicoló Paganini himself; a man deemed the greatest violin virtuoso of all time. The myth of Paganini's greatness was known around the world in that day, even reaching the shores of the New World. He was known as the *Devil's Fiddler*, for it was said that every time he played the Devil was at his elbow.

It had been this very myth that had drawn Magnus back across the Atlantic to duel with Paganini. The challenge would take place in the home of Johann Wolfgang von Goethe himself, a famous Illuminati poet and playwright; a close friend of Paganini's.

Paganini had refused to play Beethoven's work in public. But the invitation to meet the challenge of a mysterious virtuoso in the Weimar home of his friend Goethe had proven too tempting.

Paganini had been at his vaudevillian best that night, Magnus remembered. But there had been something strange about the prankster's presence as they dueled by the light of the fireplace in Goethe's library. As Paganini danced back and forth in front of the fire, Magnus had noticed his feet gliding with the music in such a way it looked as though the soles of his buckled shoes were hovering an inch above the floor. He dismissed it as a trick of the fireplace's flickering light since he hadn't detected any supernatural presence about. But the aura surrounding the ghostly, gaunt-faced violinist at the time was unnerving, as if he were a puppet literally dancing on unseen strings. And his speed and accuracy was certainly not like anything he had ever heard before, his genius bordering on the diabolical. He had been a mystery at best.

Magnus stopped in the middle of his playing with that thought, eyes opening slowly as he looked at his violin that Stradivarius had designed with a low bridge to give it a fiddle capacity. "Paganini," he said softly. "He was there, too."

Magnus lowered the violin and its bow. He floated backward off the railing, landing softly on the balcony floor. He hadn't put it together until now. That same sense of inexplicable mystery he had felt during his duel with Paganini had been experienced one other time several years before coming to this valley. He remembered the words of the assassin during their encounter in Lebanon on that Christmas Eve night of the unholy nativity. Words he had given little heed to when he asked him if he were Old Scratch himself: "*No…. But you can think of me as the Devil's Fiddler, if you like.*" the assassin had told him.

The events of that revelatory night came rushing back forcefully, gathering with it a storm of all the other unexplained events and apparitions he hadn't been able to discern in the past.

"Michael was right," he whispered to himself, his gaze narrowing into a trance-like focus. "He's been hunting me…waiting for my weakest moment."

Magnus glanced to the left suddenly as more immediate concerns registered in his sensitive ears. He sat the violin and its bow down on top of the rail, bowing his head to pray one last time as he picked up on the unmistakable hum of a chopper in a dead-on approach.

357

Chapter Thirty-six

Grimes worked a row of buttons on the main instrument panel of his cockpit, resulting in a grating noise similar to a huge gear downshifting. The chopper's rotors spinning wildly above the jet-like canopy and its turbo shafts suddenly went quiet as Grimes engaged the chopper's experimental stealth technology.

He slowed the Apache to 30 knots before dropping down over the treetops, following the dirt road that split the tall field of grass in front of the old meeting hall. He flew the chopper almost level with the height of the sanctuary's roof.

The Apache stopped about 50 feet away from the front of the sanctuary, hovering only some 30 feet off the ground. The wind from the chopper's near-silent rotors pressed down on the grass below, rolling forward against the foundations of the old clapboard structure where the ground support team was hiding.

The pack leader below gave a thumbs-up to the Apache, turning to his men on both sides of the road, motioning for them to brace for the fire zone.

Grimes gave a quick salute, turning to focus on the sanctuary's arched window as he spoke to the pilot elevated behind him. "Switching weapons to forward systems."

"Aye, sir."

Grimes quickly dialed the chopper's chain gun into the hand controls of his cockpit. He then activated the instrument panel's PNVS display, engaging the chopper's new thermal

imaging scanner mounted on the target acquisition and desig-
nation systems turret on the chopper's nose section.

Grimes pushed his helmet's mic back toward his mouth,
squinting in surprise as the targeting eyepiece of his helmet lit up
with an unusually bright pattern of body heat emanating from
the balcony. "Target...is confirmed," he said with hesitation,
unsure if what he was seeing was real. "Thermal lock engaged."

Specter's voice was loud as it rang through the speakers
inside Grimes' flight helmet. "Fire at will, Hawkeye One. Fire
at will!"

Magnus stood in the moonlight with his head bowed, palms
facing the ceiling, finishing his prayer with a soft, "Amen."

He lowered his hands slowly, lifting his head at the same
time as he picked up on the command to fire blaring through the
Apache's com-link, eyes exploding open in a wild stare. "Fools
rush in...."

Magnus whipped around in a blurring spin, the train of his
coat flying out behind him over the rail in his run toward the
back wall. He leaped forward halfway across the balcony's floor,
extending his body at an angle as he took flight, arms stretching
out before him in a double-fisted charge.

Magnus crashed through the balcony's arched window, shattering the glass with the force of his joined fists as he sailed out
into the night air, the wind brisk against his face, gliding high
above the field of grass like a windswept shadow as every eye
gathered against him was stunned by his sudden assault. He
skimmed through the air just beneath the twisting rotors of the
Apache, pulling his knees forward to plant his right boot on the
angled panel of the chopper's canopy just above Grimes' head.

Grimes fired out of surprise as Magnus crouched beneath
the rotors on the forward section of the canopy, unable to hold
the chopper in a steady hover while unloading with the chain
gun, ripping across the sanctuary's upper facade in a side to side
pattern of tracer fire.

The ground team below watched in disbelief, drawing their weapons on the windswept figure crouched on the chopper's canopy, unable to fire.

The Apache twisted to the right and left. But Magnus remained unmoved from his crouching posture.

The chain gun tore across the sanctuary's roof in a brilliant spray of bullets again as Grimes tried to steady his panicked grip on the controls. "Wolf Den, this is Hawkeye One, do you copy?!" he shouted into the mic of his helmet.

Magnus slid his right boot sideways to look down into the cockpit, eyes glowing like emerald coals as he met Grimes' mystified gaze. He grinned at him before leaning forward in a sudden jolt, fluidly unsheathing his sword, slicing through the chopper's blade pitch control rods and the main rotor mast in a shear of sparks.

Magnus shot off the canopy to the right as the rotor blades were catapulted upward from the top of the severed mast, the Apache pitching to the left, crashing to the ground on its side in front of the old worship hall. The pack leader and his split team had no time to scramble for cover, the chopper's Hellfire missiles detonating on impact as the Apache's self-sealing fuel cells exploded open, consuming them all in a rolling wave of flames that leveled the entire sanctuary in one swift blow.

361

＊•＊－ ➤○➤ ＋•＊＋

Specter, stunned, watched as the Apache's camera went static. He stepped back several paces toward the center of the communications room, mouth gaping in horror as he stared blankly at the snow-covered screen.

The technician working the terminal in front of him turned around in his swivel chair with the same look of disbelief. "Di...did you see that?"

Specter didn't answer. He had only seen one other person display such superhuman abilities, and he was dead.

"Sir?"

Specter looked at the wide-eyed technician, his face twisting with a familiar look of fear. "Alert the Sentinel Corps," he said softly. "I want containment teams on the southern road in five minutes."

The technician hesitated as if he hadn't heard the command.

"Now!" Specter shouted.

"Yes, sir," the technician replied, whipping around in his chair.

Specter stepped back another pace, burying his face in his hand as he thought of the consequences to come.

Sodom stood perplexed on the clock tower's obelisk, the moon craning high above his dark head, wings drawn snugly around his body. His black and yellow eyes were transfixed on a spiral of flames ascending from the middle of the valley's eastern mountain.

Sodom turned, focusing on the air base north of the town where pilots were scrambling toward Black Hawk helicopters that had come in for refueling.

Sodom resumed his position, glancing down at the courthouse square where heavily-armed agents were running from the glass building facing the southern section of the town, piling into a line of Suburbans in groups of four.

Another explosion from the eastern mountain lifted Sodom's head from the activity below. His warriors nesting in the Masonic Temple's redwoods had turned from the singing and dancing on the roof below, staring in the direction of the explosions.

Sodom gave no order to his warriors to investigate. Instead, he looked to the other mountain ranges, waiting to see if another certain power would respond to the disturbance.

The assassin stepped from the shadow of the two trees behind the rock where the Archangel had been sitting, stopping short of the edge as a familiar, crystal-blue force field wrapped around him in a sudden flash of light, barring him from going any farther.

He angrily struck the cylindrically-shaped force field with a thunderous blow of his right fist, its bright field rolling like an impenetrable wall of watery fire. It was a divine prison that had restrained him many times in the past.

He gazed hotly at the eastern mountain range as the field continued to roll around him from the aftershock of his punch. Flames and smoke climbed high above the treetops of the distant peak, taunting him where he stood. But his temporary incapacitation didn't leave him without other options.

The assassin crossed his thick arms over the expanse of his chest, raising his heated glare to the heavens to cast a telepathic message across the stars. "The hammer of judgment is falling sooner than anticipated."

Lucifer sat on his black throne somberly, head bowed slightly, hands gripping the silver dragon-head busts on each armrest. The two warriors from his Imperial Guard still hovered above him, their hallucinogenic wings remaining fixed in a fiery canopy over the Archrebel.

Dragylon's court of Shadow Kings were assembled on the railed walkways running along the sides of the library's roof, whispering telepathically amongst themselves as the sphere sailed slowly through the Earth's upper atmosphere toward the Middle East.

Lucifer lifted his dark head slowly, the fire in his eyes boiling outward in crooked streams of crimson light, curling back around the sides of his golden face. A familiar voice had whispered across the breadth of his cosmically-crowded mind, merging with the pattern of his own thoughts that allowed him to see a distant mountain partly aglow with flames through the eyes of another.

Lucifer dug his emerald nails into the top of the armrests, the golden irises of his crimson eyes flashing with a patiently aged hate as he remembered how the deeds of the Shekinah Champion had frustrated many of his plans throughout the centuries. "No more," he sneered, the flames on the distant

mountain spiraling through his cosmic mind. "The season for stalking has come to an end."

He shot forward suddenly in a flurry of wings, arcing upward over the mammoth trees beside his throne, a deep scowl of vengeance etched into his bright face, leaving the Shadow Kings and the legions below confused as he disappeared through the galactic archway in a splash of light.

Chapter Thirty-seven

Magnus hovered nearly 10 feet above the peak of the flames, the split train of his coat swishing back and forth in the drafts of heat. He watched as the fire quickly consumed what was left of the sanctuary's old frame. The ashes of the meeting hall's burning timbers and his ancient books ascended all around him in the heated drafts, swirling across his eyes and face as they spiraled to the heavens like the incense of a precious offering.

Magnus' face was vacant of all mercy as it glowed in the brightness of the enormous pyre licking at the soles of his boots from below. The Apache had become a blackened hull, the bodies strewn about in the ruins rapidly melting down to their skeletal structures from the fire's intense heat. The embers of the sanctuary seemed to hiss above the other noises of ruin, almost crackling with praise as the bones of the wicked lay *hip and thigh* in a great slaughter at the foot of its foundation.

Magnus inhaled the fire's aroma with a sudden breath before turning around quickly in the air, scattering the embers floating up around him. He flew toward the trees on the right side of the dirt road, skimming over the tops of the pines as he vanished down the side of the mountain to meet the enemy's main force that was sure to be en route.

Specter glared at the snow-covered screen in the situation room while the technician in front of him worked the central terminal. "Punch up the satellite feed!" he ordered.

"Yes, sir," said the technician, pounding away on the keys of the terminal.

The large screen above them flashed clear, projecting an aerial image of the valley.

Specter took off his coat and rolled up his sleeves, crossing his arms, sweat forming along the bridge of his forehead. "Bring up the target area of the southern road."

The technician complied instantly, rattling the keyboard with frenetic speed.

The image was quickly condensed to focus on the immediate areas surrounding the valley's southern road. Three Suburbans raced into view from ground level, with three Black Hawks pulling up the rear from the air, flying low to the treetops.

Specter watched silently, waiting for the moment of interception, the beads of sweat breaking into streams down the sides of his face.

Chapter Thirty-eight

Magnus crouched in a steep ditch in front of the valley's southern road, shrouded in the shadows of the thick pines behind him, his back facing the meadow on the other side of the trees where he had rescued April.

He looked up to his right, spying three groups of headlights racing in his direction. Behind them, flying low over the trees on each side of the road, was a cluster of Black Hawk helicopters providing air support.

Magnus waited, stretched on the grass bank.

Just as the first of the three Suburbans were about to pass in front of him, Magnus sprang up in a burst of preternatural speed, hitting the left side of the road running. He lowered his shoulder as the front end of the vehicle was passing before him, his face and arms a blur as he slammed into the left front fender of the lead Suburban, shearing through the metal, pushing forward like a buzz saw, using his shoulder to cut through the entire engine block, shattering the windshield as he exited the opposite fender. The entire moment was faster than the blink of an eye, causing the other two people in the SUVs to hit the brakes when the lead vehicle careened out of control. The agents in the lead vehicle were killed as the vehicle flipped and roll down the steep bank on the left side of the road.

Specter ran forward and gripped the back of the technician's chair, staring up at the devastation playing out on the projector screen above him. "Block the road!" he shouted. "Block the road!!"

The eight remaining Sentinel Corps agents jumped into the debris-covered road from the other two SUVs, slamming the doors shut as they turned their backs against the right side of each vehicle, weapons cocked and ready. The Black Hawks hovered in a triangle above them, shining down giant spotlights into the surrounding woods.

Magnus watched through the trees on the right side of the road as the agents lined up beside one another. The lead agents were peeking over the hoods of both vehicles at the same time, looking to the left side of the road, hoping to glimpse his position with the Starlite sunglasses they were each wearing.

Magnus searched the shadows to the left and right of him, wondering where the real enemy was.

He turned his attention to the road again as one of the spotlights from the hovering Black Hawks panned across the trees in front of him. He probed his fingers through the pine needles covering the valley floor, finding two smooth stones at the base of the nearest tree.

Magnus raised his head, fixing his eyes on the agent who was peeking over the hood of the new lead vehicle. He studied the openings between the trees in front of him for a moment, finding the best path possible. With perfect aim, he reared back and threw the stone in his right hand, watching as it sailed with the speed of a bullet through the path he had chosen. The rock exploded through the right temple of the peeking agent, shattering his skull, blood splattering across the hood as his body flailed forward.

Magnus took aim again before the rest of them could react, throwing the other rock in his left hand with ambidextrous ease, watching as it took the same path as the other one. It hit the agent beside the fallen one the moment he turned toward Magnus' hiding place, snapping his sunglasses in half as it pierced the flesh and bone between his eyes. The rock exited the back of his head, exploding through the passenger side window behind him like a gunshot that caused the other agents to duck.

Magnus broke into a forward run through the trees as the agents stood to their feet and started firing in his direction. He snapped some of the tightly knit pines in half with the motion of his shoulders, his pace unhindered as he charged into the fray, the seals of his golden armor chiming like the emblems of *Death's* approaching horse. Their bullets lit up the forest like speeding fireflies, zipping by his blurred face in near misses. Very few found the target as they bounced off his face and armor like pellets of sleet.

Magnus vaulted into the open in another pine-snapping explosion, leaping through the air, a silent roar in his bright eyes. He hit the pavement in front of the two agents still standing against the lead Suburban, slowing enough to appear as a wraith-like shadow charging toward them.

Magnus hit the two agents in their chests with the palms of his hands, slamming them against the vehicle in a window-shattering impact, killing them instantly as he pushed the Suburban over the bank on the other side of the road.

The remaining four agents rushed around in front of the other vehicle, firing in sporadic streams as the other Suburban crashed into the woods.

After a barrage of constant firing, a tall, brutish looking agent threw up his fist, signaling for a cease fire. The agents reloaded their HKs with tape and turn clips, standing down to investigate the fire zone through the plumes of smoke ascending from the barrels of their weapons. The brutish agent stepped forward a pace, chambering the first round of his new clip, his weapon held ready to unload once more as he studied the shredded trees on the other side of the road's steep bank.

Without warning, a shadowy pocket of air blew by the brutish agent with a chilling force. Before he could turn to follow the strange anomaly, a bone crushing thud echoed behind him. He turned just as two of his comrades fell dead in the middle of the debris-covered road, their necks broken instantly.

369

The brutish agent snapped his head to the left only to see his last comrade fall before him, neck broken by the same anomaly that swept between them again.

The agent spun wildly as his comrade hit the pavement, unloading with his weapon again in a horrified scream, desperate to destroy an enemy that defied belief.

* * *

Magnus hovered lightly on a branch near the top of a pine on the right side of the road, arms crossed over his chest, eyes aglow in the shadows. The wind from the choppers above him pressed down on the top of his perch as they frantically searched the woods of the fire zone with their spotlights, hoping to fix their own guns on the elusive target.

He stood on the branch for several minutes, back propped against the trunk of the tree, waiting until the petrified agent below exhausted the last of his ammunition.

Magnus' demeanor quickly shifted to impatience as the agent threw his empty weapon aside and picked up an HK in each hand from two of his fallen comrades. He lunged forward from the tree's long branch, arms extending behind him in his drop toward the road, the train of his leather coat spreading out in an aquiline manner on each side of him as it was designed to do.

He landed softly on the surface of the road as the brutish agent turned to the left bank, quickly depleting the ammo clips of the two HKs he was waving wildly.

The agent stood there for a moment, breathing heavily as spirals of smoke floated in front of his feverish face from the barrels of each weapon. His breathing slowed to a haunted pace, sensing suddenly that someone was standing behind him. Close behind him. He swallowed hard as he started to turn around, hesitantly. The hair stood up on the back of his neck when he glimpsed a silhouette from the corner of his right eye. He stopped immediately, his breathing accelerating even more, mind racing out of control. He glanced down to his right, spotting another weapon lying on the road several feet away. He threw the empty weapons aside and dove for the other HK lying in the road.

Magnus reached out and grabbed the agent by the tails of his suit coat before he could hit the road, jerking him backward. He snatched him by the back of his thick neck with his left hand in his rebound toward him, rendering him immobile with the strength of his grip. He lifted him into the air with ease, grabbing the back of the agent's pants legs with his right hand, cinching them together tightly as he pressed the large man above his head horizontally.

Magnus held him aloft for several seconds, listening to the agent's horrified curses a moment before falling to his left knee suddenly, bringing the agent down with him. The agent's curses stopped short in his mouth as his back exploded in a terrible snap across the champion's right thigh that was extended outward, blood spewing against Magnus' coat and armor from a crack that was ripped open in the large man's chest.

He shoved the broken body off his leg, standing back up just as one of the Black Hawks got a fix on him in the middle of the road with its spotlight, bodies piled around his feet. The smell of brimstone filled the air as the soul-crowned spirits of the dead agents were sucked down into Hades. He ignored the portals opening and closing all around him as the other two Black Hawks focused their spotlights on him as well, pulling together in a tighter formation with the other chopper. The bay doors of each aircraft slid open as he stared up at them, revealing a gunman standing in each of the hatchways. M134 multi-barrel miniguns were mounted on the decks in front of them, poised to fire.

Magnus stood motionless in the combined spotlights, the wind from the rotors whipping his hair backward as he looked up, his coat flipping back and forth. "Well?!" he taunted, throwing his arms out to the sides.

The deck guns from each chopper ignited in unison, unleashing a shower of armor piercing rounds at the lone champion.

Magnus somersaulted forward, grabbing his knees in his roll through the air, bullets piercing the webbed sections between the flexible rods of his coattails. He landed mere inches from the front bumper of the last Suburban, quickly dropping to one knee. He reached down beneath the chrome bumper with his left hand,

371

clasping the front portion of the vehicle's chassis. A spray of bullets ripped across the metal in front of his fingers as he crinkled the hood with the grip of his other hand.

Magnus lifted the vehicle off the road with little effort, pointing the back end of the Suburban straight up into the air when he stood to his feet. He cocked his head to the left past the glare of the headlights, looking up across the bottom of the vehicle as another barrage of bullets shredded the right front tire near his head.

He threw the vehicle as if it were a javelin, rumbling the surrounding treetops with its wake.

The target chopper had no time to react. The airborne Suburban struck it square in its nose section, causing a chain reaction as it spun around out of control in a terrible explosion of flying debris that crashed into the other two Black Hawks.

Magnus darted to his right, leaping forward several hundred feet, landing with a nonchalant walk as heaps of metal crashed to the road behind him in a mushroom of flames.

372

Specter bowed his head, turning his back to the projector screen, removing his glasses to hide his face in his hand.

The technician turned toward Specter, struggling to speak. "Si...sir?"

Specter turned back around, holding his glasses by his side, face wet with the fear of what he had just witnessed. "How many choppers do we have left?" he asked.

"One, sir," he answered nervously.

Specter closed his eyes to think. "I want the other prototype for the A-6 Mark loaded on that chopper in five minutes," he ordered, looking back up. "Once that is done, have the pilot fly to the chateau and evacuate Mr. Alchemy immediately. The rest of us will hold our ground."

The technician hesitated in his response to the orders.

Specter's eyes widened angrily when the technician didn't respond immediately, looking as though he were in a state of shock. "DO IT!!" he shouted.

The technician whipped around in his chair, grabbing a communications headset to issue the orders.

Specter turned his back to the screen again, covering his face as before. He knew death was certain no matter what the outcome. And he had no desire to face it alone.

Chapter Thirty-nine

Sodom stared at the second set of fires burning on the valley's southern road. He threw open his wings indignantly, reaching for the large blade hanging from the belt of his armored apron. He jerked the weapon from its sheath, calling in a thunderous voice to one of his warriors. "Tribune Massakur!"

A lone rebel rose from one of the redwood trees protruding through the roof of the town's Masonic Temple, making a quick flight to the clock tower's obelisk. Massakur was over eight feet tall, with a sleek body resembling granite. His warlike, humanoid face was accented by star-shaped irises of red fire rotating in the center of his black corneas. A mane of fiery-red hair competed with sharp, black wings billowing together in waves behind him. A golden trident with blue fire streaming from its three-pronged head was carried in his right hand, accompanied by a round black shield attached to his left arm.

Massakur hovered in front of Sodom. "I am yours to command, my king," he said, bowing his head.

Sodom pressed the flat of his sword's curved tip beneath the rebel's stone chin, eyes glowing with a yellow confidence as he lifted the warrior's head with the edge of his blade. "Kill the champion," he ordered.

Massakur smiled wickedly, revealing a golden pyre that licked at the spaces between his shark-like teeth. "With extreme prejudice, my king?"

"Is there any other way?"

"I will bring you his head," he vowed.

"Boast afterward," Sodom replied.

Massakur nodded before whipping around in the air, his black wings flapping wildly behind him as he soared over the roof of the Masonic Temple. The other warriors cheered him when he passed, hoisting his forked trident and shield as though he had already won the battle.

"Go!" Sodom shouted to the rest of his warriors. "Follow your tribune!"

The remaining warriors shot up from the tops of the redwoods protruding through the corners of the temple, following Massakur toward the southern road.

Sodom watched his elite band forge a wall high into the air, its foundations starting at the edge of town on its southern road. He glanced around at the surrounding mountain ranges one last time. There was still no movement from the assassin.

He looked below, sensing activity beneath his tower again. A low, gurgled hiss escaped his fangs as an agent in a green flight suit scurried across the roof of the Omega Group's southern glass building toward a newly-landed Black Hawk helicopter. He ducked beneath the chopper's twirling blades while carrying a small metal case with both hands.

Sodom glared venomously at the mountains, searching the distant treetops for the slightest glimpse of the assassin. "Project Palladium has been compromised!" he growled. "Where are you? He's coming!"

Magnus strolled along the valley road at a normal pace, peering up at the Hunter's moon still hovering in the sky. The trees were vacant of rebel hosts. But he expected that to change the closer he got to town.

Magnus rounded a bend in the valley's southern road, lowering his gaze with his first glimpse of what awaited him. A tightly-constructed wall of rebels stood in the straight stretch of road before him some distance away, burning into full view against the sleepy backdrop of the town. They were stacked six groups high, reaching nearly fifty feet into the air, with four in each group.

Magnus did not slack his pace. He focused on a particular rebel standing in the middle of the road several feet in front of the other fiery-eyed rebels, magnifying his image.

Magnus walked several more minutes before coming in range of the stone-like warrior, stopping about a hundred feet away. He stood there for a moment and studied the wiry titan, crossing his hands behind his back.

Massakur smiled at the champion, pointing his golden trident as he spoke. "Is this the legendary king that has made the powers of darkness tremble for centuries?" he mockingly inquired, vapors of blue flame rolling from the forked head of his trident. "I am unimpressed."

Magnus glanced at the black shield on the warrior's left arm, recognizing it as one of the shields of the rebels that were perched on the roods outside the broken walls of Jerusalem the day it finally fell to Titus. "I suppose you're the champion of the ranks?" he remarked.

"I am Massakur, Tribune of the Nekros Order under Sodom the Sullier's command."

Magnus checked the trees on each side of him again as the lead rebel boasted of his authority. There was no hint of the assassin's presence anywhere nearby. But that had never been a luxury afforded him in the past, he remembered.

Magnus quickly fixed his sights on the lead rebel again, reaching to his left to draw the blade hidden beneath his coat. He gazed at the angelic wall behind Massakur, lifting his sword slowly, the blade shining with a lethal sheen in the moonlight as he pointed it at them all.

The warriors behind Massakur moved their clawed right hands with lightning speed to the pistol grip stocks of their infernal crossbows, drawing their weapons simultaneously. Each bow folded outward from the sides of their large, barrel-shaped ends with thunderous snaps as they were released from their armored holsters.

Massakur glanced back at the wall behind him as the uniform sound of the drawn weapons echoed throughout the night air, his black and red eyes wide with pleasure when he looked back at Magnus. "My brethren are a little anxious as you can see," he taunted.

Magnus eyed the diabolically-crafted crossbows aimed at him throughout the wall, taking note of the blue fire glowing in the rims of the widely flared muzzles of each bow that resembled the short, large-bore blunderbuss guns of the 18th century.

"Don't let my brethren frighten you into submission," Massakur sneered. "The battle is between us."

Magnus stood his ground.

"The first move is yours, champion," Massakur replied. "But know this: You will only get one."

Magnus grinned as he lowered his sword in front of him, dropping his chin in a subtle aim. "I only need one," he uttered.

The champion began to channel his breaths into a calculated rhythm, sensing his drawn blade had sufficiently lured them into his trap, distracting them from the sword hidden within, used only in secret throughout the ages. " *'Wail, O oaks of Bashan!'* " he said, quoting from the Book of Zechariah, the pitch of his voice building, picturing in his mind the force and direction of his strike. " *'For the thick forest…HAS COME DOWN!!!!!!'* "

A sonic wave burst forth from his mouth as he shouted the last portion of the verse, rolling toward the wall like the vaporous ring on the edge of an atomic explosion.

The warriors who made up the wall, each who had been in Jerusalem the day it fell to Titus, remembered the champion's hidden sword too late as they tried to scramble before the wave struck. Its force and speed shattered Massakur like a vainly posed statue, ripping upward through the retreating ranks in black explosions. The wave pushed straight up through the sky, tearing a temporary hole in the ionosphere before fading across the reaches of the Outer Realm.

The glowing eyes and the ashy remains of the rebels were sucked downward like falling stars as the road's surface twisted like water in a counterclockwise motion, opening into a dark, vacuous pit.

Magnus watched Sodom's warriors fall in fiery clusters through the gateway of the Abyss, the rim of the pit having hardened just short of the toes of his boots; its mouth of wailing torment yawning wide enough to catch each of the falling hosts.

＊•••＝◦═••＋＊

Sodom wrapped his left arm around the clock tower's obelisk as the vacuum of the Abyss swept across the entire airspace of the town, roaring with the sounds of the damned as it ripped at his evil substance. His false wings flapped madly against the sides of his face as he watched the remainder of his warriors fall helplessly into the pit, eyes bulging from their sockets in a black and yellow rage. He spit curses at the champion as the pull of the vacuum blistered the surface of his Morganite skin.

379

Chapter Forty

The black nails on Sodom's left hand dug deep into the ivory-layered obelisk, the winds of the Abyss fading as the rim of the pit started to shrink.

He slammed against the obelisk as the pit finally closed.

Sodom glanced out toward the valley's southern road while he hung there, his wings having deflated into a ripped and torn robe; their true form. Black ooze poured from the bubbling holes in his face and scarlet-colored muscles, dripping across the miniature shield of gold in the center of his cuirass breastplate.

An exhausted growl escaped through his fangs when he caught his first glimpse of the champion's dark silhouette at the edge of town. "You wretched heap of clay!" he snarled.

Sodom pulled himself to the top of the obelisk, clamping his taloned feet down on the structure's triangular point, slowly standing upright against the backdrop of the moon and stars. He hesitated in his response to the attack, his stare falling down on the sprawling rooftops of the town beneath him, pondering the champion's power that had destroyed his warriors in a single blow. The historic Victorian homes of Imperial Lane struck him with a sudden revelation, reminding him of those on Nob Hill that were destroyed in the San Francisco Earthquake of 1906. "It was you," he whispered hatefully, snapping his glare toward the champion again. "It was you!"

He lifted the curved sword in his right hand, black ooze dripping from his thick arm as he pointed the blade in Magnus' direction. "Come to me, clay champion!" he dared. "Don't hide behind the sword of your mouth as in the past! FACE ME HERE!!!"

"The champion is the least of your worries, Sodom."

Sodom whipped around, coming face to face with one of Heaven's mighty Book Masters.

Scriptos hovered a few feet away, decked out in a royal blue robe, silver fire streaming from the sides of his eyes as he pointed his shimmering broadsword at the rebel, his muscular arms bulging through the sleeves of his billowing garment of old.

Sodom pulled his sword over in front of him, securing it with both hands while pointing it at the angel. "Where did you come from?!" he roared.

"You should have paid more heed to the assassin's warnings," he said, arms locked straight out in front of him, unflinching.

Sodom glanced quickly to his left as the last Black Hawk passed by the clock tower, heading in the direction of the chateau on the northern mount.

He looked back at the angel. "It's not over yet!" he snapped, black ooze spitting through his fangs. "You have to defeat me first if you want to be king of the mountain!"

Scriptos lunged at the rebel prince suddenly, swinging his sword at Sodom's dark head. Sodom was able to block the blinding swipe, his foothold slipping a bit as their weapons collided in a thunderous charge. Bolts of electricity exploded in every direction across the valley's field of stars as they battled one another above the town.

Scriptos was quicker than Sodom had expected, swinging his sword in a flurry of silver blurs.

Sodom managed to block each blow with a blocking maneuver, but he was unable to move forward with any attempt at an offense. His legs, struggling to support him, weakened with each assault from the angel's relentless blade.

Scriptos circled the obelisk several times in quick rotations, lunging and swinging at the perched rebel, tormenting him with his ceaseless attack.

Alchemy once again stood in the threshold of the library's French doors, listening to the sounds of a distant thunder. Under his right arm he held the helmet he had retrieved from Tsavo's conference room under his right arm while gazing out across the back lawn.

A rush of wind suddenly swept across the patio, rolling through the French doors. Alchemy stood immovable as the wind slammed against him, charging through the library like a hurricane. The flames in the stone fireplace exploded with a roar when the rush of air hit the back wall, spitting sparks across the shadows on the hardwood floor.

Alchemy glanced up to see a dark gray helicopter approaching the back lawn, the locks of his hair blowing wildly around the sides of his face as it landed in front of the patio.

The right side bay door flew open when the Black Hawk's landing gear touched down on the plush grass. A crewman jumped from the slick, ducking his head as he passed beneath the rotors. He ran toward the stone rail that wrapped around the library's patio, hurdling over it.

"Are you, Mr. Alchemy?!" the crewman asked.

Alchemy struck the crewman with his powerful stare, stopping him cold a few feet away. He waited a moment before answering, letting the seriousness of the crewman's informalities toward him sink in. "I am Alchemy…. Speak."

The crewman answered hesitantly. "Sir…. The town's security has been compromised I have orders to evacuate you immediately…. We have the second A-6 Mark prototype on board."

Alchemy turned his back to the crewman, knowing that what he had just told him meant that the Archangel's warning was already coming to fruition. He glanced at the golden face mask of the helmet tucked against his side. "The champion," he whispered hatefully.

The crewman craned his neck, trying to see Alchemy's turned face. "Sir?"

Alchemy looked to the fireplace on the other side of the library, watching as a strange anomaly emerged in the wall. A golden light that only he could see started to seep through the narrow spaces between the fireplace's numerous stones, spreading in every direction, outshining the flames in the hearth below.

A voice spoke to his mind from the rays of light stretching throughout the library. "My son," said the voice.

Alchemy bowed his head. "I am here, father."

"It is time to leave this valley," said the voice.

Alchemy looked back up at the rays of light boldly. "What of the town?" he asked.

"Its purpose has been fulfilled."

Alchemy glanced down at the helmet under his arm. "And what of the champion?" he asked.

"He will be dealt with."

Alchemy bowed his head. "Thy will be done, father," he said.

"No one must ever see you bow before another power, be it visible or not," the voice warned.

Alchemy nodded slightly, watching the rays of light seep back through the spaces between the fireplace's many stones. He could feel the confused stare of the crewman behind him. He turned around slowly, his hair blowing backward from the torrent winds of the Black Hawk's rotors.

"Sir? Are you all right?" the crewman asked.

Alchemy growled softly as a watery ripple rolled across his face in the image of a black lion's face that had the slanted eyes of a dragon.

Instantly, Alchemy reached out with his left hand and grabbed the terrified crewman's chin, snapping it sideways before the man realized what had happened. The crewman fell to the patio at Alchemy's feet in a violent thud, his neck broken in one fluid gesture.

Alchemy pinched the knot of his gold tie with a smooth stroke, casually stepping over the crewman's lifeless body as he walked toward the Black Hawk.

<hr />

Sodom stood with his back to the moon, his tattered robe billowing behind him. He fought to keep his arms up, pointing his tired blade at the angel hovering in front of him. His sharp feet

had slipped to the sides of the pinnacle, legs all but drained of their strength.

Scriptos stared quietly at the ragged Shadow King, knowing that he was ready to fall. Without word or pomp, the angel slowly lifted his broadsword. An elongated ring of blue fire exploded around the blade when he pressed an embedded jewel near the hilt's round hand guard, promising the rebel a final punishment.

Sodom scanned the area frantically, hoping to glimpse some sign of the assassin coming to his aid. There would be no sign. He stood alone, a Shadow King ready to fall from his mountain.

Sodom looked back at the angel, hissing in a fanged snarl before leaping back from the obelisk, spinning around in the air to flee.

Scriptos streaked across the night sky after him.

Chapter Forty-one

Magnus stood at the edge of town like a thief in the night, watching as Scriptos chased the town's deposed ruler across the horizon. Both disappeared quickly over the peaks of the eastern mountain range.

He slowly lowered his stare toward the sleeping town that lay before him, magnifying his focus on the roof of the town's Masonic Temple. The faint odor of burnt flesh lingered in the air from the smoke rising from the fire of the temple's rooftop altar. The demon possessed men he'd seen entering the temple the other night were dressed in the same Druidic garb as before, still dancing and playing their stringed instruments in maddened celebration; a scene reminiscent of how Belshazzar and his guests feasted on evil delights the night Babylon fell stealthily to the armies of Persia.

The only other signs of life were the town's glowing street-lights. Above street level, beyond the sloping roofs and vaulted gables of the Victorian sector, stood the Omega Group's southern building. The clock tower rising up through the center of the courthouse behind the building was flooded with light from below, its ivory exterior glowing against the dark sky. The blue and gold colors of the Zodiac clock face were bright as well, with its mechanical moon nearing the first quarter half of its elliptical dragon orbit.

Magnus checked the main road leading into town, picking up on the distant sounds of approaching vehicles.

He lowered his sword, standing its angled tip on the road's surface, resting his hands on the ivory hilt while steadying it at the lowest level of his chest. He stared at the vehicle lights in the distance as a soft wind brushed across his face, pushing back strands of his black hair.

Magnus thought of the families sleeping in their beds while the SUVs were racing toward him, unaware of the wrath that was about to be unleashed on them all.

He bowed his head and closed his eyes to push back the images in his mind, hardening his stance when a whispered reminder from the Holy Spirit brought to mind the Ichabod curse levied against the town. "So be it, Lord. *Lo-ruhamah.*"

Magnus lifted his head with a slow breath, looking above the SUVs barreling towards him, squaring his shoulders as they drew closer. He gripped the sword's elongated hilt, eyes glowing in the shadow falling across his face as he concentrated on the town's ivory tower. " *'A lion has roared! Who will not fear?'* " he said, quoting from the Book of Amos as the lights of the approaching vehicles grew brighter. " *'The Lord God has spoken! The Lord God… HAS SPOKEN!!!!!!'* "

The road collapsed beneath Magnus' feet at his shout, forming a crater five feet deep and 40 feet wide as he unleashed the full power of his voice. The seismic sound exploded from his mouth in a vaporous apparition, rolling forward like a giant tidal wave, plowing up the road as it went. The trees exploded into embers as the wave stretched across each side of the road for several miles.

Magnus was pelted with a shower of bark and pine needles, watching the wave hit the oncoming vehicles first. The Suburbans were shredded in half, sending bodies and sheet metal flying into the air.

The town was now nothing but a rippled picture of its former glory as the wave rolled towards it, reaching high into the twilight sky. Its rumbled approach was so loud it shook the foundations of the surrounding mountain ranges, bringing the bells of Sodom's tower to life in tolls of unescapable death.

***

Specter, deathly pale, stood paralyzed in front of the projector screen in the situation room. The valley's southern road was being plowed up into mounds before him by the strange wave, watching it instantly eviscerate the first structures near the town's city limits.

The technician in front of Specter jumped up and ran from the room to try and save himself.

Specter did nothing to stop him. He just stood there watching in horrified wonder, knowing there would be no escape.

—•⋯ ≍◦≍ ⋯•—

Mortar, plaster and painted wood exploded across the reflections of Magnus' emerald eyes as the gematria phrase, *My Wrath*, burned with an ember's glow on the surface of his lips. He watched the wave hit the heart of the town's most lavish sections, rolling undaunted toward the storefronts. Debris filled the air as the rippled wall of sound tore through everything. Plumes of explosions followed as gas lines and fuel pumps were uprooted from the ground.

The wave quickly demolished the Victorian homes of Imperial Lane and the Masonic Temple nearby, catching the Druid revelers by surprise as it pushed towards the Omega Group's square of glass buildings. The wave ripped through the southern building as if it were paper, expelling glass everywhere while bearing down on the courthouse and its clock tower. In less than a second, the frontal facade of the Abbey-style courthouse was blown apart in a storm of bricks. Sodom's ivory tower was next to fall, exploding into millions of pieces as the wave crushed the rest of the courthouse and the other three glass buildings hedging in the courthouse square. The entire town shifted in sudden violence as the wave fell on the tower and its surrounding buildings like a great millstone. It collapsed into an enormous crater as the walls of the town's subterranean tunnels that were fractured by the aftershocks of the San Francisco Earthquake of 1906 gave way at the peak of the wave's rumbling destruction.

Magnus leaned against his sword, lowering his head as the wave descended on the northern reaches of the town, its height and energy finally decreasing.

Alchemy sat down in the bucket seat next to the chopper's open bay door. The wind of the rotors tore at his hair and clothes while he reached behind him for the seatbelt harness, pulling it down over his head to strap himself in.

The pilot in front of him was staring out his window, staring at the body of his crewman lying dead on the library's patio. He turned around when Alchemy slammed the bay door shut, silencing some of the noise of the churning rotors. "Is everything all right, sir?" the pilot asked.

Alchemy palmed his hair to the sides of his handsome face, giving the pilot a cold stare. "Yes, captain," he answered. "I had to indulge myself in some much needed aggression…do you mind?"

The pilot hesitated. "Uh…no, sir," he answered.

"Good. Now, where's the prototype?"

"It's in the lock down at your feet, sir."

Alchemy peered down at a square panel that was cut into the bay's steel floor beside his left shoe. He placed the helmet on the seat to his left while reaching down to grab the panel's black latch, ripping the steel cover off angrily and tossing it aside. A small case was sitting inside the compartment, shining with the same silver color as the Tyrian shekels concealed in the inner breast pocket of his coat.

Alchemy picked up the case and placed it in his lap. A familiar symbol of broken infinity was etched in multiple colors in the center of the case's lid. He cradled his hands around the front of it, caressing the silver exterior before flipping the latches on each side of the case's small handle. He lifted the lid slowly, looking down at a tiny glass cube fixed in the center of a thick piece of black foam. The prototype for the group's Quantum nanochip was secured inside the glass. A sleek silver tube with a red button on top was positioned next to it, with a raised symbol of broken infinity two inches long and an inch wide protruding from the bottom of the device in a sharp gleam, the structure of its design intersecting with a small, needle-like delivery hole nestled in the center of its 8-style icon.

Alchemy slid his fingers across the tube's surface, eyes smoldering deep into the future as he thought of the god he would become. Armies would align to his call. Empires would merge under one banner. All would find security from the stability his Mark would offer in a world plagued by chaos and judgment.

The steel floor beneath Alchemy's feet began to vibrate with a precursor to those very plagues of judgment he thought to defeat.

Alchemy peered through the window as shingles started to slide from the chateau's segmented roofs, its windows exploding suddenly. The entire back lawn where the Black Hawk had landed was trembling violently.

Alchemy spotted a giant, rippling wave of sound cresting over the chateau's rooftop. "I suggest you take off, captain," he said as the wave started to descend on their position.

The pilot grabbed the controller, glancing out his own window. He pulled back hard on the stick, watching in disbelief as the chateau started to shake apart.

Chapter Forty-two

Magnus lifted his head. The wave finally started to dissolve against the northern mountain range. Hundreds of large and small fires ascended into the sky from the mounds of rubble in the distance, turning the moon blood-red in color. The town was a wasteland. Flaming debris fell back to the ground like shooting stars, reminding him of the Leonid Meteor Shower that had so stunned the entire planet on November 13, 1833, sparking a religious revival in the western hemisphere from those who thought Judgment Day had arrived.

The champion spoke in a low voice as he recalled a familiar passage from the Book of Jeremiah. " *'O you sword of the Lord, ... how long until you are quiet?'* " he wondered, the Hebraic embers on his lips fading from view.

An approaching sound caught Magnus' attention while he contemplated the destruction he had unleashed. He looked up to see the running lights of a lone helicopter approaching from the north, flying high above the town's fiery remains. Judas, he thought. It had to be.

Magnus turned away, fighting the urge to lunge through the air and destroy the chopper before it could flee the valley. He could feel the Holy Spirit's restraint on his heart. Judas must escape. He had a destiny to fulfill. God's justice and holiness demanded it.

Alchemy looked down on the town's flaming ruins. There was no remorse in his gaze for the families lying dead beneath the piles of rubble. The only regret was the loss of the nanochips they had been implanted with.

The pilot was looking at the fiery landscape below through the chopper's windshield, shaking his head in disbelief. "Holy...." He glanced back over his left shoulder. "Sir, what should I do?"

Alchemy looked at the pilot impatiently. "Fly on, captain," he answered.

The pilot noticed something when he looked forward again. A lone figure was standing in a crater near the edge of the town's southern border, his silhouette lit up by the many fires burning throughout the debris. "Sir, I see a survivor!" he said, glancing back at Alchemy. "Shall I set it down?"

Alchemy turned to the helmet sitting in the seat to his left. He knew it was the champion without even looking out the bay window. "Fly on, captain," he repeated.

"But, sir?"

"I said fly on, captain!"

The pilot turned back around. "Yes, sir."

Alchemy gave his attention to the silver case sitting in his lap, fingers charged with memory as he caressed the lid's dragon-marked surface. "You were right, Michael.... *The love of silver is the root of all evil,*'" he said softly, quoting the Greek translation of the Scriptures. "Its gleam of opportunity is irresistible.... One that shines more brightly in the darkness."

Chapter Forty-three

Magnus waited until the chopper passed out of range of his powerful hearing.

He leaned back from his sword to stare up at the heavens. "It is done, Father," he said. "It is done."

"NOOOOOO!!!!!!!!!!!!!!" a voice echoed. "IT IS NOT DONE YET, CHAMPION!!!!!"

Magnus stepped back a pace, lifting his sword in front of him, scanning the outside of the crater for the source of the voice. He turned his back to the town's scorched landscape, looking down the dark southern road while holding his sword with both hands.

"COME TO ME, CHAMPION!!!!!" the voice dared. "FACE ME LIKE A KING!!!!!!"

Magnus snapped his head to the right, looking above the tops of the pines to hone in on the peaks of the western mountain range. The emotion of his heart was stirred suddenly as the infernal voice of his nightmares taunted him from afar.

He gritted his teeth angrily. "The way of kings it shall be, then!"

Magnus spun to his right and leaped from the crater, bursting forward in a blinding sprint through the sections of the neighboring forest that hadn't been destroyed by his voice.

Chapter Forty-four

Magnus made his way slowly through a cluster of pines, his sword leading the way as he climbed a small hill to a moonlit clearing. He found himself standing on the bank of a large pond which barred his immediate path, surrounded by chirps, croaks and soft whistling sounds from the pond's nightlife. The water in front of him was over 50 feet deep and at least a quarter of a mile in circumference. It stretched to a tree-covered slope spanning the face of the western mountain range. Its borders were hemmed in by more of the valley's familiar pines, their branches intertwining tightly to form an arena-style barrier around the banks of the pond.

A crisp wind swept down from the mountain across the water's moonlit surface as he stood on the bank, silencing the pond's natural residents with its icy entrance. The wind gripped the champion's stern face like a clawed hand.

Magnus raised his line of sight, panning up the mountain's beginning slope, noticing a narrow bluff overlooking the pond some 60 feet above it. A black figure was crouching on a large flat rock near the bluff's ledge. Its outline was shaped by a metallic wingspan that rolled outward with a slow, liquid motion in the moonlight. The sharp tips from each wing arced high above the figure's golden head like horns trying to curve together.

Magnus locked gazes with the bright-eyed assassin, driving the tip of his curved sword into the ground beside him. He threw open the sides of his leather coat, allowing the silver buckles and the golden seals of his armor to be seen more clearly, taunting the assassin to test their strength.

The assassin stood up from the rock he was perched on, wings billowing outward in bronze flashes of adamantine sharpness. He vaulted forward from the ledge, gliding toward the pond's bank below, wings howling straight up above his head with piercing screams of descent. He landed on the bank in a display of thunder and great power that shook the ground.

The locks of his golden hair flailed around the sides of his masked face as he lifted his head toward the champion, wings collapsing behind his shoulders. His black, marble-like sheen reflected the moon and stars as easily as the pond's surface did, making his density appear deeper than it was.

A diamond-fanged smile lit up the bottom half of the shadow covering his face, stretching to a jester's width. "Nice armor," the assassin replied, his voice echoing across the water's surface. "I see you have already dipped it in the blood of some of your enemies. But be warned: I am not weak like they are. Your gilded armor will not save you from my reach."

Magnus took a step toward the water's edge. "Shall we find out?" he echoed back.

The assassin nodded with a fiery glare, reaching behind with his right hand to grab the long spine on the outer edge of his right wing, separating it in a flash of light from the rest of his metallic appendage. He pulled it over his shoulder, cradling it with one hand. He started to work the spine with a smelter's grace, shaping and folding it with the diabolical speed of his hammering fingers, cutting its length in half as he mastered it into a flattened and slightly curved design similar to the dadao dragon swords of 17th century China. He then gripped the razor edge of the flattened spine just above its severance line, feeling its fire as he formed grooves for his fingers with the pressure of his hand. Shards of electricity emanated from the gripping flex of his forearm, spiraling down across the bronze-colored weapon in a snake-like fashion, leaving behind a Quicksilver enamel as it disintegrated off the blade's angled tip. He slashed at the air several times with the weapon, expelling frigid vapors and streaks of silver light across the pond.

The assassin glared at the champion in the distance again, lowering the blade in front of him, black smoke rising through his fingers. "I am the darkened shore…crash against me AND BE BROKEN!!"

The assassin leaped forward onto the pond's reflective surface, boiling it with the touch of his oval, cleft-shaped feet as he broke into a thunderous run, wings fanning high behind him.

Magnus grabbed the ivory hilt of his sword, gripping it tightly in his right hand before breaking into a similar run over the water's surface, the seals of his golden armor chiming in unison with the motion of his torso. The blurred force of his boots created a wall of water to the right and left of him, soaring above his head in his race across the pond. His image reflected in the watery walls, giving him the appearance of a trinitarian freight train being led by a sword bobbing up and down with flashes of silver and crimson light.

Magnus reared the sword back to his right just as the assassin did the same. He seemed even taller than before, the champion thought, watching as the assassin's golden head eclipsed the distant moon, his eyes barreling toward him like spears of white fire, fangs gaped wide to devour.

Magnus leaped forward through the air just as the assassin started to swing his blade. He met the assassin's weapon with equal force, their blades exploding in a brilliant charge of electricity that spread across the water's surface like two lightning bolts crossing paths.

Magnus twirled around backward in the air to the right of the assassin as his sword sheared off the rebel's blade, bypassing the charging juggernaut in a move similar to the *petrinos* maneuver taught to him during his days in the *hippika gymnasia*. He landed some 30 yards behind the assassin, skidding on the soles of his boots even farther across the surface of the pond with the force of his motion, spinning around several times in wild sprays of water.

When he finally stopped, Magnus was facing the bank where he had been standing only moments ago. He slashed his sword through the air, watching the assassin spin around on the water in his direction. "Is that the best you've got!" he said in a reined shout, water exploding in pockets around him.

The assassin laughed with the force of a volcanic eruption, fangs bright in the moonlight. "You scream as loud as that little whore wife of yours," he sneered. "Do you also whimper like your father and brother did when I killed them, too?"

Magnus' arrogance faded instantly, eyes hardening with emerald fires as the hurt and separation of the last two millenniums were flung in his face with devilish timing. He plunged forward in a blind rage, his face blurring as he sped across the pond's surface, creating walls of water that soared even higher than before on each side of him. He pushed his sword straight out in front of him.

The assassin met him at the center of the pond with equal speed, their blades crashing together in an explosion of water and lightning.

Magnus held his ground on the water's surface this time, swinging his ancient sword in upward arcs at the assassin. His blinding swipes were met with blocks from the assassin's blade each time, the stream of blood on his sword's edge absorbing the impacts of their colliding weapons, preserving the stability of the blade and its tang beneath the ivory hilt. Their movements were so fast that both weapons were nearly invisible, expelling shards of lightning as they struck one another, charging the air and water beneath them with all the straying currents of electricity.

Magnus paced backward bobbing from side to side with blinding speed as the assassin swung relentlessly for his head in angled swipes, the blade's frigid heat brushing sharply close to his face each time. He somersaulted backward as the assassin swung for his legs, touching the water's surface with his left hand in his flip through the air, the assassin's blade slicing just beneath his coattails. He landed on one knee on the pond's surface with a splash, bringing his blade up in front of him as the assassin swung back around in a counter swipe, their weapons exploding in a thunderous wave of light and sound.

The assassin glared down through the crux of their crossed weapons as the champion held his ground against the weight of his locked arms, streams of electricity rolling off the their blades like water. "Excellent execution," he sneered, eyes flashing with bursts of white heat as he glanced at the image embroidered in gold velvet on the left breast of the champion's crimson-colored coat. "I have taught you well over the centuries, *Great Lion*."

"You have taught me nothing!" said the champion, the streams of electricity from their crossed blades casting strobes of light across his angry face.

The assassin leaned toward the crux of their blades, barreling down on him with the heat of his eyes. "Oh, but I have, son of my heritage," he argued. "More than you know."

"Your lies have no power over me any longer!" Magnus replied, arms trembling under the assassin's arcing weight.

"Really?"

"I know you've been hunting me in the shadows throughout history! But I am no longer a boy so easily frightened by monsters lurking in the dark! Tonight, I am the hunter!"

Magnus shoved the assassin's blade with all his might, standing to his feet, moving forward in a frenzy of swipes and lunges. He spun to the left and right with his sword, the assassin meeting his frenetic blade each time as he lost ground to the champion's determined charge.

The assassin batted away one of the champion's swipes with his right wing, halting his charge forward, pushing him back with the sudden blow.

Magnus retreated another step from the assassin, arcing backward as the spirit swiped down at him from left to right, missing his throat by an inch. He recovered his step as the assassin came back across with his blade, swinging his sword with terrible strength. He met the *dadao*-style blade with greater force this time, shattering it in a horrendous explosion, spewing silver and bronze shrapnel to the left and right of them.

Magnus quickly followed with another swipe of the sword, swinging the weapon back to his right with the same force.

The assassin snapped his wings forward as the champion brought his blade around to strike at his vaulted chest, forming an impenetrable shield around his body. The sword shattered as it struck the spiral-shaped wingspan, leaving only half a blade in the champion's hands.

Magnus leaped backwards as the assassin threw open his wings again, barely escaping the reach of the wingspan's sharp edges when they exploded outward. He glanced at his broken sword in disbelief. Other weapons had failed him in the past during the heat of battle, but never the ones forged with the Shekinah Wine in his blood.

The assassin stooped forward wrathfully, clenching his large fists, wings spread wide.

Magnus watched as two large rings of silver fire appeared around his thick forearms. His mind flashed back to their last meeting in the sewers beneath the town, remembering the power hidden in the smaller rings orbiting the two larger ones. He dove forward through the surface of the water just as the larger ring around each of the assassin's forearms spun quickly, discharging a familiar spray of stiletto-shaped bolts of silver fire from the smaller rings.

Magnus flew through the water just beneath the projectiles, turning his back to the pond's bottom to see the assassin's bright-winged form rippling above him on the surface. He thrust his arms in a powerful stroke, exploding back up through the water's surface, flying straight up through the air behind the rebel. He looked down as he flew upward, spinning into a backward flight, watching the assassin turn in the other direction at the sound of the exploding water.

The split train of the champion's soaked, specially-designed coat flapped as he descended behind the assassin, giving away his position as he landed back on the pond's surface.

Magnus still held his broken sword as the assassin whipped back around in his direction with a blistering right hook. He managed to catch the his large fist with his left hand, plunging forward with the sword in his right. He stabbed him in the chest, cracking a small portion of the preternatural flesh as though it were glass.

The assassin stumbled backward a few feet from the blow, growling angrily from the pain in his chest.

Magnus was relentless, following up with thunderous body blows to the assassin's midsection, cutting the flesh of his hands with each blow. His own blood splattered against his face as the Shekinah-hardened bones of his knuckles protruded back and forth through his skin like the pistons of a roaring engine, the pain hitting him like jolts of lightning, his hands cutting and healing with tremendous speed.

He raged forward forcefully, pushing the assassin backward with the power of his voice, causing the water to explode in pockets all around them while calling out the name of his murdered wife. "Rachel! Rachel!! Rach…."

The champion's passionate flurry of blows ended abruptly as something the size of a small boulder came crashing down on the back of his head, sending him face first through the water's surface.

◆–••–≡◦≣–••–◆

Magnus sank quickly from the weight of his golden armor, the motion of his impact rolling him over on his back as he went under. His body had been partially paralyzed from the unexpected blow, arms and legs floating uselessly as he drifted downward, nearly unconscious. The power of the Shekinah Wine in his bloodstream had acted with an instinctual speed beyond anything he had experienced before, closing his mouth before he hit the water to preserve the Edenic oxygen flow in his body. He would be able to hold his breath for an inordinate amount of time.

Magnus hit the bottom, the back of his head landing on a sloped surface of gray sand. His weakened arms and legs became tangled in tendrils of pond weed enveloping him in the water's murky depths.

He could barely hear his own thoughts. He tried to pray inwardly for help, wondering who had surprised him so quickly from behind.

A rapturous melody permeated the water suddenly as Magnus tried to pray, the pond floor trembling with powerful, methodic beats. Its resonance gave a binding surge of power to the vines wrapped around his arms and legs, electrifying his body with a fiery sensation.

Magnus managed to lift his head from the sloped surface enough to see a golden light appear in the distance, moving slowly in his direction. The pond floor grew brighter from the rays of the approaching light, music building symphonically as it drew closer.

The light started to take shape a few yards from where the champion lay bound to the pond floor. It morphed into a being of translucent gold, moving like some deposed king of old traversing the depths of the Pre-Adamic Earth laid waste when sin first entered the universe.

The rebel glared at him, his dragon eyes as bright as crimson suns, with vertical, fang-shaped irises of golden fire, encrusted with a vertical row of nine black pupils shaped like six-pointed stars, each pupil rotating counterclockwise. His velvet wings were incrusted with eagle-like feathers and scale-covered gems, stretching high and wide above his shoulders, increasing the outline of his muscled form. Stacked rows of ruby, horizontally-shaped vents protruded several inches from his muscular midsection, whistling with chords from a familiar violin concerto as each vent pumped back and forth fluidly.

Magnus watched in awe as the being crouched to his left knee over him. His face was smoothly human, strangely resembling the Apollo frieze he had once seen in the Temple of Apollo in Didyma, Turkey centuries ago, his reflective black hair swimming wildly through the water like a nest of vipers bound by their tails. But his brightness reminded him more of the multi-named sun god of the Zodiac. He was more beautiful and frightening than any being he had ever seen; a vision strikingly similar to the descriptions of Lucifer recorded in the writings of the Prophet Ezekiel.

Magnus listened to the concerto playing flawlessly throughout the water, its texture matching the virtuosos grace Paganini had displayed that night in Goethe's library. He stared at the rebel's bewitching face, believing that he was seeing the assassin's true form for the first time. Although he had never seen this image of him before, he could sense there was something deceptive about his appearance if he was who he now believed him to be.

Lucifer smiled with a gleam of diamond fangs, his laughter rolling through the water with infernal clarity.

Magnus struggled to free himself from the vines, feeling some of his strength returning. Before he could break away, Lucifer lunged forward with his right arm, the movement too fast for him to counter. He wrapped his golden fingers around the back of his neck like a fiery noose, digging his emerald nails into his hardened skin, slamming his head down through the slope's soggy surface. Everything went black as the gray sand covered his face. The pressure on his throat was like nothing he had ever felt before, water and sand seeping into his mouth, choking him.

This must be what it's like to die, he thought, feeling his head sink deeper into the sand. It felt as though he were being pushed into Hades itself. He had swallowed the assassin's bait with all the hatred that was within him, forgetting what John had told him, letting his pride and desire for revenge dictate the course of the battle.

The assassin had indeed taught him something. He had taught him how to wallow in the fullness of his fallen nature. Pride and personal vengeance had tempted him many times in the past, but its allure had never been brighter than when he struck the assassin's Quicksilver blade in that first moment of avenging rage. The power to exact justice had seemed within reach in his blinded passion. But now it seemed he would pay a terrible price for his sins: Death by disgrace.

Chaos clouded his thoughts while he struggled against the power of the Archfiend, his sharp laughter mocking him through the music still playing in his pipes, its texture layered in the swishing sand and water raging back and forth through his powerful ears.

Magnus surrendered his struggle suddenly, closing his eyes beneath the sand's grainy darkness to turn his battle inward. "Forgive me, Father," he prayed in his mind, arms and legs going limp beneath the weight of the Archrebel's fiery hand. "Forgive me for my arrogance. Forgive me for grieving your Holy Spirit."

405

The chaos and the pain did not lift, the Archrebel's laughter vibrating louder through the music, sand and water.

"Help me, Father. Help me!"

Just as he felt his neck would snap, the weight of the chaos finally lifted for a moment. It was as if his spirit rose to the thinnest layers of his hardened flesh, probing outward as the memories of his long life paraded before him in a funeral march.

A soft, familiar voice descended into the pit that his pride had dug for him, driving back the funeral procession in his mind. *"No one can take away that which I have given,"* the Lord whispered. *"Rise up, you beloved son of The Way!"*

Magnus' eyes flew open, glowing hotly through the sand covering his face as the voice of God echoed through his heart and mind, the chaos of his struggle crashing back down on him. But his Shekinah Strength had returned in full, the Spirit of the Lord's magnified presence energizing him. Forgiveness had been instant. And inspiration, if only for a moment, had returned.

Magnus pulled his knees toward his chest, ripping the vines with child-like ease. He pushed them forward with his renewed strength, guiding them on instinct. The soles of his boots struck Lucifer's wide chest with thunder, their impact repelling the Archfiend backward.

Magnus pulled his head from the sand as the fire around his neck was quenched, ripping his arms free of the other vines. He shot to his feet through the currents of water, standing on the pond floor. He searched the water's depths with a brightened vision. There was no sign of the golden foe.

Magnus pulled his arms behind him, propelling himself toward the pond's surface.

Chapter Forty-five

Magnus emerged slowly through the pond's surface until his feet were firmly planted on top of the liquid plateau once more, the water rolling from his face and clothes. The golden foe who had nearly choked the life from him moments ago was standing only a few yards away.

He stared at the jeweled figure before him that outshone the moon itself, his heart beating wildly as he glanced at the symbol in the center of the rebel's chest that had shadowed him all of his life. "So, you are the Devil under all those pretexts of shadows after all?" he remarked, looking back up into Lucifer's face.

"Of course," he said with a bright smile, extending his left arm to the side. "But so is he."

Magnus' gaze narrowed with momentary confusion as a tornado of shadows burst through the surface of the pond beside Lucifer, spinning wildly for several seconds. The shadows exploded suddenly with flakes of frigid light, flying in every direction to reveal the pilot inside. The assassin stood evenly with Lucifer, matching his height and muscle mass perfectly. The *Omega*-style symbols carved into his wings flexed with a peculiar motion, resembling the crescent moons he had seen on artifacts from the temples of the Akkadian moon god *Sin*.

The assassin smiled maniacally, the water rolling softly beneath his feet. He opened his large hand to reveal the champion's broken blade that had been lodged in his chest.

The assassin laughed at the champion's bewilderment, tossing the broken sword to the bank behind Magnus. "We are above your comprehension," he replied, fangs gaping lustfully as the everpresent shadow masking his face finally melted away, revealing the brow of a man and the blackened face of a lion that had the slanted eyes of a dragon. Countless pricks of black fur briefly folded outward from his muscled physique before melting back into the glossy luster of his body.

"Far above," Lucifer added. "But there is one greater than both of us…for separate, we are two. Together…."

It came to him in that moment as Lucifer paused in his boasting. That was what had been deceptive about his appearance, he thought, flashing back to just moments ago when the Archfoe tried to choke the life from him. On the Pre-Adamic Earth, before his fall from Perfection, Lucifer had been the Anointed Cherub, the highest Seraph of the Zoa. He was the champion who protected and covered God's earthly throne on the Holy Mountain that loomed above the center of the jeweled city of Eden and its palatial garden, a kingdom similar to the New Jerusalem to come in both likeness and location. But like the holy Cherubim who stand before God as representatives of the four tribes of Earth to be spared annihilation in the Noachian Covenant, his former title and office of function would be interchangeable with that of a seraph. And a seraph would have six wings and not just four like the smaller ones in the middle of Satan's chest seemed to suggest, a mystery found in the Book of Ezekiel that would be revealed more fully in the Revelation of Jesus Christ given to the Apostle John.

"Impossible," Magnus whispered, eyes widening as he recalled the assassin's words again from that Christmas Eve in Lebanon: "*No…. But you can think of me as the Devil's Fiddler, if you like*," the assassin had told him. It had been a play on words he had used to both confirm and deny who he truly was.

Both of them laughed in unison, their voices merging in a ghostly echo. "Noooo, champion…I was the first," they echoed.

Magnus watched as they both rose several feet in the air, hovering before him with their arms stretched out in cross-like fashion. The assassin slowly floated to the left in an eclipsing motion. Lucifer moved forward from behind, sifting through his winged back, the translucent density of his glorious body merging with his darker form, increasing his height by another foot as the sun became one with the moon. Bolts of electricity surged up and down the amalgamated form as Lucifer's ruby vents bulged through his midsection. A long, jewel-encrusted apron of crimson strips of fabric swirled down around the tops of his knees, hanging from a diamond, chain-link belt that materialized around his waist in tiny bursts of light, with an empty black scabbard emerging through his left thigh. A golden flame burst through his sculpted chest, splitting in half like separate fuses, expanding through the crevice between his pectorals as it formed a broken symbol of infinity. Two dragon heads with sharp wings appeared at the ends where the flame had split.

It was as if scales were falling from his eyes as Magnus watched the strong-jawed countenance of Lucifer's man-shaped face ripple into prominence over the assassin's. The dragon heads crowning the split symbol in the center of his chest merged with one another, taking the shape of the assassin's lion veneer as the insignia fused together in its 8-style structure, followed by wings sprouting from the sides of its smaller-sized head. The dragon eyes of the Archfiend's crowning face turned golden, their vertical irises burning with crimson flames. His wings morphed from bronze to a fiery shade of metallic crimson. The feather-like segments and the glassy, eye-shaped scales of Lucifer's submerged wings protruded through the adamantine during the transformation, showcasing jeweled, five-pointed stars in their centers. The assassin's silver moons arced over the jeweled feathers, completing the vision of that rebel who had tempted Magnus to avenge his wife's murder as he cradled her lifeless body in front Jerusalem's broken walls.

His wings rippled with dual motions. The wings in the middle of his chest were animate as well, curving around the sides of the lion's face like fiery banners, leaving only the white eyes and golden brow visible.

The revelation deepened as Magnus remembered the visions of the Prophet Ezekiel, and how he had described the image of a certain cherub in his book of prophecy depicted in carvings on the walls of a future Temple. Unlike other zoons described in the

Scriptures, the one portrayed on the Temple walls of Ezekiel's visions had only two faces instead of four. One was that of a man, and the other of a lion; a vision similar to the one standing before him now.

The fullness of the ancient dream he'd had in the belly of that Roman slave galley was almost complete when he remembered those passages of Holy Writ. The image of the two-headed dragon which had shadowed him all of his life had risen from symbolism to reality. But it had merged into a monster greater than he could have ever imagined. It was a beast who had no doubt come to collect his flesh for the funeral pyre he had seen so many times in his dreams. For he always knew deep within him that he would only die at the hands of that old dragon the Devil.

The amalgamated fiend glared down at the stunned champion as strands of electricity still coiled around his black biceps. "To the Jew, we are Alchemy and Satan," they echoed again, their voices bonding in one hollow resonance. "To the Gentile, we are Alchemy and the Devil. But you may call us…AVENGER!!!"

The name hit Magnus with a concussioning spell, bringing to mind the eighth Psalm of King David his father and mother had taught him as a child.

The evil one curved his sharp wings outward while the champion stood mystified before him, bending forward to compress the ruby pipes in his midsection. A soul-shattering blast of sound exploded through the ruby vents in his midsection, hitting the hypnotized champion with an intense wave of energy.

Magnus gritted his teeth as the fiery pain engulfed his skin beneath his armor and clothes, knees nearly buckling from the force of the vapor-like wave. His head was reeling, vision blurred. But he was still standing. The Holy Spirit was keeping him on his feet, wrapping what felt like an enormous hand around him.

The Archfoe extended his black arms forward, muscles bulging like liquid marble as he slammed the sides of his large fists together, expelling a clap of thunder throughout the air. The streams of electricity still coursing over his body were channeled to his thick arms, circling down around his forearms in large rings several times before exploding forward in funnels of silver fire this time instead of stiletto-shaped projectiles.

The funnels hit the champion in the chest with a power greater than that of a thousand lightning bolts. He felt suspended in place as the funnels engulfed his chest and head, its power pressing him backwards in a torturous vice, squeezing the marrow of his hardened skeleton.

Magnus snapped forward as the funnels of lightning finally passed over him in a torrent of wind, blue smoke rolling from his face, spiraling off the golden seals of his unscathed armor. He should have fallen forward through the pond's surface from the rebound, but still he didn't. As before, the champion could feel the Spirit of the Lord holding him on his feet while his arms and head dangled weakly.

His eyes cleared while his torso hung forward, knees bent and exhausted. He could see his charred skin healing in a matter of seconds in the water's reflection. The divine fingers of the hand holding him up started to apply a special pressure to the left side of his armored chest, pressing the spikes on the inside of his coat closer to his heart.

411

The Archrebel stretched his wings forward again, curving their sharp edges around the sides of the champion. "You stand alone at the end of your journey, Magnus," he boasted. "But the chance to exact your vengeance was worth it, was it not?"

He bent forward toward the champion. "Ahhhh…glorious pride. It is a sweet elixir, no?"

Magnus gave no reply.

The Archrebel smiled wickedly, his golden stare burning into the back of the champion's skull. "Of course it is," he answered for him. "Only when humbled does it lose its damnable taste."

Just as the evil one's taunts were starting to make their cut along the seat of his heart, different words came to his aid; ancient words that surged through his spirit like a whispered vaccine to combat the guilt before it could spread. "*Blood-stained spikes are the keys to victory*," said the Lord, the fingers of his unseen hand pressing into the left side of his chest.

Magnus stared at his reflection in the water with a sudden enlightenment, the Lord's voice sparking his memory of the Archangel's words about the Proto-Evangelum Prophecy in the Book of Genesis; the first and greatest of all God's prophecies.

The Archfoe noticed Magnus' renewed reflection at his feet. "Hope is for the weak," he sneered. "Those with real power yield to no such plight. Haven't you learned that lesson yet?"

Magnus lifted his right arm slowly, reaching for the inner left pocket of his coat. He gripped the squared heads of the spikes between the spaces in his fingers. A building surge of power coursed through his mind and body as he held each spike, knees locking straight as he remembered the vision of the spikes protruding through his knuckles in his ancient dream.

Magnus remained slumped over, appearing still injured as the evil one took another step closer to him, closing the sides of his wings around him tightly.

The evil one leaned his reflective face closer to the champion. "Sing me a song of wars and kings, brave champion," he taunted, eyes flashing with bursts of golden fire. "Sing me a song of your greatness, your power and your nobility. Sing me a song!"

The Archfoe's laughter echoed off the curved interior of his encompassing wings as the champion said nothing.

He leaned forward some more until his smooth face was able to reflect the image of the stooped-over champion. "Know this, young lion," he said in a seething hiss. "I am the Anointed Cherub. The first of God's champions...and the greatest. I have defeated all those who tried to take my place. Though millenniums may pass, none have ever escaped my wrath. For vengeance, like wine, is best served with age."

Magnus gripped the spikes in his pocket tighter, the power of the Blood amplifying the Shekinah Wine in his body. He could feel the Lord's hand behind him now, urging him to strike.

Magnus channeled his breaths toward the water, sensing the Archfiend's head was within reach. " *'Vengeance is mine!!'* " he roared suddenly.

The water exploded around them as Magnus reared backward, jerking his hand from the pocket of his coat. He lunged through the wall of water in front of him before the evil one could draw back, swinging his spiked fist in a backward swipe. The tips of each spike cut across the forehead of the Archrebel's perfect face in a spray of golden blood, slicing through the edge of his left wing as the champion's arm swept to the side, scattering a portion of the wing's eye-shaped gems like glitter.

The evil one stumbled backward several paces in a terrible roar, falling to one knee, grabbing at the deep gashes on his forehead, golden blood bubbling over his black fingers.

Magnus held his station on the pond's surface as the wall of water crashed back down over his head and shoulders, curling his spiked fist in front of him for the Archrebel to see. " *'Vengeance is mine, I will repay, saith the Lord!'* "

The Archfiend's golden eyes were wide with disbelief as he gazed at the jagged weapons protruding between the champion's knuckles. The familiar Blood on each spike shimmered in the fading moonlight, testifying to the sacrifice of the Son of God which had already spiritually wounded his head at Calvary first prophesied in Eden.

He recoiled from the ancient spikes the champion was wielding, hissing with his greatest fear. "The Blood...the Carpenter's Blood!!!"

Magnus took a step forward as the evil one recoiled defensively. He gazed at the secret name of God pressed into the spikes. The squared prose of poetic symbols on each spike started to pulsate with beads of light as he stared at them, fueling his mind with one final maneuver.

Magnus jabbed his spiked fist through the air suddenly, pointing it at the Archrebel with a wild glare. " *'The Lord rebuke you,'* " he said, feeling the power of the Blood surge through his chest even more than before, calling up one of the strategies used by the Archangel Michael himself when contending with Satan over the body of Moses as recorded in the Book of Jude.

413

" *'The Lord rebuke you!'* " he repeated, his voice building with an amplified power as the surface of the pond boiled beneath them. " *'THE LORD REBUKE YOU!!!!!'* "

The pond floor was electrified with a brilliant, white flash, rising to the top in a matter of seconds. The Archrebel wrapped his adamantine wings around himself as the bright anomaly exploded through the surface of the water beneath both of them, each blinded from the other's view. The Holy Spirit reconfigured the power of the champion's voice into an apocalyptic wave of light and sound that spread outward through the surrounding trees, funneling high into the heavens above them.

Magnus was catapulted into the roaring light that continued to funnel up through the surface of the water, unable to hear the powerful pitch of his own voice. His spirit pushed against his hardened skin as he rose into the light-filled air. The power of God's hand was lifting him again like it had done before when he was in the throes of death on the bottom of the pond floor. He could feel his all-powerful warmth beneath him. Above him. On every side of him.

⊷•⊷⊷≖○≊⊷•⊷

Magnus floated back down to the pond's surface as the light began to dissolve around him, fist still poised in front of him as the noise subsided, the gematria phrase, *My Wrath*, burning brightly in the flesh of his lips. He looked around at his surroundings, the remainder of the light withering away like windblown ash. The Archrebel was nowhere to be seen, as if he had been swept away to the farthest corners of the universe by the force of the divine explosion.

Magnus looked to the cliff where he had seen the black lion perched earlier, not willing to trust his eyes this time. He kept the spikes clenched tightly between his fingers as he searched for his adversary, looking to the trees surrounding the pond. But there was no sign of his adversary in the fading shadows.

Magnus glanced down at the pond's dark surface, taking a quick step backward, half expecting to see the evil one lunge upward through the surface like some savage predator lurking in the deep.

Magnus lowered his guard slowly, sighing with a soft relief as the Holy Spirit dwelling within him made the truth clear to him. It was done. He *had* won. But it was a victory that hadn't come by the power of his arm or his sword, but by the power of the Lord Jesus' Blood shed in humility so long ago.

Magnus bowed his head humbly, dropping to his knees on the water's surface, the weight of his legs sending large ripples outward on each side of him.

He watched the first rays of sunlight start to crawl across the dark surface of the watery hell all around him, filtering through the trees on the bank behind him. His words came prayerfully as he quoted part of David's Psalmidic subscription about Muth-labben, the death of Goliath. " *'Out of the mouth of babes and nursing infants you have ordained strength because of your ene-mies, that you may silence the enemy…and the avenger.'* "

415

A town lies in ruins.
Lives are lost in a breath,
yet some are saved
by the shedding of Blood.

The Shekinah Chronicles
Book Master: Tower Valley 2006 A.D.

Epilogue:

The night air was sharp and frigid as it swept across San Francisco's Golden Gate Bridge, stirring heavy caps of snow piled up on the bridge's guide wires and spire-crowned towers. The Bay City was blanketed in white from a freak snow storm that had swept down from the north, giving the city an unseasonal Christmas Eve.

The bay was quiet except for a few ferries making their way slowly across the surface of the dark water.

The city itself, however, was bustling with the nightlife of holiday shoppers snatching up last minute gifts, their frantic activity mirrored in the realm of the supernatural. Word of the loss of Tower Valley had spread quickly throughout the ranks of the powers of darkness. Sodom's proudest principality had been left in a state of division. With their Shadow King missing in action, the city's hosts of wickedness had split into different factions, dividing up territory among themselves in a summit of the Dominium Gate Masters being held at Mount Diablo miles away from the city. The legions were drawn together in tight rings, stacked on top of one another while rotating above the radio and televison antennae on top of the mountain. A sentry watch, with warriors from each of the city's newest ruling factions, was posted closer to the city at a former U.S. military base known as Angel Island.

⚊⚊•‡•◇‡•⚊⚊

Magnus made his way down a sidewalk near the heart of San Francisco's Financial District. Department store signs and

Christmas decorations stretched above his head as he moved in and out of the holiday crowds. Such weather was a surprise to him here in the Bay City. But he had come down from Canada after a brief sabbatical, and was more than prepared for the snow piled up all around him with the long, dark brown coat of 19th century design he was wearing. A bright red scarf was draped around the collar of his blue shirt, their ends crossed and tucked beneath the coat's closed breasts.

He read the current headlines of the city's main paper while he walked, tapping along the way the golden tip of his Malacca cane which had a slender blade hidden in its hollow shaft. He kept his head down as people passed by, having no desire to draw any unwanted attention with his ghostly eyes. Even with the many streetlights and lighted decorations surrounding him, his eyes would still flash with bright sheens of emerald fire when he passed through the shadows. Thankfully, the city's rebel hosts were preoccupied with something high in the atmosphere over Mount Diablo and Angel Island when he first arrived, which was more than a welcome relief after all he had been through lately. But that didn't mean the city's demon spirits weren't still roaming the streets as usual.

The past two months had been a drain spiritually. The carnage he had left behind in Tower Valley was still fresh in his mind. He had never forgotten any of the cities that he had brought judgment upon throughout the centuries. It was impossible, especially the city he was walking through at the moment. But even with all he had experienced throughout the last two millenniums, nothing had ever truly prepared him for what he had seen and experienced on the surface of that pond. With the exception of his wife's grisly murder, no memory would ever hold a darker place in his thoughts than his battle with the Archrebel. It would be with him for as long as he walked the Earth, stalking him with the promise of the evil one's return.

Magnus kept his focus on the folded paper as he continued to walk, tapping his cane casually, trying not to think about such a promise.

He suddenly detected something unnerving in the crowds behind him. He lifted his head slowly from his paper as he kept going, picking up on a frigid voice through the clamor of the passing crowds, seeming to whisper his name.

He stopped beneath one of the sidewalk's lampposts, turning around slowly to see if he was being followed. He noticed a tall figure in a black fur coat, facing his direction in front of a lamppost a half a block down, holding a red shopping bag in his right hand. A halo of horn-like beams of golden light emanated from his dark head while he stood in the glow of the lamppost, the lower half of his face hidden behind the covering folds of his fur coat's high collar.

A crowd of shoppers stepped in front of the tall figure in the fur coat before he could bring him into a magnified focus, covering him from view for a moment as one of the city transits pulled up beside the lamppost where he was standing.

Magnus gripped the curved lion's-head handle of his cane tightly, waiting for the shoppers to board the transit, his heart skipping a beat. He could imagine those familiar eyes of white fire staring at him from behind the covering folds of the stranger's fur coat. But the stranger was nowhere to be seen when the last of the shoppers filed into the transit.

He hesitated before turning back around, shaking his head dismissively. Exhaustion, he thought. But he would keep a watchful spirit.

He walked for several more minutes until he came to a store on the left of him with a large showcase window. A big-screen television sat on the other side of it, projecting the image of one of the national networks' famous anchors who was recounting the current crisis the world was engulfed in.

Magnus tossed his paper into a trash can nearby and stepped toward the large window, propping his black-gloved hands on top of the cane's handle in front of him. He quickly tuned out the sounds of the city, focusing his powerful hearing solely on the veteran anchor's deep voice.

A picture of troop movements appeared on the screen along with the commentary. "The world continues to teeter on the brink of what promises to be a full scale conflict in the Middle East.... The fractured Arab League has promised retaliation against Israel for their alleged involvement in the covert incursions that brought down the governing regime of Lebanon, including the assassinations of President Abydos of Egypt and King Al-Saud of Saudi Arabia.... The United States and its allies have also been condemned for allegedly spearheading the covert operation which caught the world off-guard nearly two months ago. It was an operation, according to strange accounts by eyewitnesses, that included the use of horses, swords, and crossbows."

"As a result, the coalition forces currently controling Syria and Iraq have stepped in to assume control of Lebanon during the chaos. It was a move partially motivated by the rash of assassinations of Europe's top leaders. EMU defense ministers are blaming the deaths on Muslim fanatics who they say are bent on revenge against all who are allied to the U.S. and Israel. Muslims from around the world cry out for the destruction of Europe and its Jewish allies. But on the other end of the spectrum, Israel has been pointing a finger of blame at members of the Arab League for the death of Prime Minister Shamur...Shamur's plane exploded over the Mediterranean shortly after news of the incursion broke. The IDF and Shin Bet security forces seized holy sites all over Jerusalem shortly after that, including the Temple Mount."

"Though the United States and its allies have been condemned by the rest of the world for the chaos in Lebanon, the U.S. Secretary of State has been dispatched to the Middle East to meet with Israel's new Prime Minister. The secretary will call on Israel to step down their alert to help ease tensions with the Arab League and decrease violence from Palestinian militants."

Magnus watched the reporting with intensity. The news switched briefly to a follow-up report on a car bombing which took the life of a young CEO of a media conglomerate.

The picture of a devastated town in a valley surrounded by familiar mountains appeared on the screen next as the anchor continued. "In other news tonight, the President has authorized a federal investigation of Tower Valley, the small town in the mountainous regions of Northern California thought to have been laid waste by a massive earthquake almost two months ago. Seismologists from the U.S. Geological Survey have estimated that the strength of the shallow cataclysm was at least a 9.6 on the Richter Scale. But experts from the West Coast & Alaska Tsunami Warning Center and the U.S. Geological Survey who monitor the Cascadia Subduction Fault Zone that runs through that area, remain baffled as to why a Tsunami wave didn't appear along the Pacific Coast as a result of the cataclysm. Their initial findings have shown no evidence of ruptures in the fault line running between the Juan de Fuca and North American lithosphere plates that would have created the wall of water expected with such devastation. And the mystery is amplified even more by the lack of any residual aftershocks. They also remain in the dark as to why a rift appeared in the ionosphere above the valley just before the push-pull waves of the quake struck, an anomaly that hasn't been seen since the earthquake that shook Hawaii in 1973. Some are even comparing the cataclysm to the mysterious quake of 1908 that struck the plains of Siberia with the power of a 40-megaton explosion. But even stranger than that, is the hour in which the earthquake struck...5:13 a.m.: The exact moment when San Francisco was devastated by the great quake of 1906 that had its one hundredth anniversary earlier this year on the Eighteenth of April. But ignoring all the elaborate conspiracy theories of a coverup which have sprung up as of late, FBI agents investigating the site have yet to rule out a possible act of terrorism since, by even stranger design, the main area of devastation seems to have been mostly limited to the valley floor and its town."

Enough, he thought.

Magnus turned and started walking again, tuning out the news to let the city's banter come rushing back in as a distraction. He eventually passed by the narrow alleyway of Commercial Street, unaware of the eyes watching him.

Plumes of steam billowed up through a small vent in the street near the alley's entrance, curling around a nearby lamppost. A tall figure of a man in a luminous, hooded robe of sky-blue flax sat quietly atop an armored horse standing amidst the plumes of steam. Eyes of jeweled fires burned brightly in the rider's hood, watching Magnus pass.

Six other figures in the same apparel emerged like ghosts in the wall of steam where Michael was stationed, the armored hooves of their red, white, and black horses clattering in soft echoes off the walls of the buildings rising up on each side of the historic alley.

One of the six moved forward to the right of the Archangel, small streams of blue and white fire curling around the sides of his hood, watching from his vaulted saddle as clusters of mortals passed by after the champion. "His spirit is tired, great prince" Gabriel replied.

"Yes," Michael agreed.

"Magnus will resist the very thought of his new mission."

Michael nodded. "It is an unenviable task required of him," he noted. "But the Lord will strengthen him when the time comes…the Beast must be protected."

Magnus continued down the tree-lined sidewalk, crossing over an angled walkway in the street towards the historic Jackson Square District. He passed the black columns of the rounded portico and the caduceus-marked windows of the old Transamerica building belonging to the satanic *Church of Scientology*, crossing a small side street past the site of California's first Masonic Temple. He turned the corner, walking past a host of seasonally-decorated antique stores, each occupying buildings that had survived the great quake of 1906.

The crowds of shoppers buffeting him earlier were no where to be seen now as he passed underneath the awning of the Challiss House antique store.

He was about to walk by the famed entrance to the alleyway of Hotaling Street when he stopped suddenly, turning to the right at something small and out of place that caught the attention of his powerful hearing.

He walked down the narrow alleyway past antique streetlights and horse-headed hitching posts, walking past small banks of snow pushed up against the sides of the alley's old buildings where part of the city's shoreline used to be. This was an old and very familiar alley to him, a picturesque place where luxury and hidden evil had been married in the shadows of commerce for quite some time.

He followed the sound of faint heartbeats and weakened breaths he had detected moments ago until he came upon another antique store about halfway down the alley. What he saw stunned him. There before him, huddled between two small piles of snow, lay a little girl wearing nothing more than a pair of tattered overalls and a thin, soiled sweater.

Magnus closed his eyes with a deep sigh, bowing his head for a moment. When he lifted his head again his heart skipped a beat as he was momentarily drawn to the tall glass window in the middle of the antique store's showcase entrance. A halogen light cast an eerie glow on the lower panes of glass near where the child lay, spotlighting a stone dragon frozen in its lunge from the store's shadowy interior. It was propped on top of an old book sitting on a small table, its clawed right hand stretching out toward the window just above the child's head. That image quickly brought to mind the evil rituals being celebrated tonight, the High Grand Climax of Christmas Eve.

He turned and noticed a familiar, cobblestone structure. A large rectangle of sand-colored stone was carved into the wall above its sunken doorway, depicting the head and shoulders of a Virgoan goddess, with a serpent coiled around each of her outstretched arms and symbols of agriculture clenched in her hands that reached out to the imposing lanterns posted on both sides of the doorway. The building itself was located next to the rear section of the Masonic Temple he had passed by earlier. It was a private club known as Villa Taverna where the city's elite gathered together.

Magnus turned and squatted in front of the little girl as she lay in a trembling stupor. He laid his cane down and listened to the child's heartbeat. He pulled the long brown hair away from her face, drawing back in surprise as he uncovered it. Her face was

425

covered with swells of black lesions, something he hadn't seen since the days of the Black Plague.

He snapped his gaze back to the statue of the dragon, knowing that something unnatural had touched her, something completely and utterly unholy. It was almost as if she had been dropped here at the very moment he was passing by the alleyway, the city's cultivated center of hidden evil that survived the judgment he had brought upon San Francisco over a century ago.

Magnus grabbed the lion's-head pommel of his cane with his left hand in a sudden rage, whipping out the blade hidden in its hollowed out shaft as he shot to his feet, whirling back around toward the rear section of the Masonic Temple and the private club next to it. He turned to his left to search the dimly lit doorways at the other end of the alley where the new Transamercia building stood against the night sky, brandishing his slender blade defensively, half expecting to see the Archfiend come barreling forward from some darkened corner.

But he didn't.

He bowed his head with another tired sigh, turning his attention to the child again. The blade and the cane's hollowed out shaft fell from his hands, clanging against the street as he squatted down in front of her. He reached forward and scooped the child up in his arms, lifting her into the air. Her long brown hair fell to the sides of her lesion-covered face as he cradled her trembling body close to his chest. She couldn't have been more than six years old, he thought, quiet tears rolling down his face from listening to the labored beats of her dying heart. She would probably be dead within the hour.

Magnus reached back with his right hand and pulled the red scarf from around his neck, placing it over the child's shivering body.

The child's eyelids fluttered open as the champion snuggled the scarf up to her neck like a small blanket. Her eyes were brown, but fading slowly to a gray color of death. She seemed frightened at first by the champion's glowing stare. "Please...don't hurt me," she said in a quivering voice.

His tears came even harder with her words. "I wouldn't dream of it, child," he replied in a near whisper.

The child stared at the champion's bright eyes. After a month of abandonment and abuse, she no longer had the will to resist the strength of those larger than her.

Magnus was careful not to crush her tiny body as he hugged her, trying to warm her the best he could. His heart ached when he looked at her thin face. Though he had been born a prince in the House of Sheshbazzar, he had also tasted the loneliness and despair of being homeless. And it didn't matter who you were, or who you used to be, such circumstances were hard on anyone, especially the young and defenseless. They were always the first to die. The world was no respecter of age. It devoured the weak with an insatiable appetite for more, spitting out the remains of the poor in its gutters.

In the softest of movements, Magnus started to float upward, a slight wind pressing down on both of them as they rose through the air in a backward angle. The child's eyes widened when she saw the night's twinkling skyline coming toward her.

"Are you...an angel?" she asked softly.

Magnus smiled through the tears that were starting to dry on his face. "No, child," he replied. "But they're all around us."

She smiled faintly, snuggling against the champion's chest as they drew closer to the stars above the alley's dual roof line.

Magnus floated upward until his shoes passed above the cobblestone ledge of the private club behind him. He whisked backward, stirring up white swirls in his skim above the snow-covered roof.

He turned completely around as he approached the far end of the building, soaring out over its edge in an angled flight, passing over the side street below, sweeping over the three story roof of the old Transamerica building. He climbed higher into the sky, passing over other rooftops, caring little if anyone below saw him or not as he flew over Union Square where small holiday crowds could still be seen at such a late hour. He would give the child an aerial tour of the city, lifting her above its oppression for once.

Magnus did give a quick look at Mount Diablo and Angel Island while ascending over the rooftops of Nob Hill, making sure the enemy hadn't broken from their guarded conclaves yet. Those who kept watch at Angel Island didn't notice him as he made his way toward the Top of the Mark restaurant positioned atop the enormous, gothic-style roof of the 19-story Mark Hopkins Hotel built with terra cotta mastery on the premier crest of Nob Hill. He landed on the ledge of a corner niche roof just below the hotel's enormous, trapezoid-shaped dome that intersected with other sharp-angled roofs decked with stone arches that loomed above the restaurant's picture windows. A bright, needle-like spire rose high into the air behind him from the center of the main roof.

In the distance before him lay the dark-hued mansion of the Pacific Union Club and the twin bell towers and daunting arches of the enemy's Notre Dame-style stronghold known as Grace Cathedral. To the left of the cathedral was the marble behemoth of the city's Masonic Memorial Temple. Beyond the rest of the historic structures of Nob Hill was one of the grandest views of the bay and its Golden Gate Bridge.

***

Magnus stood motionless on the corner ledge, praying quietly for the child in his arms as the midnight hour approached. Now and then a brisk wind swept across his lofty perch, blowing the split train of his brown coat backward as he gazed out at the Golden Gate Bridge and the city's bright skyline sprawled out beneath them.

Magnus held the child so she could see the Bay City in a way she had probably never seen it before as her breaths became fainter and more labored.

The child looked at Magnus as he hugged her, showing her a love she had never known before. Her eyes glazed over suddenly with a vision of another world, uttering a wisdom that was not her own with the last ounce of her strength. "Please remember me, Jesus," she said softly. "Re…remember me…."

Magnus closed his eyes as the child breathed her last breath, feeling the warmth of her soul-crowned spirit being released when her head rolled to the side against his chest. "The Lord will greet you, little one," he whispered.

Magnus held the child in a mournful silence, kissing the top of her forehead before covering her face with the scarf.

"I see you found my gift," a voice said from behind.

Magnus lifted his head slowly at the sound of the voice, eyes hardening with anger. He turned around on the ledge, the look on his face turning from anger to total surprise. The man in the fur coat he had seen from a distance on the street earlier in the night emerged from the shadows of the corner rooftop's angled walls. But it was no ordinary man walking toward him. It was the Wicked One himself. The Mystery of Iniquity.

Alchemy, wearing a full-length fur coat of black wolf's hair, cut an intimidating figure against the gothic backdrop of the hotel's main roof. His contoured, slightly unshaven face was voguishly framed by his wind-swept hair that still had faint beams of golden light emanating from the translucent strands of gold mixed with his black locks. The red shopping bag he was holding earlier was still clutched in his right hand, supporting something inside that bulged heavily against its sides.

The soles of Alchemy's Italian shoes crunched the roof's snow as he stopped a few yards away from the raised ledge. "I found her in a sleazy hotel in the Castro District as she was about to be tortured by one of the master's servants," he said. "So, I thought I would show her my own touch of mercy. She wasn't exactly the perfect sacrifice for the High Grand Climax, but things seem to have turned out well since you brought her to this high place to die. It's almost as if you have brought back the glory days of Chemosh."

Magnus stared down at the Master's betrayer in an unbelieving silence, a moment which had been manipulated with diabolical skill. It was the first time he had seen him up close since his battle with the Archrebel. And it was a frightening revelation. For his face was an exact replica of Lucifer's man-shaped veneer that had dominated the countenance of his amalgamated foe during their battle.

Alchemy smiled playfully at his hardened look of surprise. "It's nice to finally meet the legend up close and personal," he said. "The slayer of kings and kingdoms…. Such a legacy makes us brothers, doesn't it? I would almost venture to say there's even a family resemblance in our faces. And though it is *not in my heart to be so*, we are both rods of God's anger, are we not?"

Magnus said nothing. His fiery stare at the Beast was more than enough of a reply.

Alchemy gestured at the bell towers of Grace Cathedral behind Magnus, and at the other historic buildings of Nob Hill where empire builders of the past had once lived lavishly. "Shall I tempt you to serve me since we are so much alike?" he mocked. " *'All these things will I give thee, if thou wilt fall down and worship me.'* "

Magnus' reply was the same, wrath provoked, yet chained by silent submission to the Spirit of the Lord.

Alchemy moved closer, stoking the champion's fire a little more. "You do know that your victory in the valley was minimal, don't you?" he continued, his eyes pulsing with a blue fervor. "The *Covenant Harness* still rests firmly upon me. My time to travel the King's Road is near. The delays will soon end. And then…Then the great Seraph and I will be one as I claim the Throne of David for the Serpent Tribe of Dan."

Alchemy glared at Magnus with supreme pleasure, daring him to retaliate as he took yet another step forward with more of his taunts. "There's something else you should know. Just as Apollo skinned Marsyas for challenging him with inferior music according to the fable, so, too, shall the master skin your hide in the rematch of chords and swords to come," he said. "Only this time, I will be the *Devil's Fiddler*."

Magnus could feel the Holy Spirit's restraint on his heart with the Beast's words. He could have had him in his grip in the blink of an eye, crushing the vile breath from his throat with a single hand. But he would not act on his desire. Such vengeance belonged to the Lord. And at the appointed time, it would be poured out in full.

Alchemy turned sideways, throwing a casual wave as he started to leave. "Farewell, champion. The King's Road is calling."

Alchemy stopped abruptly after walking several feet, turning back around toward the champion. "Oh, I almost forgot. I have one more present for you," he said, smiling with another devilish gleam as he reached inside the red shopping bag he was holding. "I wanted to thank you for being a part of the procession that welcomed me at my resurrection on that Christmas Eve night so long ago. It's not frankincense or myrrh, but it is fitting for a nomadic king of your particularly cursed bloodline."

Alchemy pulled out a bronzed helmet with a gilded face mask from inside the bag, tossing it in front of the ledge where the champion was standing. "Merry Christmas, *Great Lion.*"

The champion glanced down in surprise at a helmet he hadn't seen in centuries as it lay wedged in the snow in front of him.

The look of surprise was frozen in his face as he snapped his head back up, catching a faint glimpse of ghostly shadows that swept up from beneath the Beast as he was walking away in a bout of laughter, swirling around him like a tornado that was hauntingly familiar.

Alchemy vanished as the shadows exploded outward in a twisting flurry of snow, his laughter fading with vapors of stringed music.

Magnus stood motionless for a moment as he watched the last of the twisting snow fall slowly to the spot where Alchemy had disappeared.

He could still hear the Beast's laughter and the scorched chords of music in his mind as his eyes fell on the ancient helmet again. Its golden mask and emblems were bright against the backdrop of the snow that covered the roof. He peered into the hollow eyes of its mask that reminded him of other eyes that had hunted him from behind similar masks throughout the ages, reaffirming the Beast's vow that the score would be settled. For there was still the vision of the funeral pyre in his ancient dream that promised to task him.

A brisk wind swept across the rooftop as he stared at the gilded mask, pushing the ancient helmet on its left side in a flurry of snow. The golden emblem of the warrior lion that was embossed on the left side of the bronze helmet shimmered brightly in his eyes as he stared at it, its powerful mouth clenched fiercely around the image of the circular ring that held the keys of Death and Hades.

Magnus turned on the ledge as a gust of wind bloated the train of his brown coat with a frigid blast of air. He still held the body of the lifeless child with an unflinching embrace as he gazed up at the sky, listening to the bells of Grace Cathedral announce the stroke of midnight. He yearned to see the Lord Jesus pierce those stars above him, coming forth to rescue him from the shadows of his pain once and for all. "How long, my King?" he asked somberly. "How long must we wait?"

"I am with you always,
even unto the end
of the age."
Amen.

Matthew 28: 20

Author's Note

Though it has taken almost seven years of writing, rewriting and research, it has been an enormous pleasure to write this particular book. But it has taken me ten years to get published. I worked on the second novel in the series during that seven year period, but the majority of my time was spent on *Wayfarer*. And I would like to thank my parents for first sharing the love of Christ with me, the same love I have tried to share in this epic story. They nourished my love of all things heroic and noble. And there are a host of others I owe many thanks to as well: My brother Richard, my brothers and sisters in Christ—Bobby, Pam, Keith, Craig, Karen, Pat Tillet and many more. I also would like to thank my cover artist and brother in Christ, Mario Ruiz, for his awesome design of the book jacket. May the Lord be with you, Mario, as you start your own company, Valor Press. And I thank Dr. Akin for his endorsement of this book as well, with careful note being taken that he does not personally hold to every doctrinal issue expressed in these pages. Above all, I would like to give thanks to the Lord Jesus. He stood by me more than anyone. I can do nothing without Him. All glory belongs to Christ Jesus.

There are things of great and eternal interest woven into the book that I wish to elaborate on. I wanted this book to be something that had never been seen before in the market, something that would transcend this time in history and impact those on the other side of the Age of Grace, especially those born during the Millennial Reign of the returning Christ. Though nothing will ever replace the prominence of Holy Writ, I do want people both now and then, and even those during the Time of Jacob's Trouble,

435

to see how we viewed things on this side of eternity. I hope it will be one of many teaching tools for the ages to come, especially that age at the end of the Millennial Kingdom when satan will be loosed upon the world one last time to fulfill the rest of God's master plan.

There are phrases and descriptions in this epic that point to more obscure and deeper meanings of truth than some may have discovered as they read the book. I also chose to structure certain words and phrases according to my own design. Other examples of parabolic phrases and images incorporated into the book are listed in the following categories:

Symbols & Foreshadows

1. The main story of the book, though it covers thousands of years of history, takes place over a period of roughly three days. In it you see Magnus foreshadowing the Lord in many ways. I portray him as having the skills of a carpenter as demonstrated by the one of two war-cabinets he crafted from acacia wood. The acacia tree was used to construct the Ark of the Covenant that carried the manna, the rod of Aaron and the tablets of Moses. In the Old Testament, the Ark was also seen preceding the Israelites as they were called on by the Lord to do battle with the enemy, just like Magnus' war-cabinet was portrayed as being transported to the old church building before he arrived, a parallel that was totally unplanned during the writing of that particularly significant scene. Magnus' body is also similar to the Shekinah body the Lord has in its bronze appearance and the fire of his emerald eyes. Magnus' arrest in the first Origins section also parallels some of the events which happened to the Lord in the 18th chapter of the Gospel of John. That particular passage has even greater significance when you compare what Magnus does to Tower Valley at the end, which points

to Judas' greatest defeat first glimpsed in John 18, to be expanded in Revelation 19. I'm sure John was greatly inspired in his Gospel story to show how Jesus made Judas and his army fall back at the sound of his voice when he was being arrested in the garden, especially considering that John's retelling of those famous events was written after he had penned the Apocalypse account, which is more than a little striking when one ponders what John was seemingly trying to say to his readers. He knew exactly who the pseudochrist would be.

2. The dream sequence that Magnus has in the first Origins section of the book is a compilation of actual images from the Scriptures. I portrayed it as being pulled from his own knowledge of the Scriptures so that people wouldn't think I was trying to write some sort of new prophecy. I wanted it to be an overall image of an evil triangle that would task him throughout the ages, while at the same time expressing the truth of what the Bible says will happen in the future.

3. As Christians we walk by faith and not by sight. Because of this, I felt it necessary to let Magnus' conversation with April in Chapter 12 about believing what she had seen of his powers be symbolic of what the Apostles and the others of that day saw of Jesus. The miracles Jesus and the Apostles performed were for the proclamation and presentation of the Messiah and his Kingdom. They were for the fulfilling of prophecy even up unto the writing of the book of Acts. As one scholar has noted, signs and wonders did not end with the Apostolic era of the early Church. But the majority of these signs and wonders are from the enemy. This will increase with the arrival of the Beast. I wanted Magnus' abilities to be symbolic of what was holy. This is explained to a degree in

Chapter 9. His displays of supernatural power are also symbolic of the signs that will be shown to the Jewish remnant after the Ascension of the Church.

4. I used the word bronze quite a lot in the book. Magnus and Alchemy both have bronze skin. Avenger's wings are made of bronze-colored adamantine. The Hebrew symbols inscribed on the signet-like seals of Magnus' special armor are Christaloy bronze, along with other examples. I did this because bronze is a symbol of judgment in the Bible, which is why it appears so often in the story. The signet-like seals of Christaloy gold that make up Magnus' armor comes from the seven seals of wrath and judgment in the Revelation. The use of the imagery of palm trees in the book, such as those featured on Magnus' helmet and his coat, along with his Malacca cane made from a rattan palm, is significant as well because of that particular tree's prominent portrayal on the walls of the Lord's throne room in the Millennial Temple.

5. I portray Magnus and Lucifer as the Lord's anointed in the book, somewhat paralleling the struggle between Saul and David. Even the battle scene at the end shows Magnus slicing off a portion of the Archrebel's wing just as David sliced off a section of Saul's robe in a cave in the Wilderness of En Gedi as told in I Samuel 24. Magnus' choice for dispatching his adversary at the end also parallels how David chose to deal with Saul in that same chapter from I Samuel, linking it to the Book of Jude where Michael defeated the devil by saying, "*The Lord rebuke you.*"

6. Tower Valley, a name derived from the Tower of Babel, is also comparable to Apostate Jerusalem of the latter days. In the book, the town was once known as Tsidkenu Valley, which is one of the

titles for the city of Jerusalem during the Millennial Kingdom; a name recorded as Jehovah-Tsidkenu in the 23rd and 33rd chapters of the Book of Jeremiah that is translated as *the Lord our righteousness*. Tower Valley is also ruled over by a Shadow King known as Sodom, the same name of that infamous city of evil that Apostate Jerusalem is compared to in the latter days by the Prophet Isaiah before the commencement of the Kingdom Age. The town's original settlement is significant as well. I wrote it as being founded in 1860 to give it a forty-year period of righteousness and peace before the townspeople allowed a Masonic Temple to be built in the midst of their newer settlement in the center of the valley in 1900. This coincides with the 40-year periods of peace the Hebrews often enjoyed in the Book of Judges, before turning to idolatry and being enslaved by the Philistines again and again. Because Tower Valley is a foreshadowing of Babylon as well, I also show the rebel angels that Magnus destroys being sucked into an imprisoning portal to the Abyss located beneath the town. This looks forward into the future when the real city of Babylon, which is currently being rebuilt, is destroyed and becomes a prison house for the demons as foretold in Revelation 18. There is some debate about rebel angels and demons being separate entities. There is ample evidence that suggests this. That's why I chose to portray them as being separate.

7. The choice I made by ending the story in the year 2006 has nothing to do with trying to write some sort of new prophecy. I chose this year to coincide with the 100th anniversary of the 1906 Earthquake that struck San Francisco. It worked out better than I had originally anticipated since the quake took place on the 18th of April. The destruction of

439

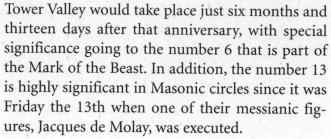

Tower Valley would take place just six months and thirteen days after that anniversary, with special significance going to the number 6 that is part of the Mark of the Beast. In addition, the number 13 is highly significant in Masonic circles since it was Friday the 13th when one of their messianic figures, Jacques de Molay, was executed.

8. The car I chose for April at the beginning of the book also has some special significance. The Aston Martin portrayed in the book was featured in a magazine I bought in 1997. Nearly six and a half years later, while doing a revision, I chose to use it, replacing the Volvo that was written into the first draft between September of 1997 and September of 1998. Significantly, the makers of the car from the magazine article referred to its color as cheviot red, which is tied to the Cheviot Hills between England and Scotland where breeds of hornless sheep roam. The special color of the car could somewhat parallel the Blood of the Lamb that was already predestined to wash away the sins of April and her daughter. Another interesting parallel can be drawn to the final state of the car shown in Chapter 12. I portray one of the star-shaped wheels of the Aston Martin being imprisoned by a square of red metal. If you go from there and compare that image of the square of compressed metal to the square altar featured in the Millennial Temple you see an intriguing symbol. The altar of the Millennial Temple, where ceremonial sacrifices of lambs and other animals will take place, is interestingly called *Ariel*, a name in Hebrew meaning *lion of God*. According to John W. Schmitt and J. Carl Laney, authors of the book *Messiah's Coming Temple*, the sacrifices prophesied in the Book of Ezekiel, and the name of the square-shaped altar itself, will serve as a memorial to the original and

permanent sacrifice for sin accomplished through Jesus' death and resurrection, which also brought about the defeat of satan and his one-third army of star angels as first prophesied in Genesis 3 and later in Revelation 12.

9. The mysterious rider in Chapter 19 was described with certain Scriptural phrases so as to portray all *Four Horsemen* mentioned in *Revelation*. This is actually a fourfold picture of the *Antichrist* just as the Gospels are a fourfold picture of Jesus.

10. Dragylon, lucifer's Imperial Fortress in the book, is a mock attempt to create something comparable to the New Jerusalem. This was not something I had originally intended. It just turned out that way in the process of my research and the inspiration the Lord gave me on a daily basis.

11. The *Sword of the Lord* phrase in the book was used only three times. I did this because the number 3 is a divine number. I wanted to use it nine times since that number is equated with judgment in the Scriptures, but I felt it was just too much. I also used the phrase *Great Lion* three times in reference to Magnus' name and surname to represent Jesus' title as the Lion of the Tribe of Judah since Magnus is a foreshadowing of what the Lord will be like at His return.

12. April's catching away with Raptos, in case some missed it, was a type of the ascension to come when the Lord Jesus returns for the Church. April's full name is also significant. Her first name represents the celebration of the Lord's resurrection. Her last name, *Wedding*, represents the Marriage Supper of the Lamb that is to come, in which all saints will participate.

13. The revelation about satan at the end of the book is based upon a theory I came across in one of

441

Dr. Danny Akin's systematic theology books many years ago. It is merely a theory I expanded for dramatic purposes. There are parallels for this theory in the Book of Ezekiel as well. I wanted to do something that had never been done before with this king of all villains. The spiritual warfare during the writing of this book was quite difficult, and continues to this very moment as my fingers glide across the keyboard. I tried my best to show him in all his truest forms without portraying him as some glorified antihero as so many other writers have done in the past.

14. I used Judas' surname, *Iscariot*, for the first part of his new name Iscarius. Some believe that his surname was actually Sicarius, and is perhaps the root word for the name of an ancient guild of Jewish assassins known as the Sicarii. The last part of his new name, *Alchemy*, is an early form of chemistry that sought to turn base metals into gold and to create an elixir for eternal youth. It also has links to the name lucifer as I touched upon in Chapter 25, which connects it to that famous passage in Isaiah 14 concerning his fall. And the *Mystery of Iniquity* phrase that is used in the book is meant to define the spirit of Antichrist that permeates this wicked world system, while also being fulfilled in the resurrection of Judas. And as for Judas being from the Tribe of Dan, that was merely used for drama. There is no evidence for him being part of the Tribe of Dan. Some scholars believe the antichrist will come from this tribe because of its sordid history, and because of a certain passage of Scripture about the swift horses of Dan.

15. If you remember from the story, I mention seven future Jewish Assemblies several times. This was done to tell an important truth about the Revelation

of Jesus Christ. The seven assemblies John writes to are not seven stages of Church history as I was taught most of my life. Careful study of the text will prove that. There are many people with a list of professional degrees longer than both of my arms who shouldn't be writing books on this topic because of their biased favor for tradition. They want to take from Israel and give to the Church what doesn't belong to the Church, such as the Church being the Bride of Christ. That's a mockery of God's Holy Word. There are 285 Hebrew idioms in the Book of Revelation, thus giving it a distinct Jewish character. And it doesn't just begin at Chapter 4. It starts from word one of Chapter 1 and proceeds to the end. From the marturia testimony of Jesus Christ to the Old Testament references applied to the seven assemblies, we can see a deliberate process of elimination. An elimination of all possible confusion with the Church. At least this is the case from God's point of view as it was given to the Apostle John, who, by the way, was not a political prisoner on the isle of Patmos as tradition likes to claim. He was taken to the island by God himself to go forward into the future to the actual Day of the Lord, and then record what he had seen. Certain revisers of Holy Writ have done a great disservice to the people of God on many occasions by inserting words into the text that do not stand up to the original languages in which the Word of God was written. Now, I do not claim to be scholar by any stretch of the imagination. But I know that much of what I have been taught of prophecy is just simply wrong. It doesn't match up to the text. Just because someone has a television show or sells millions of books doesn't mean they know what they're talking about when it comes to this important topic. What matters is whether or not their words match up with the text,

443

and that doesn't include anything which is forceably made to fit. I have learned much from the writings of E.W. Bullinger and A.W. Pink, with careful note to the reader being that I do not agree with all that they wrote of the Scriptures. The greatest authority in my life is the inerrant Word of God itself.

16. As one last side note, all these symbols and fore-shadows travel back and forth to the past, present, and future during their unfoldings, just like the prophecies of the Bible so often do. But please don't get the wrong idea. There is no replacement for the Scriptures! This story is merely an allegory of what has already been written in the Bible. It is meant to entertain and challenge my brothers and sisters in Christ, while sharing the Gospel with the lost and exposing the enemy in a way that's never been done before.

Author's Biography

Like the character in his book, Matthew Dickens has had many wanderings, spanning from one end of this country to the other. Saved at an early age, he now serves as a teacher for a home-based Bible study. He loves the Word of God, as well as contemplation of God's creation, especially the animals. Matthew longs for the return of Christ. In the meantime, he resides in his hometown of Roxboro, North Carolina. He enjoys swordsmanship, basketball, and boxing.

THE SHEKINAH CHRONICLES SERIES

WAYFARER
BOOK ONE OF *THE SHEKINAH CHRONICLES*
ISBN:0-7684-2234-5

ASCENSION
BOOK TWO OF *THE SHEKINAH CHRONICLES*
ISBN:0-7684-2243-4

Prepare yourself for a ride that will take you from one end of the galaxy to another in a riveting battle for the Kingdom of God.

BOOK THREE
THE SHEKINAH CHRONICLES
ISBN:0-7684-2244-2

Witness the Day of the Lord as the Christos Champion returns like a thief in the night.

BOOK FOUR
THE SHEKINAH CHRONICLES
ISBN:0-7684-2245-0

The rise of the Millennial Kingdom is sure. But an old hatred is stirring under the guise of submissive subterfuge.

BOOK FIVE
THE SHEKINAH CHRONICLES
ISBN:0-7684-2246-9

A secret society has arisen at the halfway point of the Millennial Kingdom. The Covenant Harness has been rediscovered. The past is taught, but little is remembered.

BOOK SIX
THE SHEKINAH CHRONICLES

ISBN:0-7684-2247-7

The tides of war are mounting. Arm yourself for the final conflict, for the Abyss has been opened.

BOOK SEVEN
THE SHEKINAH CHRONICLES

ISBN:0-7684-2248-5

Bear witness to the Great Judgment as you are taken on a journey through time and eternity.